William Alexander Hammond, Wiliam Alexander Hammond

Mr. Oldmixon. A novel

William Alexander Hammond, Wiliam Alexander Hammond

Mr. Oldmixon. A novel

ISBN/EAN: 9783743303218

Manufactured in Europe, USA, Canada, Australia, Japa

Cover: Foto ©Raphael Reischuk / pixelio.de

Manufactured and distributed by brebook publishing software
(www.brebook.com)

William Alexander Hammond, Wiliam Alexander Hammond

Mr. Oldmixon. A novel

A NOVEL.

BY

WILLIAM A. HAMMOND,

AUTHOR OF "LAL," "DOCTOR GRATTAN," ETC.

NEW YORK:

D. APPLETON AND COMPANY,

1, 3, AND 5 BOND STREET.

1885.

CONTENTS.

MR. OLDMIXON.

CHAPTER I.

WHY BARBARA LAUGHED.

" Do you think that head is thrown far enough back, father ?"

The speaker was a young woman of apparently twenty years of age or thereabouts. She was neatly but plainly dressed, and she was seated in front of a long table or work-bench, moulding into a natural attitude the stuffed skin of a canary bird that was nearly ready for mounting on the little wooden pedestal that stood close at hand.

The room was evidently the workshop of a taxidermist, for there were lying about it, on tables and chairs, and even on the floor, several skins of animals of various kinds. There were also half a dozen or more mounted specimens in different stages of forwardness. There was a Skye terrier ready to be sent home to his disconsolate mistress so soon as his hair should have received its final combing and brushing, and there was a diminutive black kitten, that had doubtless once been the playmate of some rich man's little daughter, if a judgment could be formed from the fact that there was a silver collar about its neck with the name " Georgiana" marked upon it in blue enamel letters ; and there was a bull-dog rather the worse for his troubled existence in this world of sorrow, for one ear was entirely gone, and the other had been so materially damaged as scarcely to bear, aside from its position on the beast's head, even a remote resemblance to an auricular appendage, while his body at various places was denuded of the hair that nature had originally given him, allowing long and deep scars to be seen, that were the honorable evidences of the glorious battles he had fought. Then there was a rattlesnake, probably a hunter's trophy, coiled as though about to deliver a blow to an adversary, its jaws opened to their fullest extent, and its ugly-looking fangs elevated to the position requisite for penetrating the flesh and discharging their venom into the blood of its victim.

At the other end of the room from where the girl was working was an old man, the one whom she had addressed as "father." He was intently engaged in setting up on its platform a magnificent specimen of the royal Bengal tiger. So busy was he, that he did not apparently hear the observation that she had addressed to him, but went on with his work, bending one leg of the beast and straightening another, and giving the neck a little turn here and another in a different direction there, until he had succeeded in getting the posture that he thought would best display the nature of the animal. Then he went off to a little distance and surveyed his work from various points of view, going up to it occasionally to change the position of some part that did not give him entire satisfaction.

In the mean time the girl went on with her work.

She was not what would have been called beautiful by the majority of those who set up as judges of the faces of women. She would never have been selected by a dressmaker or by one of those purveyors of fashion that clothe lay figures in their æsthetic productions, to stand in a bay-window or a show-case as a displayer of their chromatic and morphological structures. I have a friend who insists upon it that the faces and forms of these lay figures are more beautiful than those that nature produces. For him the worker in wax has no superior as a delineator of the human form divine, and he goes down-town every morning to spend an hour or so in the contemplation of the lovely pink and white compositions, clothed in tissue-paper gowns, that stand in the windows of the pattern-makers. He would never have looked twice at Barbara Henschel.

But an artist, a painter or a sculptor, a poet, any man with brains in his skull, would not only have looked twice at Barbara Henschel, but he would have looked a dozen times or more if he had had the opportunity, and even then he would not have been satisfied, for there was something in her face that was irresistibly attractive to a thinking man. It was not, perhaps, in her large gray eyes, for there was nothing particularly remarkable about them. A thousand such can be seen any fine Saturday or Sunday afternoon in Central Park. It could scarcely have been her hair, which was red—unmistakably red; not auburn or golden, but red like that that Titian has put on the heads of some of his Venetian women, only a little redder. A lock of it under a glass case would not have been a beautiful object. It might have decked the head of one of my friend's magnificent figures that stand in Madame Félicie's shop-front, and no one but he and others with his materialistic notions would have admired it. But on Barbara Henschel's shapely head it was quite another thing. It seemed to have a life of its own that it got from sympathy or association

with the rest of her, just as an eye or a hand receives its
beauty from the soul that flashes through it and the blood
that courses through its veins and arteries. Nature had
not been miserly in the matter of quantity ; for although
it was all, save a few irregularly placed curls on her forehead, gathered together into a knot at the back of her
head, it was easy to see that the growth was sufficiently
luxuriant to excite the envy even of the " Fair One
with Golden Locks," had that magnificent fairy being
caught a glimpse of it.

As to her complexion, it goes without saying that it
was fair. It was of the kind that red-haired women
usually have, though perhaps a little paler. The skin
was of course thin and delicate, so that under the influence of the adequate emotions it would blush or become
pallid with a promptness and a thoroughness that would
leave nothing to be desired on the score of passional
manifestation.

As she uttered the words with which this chapter begins, the faintest beam of a smile passed over her countenance ; and then it was seen that her eyes lighted up with
a wonderful beauty that in their condition of repose they
gave to the commonplace observer, such as my friend, the
admirer of Madame Félicie's lay figures, no indication
of being able to exhibit. But the artist, the poet, and
the man with brains would not have been surprised except, perhaps, at the extent of the change. He would
have known all along that the power of expression was
there, not only in her eyes, but in every feature of her
face. It was that knowledge that would have made him
want to look more than twice at her, hoping that something would stir her emotions or her intellect, and bring
out the latent beauty that lay hidden in her face.

And the like was true of her mouth, that most expressive of all the features, not even excepting the eyes. As she spoke and smiled, the parting of her lips showed two rows of white and regular teeth, that appeared to be as satisfactory from a masticatory as they evidently were from an æsthetic point of view. There is no middle ground so far as teeth are concerned. They are either good or they are bad. If they are not the one they are assuredly the other. This girl's teeth were good.

It must have been something remotely connected with the bird she was mounting, rather than the bird itself, that made her smile. The work of the taxidermist is not particularly enlivening any more than it is especially healthy. Indeed, the continual handling of the skins of dead animals must tend, one would think, to produce a melancholy, or at least a grave frame of mind, just as the contact with arsenic, corrosive sublimate, and other poisonous but preservative substances is calculated to exert a deleterious influence on the bodily health. Barbara Henschel had, however, evidently been endowed with sufficient mental and physical stamina to resist both categories of depressing influences, for she was sound of health in mind and body. Her organs worked with all the regularity of a dynamo-electric engine, and the consequence was that she had the superlatively healthy body that insures the superlatively healthy mind.

Yes, there must have been something directly or indirectly associated with the bird that tended to excite her risible faculties; for as she moulded the plastic form of the little creature with her slender fingers, and scanned it from time to time with a critical eye as she pursued her work, her face appeared to be constantly on the point of again relaxing into a smile, until at last, unable

1*

to restrain herself, she dropped the object of her skill and, throwing herself back in her chair, burst into peal after peal of merry laughter.

The old man who was working on the royal Bengal tiger at the other end of the room now ceased his labor, and, raising his spectacles from his nose, looked at the girl in utter astonishment. As the laughter continued, he rose from the bench on which he was sitting and softly walked over to where she was at work. He stood behind her for a moment, looking over her shoulder at the bird that still lay on the table. Then he picked it up and carefully examined it, holding it in various positions, adjusting now the head and again a wing, but so slightly that no appreciable change was made in the attitude as given by his daughter.

"I don't see anything to laugh at," he said at last to the girl, who had in the mean time ceased to manifest her mirth, and was, with him, looking critically at the bird. "It's very well done, much better than I could have done it, and I've been at the business close on to sixty years, as apprentice, journeyman, and master. You've got the true instinct of the artist, my dear. Ah, how often have I told you that the art of the taxidermist is as high and as subtle as that of the sculptor! Look at that bird! Could the English Lawson, or the French Barye, or even the American Kemeys, who stands a head and shoulders above them all, have done better in marble or bronze? Couldn't you swear that it was just about to pour forth its piping notes—indeed, that you must have suddenly become deaf, for that otherwise you would certainly hear it singing away at the top of its little voice? You can see the delicate throat swell with the expansion of the larynx, and almost move as it varies the inflections and tones of the notes that you are sure are coming out. Can the sculptor do as much with his clay as you have done with the skin of that bird and a little cotton wool? Ah! my dear, you are an artist, a true artist, for you know how to interpret and to depict nature, and to put into your work a living spirit."

"I'm glad you think it's good, father. I'd rather please you than all the rest of the world, for you know what is good and true in art; and if I've been able to get a little of your inspiration, I am satisfied."

"What I know, Barbara, I've acquired by hard work, with stern necessity to urge me on rather than genius. But you could not remain idle if you tried, for you have a soul that needs no spurring to make it plunge forward in the race of life. But you must go away from here to some place where you will have a chance to expand. Here you will never be appreciated by the public. You'll always be regarded just as I am—as a mere 'animal-stuffer'—and you'll wear out your young life in the old shop mounting pet birds and dogs and cats, without ever getting even the name of 'artist,' while others with a tithe of your talent and none of your genius carry off the prizes of life."

"But, father dear," said the girl, patting his cheeks with both hands as she stood erect before him and looked fondly into his face, "I'd rather work here with you than to go away and try to be great. Perhaps, after all, I'd fail, and then where would we both be? No, no; let me stay with you. I like my work, and I like to be with you; I'd rather be happy than famous."

"Ay, girl, that's all very well," resumed the old man, stroking her red hair with his old withered hands, and lingering over the action as though it afforded him

infinite pleasure ; " far be it from me to drive you away
from your old father, for you are a good girl, Barbara,
a good girl, and you've always been good since the day
you were born. But you might be famous and happy
both, my dear. How would you like that ? Famous
and happy ! For, you see, fame brings money, and
what would we be without that ? There's a good deal
of competition now in our business, and I'm getting old ;
and though I'm good yet, it won't be very long before
I'll have to give up. Not but that you could carry on
the work. I know you could. Professor Ricketts at the
Museum told me the other day that the flock of quails
you mounted for him was the most artistic group of birds
in the collection. I heard him pointing out its beauties
to several ladies when he didn't know I was standing behind him, and he said there wasn't a taxidermist in
Europe or America that could equal it. That's high
praise from him, for he's seen all the famous museums
of the world. But, after all, what is it ? He and you
and I know that no one but an artist could turn out
such a gem ; but to the world it's only a piece of bird-
stuffing, with which your name is not connected. He
paid a good price for it, though—good, that is, for our
work ; but if it had been in bronze you'd have got a
thousand dollars for it."

" Then let me stay, father. When you get too old
to bother yourself with work I'll carry it on, and all
you'll have to do will be to give me your advice and instruction."

" Ay, but I want to see you famous before I die. I
want to see your name in the newspapers. I want to
hear people talking of the great artist Barbara Henschel.
I want to see your work in the exhibitions and engraved

for the illustrated magazines, with biographies of you, and your portrait at the head of the articles. Then I think I could die in peace. And I wouldn't leave you a pauper either, Bab. I've got a nice little sum all for you, dear; enough, too, to keep you in comfort while you are studying, so that the wolf would never be at your door. Old Christian Henschel hasn't been a taxidermist for more than half a century for nothing."

"Then you shall give up work whenever you choose. We'll buy a little farm like the one near New Rochelle, that you were looking at last summer. Peter shall look after the shop and do the hard work, just as he does now; and I'll come into town every day and do the mounting. Then, you see, I could bring out with me the smaller animals, and you could show me how to display them to the best advantage. Wouldn't that be nice?"

"Yes, yes, very nice; but it would be still nicer if I was to sell the business to Peter, and instead of your coming to town every day to stuff animals, you came to take lessons in sculpture from Mr. Maurice. I was speaking with him about it yesterday, and he said nothing would give him greater pleasure than to have you as his pupil; and then in a year or two you should go to Europe and study the works of the great masters. I've enough to pay for it all—oh yes, quite enough."

"And leave you here! I couldn't do that, father."

"I didn't say that, my dear," said the old man, with a low laugh. "As I get older a longing to see old Denmark again comes over me. We have glorious sculptures in Denmark. There is no one since the ancient Greeks that has equalled Thorwaldsen. We'll go together, and perhaps spend a year in Copenhagen.

Wouldn't you like that better than wasting your talent in stuffing pet canary birds?"

"Perhaps I would, father," answered the girl, while her face showed the pleasure that the picture held up by the old man gave her, "if I thought—"

"If you thought I'd like it too? That's what you were going to say. You think too much of me, and not enough of yourself. My race is nearly run, yours is scarcely begun. I can never be anything more than I am—an 'animal-stuffer,' as they call me—while you can be, and, please God, you *shall* be, the admiration of kings and emperors, and, better still, of artists. Think of it, dear! think of it! There's time enough; I'll give you a month from to-day to decide."

"O father, you're so loving and kind to me!" she said, while her eyes filled with tears. "I'll try to do what's right for your sake."

"In one month, then, from this day and hour you shall give me your decision. But you haven't told me what you were laughing at," he continued, laughing himself at the idea of his forgetfulness. "It's not often that you laugh so heartily as that. It put me quite in mind of your poor mother, of the time when she was a Danish peasant girl and I was a journeyman taxidermist for old Rasmus Olafsen, in Copenhagen, nigh on to fifty years ago. Yes, she laughed just like that; just like that fifty years ago."

The old man seemed for a few moments to be entirely overcome by his recollections of the past; and then, without waiting to be told the cause of his daughter's mirth, he shuffled back to his work on the royal Bengal tiger.

"Then you don't care to hear what I was laughing

about?" inquired Barbara, as she picked up the bird and began to adjust it to the little perch on which it was to stand. "You know I always see the funny side of everything."

"Oh yes, I want to hear! You're a jolly girl, Bab. Sometimes I think that, in view of all the serious matters of life, you are too light-hearted; but it's good for you, after all, perhaps. When your mother was Olga Heiberg, she was always laughing at something; but after she married me and came to America she tasted the realities of life—mostly sorrows, as they are—to their full. We had a hard time of it here the first three or four years after our arrival. There was very little demand then for my work, so that we suffered; but, thank God! we conquered a good place in the world at last."

"That was because you knew more about taxidermy than any one else in the country; because you had an artist's eyes and head, and because you were not afraid of work. Now you have orders from all parts of the United States."

"Yes, and have had for thirty years. That tiger is to go to the Academy of the Natural Sciences in Philadelphia, and that ornithorhynchus to the Museum of Comparative Anatomy in Cambridge. Oh, I've had orders from Mexico and South America, and Europe, too! We'll see some of my work in the Prindsens Palace in Copenhagen. I sent a buffalo to it last year—the only specimen of the animal they have ever had. Yes, they've plenty of my work in Europe, and they've paid pretty well for it, too, as prices go in our business. I got three hundred dollars for the buffalo, but it cost me fifty to get the skull and the skin."

He went on with his work at the tiger after this speech,

while Barbara, having finished mounting the canary, placed it under a glass shade and went to where her father was sitting surveying the result of his labor.

"I haven't told you yet what I was laughing at," she said, with a smile on her face. "I don't believe you care to know."

"Yes, yes, I do!" exclaimed the old man, with every appearance of interest. "I forget; my memory is very bad, and it gets worse every day. Things that took place sixty years ago I recollect as distinctly as though they occurred only yesterday; but the things of the moment escape me. I was talking with Professor Laird about it yesterday, and he said that I don't register impressions as well as I did. My brain is not so sensitive. You see, my dear, I'm over seventy years of age; but I'm a pretty strong old fellow for all that, and my eyes, when I've got my glasses on, are just as sharp and just as true as ever. Now, look at that tiger! Isn't he splendid? How they'll crowd around him at the Museum next Saturday! I have the consent of the Academy of the Natural Sciences to show him at the Central Park Museum before he goes to Philadelphia. But then," he continued, as he resumed his seat on the bench, while Barbara remained standing by his side with one hand resting on his shoulder, "what were you laughing at?"

"I was thinking," answered Barbara, laughing again at the remembrance, but not so heartily as before, "of the old gentleman that brought the bird here to be mounted. He was very old—older than you, father, but dressed like one of those young men that we see in the Park driving his horses tandem and with a pretty young lady by his side. He told me all about the bird, and he

wept over his story as though his heart were deeply
touched ; as it was, no doubt."

" But, Barbara, my dear, it isn't kind to laugh at the
grief that a person feels when a pet animal has died.
It's strange how these dumb creatures do creep into our
hearts ! And it's well for us that it's so, for more than
half of our work comes from the mounting of dead pets.
Yes, a good deal more than half. It's an honorable
feeling, and we should be the last ones to laugh at it."

" I wasn't laughing at his grief, father, but at the
story he told ; and it was so strange that he should
have told it to me, a perfect stranger. He lives opposite
to a very beautiful young lady, and he's in love with
her. He's seventy-five if he's a day, and she's my age.
He's an old bachelor and, as he told me, has been in love
more than forty times, but could never quite make up
his mind to propose. And so some young fellow has at
last, in every case, come along and married the lady, or
else she has died while he was trying to get his courage up
to the point of asking her to be his wife. He says there
are over forty ladies, any one of whom could have been
his wife if he had had the daring a man ought to have.
The oldest is seventy-four and the youngest twenty."
And again Barbara laughed.

" He seems to have a brave enough idea of his power
as a lady-killer, and I think he's an old fool !" exclaimed
Mr. Henschel, with some degree of irritation in his
voice. " He ought at his time of life to be thinking of
the grave instead of marriage, and to a woman of
twenty at that !"

" Well," continued Barbara, " the young lady who
lives opposite to him had a canary that she prized very
highly, and that every morning, in full sight of her old

admirer, she hung out of her window. Then he used to
sing while the gentleman sat at his window and listened
to each note, as though it came, as he really imagined at
times it did, from the lady herself."

"What, you don't mean to say that he was quite
such an old idiot as that!"

"Yes; that's exactly what he told me. It seemed to
him as though the bird were telling him what the lady
had said, and he used to sit behind the curtain of his
window and listen to it till the sun got round and the
lady took the bird in."

"He imagined the bird to be a medium for the lady
to communicate her thoughts to him?"

"Yes, that was it."

"But did he have no way of replying?"

"That is coming. Every day the bird used to sing,
and, as the heart-sick swain imagined, tell him that his
love was returned, and that all he had to do was to ask
for the lady's hand, and that she would gladly give it to
him with her love. But for all that he could not muster
up courage enough to do as he thought he was told. In
fact, he had never spoken to her in his life, and did not
even know her name—her first name, I mean."

"He's a lunatic, my dear! Oh, there's no doubt of
that! When I was a boy in the little village of Thune,
where I was born, there was an only man named Jan
Petersen, who used to think all the birds were talking
to him. Hour by hour he'd sit in the fields listening
to them and talking back at them. At last he got to
throwing stones at them, for he thought they were abus-
ing him; and one day a stone that he threw at a thrush
struck a little child in the head and killed him. Then
they shut Jan Petersen up in a lunatic asylum, and

that's what they'll do with your old beau if he doesn't mind."

"I shouldn't be surprised. But hear what he did. He was too bashful to talk to the lady, but he bought a canary bird and hung its cage up in his window and talked to it of his love for the lady while he was sitting behind the window curtain. Then, when the bird sang, he thought it was telling the lady's bird how all its words of love were reciprocated, and that thus she would know the state of his heart. But one day the lady left the door of the cage open, and her bird flew away and came across the street; when, finding the window open, it went into the old gentleman's room. The moment he saw it he shut the window and opened the door of his own bird's cage, hoping that the lady's bird would go in. It did go in just as he hoped; but no sooner had it entered than the other bird flew at it, and, before the gentleman could interfere, had killed it. This was the end of that love affair, and that is the bird that I have just mounted. His only happiness now consists, he says, in thoughts of the past. He never intends to fall in love again, but he means to soothe his troubled spirit by looking at the dead canary under a glass shade. It isn't a bad story; but the idea of that spruce-looking and dandified old gentleman thinking of his lost love by gazing at a dead canary made me laugh."

"He's an old fool."

"He'll be here in a few minutes to get his bird. He said he preferred to call for it rather than to have it sent home. Oh, there he is now!" as a carriage drove up to the door of the office—the front room of the establishment—"and Peter is talking to him."

"Mr. Oldmixon would like to see Miss Barbara," said

a young man, appearing at the glass door that opened from the show-room and office into the work-shop.

" He only wants his bird, Peter, and there it is. The price is five dollars."

Peter took the bird, and passed with it into the front room.

" Five dollars for that work of art !" exclaimed Mr. Henschel ; " it's worth fifty."

But at this Barbara only smiled.

CHAPTER II.

ALTHOUGH the door between the two rooms was closed, Mr. Oldmixon's expressions of delight at the appearance of his bird were so loud that it was impossible for Barbara and her father to avoid hearing them, in part, at least. Mr. Henschel's face lighted up with pleasure.

"Ah!" he said, in his slow, deliberate way, "he's not such a fool as I took him to be. He knows a good thing when he sees it. You did not charge him enough for it, my dear."

"Five dollars seems enough for an hour's work, father."

"But the genius! the genius, my dear! You should charge for that, not for the mere manual labor that you put on your work. Unless genius is charged for, Meissonier would get no more for a picture than would a sign painter; not so much, in fact, for he puts a few hours' work on a piece of canvas, while the sign painter is several days at his job. But the one gets ten thousand dollars, and the other the thousandth part of that sum."

"But there is only one Meissonier, while there are a dozen taxidermists here in New York alone."

"Ah! but only one Barbara Henschel. You should assert yourself, my dear. The world generally takes a person at his or her own valuation."

"Mr. Oldmixon would like to see Miss Barbara," said

Peter, putting his head in through the half-open door, and instantly withdrawing it.

"I don't want to see him, though," exclaimed Barbara, with a little tinge of vexation in her voice. "Why can't he take his bird and go!"

"Oh, see him by all means!" said her father, with something of an imploring tone in his voice. "He may want to give you a more important order. Never neglect business, my dear. While we are taxidermists, let us not be forgetful of our interests."

Thus adjured, Barbara gave a little look at herself in a rather dilapidated mirror that hung on a nail driven into the wall, and without further words went into the front room.

"I am everlastingly obliged to you, Miss Henschel," said Mr. Oldmixon, in a melancholy voice, as soon as he caught sight of her. "I felt that I could not go away without thanking you in person for the beautiful manner in which you have mounted this poor bird. It is the one thing that is left of my—my— Would you mind asking your assistant to leave the room for a moment?" he continued, in an altered tone. "Thanks," as Peter, without waiting for a stronger hint, went out, shutting the door after him. "My unhappy passion," resumed Mr. Oldmixon, in the lugubrious accents with which he had begun—"unhappy in more ways than one, and to-day rendered additionally hopeless."

As he finished speaking Mr. Oldmixon took from the breast-pocket of his coat a cambric handkerchief with a wide black border, and gently pressed it to his eyes to absorb the tear that stood in each. Then he very carefully folded and returned it to its place, leaving just the least bit of the black border visible.

He was certainly seventy-five years of age if he was a day, as Barbara had said. In stature he was scarcely five feet, but was as prim and as neat as though he had just stepped out of a band-box. He had removed his hat on Barbara's entrance, and had thus displayed a head absolutely as devoid of hair as was the palm of his hand. His face was shaved clean of all capillary growth, and was as red as a boiled lobster, as was also his scalp; and this hue extended down his neck as far as his clothing permitted it to be seen, and doubtless a good deal farther. He was dressed in the height of fashion, and with an affectation of youthfulness that was ludicrous when contrasted with his evidently advanced age. He sported a blue necktie, with a Roman gold pin representing the head of Medusa, and wore salmon-colored gloves and patent-leather shoes, that he kept tapping with a slender cane all the time he was speaking. Altogether he was a very extraordinary-looking personage, though certainly a gentleman, and entirely sincere in the emotion he was showing.

For a moment Barbara scarcely knew what response to make to this declaration of his unhappiness; but she was a quick-witted young woman. She really felt sorry for him, and she was ready to sympathize with him, or any one else, in fact, that suffered in her presence. She thought it better, however, after a little reflection, to ignore the existence of his grief; so she answered very gently that she was glad he liked the bird.

"Of course I like the bird! It is beautifully, most artistically mounted, and I thank you from the bottom of my heart for all the care you have given to the—the —carcass, shall I say?—of my poor little friend." Then he again took the handkerchief from his pocket, again mopped up the standing tears, and again, folding it exactly in the creases the laundress had given it, put it back into his pocket.

"May I sit down, Miss Henschel?" he asked, after he had completed these actions. "My feelings quite overpower me."

"Of course, Mr. Oldmixon," said Barbara, bringing a chair and placing it by his side.

Mr. Oldmixon regarded it for a moment somewhat ruefully, then he looked at Barbara, and then glanced slowly around the room. Espying what he had evidently been looking for—another chair—he made a dash for it, and, though it was heavy and apparently about as much as he could comfortably lift, brought it to where Barbara was standing.

"I never sit while a lady stands," he said, with a low, old-fashioned bow and a little wave of his hand toward the chair. "I wouldn't do such a thing if I were dying of fatigue. Will you kindly be seated, Miss Henschel?"

Barbara blushed a little at this attention, and sat down. Mr. Oldmixon couldn't blush any more deeply than was his natural manner, even had he felt like doing so; but he followed Barbara's example so far as sitting down went.

"Miss Henschel," he said, after he had crossed one leg over the other, while he continued to switch first one shoe and then the other with his slender cane, "I am about to make you a very important communication, no word of which must ever pass your lips except so far as your father is concerned. Always confide in him. A daughter can have no better friend, at least till she is married to a good man, than her father. Tell him as much as you choose, but be silent while I live to every one else."

Barbara started. The idea flashed through her mind that he was going to do what he never had had the requisite courage yet to do—make her a proposal of marriage. He had already intimated that his late affair had had an unhappy termination. His manner was so impressive and, at the same time, so mysterious, that it was not strange that such a notion should occur to her. Besides, she had strong reasons for believing that he was not entirely of sound mind. She did not believe him to be insane, but she was quite sure that he was very eccentric, and therefore of that form of mental constitution that prompts to the doing of singular and erratic deeds.

But a moment's consideration sufficed to show her that such an act on his part was not very probable. In all the instances—over forty in number, or, to be precise, forty-three—in which Mr. Oldmixon, according to his confession made to her a few days ago, had been in love, he had never been able to master sufficient heart to declare his passion. It was scarcely probable, therefore, that if he were in love with her—of which, indeed, he had given no evidence—he should all at once find his courage developed to the extent requisite for making a matrimonial offer. What he had failed in doing forty-three times he would not be likely to succeed in accomplishing on the forty-fourth occasion. Forty-three defeats argued the existence of a constitutional peculiarity that no mental efforts could subdue. The soldier who has run away in forty-three battles could not possibly fight bravely in the forty-fourth. Besides, as she watched him while he was speaking, she saw that he was in a condition of nervous trepidation that was almost pitiable to behold. Not only was he slashing his patent-leather shoes with his cane, but his face was twitching as

2

though each individual muscle were tacked on to a wire through which an interrupted galvanic current were passing. No, he could not be about to venture on a declaration of love. If he were, he would certainly break down before he began. Besides, there was an accent of sorrow in his tone that was incompatible with the joyousness that should accompany an intention of the kind in question, and a tear was running down each rubicund cheek—a tear that seemed to be amply supplied at its source, for it showed no signs of a diminution in the force of its stream, and, so far as appearances went, would keep on in its meandering career till it was absorbed by the stiff " choker" that encircled his neck.

But Barbara was not suffered to remain long in doubt ; for after going to the door between the two rooms to see that it was entirely shut, and then turning the key in the lock of the street door, Mr. Oldmixon again sat down, again crossed one leg over the other, and again, resuming his pedal castigations, began to unburden his mind.

" Miss Henschel," he said, as—doubtless feeling the water-courses on his cheeks—he again took out his handkerchief and pressed it lightly to his eyes and face, " I think I am in a position to exclaim with the poet— Addison, I believe the author of that admirable series of essays entitled the " Spectator," as well as of several plays, from one of which, *Rosamond*, the lines I am about to quote are taken—I think," he repeated, " that I am in a position to exclaim in regard to love,

> ' Endless torments dwell about thee,
> Yet who would live and love without thee !'

For I have met with a misfortune so sudden and overwhelming, a catastrophe so dire, so agonizing, and altogether so cataclysmic—if you will permit the expression

—that it appears to me as though the end of all things is approaching, and as though—if I may say so without perpetrating an anticlimax—my heart-strings were torn loose from their attachments."

" I am very sorry, Mr. Oldmixon, if anything has occurred to distress you," said Barbara, with the tenderness of voice and look that at once showed that she was sincere.

" You are very kind; so kind, in fact, that I am tempted to confide in you. Indeed, Miss Henschel, you will recollect that on the occasion of our first meeting—when I brought my poor little bird to be restored, as far as your artistic mind and hands could accomplish the object, to the semblance of what it once had been—I ventured to give you a few details of my life, which I was not without the hope would arouse in your sympathizing heart a little spark—scarcely a flame, Miss Henschel—a little scintillation—if I may employ the simile—of pity for one who is, I trust, not altogether unworthy of such an emotion from such a woman."

As he uttered these words Mr. Oldmixon's voice, which had never been strong, became more and more squeaky, till at the end it was not far different in timbre from that of a very infirm and juvenile pig. He stopped, and taking a little vial from his waistcoat pocket, and with an inclination of his head toward Barbara, as though to ask her permission, removed the cork, and, holding the open mouth to each nostril alternately, sniffed the vapor that arose from the few drops of liquid. The effect was to make his face still redder than before; but it appeared to give him renewed strength; for with an air of relief he recorked the little vial and, holding it in his hand in readiness for another emergency, he again spoke, and with an increased force of voice.

" Pardon this little episode, Miss Henschel," he said. " The fact is, I have a weak heart physically as well as mentally, and I am obliged upon occasions of a trying character, such as is this, to resort to the nitrite of amyl as a roborant."

" Can I do anything, Mr. Oldmixon ? Will you have a glass of wine ?"

" No, Miss Henschel ; material aid is not what I require. I am in search of a receptacle into which I can pour my sorrows ; not a mere inanimate vase, but a living, breathing, heart-possessing repository, such as I have every reason for believing you to be. May I presume that far on your benevolence and my impressions of your disposition ?"

Barbara began to feel some degree of embarrassment. She was sorry for Mr. Oldmixon more from seeing in his face and manner the evidences of his grief than from any consideration of the subject that had brought him to his present state. That subject she had strong reason for believing was another disappointment in love, and she really had no desire to hear the details of the forty-fourth misfortune that had befallen her susceptible visitor. There was something, too, that was excessively ludicrous in the idea of this little, desiccated and eccentric old gentleman making her the confidante of his amatory adventures, or, indeed, in his having any such experiences at all. Still, what was she to do ? She could scarcely refuse to hear him. He was so gentle, refined, earnest, in his deportment and language, that she could not find it in her heart to repulse him. She was not the kind of a woman to submit to imposition or intentional annoyance. She had a high spirit and plenty of it when occasion required it to be manifested ; but she

had also one of the tenderest hearts that ever beat in a
woman's breast, and hence the wounding of the feelings
of any one, for the small object of securing relief from a
tiresome experience, would have been almost an impossibility with her. As was to have been expected, her
good-nature prevailed.

"If you think I can help you, Mr. Oldmixon," she
said at last, "I shall—"

"If I think you can help me!" he exclaimed, interrupting her. "Miss Henschel," he added, with an increased gravity approaching solemnity, "I *know* you
can help me."

"I will do what I can."

"Then listen! This morning I was looking out of
my window, thinking of her upon whom my heart was
fixed, and trying to get a glimpse of her as she passed
back and forth in the sitting-room on the second story,
when I observed some unusual signs of an intra-mural
activity new to the house. Men with flowers in baskets
and in the form of bouquets, others with models of tem-
ples and of doves, Cupids and other things in confection-
ery, and women carrying big paper boxes of various forms,
entered the house. Then several wagons arrived with
the names of Delmonico, Tiffany, Howard, and other
purveyors to the gastronomic and æsthetic tendencies of
man and woman, painted on them; and ice-cream freezers
and a multiplicity of packages were handed into the
house. Finally, one after the other, a half a dozen
carriages drove up to the door, and as many young ladies,
dressed in white and carrying bouquets, got out and
went in. Then, as did Hamlet, I said :

> ' All is not well ;
> I doubt some foul play.'

But in what shape it was coming I could not divine. The real cause for all the exhibitions I had witnessed never occurred to me. It only shows how unsuspicious I am."

He ceased talking, and again applied the restorative vial to his nostrils, while Barbara, who was quick enough to perceive to what finality his story was tending, listened with increased interest, when, after a moment or two, he resumed his discourse.

"I stood and watched, my soul filled with the most gloomy but ill-defined forebodings. What could it all mean? I paced the floor! I struck my forehead! I rubbed my head with a piece of cocoanut cloth, in the hope of rousing my dormant intellectual faculties to the comprehension of what was going on; but all to no use. My brain appeared to have sunk into a deep lethargy, with all its faculties, save those of perception, benumbed. I could see and hear, but I could not understand. But the necessary goad to my slumbering wits was soon to be applied without mercy; for after I had gnawed my heart till the agony became insupportable, the door opened, and *she*, clothed in white, wearing a white veil and with orange blossoms in her hair, descended the steps and entered a carriage that had a moment before driven up to the sidewalk. The sun came out brighter, and

> ' In the warm shadow of her loveliness,
>   He kissed her with his beams.'

Fool that I was! Had I known what all those preparations meant I might even then have stopped it, for I should have rushed across the street, have entered the house, have thrown myself at her feet, and have declared my passion. Who," he added, looking complacently around the room, as though he had been addressing a

dozen or more auditors, but finally fixing his eyes on Barbara, " can doubt what would have been the result ? The
wedding would have gone on, the reception would have
taken place, the ice-cream, and the cake, and the chicken-
salad, and the terrapin, and the boned turkey would have
been eaten ; the champagne would have been drunk ; the
band would have played its gayest music; the epi-
thalamium would have been recited ; but the bridegroom
would have been me—Victor Constantine Oldmixon—
and not the despicable wretch who, like a thief in the
night, had stolen into another man's fold and robbed him
of his best beloved."

Mr. Oldmixon fairly broke down with the emotion
consequent on the recollections evoked by these words.
He covered his face with his handkerchief, upon which
he had poured the contents of his remedial vial ; and thus
while he sobbed out the expression of his feelings he
sniffed in the salutiferous exhalations that were to en-
ergize his heart.

Barbara did not know what to do. It was impossible
for her, a stranger and a woman of twenty, to offer sympathy in a love affair to a man of seventy-five, whom
she had seen but once before, and whose very existence
was till a few days ago unknown to her. Besides, the
commiseration that she had felt for Mr. Oldmixon when
he began his recital, and when there was more or less
uncertainty in her mind relative to the actual details of
the disaster that had overtaken him, had rapidly disappeared under the influence of the comicalities of the
situation, as they had been revealed to her by his extravagant though certainly graphic description. Indeed,
it was with the utmost difficulty that she restrained herself from bursting out into a fit of just such laughter

as she had indulged in that very morning over recollections that had not one tenth part of the ridiculousness of the mental pictures now before her. As it was, a smile, that was several times on the verge of becoming audible, sparkled on her face. Fortunately, Mr. Oldmixon could not see through his handkerchief; and after he had vented his grief sufficiently, and inhaled an adequate quantity of the nitrite of amyl to invigorate his heart and nervous system, he proceeded with his story.

"I was determined to find out who the destroyer of my happiness was," he resumed, with more firmness in his voice than he had yet exhibited. "I am a coward, I admit, so far as women are concerned. Any member of the female sex, if she is good-looking, can twist me around her little finger; but with men I am a different sort of a person altogether. When I was a student at Heidelberg I fought three duels. The scars I received in those contests I shall carry with me to my grave. Do you see this?" as he laid his finger on a fine line that crossed one cheek; "and this?" as he indicated another on his chin; "and this?" pointing out one that must have been the remains of a cut that one would think could not have done less than sever his nose from his face. "There are others that have faded out with my advancing years. They are all, however, as nothing to those that I bear on my heart.

'The heart's bleed longest and but heal to wear
That which disfigures it.'

So I rushed out of the house to a livery stable in the next block, and jumping into a coupé that was standing ready I ordered the driver to follow the procession of carriages that was then passing in sight down the Avenue.

I soon overtook them. They turned into Twenty-fifth Street, and stopped at Trinity Chapel. *She* entered the church leaning on the arm of an old man—her father, I suppose. I followed. There was an immense crowd awaiting the entrance of the bride. It seemed as though all New York knew of the wicked act that was about to be committed, while I had been kept in ignorance. I pushed forward as near as I could to the chancel, and whom do you think I saw standing there with his best man awaiting the entrance of my beloved? Whom do you think I saw? Miss Henschel, you are an innocent-minded girl; the contaminations of the world have not touched you. You are one of those pure spirits that think no evil. As I looked at him I felt, in all their force, the words of the poet, that

'Sharper than a serpent's tooth it is
To have a thankless child.'

To be sure, he is not my child; he is only my nephew. Jack Oldmixon, my poor brother's son, is the man who has robbed me; but the words spoken by old King Lear lose none of their force, even though the miscreant be a nephew instead of a son."

"But did you know nothing of all this?" said Barbara. "Is it possible that your nephew would get married without letting you know anything about it?"

"I knew he was going to be married. I've talked the matter over with him half a dozen times; but I had no idea that when he told me he was going to marry Miss Camilla White that she was the object of my heart's desire. White is a common enough name. I know fifty Whites."

"But surely," rejoined Barbara, who had now sufficiently obtained control of herself to converse on the

2*

subject, "he did not know that you were in love with the lady!"

"Of course he did not! How could he? I never mentioned her name to him."

"Then I don't think you ought to be angry with him."

"That seems to be very logical, Miss Henschel; but what has logic to do with love? The more love the less logic. Now, as in my case there was more love than had ever existed before in any similar case, there is an absolute absence of logic. Jack owes everything he has in this world to me. His future is in my hands, and I am going to punish him.

> ' I hate ingratitude more in a man
> Than lying, vainness, babbling, drunkenness,
> Or any taint of vice.'

"I went home at once, determined to let him feel the lion's claws, and I altered my will, so that, instead of getting a half a million when I die, he will get exactly nothing. Nothing—that is, but one dollar."

"Oh, you are too hard on him!" exclaimed Barbara, whose sympathies were now entirely diverted to the young man and his youthful bride. "Doubtless he had taken every means to inform you of what he was about to do; and if you did not understand, I do not think you should blame him."

"But, my dear Miss Henschel—if you will kindly permit a broken-hearted man to address you in that paternal phrase—have I not already told you that this love is absolutely devoid of logic? It has nothing to do with reason. It is a matter of the heart alone. To be sure, when I got home and looked over my invitations—as a rule I never open them—I found the cards from the

Whites, a note from my nephew, and a pretty little one from Camilla, hoping that I would break through my habit and come, not only to the church, but to the reception afterward. But all that doesn't make the matter any better. I shall make him feel it.

> ' Though those that are betrayed
> Do feel the treason sharply, yet the traitor
> Stands in worse case of woe.'

Never shall a cent of mine go into his pocket."

"O Mr. Oldmixon, you will not be so unjust—so cruelly unjust!"

"Yes, I will. That is exactly what I will be—cruelly unjust. You have used the exact words. From this time on, so far as Jack Oldmixon is concerned, I shall be a changed man. Neither kindness nor justice shall ever find a place in my bosom"—striking his breast over his heart as he spoke—"for that traitor, that robber, that wolf in sheep's clothing! The well-spring of benevolence that bubbled in my heart for him is frozen deep down to its very source. He will starve, I am happy to say, if I cut off his allowance—and cut it off I shall."

"I am very sorry," said Barbara, rising as though to leave the room. "I suppose he loves her with all his heart. Poor fellow! I wish I could help him."

"And is all your sorrow for him?" cried Mr. Oldmixon, also rising. "Have you none for me? He has been victorious. I am defeated, heart-broken, and yet you lavish your pity on him! I must confess, Miss Henschel, that I expected something different from you."

"I feel sorry for you," replied Barbara, who now brought her good sense to bear on the subject, and who thought that Mr. Oldmixon's absurd conduct and ideas should not be allowed to pass as though she approved them, "for I think you acted very foolishly. You never told the lady that you cared for her; your nephew informed you of his attachment, and then, when you accidentally find that you are both in love with the same woman, you unjustly blame him, and you announce your intention to treat him cruelly. It appears to me, too," she added, "that—that—"

"Out with it!" interrupted Mr. Oldmixon. "You think he is better suited for her on account of age, and perhaps you would also have said intellect, than I am. I admit it all. I am seventy-five—he is twenty-eight. He is of sound mind. I am of unsound mind, or at least queer, cranky, off my balance, or, to use a more polite and scientific term, eccentric. Yes, he is better suited to her than I am. His conduct throughout the whole affair has been excellent, and mine has been absurd; but, as I told you, love is not a matter of logic, and I'm going to disinherit him as sure as my name is Victor Constantine Oldmixon; and I have documentary evidence of the strongest character that that is my real appellation. I shall leave the whole of my fortune to my other nephew, Hogarth Oldmixon, and to one other person, in equal parts, share and share alike; and Mr. Jack shall not have enough to buy him a coffin. Hogarth is a wild fellow, and I had not intended to give him a cent. I've altered my will so far as Jack is concerned, for I did not know but that I might die to-night—all the Oldmixons die in their sleep, unless they are shot or hanged or commit suicide—and I wanted to make sure of him. If I die to-night my whole estate will go to a new society that I have established—'The Society for the Relief of the Widows and Orphans of Deceased Plumbers ;' but if I live till to-morrow I'll make a new will such as I just mentioned."

" Is your other nephew an honorable man ?" inquired Barbara, while Mr. Oldmixon, in his agitation, walked up and down the floor, slashing his legs with his cane.

" Honorable ! Yes, I suppose so ! Honorable enough for this world, at any rate. To be sure, he drinks and gambles and runs into debts that he can't pay, and does other little things of the kind. But why do you ask ? What has honorable got to do with it ?"

" Only," answered Barbara, " if he is an honorable man he will not take his brother's fortune, when he knows how unjustly you have treated him."

" Ha ! ha ! ha !" laughed Mr. Oldmixon. " You don't know Hogarth, that's clear. He'd take it if every piece of gold was lying on the eyelids of my corpse. So that he gets money he doesn't care where it comes from. I had a thousand dollars stolen out of my room a year or so ago, and I am very sure that Hogarth Oldmixon was the thief."

" And that is the man," exclaimed Barbara, indignantly, " you are going to reward with the fortune that ought to go to his honest and honorable brother ! Mr. Oldmixon, I am ashamed of you ! Yes, ashamed of you ! Good-morning !" and she moved toward the door, evidently with the intention of ending the interview by leaving her visitor alone.

" Stop, Miss Henschel ! For Heaven's sake, stop ! I have not told you all yet ; and the fact is," he continued, as Barbara stood by the door with her hand on the knob, " I must ask your forgiveness for having slightly misled you. The nephew who stole my treasure from under my very nose is the same one that took my money. It's the drunken, worthless, gambling fellow, Hogarth, whereas Jack is as innocent as a babe. It's Hogarth I'm going to disinherit. Jack I disinherited long ago. Now I'm going to reverse the proceeding. But, of course, it would be just as cruel and unjust to poor Hogarth to deprive him of his fortune for marrying the woman I loved as it would have been to cut Jack off, eh ?"

As Mr. Oldmixon uttered these last words he looked at Barbara with a degree of sharpness in his expression that was something of a revelation to her. What did he mean ? Why had he come to her with this false story, and then with a correction that he said embodied the truth ? Was the whole account only the delusion of a lunatic ? What was her opinion to him ? Why should she be called upon to judge between the two nephews ? All these questions, and others, too, suggested themselves to her, and to none of them could she give answers that were satisfactory to herself. She was in the midst of her cogitations when Mr. Oldmixon's voice again struck upon her ears.

CHAPTER III.

A FAMILY PICTURE.

"I suppose, Miss Henschel," said Mr. Oldmixon, coming up to Barbara and standing by her side, his head scarcely reaching above her shoulder—"I suppose that a bad man can be treated unjustly as well as a good one, eh? An act that would be cruel and unfair to a model of all the heavenly virtues would be just as cruel and unfair if committed against a son of Belial, eh? You would advise me, then, not to disinherit this blackguard that broke his poor mother's heart, stole my money, is drunk nearly all the time, is the associate of the vilest men in the city, and has now married a lovely girl upon whom I had placed my affections? What is sauce for the goose is sauce for the gander, eh?"

"You have already shown me, Mr. Oldmixon," answered Barbara, "that my opinion has no influence with you. It is scarcely worth while, therefore, for me to say anything more. Please allow me to go."

"No, not yet, please! I rely on you, Miss Henschel, to help me with your clear judgment, based, as it will be, on such power of comprehension as few, in my opinion, possess. You will kindly call to mind that when I first had the pleasure of meeting you I took advantage of the occasion to indulge in a little philosophical display. If I have a weakness for anything, it is philosophy. Well, your answers to my interrogatories were so exactly in accordance with my own views that I said to myself, 'Here is a woman who has learned how to make use of her brain. I must not lose sight of her, for perhaps some time or other I may want to use her.' The time has come sooner than I expected. I want to use you just as I would use a microscope or a telescope, or a fine chemical balance—to enable me to get at a result as nearly perfect as may be. Now, kindly allow me to state the case without all the non-essential details that may, by their obtrusiveness, interfere with the power to comprehend and, consequently, with the ability to judge, and I pledge myself, in advance, to abide by your decision and to carry it out in all its details with the utmost fidelity."

Barbara was troubled. What right had this man to come to her with his disputes, and his love affairs, and his nephews, and put upon her the responsibility of disposing of his estate? For a moment she felt indignant; but then she soon recognized the fact that she had encouraged him already to the extent of warranting him in asking her to go farther. In his misstatement of the facts she saw, or thought she saw, that his prejudices were all in favor of the wicked nephew, to whom he had already given by his will the whole of his estate. It was easy for her to perceive that this was the one whom, in spite of his badness, Mr. Oldmixon loved. Probably there were some good qualities about the young man that the other nephew did not possess; but she had already seen sufficient of Mr. Oldmixon to cause her to form the opinion that his mind was of so badly balanced a character that he would be extremely likely in any given case to do exactly the opposite of what ninety-nine men in a hundred of normal mental organization would do under like circumstances. In a moment of irritation he had gone home from the church and had altered his will; but why had he come to her with a misstatement of the facts of the case? She felt angry that he should have thus played upon her, and she at once determined that she would express no further opinion in regard to the matter till he had given her a satisfactory explanation of his conduct. At the same time she was forced to admit that there was a strong possibility that the whole story was manufactured either from a very small groundwork of fact, or without there being the slightest element of truth in its composition. She did not take long to make up her mind. There was always a degree of directness in Barbara's conduct that was one of the strongest marks of the integrity of her mind and nervous system. She thought promptly, as well as with perspicuity and force.

"Mr. Oldmixon," she said, "I do not think you have treated me with entire frankness. You appear to me to have endeavored—and with success, too—to lead me into a trap. You have obtained from me an opinion which, as you now admit, was based upon erroneous premises—intentionally erroneous—that is, false premises given me by you. I don't like such treatment, and unless you can explain your conduct to my satisfaction I shall certainly leave you to settle your troubles in your own way."

"And you would do exactly right if you did. But mine, I respectfully submit, is not a case for justice so much as it is one in which mercy should be exercised. I admit that I was wrong, and I throw myself entirely on your charity and forbearance. Besides, think of the opportunity now given you of doing a service in the cause of fair-dealing."

"But why did you place the matter before me in a false light?" said Barbara, adhering to the point she had made. "I do not see the necessity for such a procedure. I like to be treated frankly."

"I will tell you, Miss Henschel," replied Mr. Oldmixon, lowering his voice almost to a whisper. "I was a little in doubt relative to the correctness of the motive that had actuated me in changing my will. I knew that that worthless scamp would be left out in the cold; but when I came to think the matter over I was afraid that the manner in which he had treated me was not the cause that should have moved me to alter my intentions. I thought, therefore, that I would make his case out to you as that of a thoroughly good young man, knowing that if your opinion was for me from the aspect of the case I should give you, that it would be still more in my favor when the matter was placed correctly before you. But you decided against me, very much to my surprise, and notwithstanding my repeated assertions that there was no logic in the affair. Consequently, unless you will hear me further—as I have now determined to be guided by you—I shall go home and write a new will, restoring that wretch to his former position as my heir, and leaving his good, noble-hearted, and honorable brother out in the cold without a dollar to bless himself with. Now, what do you think of that?"

"It seems to me," answered Barbara, "that you are a very unjust man. Why did you make such a will, in the first place?"

"Because I have no sense of justice in me. You are entirely right when you say that I am an unjust man; I am governed entirely by feeling and impulse. That is why I came to you. I want justice; having none in my own composition, I ask you for it. Look at the matter, therefore, with your sense of truth, and decide for me, according to the principles of justice—retributive or tempered with mercy, as you may think best adapted to the case in question."

"State the case to me, Mr. Oldmixon," said Barbara, with an awakened interest. "You shall have my opinion, and you can then do as you see fit."

"Thanks; I shall do exactly as you say. Now, listen! But won't you sit down again? Allow me!" And Mr. Oldmixon brought the chair that she had just vacated to her; and then, placing his own beside it, sat down—after her, however—and resumed his recital.

"As I said just now"—beginning again to strike his shoes with his cane as he spoke—"I did a very unjust thing when I made a will leaving everything I have in the world to my nephew Hogarth, and nothing whatever to my other nephew, Jack; but I did not act without reasons, although, as you will doubtless perceive, they were of a very inadequate character. They are both the sons of my only brother, Morley Oldmixon, who was killed in a duel, many years ago, that he had himself provoked. Jack is the elder of the two by three years, but he takes after his mother; there does not, in fact, seem to be a bit of the Oldmixon stock about him, except his name. Hogarth is, however, a true scion of our house in appearance and in character. We were all a rather bad lot, I think. The founder of the house is said to have been a pirate; one of my ancestors was beheaded for treason; another was burnt at the stake for heresy; another broken on the wheel for highway robbery in France; others have suffered the penalties of the law in various ways; and Hogarth, if he has a fair chance, will certainly be hanged. I myself am a somewhat irregular sort of an individual, as you probably have already perceived; but in me the strain has been modified by the fact that my mother was the descendant of a race that has always been noted for their virtues, and was herself the daughter of a bishop. I am not, therefore, quite so bad as some of my ancestors.

"We have always, however, notwithstanding the black sheep in the family, been noted for our pride of ancestry and for a tendency to stick to our villainous members through thick and thin; to protect them by all the means at our disposal, and to lavish upon them all the good gifts that it might be in our power to bestow.

"In pursuance of this inherent trait of character, so soon as the two boys had begun to develop, and I saw that Jack was a model of propriety and excellence in everything, and that Hogarth was a combination of Jack Sheppard, Captain Kidd, and the King of Ashantee, I made my will in his favor."

"It was a wicked thing for you to do!" exclaimed Barbara, indignantly. "Very wicked and very unjust."

"Ah! that is exactly what I wanted you to say. Now, I have got an expression of opinion from you, Miss Henschel, that will warrant me in entirely reversing the provisions of my will. To-morrow morning I shall go to my lawyer and I shall instruct him to draw up another will, in which all my real and personal estate, of every nature and description, shall be given to Jack Oldmixon, under a certain condition, while Hogarth shall receive the munificent sum of one dollar for the purpose of purchasing a rope with which to hang himself. I have heretofore given him an allowance of three thousand

dollars a year, while I have left Jack to shift for himself.
I shall change all that, too."

"But," asked Barbara, "is your younger nephew so
very bad as you represent? Are you quite sure that you
have not, under the influence of the irritation you feel
at his marriage, unconsciously exaggerated his faults?"

"Oh, there's no mistake on that point. Why, it was
exactly on account of his wickedness that I made him my
heir. I have already mentioned to you some of his acts.
I could make your hair stand on end if I were to specify
to you the tenth part of his crimes, not merely offences
against good order and decency, but actual violations of
law. No, he is hopelessly and irreclaimably bad."

"And is your elder nephew altogether different?" she
inquired, anxiously, for she felt now the weight of responsibility that rested upon her, though still not by any
means entirely convinced that Mr. Oldmixon was not a
veritable lunatic.

"As different as night is from day. Jack is tall,
Hogarth is short; Jack is dark, Hogarth is fair; Jack
is handsome, Hogarth is as ugly as the devil; Jack is
honest, honorable, frank, and manly; Hogarth is a thief,
a liar, a hypocrite, and a coward; Jack works for his
living, and will, without aid from any one, rise to greatness; Hogarth never did a useful piece of labor in his
life, and if he does not die from disease induced by his
excesses, will certainly be hanged. Jack is beloved by
every one that knows him; Hogarth is despised and
hated by all respectable people as soon as he reveals his
true character."

"You did an awful wrong when you deserted the good
nephew for the bad one."

"That's right, give it to me; regard yourself, Miss

Henschel, as a physician, and me as a great big, disgusting ulcer. Don't treat me with molasses when I require aqua-fortis. Say to me, in the language of the poet,

> ' Thou shalt be whipped with wire and stand in brine,
> Smarting in lingering pickle.'

I deserve all you can say. But tell me in a few words, please ; do you think I ought to change my will ?"

"If what you have told me is true, I think the sooner you alter it the better. Such injustice ought not to stand a moment longer than can be helped."

"And you give that opinion, Miss Henschel, altogether uninfluenced by the fact that the wretch Hogarth stole my beloved away from me ?"

"I give it upon the information of his character that you have just communicated to me. If what you say is true, he must be a perfect monster. But how could he succeed in ingratiating himself into the favor of the lady whom you tell me he has just married ?"

"Oh, he's the most specious rascal that ever lived ! You may depend upon it that he has brought to bear upon her all his wiles and arts, and that she is thoroughly deceived in regard to his character. Doubtless she thinks him a paragon of all that is good and virtuous. My word for it, she will not live with him a month. My poor Camilla ! Little does she know the sorrow that is in store for her. But, my dear Miss Henschel, you have taken a load from my mind. I will leave you now, with many heartfelt thanks for your goodness, and to-morrow morning the wrong shall be undone ; I begin to feel as though the Oldmixon tendencies were being dragged out of me, and I can only attribute the change to your influence. The moment my eyes rested upon you for the first time, I said to myself, 'There is the woman that can mould me into any form she pleases.' Don't reply, I beg of you"—seeing that Barbara was about to speak. "Good-morning! Ah, my bird! I must not forget that 'emblem of stainless purity' that you have made worthy to stand amid the productions of artistic Paris or Rome. Good-by! I will, with your permission, call again." With which words Mr. Oldmixon, with his bird in one hand, unlocked the street door with the other, and passing out of the house entered his carriage, and, after speaking a word or two to the coachman, was driven rapidly up-town.

To say that Barbara was fully impressed with a sense of the importance of the interview she had just had, would very inadequately express the state of her feelings. From whatever point she considered it, she saw that it involved possibilities that she scarcely felt competent to estimate at that moment at their full value. That Mr. Oldmixon was of an erratic turn of mind was very evident; but he appeared to have a full knowledge of what he wanted and intended to do. That he would come to her with such a story as that that he had told, knowing it to be false, was entirely out of the question. There was no room for doubting his sincerity; there had been too much emotional disturbance for that. She had seen his tears, his agitation, the change in his voice, and the difficulty with which at times he had appeared to get his breath. She saw, too, how, under the influence of the vapor that he had inhaled—the strong odor of which still remained in the room—he had become more composed and able to go on with his recital.

Besides, the account he had given was too systematic and consistent to be false. She saw very clearly how

Mr. Oldmixon had impressed his own individuality on his narrative ; she saw that there were many inferences that he had drawn for which there was probably no warrant ; and these were the very strongest indications that his mind was eccentric, to a degree almost reaching a state of absolute insanity.　Thus his egregious vanity was shown in the opinion he had expressed that he might at any time on the morning of Miss White's wedding with his nephew have himself become the bridegroom had he been aware of what was going on and had declared his love for her.　The same emotion had cropped out in all that he had said, even when he had requested her to strike hard and spare not, and when he had bragged of the infamy that had been associated with many members of his family.　He seemed to revel in the depravity of his nephew Hogarth, and to be proud of the fact that there was little probability of finding his equal in wickedness.

But apart from this mental peculiarity and the extreme susceptibility to the attractions of women that he exhibited, there did not appear to be any defects in Mr. Oldmixon's intellectual processes.　His methods of reasoning seemed to her to be exact, if they were somewhat peculiar.　They might be, and doubtless were, marked by his individual idiosyncrasies ; but there was nothing in them to indicate that he did not possess a mind that was within the normal limits of soundness, however irregular it might be.　His facts were stated coherently and with a degree of precision and force that carried conviction with their enunciation, and the impression of their truth was not essentially weakened by the admission he had voluntarily made, that he had deceived her in regard to the nephew who had interfered with the course of his love for Miss Camilla White ; for the deception had been perpetrated with an object, and was only another evidence of his shrewdness.

But what did it all mean ? she asked herself. Why had Mr. Oldmixon come to her to be the repository of his secrets and to aid him in his schemes for and against his nephews ? He had said that he had been attracted by the knowledge of philosophy that she had displayed during his first interview with her a few days previously ; but she was not conscious of having shown that she possessed any such knowledge. Barbara had received a good education, though I am afraid that the majority of the young-lady graduates of our colleges would have turned up their sophomorically intellectual noses at the statement of the extent of her scholastic acquirements. The most important educational feature of Barbara's mental development was, that she had learned how to think ; whereas, the young-lady graduates aforesaid are, in general, supremely ignorant of that cerebral process. When she was about twelve years of age a sister of her father's, Fraulein Ernestine Henschel, who had been a school-teacher in Copenhagen, came over to America, at her brother's request, to take the care of his household, his wife having died a few months previously. This lady was thoroughly acquainted with the science of pedagogics, having received a very complete course of instruction in a school especially established in Copenhagen by the queen for the education of young women desirous of becoming teachers. Her aunt took charge, not only of her brother's household establishment, which, not being extensive, required very little of her time, but of Barbara's education as well, and she had kept it till Hans Callisen followed her from Denmark, married her,

3

and took her to Minnesota when she had nearly reached
her fortieth year. But by that time Barbara had had
the benefit of her aunt's knowledge and training for six
years, till she was eighteen years of age, in fact ; and
though she could neither be said to have received what
is called an ornamental education, nor one like that given
to young women at some of our institutions devoted to
the enlightenment of the female mind, she had laid in a
stock of solid information in the languages and sciences
that not one graduate of Macassar College in a hundred
can pretend to possessing. Her profession as a taxidermist had given her a love for zoology, and she had given
special attention not only to this branch of knowledge,
but to all other departments of natural history. She
was a good botanist and mineralogist, in addition to having a practical acquaintance with the science of living
beings that would have put many a college professor to
the blush.

But as to philosophy, she was about as much acquainted
with it as was the gentleman with prose, which he
found, to his surprise, he had been speaking all his life.
She had never read a line of Plato, or Spinoza, or Kant,
or Hegel, or even of Emerson. In fact, she had never,
so far as she could have told, looked into a work on
metaphysics or psychology, and she knew absolutely
nothing of the many theories of the mind that ingenious
Frenchmen like Descartes, or Englishmen like Locke, or
Scotchmen like Hamilton, had promulgated. But for all
this, it would not be correct to say that she was ignorant
of mental philosophy. Indeed, she knew a good deal
about it ; but she had acquired her knowledge not by
studying the writings of others, but by practising that
habit of introspection which, sooner or later, all thinking

people acquire, and by which more is often to be learned relative to the operations of the human mind than is to be acquired from books.

Bringing to bear, as well as she could in a brief time and in her agitated condition, the experience she had gained by her self-examinations, she came to the conclusion that Mr. Oldmixon had really been moved by a desire to obtain her opinion, having probably some doubt relative to his ability to judge correctly in a matter in which his feelings were involved. She called to mind the earnestness of his speech and the sharpness of his facial expression when he questioned her, just after he had informed her of the erroneous impression he had given her relative to the two nephews. She felt sure, too, that he would act in accordance with the views she had expressed, and she began to experience a sense of the responsibility she had incurred in advising him to change his will. What if the nephew Hogarth were neither so bad as his uncle had depicted him, nor Jack so good? Then the guilt of an unjust act—if guilt there were—would not rest on her shoulders. She had acted in accordance with assertions that she had a right to believe were true. If they were true, then she was satisfied with the part she had taken.

She looked at the clock that hung on the wall over the desk in the office. It was after twelve. Mr. Oldmixon had kept her over half an hour from her work, and she had yet a good deal to do before she could honestly say that she had done a day's labor. She therefore went into the back room, where her father, assisted by Peter, was doing the first part of the work required in the mounting of a fine specimen of that rare animal, the silver fox.

"Well, Barbara!" exclaimed the old man, as she made her appearance, "if you had thought Mr. Oldmixon was going to keep you nearly three quarters of an hour over his bird, you would have charged him ten dollars for it, wouldn't you?"

"He did not keep me about the bird, father," she answered. "It was about something of much more importance."

"Another order, I suppose," said Mr. Henschel, who under all circumstances had that keen eye to business and profit that the Scandinavian generally displays.

"No; he said nothing on the subject. I don't think he has any more work at present. But he had a good deal to say about some family matters, and he asked my advice. To-night I'll ask you to tell me whether I did right or not."

"Ah! my dear, you know more about such things than I do. But now I'll get you to give a little shaping to this fox, and Peter can go back to the office. It's a rare specimen of an animal that is every day becoming rarer. I suppose this skin is worth three hundred dollars. Did you ever see anything so beautiful? Now, the owner of this is a man after my own heart. He'd rather have it mounted as a work of art than sell it to some furrier to cut up into muffs and collars and such things for rich women to wear."

"Who is the owner, father?"

"Oh, I don't know. I didn't ask his name. He said he'd send or call for it next week; but he didn't come in a carriage, and he didn't look as if he had any more money than he wanted."

"It's a beautiful specimen; the finest I ever saw."

"Yes, the very finest. I offered him three hundred

dollars for it, but he said no ; he had killed it himself last winter while with the Hudson's Bay Company, and he wouldn't sell it.   Now, my dear, I leave it to you to put the proper expression into its face and attitude.   Remember, that in its natural state it's the slyest of all of its kind.   However, I can't tell you anything about the habits of animals that you don't know.   It's your knowledge on this subject that makes you the true artist that you are and the best taxidermist in this country, if not in the world.''

THE house occupied by Mr. Henschel as his residence and place of business, although not situated in a part of New York that would have been called fashionable, was, nevertheless, in one that was eminently respectable. Many years ago it had been occupied by well-to-do tradesmen, who lived in comfort, if not in luxury ; but in the course of time, with the constantly increasing demands of trade, most of the residences had been altered so as the better to adapt them to the newer purposes for which they were required. It was in one of these that the Henschels lived.

The lower floor was entirely, with the exception of the kitchen—situated at the extreme rear of the building—devoted to the business of taxidermy. The front room, which opened directly upon the street, served as an office and show-room. It was lined with glass cases, and in them were contained some of the most choice specimens of his and his daughter's skill ; for they not only mounted animals to order, but did a good business by keeping a stock on hand to supply the wants of museums in various parts of the country, or of individuals looking for specimens of birds or animals to place in their halls, libraries, or dining-rooms. During one year he had received orders for nearly three hundred buffalo, elk, antelope, mountain sheep, and other heads, from gentlemen who wished to use them to ornament the walls of their houses.

In addition to the work of mounting animals, Mr. Henschel had a good deal to do in the way of furnishing collections in botany, mineralogy, and conchology to colleges, academies, and private persons. He was well known to scientific men in all parts of the civilized world, and was held in high esteem by them. They took great pleasure, many of them, in sending him duplicates of the specimens in natural history that they had collected in their explorations, or had received in exchange, and he, in his turn, had given them many valuable and interesting additions to their collections, that he had received from seafaring men, with whom he had always kept on good terms, and who were in the habit of bringing him the curiosities that they had picked up in various parts of the world.

It is impossible for a taxidermist not to acquire some knowledge of natural history. It generally happens, however, that his acquirements in this direction do not extend beyond those practical points that are gathered from the collectors and scientific persons with whom he comes in contact. It was very different, however, with Mr. Henschel, as we have seen it was with his daughter. From the time when he was a boy and an apprentice to old Rasmus Olafsen, the learned taxidermist of Copenhagen, he had studied from books, and had thus obtained a knowledge of the science that the mere mounting of the animals that came under his hands would never have given him. These, it is true, served him in good stead in his studies, for he was enabled to use them for purposes of identification ; but they could never have taught him the classification and internal structure of organic beings.

Besides books, he had the advantage of much personal
instruction from Professor Bording, who not only held a
high position in the University, but was, besides, a knight
of the order of Daneborg.   This learned man took a great
interest in young Henschel, and not only allowed him to
attend his lectures, but gave him, in addition, much private
instruction.   He introduced him to Thorwaldsen, then
in the very zenith of his fame.   From this greatest of
modern sculptors the young man imbibed that love for
art that had always been a governing motive with him.
He had, in fact, gone so far as to take lessons in sculpture
and to produce two or three works that his master thought
gave evidence of his possession of decided talent ; but he
soon found that the road to greatness, or even respectable
mediocrity in the vocation of a sculptor, was not only long
and painful, but that it would be many years before he
could rely on it for a pecuniary support.   The weariness,
the anxieties, the disappointments, the rebuffs he could
have stood ; but it was necessary for him to live by his
labor.   So, when a Danish gentleman whom he knew
returned from a visit to New York and told him that
there was a fine chance in that city for a skilful and artistic taxidermist, young Henschel married the pretty
peasant girl with whom he had long been in love, and,
with less than a hundred dollars in his pocket, started for
New York.   For a time things went hard with him.
Several children were born to him, but they had all died
young, till, when he was well advanced in life, Barbara
came into the world, different, apparently, in physical constitution from the others ; for she had always been a vigorous and healthy child, and had grown up into woman-
hood without ever having had a day's sickness.   Her
father had often declared with great delight that he had

never known a day that Barbara could not eat three hearty meals.

It was very natural that Mr. Henschel should apply to his daughter the principles that had been instilled into him in Denmark. Barbara had, in fact, been reared in an atmosphere of natural science. By the time she could talk she had learned to recognize and to designate by their names the many kinds of animals that were continually passing under her observation, and ere long she could classify them into groups from the characteristics that she noticed they possessed. "Pick out all the cats, Barbara," her father would say to her, and then the little girl would go round from case to case and point out the tiger, the panther, the ocelot, the cougar, the lynx. Over the lion she was at first a little puzzled. "He looks like a cat, and he doesn't," she said. "He's got such a big head and so much hair on it ; but his wife"— pointing to a lioness that stood by the side of her lord—"looks just like a cat. I think all the wives are more like cats than the husbands." Then Mr. Henschel had chucked his wife under the chin. "Do you hear that, my dear?" he said, laughing heartily. "All the wives are more cat-like than the husbands. What a sharp little body she is !"

By exercises like these little Barbara ere long became an accomplished practical zoologist. As she grew older she began to assist her father in his work, and from the very first she developed an artistic sense that the old man declared was so delicate, refined, and yet bold, that, if she could have advantages such as had been offered him when he was a boy in Copenhagen, would bring her to the front as one of the leading sculptors of the world. Of course Mr. Henschel was prejudiced in his daughter's favor, and hence his opinions of her genius were to be taken with

3*

many grains of allowance; but for all that, there was no doubt of her having a genuine aptitude for original work. She had modelled several subjects in clay, and had done them so well that they had attracted the marked attention of several artists of her father's acquaintance. One of them—an Apache Indian hunting a buffalo, and just in the act of discharging an arrow into the heart of the animal as he rides alongside of him on his mustang—was so greatly admired for its fidelity to nature, as well as for the life and spirit that she had thrown into the composition, that her father was persuaded to have it cast in bronze. In this form it was placed on exhibition at Tiffany's in New York, at Bailey's in Philadelphia, and in like places in other large cities, and a great many were disposed of at fair prices, to the decided aggrandizement of the Henschel exchequer.

It was during a journey that her father made to the West, under the auspices of the Smithsonian Institution, and in which she accompanied him, that she obtained the requisite knowledge from life not only for the modelling of the Apache Indian and the buffalo, but for mounting many of the specimens in natural history that came to her hands. Congress had made an appropriation for constructing a road from Fort Riley, in Kansas, to Bridger's Pass, in the Rocky Mountains, and the authorities in charge of the Smithsonian Institution, ever alive to the advantages to science to be derived from such expeditions, had obtained authority for Mr. Henschel and his daughter to accompany the engineer party and troops, charged with the laying out and making of the road, for the purpose of collecting specimens of the natural history of the region of country through which the route passed. This journey had been of the utmost service to Barbara in more than one respect. It had enlarged her ideas, given her an acquaintance with nature in some of its wildest forms, which she could otherwise never have obtained, rendered her more self-reliant than she had ever been before, and put the finish to her physical organization, which, strong though it had been, was now rendered doubly so by the life in the open air for nearly six months, a horseback journey of nearly two thousand miles, and that abstraction from the requirements of civilization which always invigorates those upon whom its influence is brought to bear.

Barbara was about eighteen years of age when this journey was taken. Since her return her father had constantly urged upon her the advantages that would accrue to her were she to devote herself exclusively to sculpture and modelling; but she, knowing how necessary she was to him so long as he continued to carry on the business of a taxidermist, had resisted all his importunities. He was old; it was not likely that, in the course of nature, he would live many years longer; there was now plenty of work for them, and a good income was derived from their joint labors; but Barbara knew that if she retired from the practical part of the business that orders would fall off. It was just as her father had said. The people who required work done in taxidermy were well aware that Barbara was the artistic head of the establishment, and they wanted her to superintend the mounting of their specimens. So far as she herself was concerned, nothing would have given her more pleasure than to have entered definitely upon an artist's career such as her father desired for her. On the morning that she is introduced to the reader he had spoken more openly upon the subject and more to the point than ever before. She had previously known very little in regard to his financial condition. She knew, however, that he must have laid by enough to place him and herself above want ; but now she was well aware, from her acquaintance with his modes of speech, that he was at least a moderately wealthy man. When he admitted that he had enough to live on without work, and at the same time give her all the opportunities requisite for her obtaining proficiency in the art that he wished her to adopt as a profession, it meant that he had accumulated sufficient of this world's goods to satisfy his ambition in that direction. She knew that he was of an acquisitive disposition. The only fault she had ever been able to detect in him was a slight tendency to avarice and miserliness. This was not possessed to an extent that rendered him an object of mark among those who knew him ; but occasionally, as the reader has already doubtless perceived, it cropped out. Yes, if he was willing to stop work and spend a small fortune to place her favorably before the world as an artist, he must be rich.

It would be an easy thing to get rid of the business upon favorable terms. Peter, whose surname was Swain, had been with them in the capacity of an assistant and man of all work for nearly ten years. He had very little money of his own, but he had a wealthy friend who was willing to furnish the requisite capital for the purchase of the stand and the good-will as a set-off to his knowledge and time. Mr. Dibble, the gentleman referred to, had inspected the premises and examined the books, and had arrived at the conclusion that the fifty thousand dollars required for the purchase-money would yield over fourteen per cent profit, which, if he gave six to Peter, would leave him a net income of eight per cent. Peter, however, had other views, that were somewhat antagonistic to those of Mr. Dibble. The names of "Dibble and Swain, Taxidermists," would look well in gold letters on a black ground across the front of the house; but the name of "Peter Swain," or even those of "Henschel and Swain," would look better. Peter had come from central New York when he joined his forces with those of Mr. Henschel. At the time that he is introduced to the reader he was about twenty-eight years of age, fairly good-looking, and possessed of such an education as the majority of farmers' sons in the State of New York pick up from the common schools. He was honest and attentive to his business, and Mr. Henschel had always given him good wages. Peter was, however, ambitious to better his condition, as is every American boy of average intelligence, no matter into what station of life he is born. He wanted to succeed Mr. Henschel when the latter came to retire, and he wanted to be either his own master or to maintain only a nominal connection with the name of Henschel. The only way that he could perceive by which he could accomplish either of these ends was to marry Barbara Henschel. He was not in love with her; in fact, such an element as sentiment did not enter into his mental organization. He was a matter-of-fact man, and marriage with him, if he ever married, would be an affair of the head and not of the heart—one that would be prompted by intelligence, and not by emotion. In this respect Peter was not unlike the majority of young people, men or women, who in these times enter into the matrimonial state.

He had never hinted at such a thing to either Mr. Henschel or Barbara. While he had a very good opinion of himself, he was by no means sure that any advances he might make in the direction in question would be favorably received by either of the parties concerned.

So far as family went, doubtless his was as good as hers, perhaps better ; but in the matter of their individualities he was not so blind but that he was ready to admit that hers was superior to his, and that when she contemplated marriage she would look for a man of better parts than was he. In fact, so distant did the prospect appear of his being able to accomplish the object that stood high up in his scale of desirable things, that he scarcely ventured to consider it as within the limits of probability, and had latterly been giving more attention to the cultivation of friendly relations with Mr. Dibble than to making advances to Barbara. He had once tried to place himself in such a position as would, he thought, inevitably lead to the establishment of more intimate relations between himself and the Henschels than had heretofore existed ; but this attempt had met with such a decided repulse that it had very much the effect upon his wishes that a wet blanket has upon a fire. He lived away from the Henschels, and he had conceived the idea that it would on several accounts be desirable for him to reside with them. There was a nice room on the third floor that would just suit him, and it would be much more comfortable for him to take his meals with them than to eat in the company of the rather irreverent young men who ridiculed his profession and who constituted the band of table boarders of Mrs. Daly's establishment. In his application to Mr. Henschel to be allowed to take up his abode with him he had placed the matter on the grounds of its affording him increased facilities for attending to the business ; and that as the room that he proposed to occupy was empty, the granting of it to him would, with his board, be the means of adding a respectable sum to the income of the Henschel family.

But Mr. Henschel was very decided in the expression of his indisposition to accede to Peter's views relative to the means of becoming more sociable with his employer's family. He stated that he and his daughter were in the habit of conversing during their meals on matters that concerned them alone, and that the intrusion of a third party into their family circle would be intolerable. He was, however, kind enough to state that he would consult with Barbara on the subject and ascertain what she had to say about it, though he could not give Peter any ground for hoping that the decision would be reversed. He did lay the matter before his daughter, and her opinion was even more emphatic than that of her father against the desirability of any change in their home arrangements; thereupon Peter had seen that there was not much prospect of his ever becoming, by marriage, a member of Mr. Henschel's family. But he was a good, honest fellow, who was held in high esteem not only by Mr. Henschel, but by Barbara likewise. He was well acquainted with the art of taxidermy so far as its practical details were concerned, but he had never evinced much inclination for the scientific connections of the profession. He was literally an "animal-stuffer," and nothing more. His intentions toward Barbara were, therefore, almost as preposterous as would have been the love of a sailor on a man-of-war for the daughter of his captain. Barbara had the refinement that comes from education and association with educated and refined people. Her father's house was visited by learned men from all parts of the world, and she had been thrown into more or less intimate relations with many of them. She had thus become acquainted with their ideas on many subjects outside of taxidermy and with modes of thought of which Peter Swain had not the most distant conception. Upon one occasion she had been invited to spend a month during the summer at the sea-shore with Mrs. Lawson, whose husband was professor of mineralogy and geology in the Franklin Scientific School; and again another month with the family of Professor Senstone, at their country-seat on Cayuga Lake. It was no uncommon event for ladies whose husbands were of scientific proclivities to invite her to their houses, at which she was always treated with due consideration as a lovely, intelligent, and good girl, in whose society it was pleasant to be. From the associations thus afforded her, Barbara, without losing in the slightest degree the natural independence of her character, had acquired the polish of manner that can only come from personal communications with persons of good breeding. Her father and mother and aunt, though plain people, were not unrefined. They had that intuitive repugnance to coarseness that is so generally met with in the European artisan of the highest class; and though they might have felt out of place at a court-ball, for instance, they would certainly not have perpetrated, even in the presence of Majesty itself, any act calculated to offend the sensibilities or to interfere with the comfort of the royal guests. Barbara, therefore, had started well, and her opportunities for acquiring a gentle presence had not been neglected.

A residence of nearly fifty years in the United States had converted Mr. Henschel into a thoroughgoing American. He spoke the language with the ease and fluency of an educated native, and often said, laughingly, that he believed Danish was fading out of his memory, as the occasions for using it were so few and far between. He did not, however, altogether break with the old country.

He had been, ever since his arrival, a subscriber to a Copenhagen newspaper, and he had made two visits to that city and to the little village where he was born. The last one had been undertaken with the idea that he might possibly decide to return to his native land, and there pass the remainder of his days; but he soon found that his long residence in America had given him ideas and habits entirely inconsistent with those of the people among whom he would have to live, and, moreover, that his old companions were either dead or had ceased to take any pleasure in his society. He had, therefore, returned rather disgusted with Denmark and its people, and declaring that the land of his adoption was good enough for him, and that he hoped that when the time came for him to die, he would be found in the country that had been his home for nearly half a century; where his children had been born, and where the bones of his dead wife rested.

From all of which it will doubtless appear to the reader that the father and daughter had much upon which to congratulate themselves. He had been successful far beyond his most sanguine expectations, so far as material prosperity was concerned. The death of his wife and four sons had been heavy blows to him; but with time the sharpness of them had been blunted, to which result the constant association with his daughter and a community of interests and opinions had essentially contributed. There was very little to disturb the mental equanimity that was such a striking element of his disposition. In fact, there was nothing but one subject that greatly disturbed him, and that was his ambition that Barbara should become famous. This idea had become a passion with him—a somewhat remarkable fact, for it is not often that an old man is capable of any very intense development of feeling in a matter that does not intimately concern his personal ease and enjoyment. The aged are almost invariably selfish, and Mr. Henschel was no exception to the rule, save in the one respect mentioned. So far as his daughter was concerned, he was capable of making any sacrifice within his power to accomplish her well-being and happiness. Her future was the one theme upon which he was never tired of dilating, and he had spoken only the truth when he declared that when he could know that she had acquired the world-wide distinction to which he thought her genius entitled her, he would die content. To put her in the way, so far as he could, by any act or line of conduct, to reach the pinnacle upon which he conceived that she ought to stand, was the one all-absorbing emotion that filled his breast.

CHAPTER V.

Mr. Oldmixon was as good as his word. A night's re-flection had only tended to make him more fixed in his intention of changing his will. He began, too, to flatter himself that he was really actuated by a sense of right toward one whom he had hitherto shamefully neglected, and of stern justice toward that other, who had never in all his life done anything to deserve the unlimited kind-nesses of which he had been the recipient. He had arrived at the point of believing that no feeling of resent-ment entered into the matter, and with that facility with which people generally persuade themselves that the thing they desire to do is right, had brought himself to the conviction that whether Hogarth had or had not married Miss White he would in time, through his own self-communings, have been prompted to act toward the young man exactly as he was now acting.

" It was only a question of a few days or weeks, or at most months," he said to himself, as he was eating his breakfast at the Lucullus Club on the morning after his conversation with Barbara. " I was rapidly arriving at the knowledge that I had made a mistake. This marriage of the scamp has only precipitated matters, that's all."

He rang the bell that stood on the table.

" Bring me a morning paper," he said to the waiter that answered the summons. " Any one will do."

"Yes," he continued, as the man, having brought him a paper, had retired at an intimation that his presence was not required; "here it is!

"'Married on the 4th inst., at Trinity Chapel, New York, by the Rev. Thomas Colightly, Camilla, daughter of Jabez White, Esq., to Hogarth Oldmixon, son of the late Morley Oldmixon, Esq., and nephew of Victor Constantine Oldmixon, Esq.'

"The barefaced rascal, to dare to announce himself as my nephew! Little does he know what's in store for him. I'll give him a lesson in decency if I can't give him one in morality. I'd like to lay a horsewhip over his shoulders, and I'd do it, too, if I had one now and he was within reach of my arm."

Then, after finishing his breakfast, Mr. Oldmixon, who never walked if he could help it, got into his coupé that stood at the door of the Lucullus, and drove downtown to the office of his legal adviser, Mr. Theobald Ridley. He had in a large pocketbook the will that he had made several years since and the draft of the new one that he wished put into legal form.

Mr. Ridley was engaged when he entered the room in which clients waited till the great man of the law was ready to receive them; so, having nothing better to do, he took out the paper containing the memoranda of the provisions of the new will he contemplated making, and perused and reperused them, with the object of ascertaining whether or not he had sufficiently covered his intentions with his words. Mr. Oldmixon had a clear head for business, and, besides that, he was, in spite of his eccentricity in the matter of one-sided love affairs with women he did not know—in which he displayed a degree of imbecility that would have disgraced an idiot—a shrewd, sharp man, who could see as far into other people's motives and schemes as was necessary for his purposes. He had not been deceived by his nephew Hogarth. He had always known that he was a bad fellow, but he was an Oldmixon in mind and body, whereas Jack was not; and this fact had been the determining factor in causing him to make the will which he was now on the point of reversing.

He did not, however, find anything to change, so that when Mr. Ridley sent for him he was more than ever firmly convinced that he had done, not only what he had intended doing, but that his intentions were right.

The lawyer glanced over both papers while his client sat eying him keenly and observing, with gratification, the expression of astonishment that came over his countenance. Mr. Oldmixon's vanity was of such a high degree of development that it was gratified beyond measure when any act of his excited surprise or interest in those about him. He was pleased when he could arouse an emotion in others. It showed power.

"Do you know, Mr. Oldmixon," said Mr. Ridley, after he had made himself acquainted with the contemplated provisions of the new will, "that this is a somewhat remarkable paper?"

"Yes, Mr. Ridley, I am fully aware of that fact."

"As I understand the matter, you desire to disinherit your nephew Hogarth and to make your nephew John your heir."

"Precisely! I think that is very evident."

"Yes, yes, it's clear enough; but in conjunction with your bounty to this young man you have imposed the most extraordinary conditions that I ever heard of, and I am not a man without experience in such matters."

"Yes, they are extraordinary, I admit; but, then, the occasion is extraordinary."

"I am not quite sure that they would stand in law."

"I'll risk that. I'm something of a lawyer myself, and I am not altogether ignorant of such matters."

"I suppose you have no objection to tell me the motives that influence you in this matter?"

"Yes, I have a very strong objection to doing anything of the kind."

"Oh, well, it doesn't make any difference. I only thought there might be something in which you were misinformed or in which you were acting hastily."

"No; I am fully acquainted with all the facts of the case, and I am acting with more than my usual deliberation."

"Then," said Mr. Ridley, looking over the paper that he still held in his hand, "as I understand the matter, you wish to give by your will your entire estate, real and personal, except the sum of one dollar, to your nephew John Oldmixon."

"That is my desire," answered Mr. Oldmixon, in a tone of voice as mechanical as though he were saying his catechism, for he thought he had made his intention sufficiently plain, and that Mr. Ridley's caution was superfluous.

"And the condition is, that he shall, within one year after your decease, marry a certain lady whose name is left blank."

"Yes; I'll fill in the name; but I've no objection to telling, in the strictest confidence, that her name is Barbara Henschel."

"And in case he should refuse or neglect, from any

cause whatever, to marry the said Barbara Henschel, then the estate is to go to her."

Mr. Oldmixon nodded his head in affirmation.

"I suppose you have not overlooked the fact that if Barbara Henschel should take the initiative in the matter, and declare that she will not marry your nephew, that she would become your heiress."

"I am perfectly well aware of that fact, and I had it distinctly in view when I wrote out that memorandum."

"Then you might as well, so far as the money is concerned, make her your heiress at once, for you have put it in her power to get your money. Of course you know that the probability is, that she will prefer to be her own mistress and to marry whom she pleases."

"I know all that as well as you do, Mr. Ridley," said Mr. Oldmixon, with a little stiffness of manner not devoid of impatience, "and if the disposition of my estate had been my chief object, I should have made a somewhat different will from that that I now contemplate. Knowing you as well as I do, I suppose you are possessed of sufficient discernment to perceive that the bestowal of my money is not the prime purpose of the document I desire you to prepare."

"You wish, above all things, to secure a marriage between your nephew John and this Miss Henschel?" inquired Mr. Ridley.

"Certainly I do!"

"Then, don't you see that the provisions of the will must be kept an absolute secret from her—that, in fact, no one must know of them except your nephew John?"

"Of course I do, Mr. Ridley!" exclaimed Mr. Oldmixon, jumping up from his chair and beginning to slash his shoes with his cane. "Of course I do! Do you take me for an idiot that doesn't know his own mind? Of course I'm peculiar; I show it in many of my acts, and I suppose it is apparent in these memoranda; but peculiarity is neither imbecility nor insanity, is it?"

"No," answered Mr. Ridley, laughing; "there are many examples of eccentric wills that have stood the tests of the courts. Mere eccentricity will not affect the validity of a will. If it did, such a one as this"—taking as he spoke a law journal from the table and turning over a few leaves—"would have been upset beyond a doubt. Here," he continued, "is a man who is represented as having been a shrewd, successful business man, who had accumulated a large fortune. He had never exhibited any sign of insanity; but I think you will admit that his will is even more eccentric than yours. He disinherits all his natural heirs, and devises all his property in trust for the establishment of an infirmary for cats. A most elaborate architectural plan for the necessary buildings is attached to and made part of the will. It provides areas for that sweet amatory converse so dear to the feline heart, and rat-holes of the most ravishing nature to be kept well-stocked. The most ingenious contrivances are provided for securing to the rat a chance to escape, so that the cats may not lose the pleasure of the chase by finding their prey come too easily. High walls are to be built with gently sloping roofs for the moonlight promenade and other nocturnal amusements of the cats. The trustees are directed to select the grounds for this novel infirmary in the most populous part of some great American city, and the devisees are to be protected by a competent force of nurses from the ravages of men and dogs. No person of the male sex is ever to be admitted within the walls, and no female that has children or that is under thirty years of age. There are a hundred or more minute directions that I pass over."

"The man was crazy, of course!" said Mr. Oldmixon, contemptuously. "You don't mean to compare my will to that, do you?"

"Not exactly. I only intended to show you that there are more eccentric wills than yours. This one has just come before the courts, and has not yet been adjudicated upon. If it is sustained, you need have no fear of yours not being upheld. But I have not yet finished with the will for the protection and well-being of cats. One would suppose that in the foregoing provisions the testator had exhausted all the eccentricities of one man, however unique his nature; but the last provision of the will seems more outrageously whimsical than any that precede it. Says the devisor: 'I have all my life been taught to believe that everything in and about man was intended to be useful, and that it was man's duty, as lord of the animals, to protect all the lesser species, even as God protects and watches over him. For these two combined reasons—first, that my body even after death may continue to be made useful, and second, that it may be made instrumental, as far as possible, in furnishing a substitute for the protection of the bodies of my dear friends, the cats, I do hereby devise and bequeath the intestines of my body to be made up into fiddlestrings, the proceeds to be devoted to the purchase of an accordion, which shall be played in the auditorium of the cat infirmary by one of the regular nurses, to be selected for that purpose exclusively. The playing to be kept up forever and ever, without cessation night and day, in order that the cats may have the privilege of always hearing and enjoying that instrument which is the nearest approach to their natural voice.'"

4

"Of course," said Mr. Oldmixon, "such a will as that cannot stand, for it is contrary to public policy. The courts will make short work of it."

"And I am not quite sure that yours is not open to the same objection. Don't you think it is contrary to public policy to bribe a man to marry a woman whom, perhaps, he does not love and can never love?"

"No, I don't!" replied Mr. Oldmixon, promptly. "She will know nothing whatever of the provisions of the will, and therefore the only inducement she will have to marry him will be the fact that she loves him. If she does not love him she won't marry him, and then she will get the money. If she marries him within a year after my decease he will get the estate; if she refuses to marry him, or marries some one else, or marries him after a year has elapsed, she will get it. Surely, it's all very plain, and I don't see anything in the provisions that is contrary to public policy."

"Well, well, perhaps not; I'll do the best I can with it. You want me to put these data into the form required by the laws of the State of New York?"

"Yes, of course! That's what I came here for."

"When will you be ready to execute the will?"

"I shall be ready this evening. Send it to me as soon as it is done, and I will sign it and have my act witnessed in due form."

"And this other will, what do you wish done with it?"

"That you may destroy as well as this other that I made last night"—taking as he spoke another folded paper from the breast pocket of his coat and handing it to Mr. Ridley.

"What's all this!" exclaimed that gentleman, as he hastily ran his eye over the document.

"Oh! that's a will I made last night in case anything should happen to me before I had quite made up my mind in regard to the details of all that I wanted to do."

"It isn't worth the paper on which it is written. It isn't properly witnessed, and may as well go into the waste-paper basket"—saying which Mr. Ridley tore it into several pieces and threw them under the table. "The other, however," he continued, "is another thing. If you were to die before you execute your new will it would stand."

"And if I destroy it, what then?"

"In that case you would die intestate, and your estate would be divided among your heirs-at-law."

"Then I shall not destroy it yet. I would rather Hogarth should get my property than that it should be cut up into a dozen or more shares, as would be the case were I to die without a will. Give it back to me. I'll keep it till I sign the other. Then it will be worthless, whether destroyed or not."

Mr. Ridley handed him the paper, and in a few minutes thereafter Mr. Oldmixon took his leave, and entering his coupé directed the coachman to drive to the "Vandyke" apartment house in one of the up-town streets.

Mr. Oldmixon was a man of action. In fact, he had one of the most restless spirits that ever inhabited a human body. He was never quiet except when he was asleep, and, as a rule, he was not then in that condition, for he snored terribly and was a somnambulist—features, especially the last, that on several occasions got him into serious difficulties.

He was now on his way to make a visit to his nephew John, or, as he was generally called, "Jack," for the purpose of acquainting him with the kind intentions he had formed relative to his future financial and matrimonial relations.

He knew very little of Jack. In fact, he had not seen him to speak to him for several years. Occasionally when he had been driving through the streets he had encountered his nephew trudging along on foot ; but their eyes had not met, probably because neither the one nor the other cared to allow them to do so, and not even a salutation passed between them. Till this morning he did not even know where Jack lived, and he had been obliged to have recourse to a Directory to gain the necessary information. There he had found " Oldmixon, John, artist, 'The Vandyke,' 61 West ——th Street."

Jack had always, in addition to the other virtues that his uncle gave him credit for possessing, shown a sufficient amount of independence to extort his relative's unfeigned though silent respect. He saw, while he was yet a boy, that for some reason or other he was not a favorite. At first this troubled him greatly, for he was of a warm and affectionate nature, and he was disposed to make advances, notwithstanding the fact that they generally met with rebuffs. He was then under the impression that there might be something in his conduct or his manner that was disagreeable to his uncle, and upon one occasion had made bold to ask if there was any ground for his fear, expressing at the same time his desire to correct it if his respected relative would be kind enough to enlighten him in regard to its character.

For a moment Mr. Oldmixon had looked at the boy in astonishment, and then, with some confusion of manner, had said : " I don't think it's worth while to talk about that matter now. I'll give you an education till you are twenty-one, and then you can look after yourself. I may as well tell you, however, that all my money will go to your brother."

It was a cruel speech to make, and no one knew that fact better than Mr. Oldmixon himself. But he thought it would be as well to destroy at once and for all any expectations that Jack might have formed of coming in for any portion of his estate. He had been for some time seeking an opportunity for doing so, and now it had come to him when he had least expected it.

For the instant the boy looked as though he were about to burst into tears ; but he was a manly fellow, even though only sixteen years of age, so he controlled himself as well as he could, though his lips quivered a little and his eyes moistened.

"I thought I would ask," he said at last, "for if there is anything I can do to make you like me, I will do it. Not that I want any of your money," he added ; "Hogarth is welcome to that."

Mr. Oldmixon was not ordinarily brutal, but he felt the blood of his ancestors warming in his veins from some cause or other, and it was bad blood to get heated. He turned on the child, and with a scowl on his face said :

"I like Hogarth because he is an Oldmixon. He looks like one, talks like one, acts like one. I dislike you because you take after your mother, and I never could endure her. There doesn't seem to be any Oldmixon blood in you, and, by Heaven ! I don't believe there is."

The words were hardly out of his mouth when Jack sprang forward, and with all his young strength dealt his uncle a blow in the mouth that cut his lip and caused the blood to flow, besides loosening several of his teeth. He would have jumped upon him and have inflicted further damage had he not been grasped by Mr. Oldmixon's man and carried bodily, struggling and kicking with all his might, out of the room. That night he left the house, leaving a note for his uncle in which he declared that he would never receive another favor at his hands, nor even recognize him as a relative. "You are a liar and a ruffian," he wrote. "You insulted my mother, and if I had been let alone I would have killed you."

From that time on there had been no intercourse between the two. Jack had gone to a gentleman, a noted artist with whom he had a slight acquaintance, and had requested him to put him in the way of applying to the court for a change of guardianship. There was no trouble in effecting the substitution of his friend for his uncle, as the latter united in the application, and Mr. Winfield Bageot became Jack's legal guardian and trustee of the small property left by his mother till the time of the boy's arriving at age.

Jack's father had run through his estate in a few years after marriage, and then, as the reader has already been informed, was run through the body in a duel that he had provoked. Mrs. Oldmixon had always been delicate, so that, though her husband's death was a good riddance to her, she had only survived him a few months. She left property yielding about a thousand dollars a year equally divided between her two sons. Jack had, therefore, after the rupture with his uncle a little over five hundred dollars a year upon which to keep body and soul together and complete his education. Under the guidance of his friend, Mr. Bageot, he got along very well, and after a couple of years more spent at school he began to learn something of art, with the intention of becoming a painter, provided he showed any talent in that direction. He *did* show talent. By the strictest economy he had saved enough to enable him to pay for his passage to Rome, and once there he was enabled to live on his five hundred a year better than he could have lived on a like sum in New York. He stayed two years in Rome and one in wandering about Europe, stopping a month or two in each of Paris, Madrid, Vienna, Munich, Dresden, London, and other art centres, and working hard all the time at figure painting—the branch of the profession for which he thought he exhibited most talent, and which he greatly preferred to any other. By the time Jack returned to New York he had planted many good seeds, and planted them well, so that there was every prospect that he would be able to make his way to some degree of eminence in the line of work he had chosen.

An artist has better opportunities for bringing himself before the public than has a member of any other profession—that is, of course, if there is anything in him that the public cares for. If he paints a good picture it is hung in a prominent place at some one or more of the art exhibitions, and is, perhaps, also displayed on the walls of his club house. It is described by the art critics of the daily papers and of the magazines that are, or are not, specially devoted to art interests. It is probably engraved for the pages of some art journal or by some print-seller. It may even be chromo-lithographed. By all these means the artist is made known to society and the world at large. He is invited out, he is talked about, and his reputation is made.

Jack Oldmixon went through all this, and had achieved what most young men in his position would have considered splendid success. Every year since his return he had had one or more pictures at the annual exhibitions of

the National Academy, and they had been sold promptly
at his own prices to wealthy men in various parts of the
country.   One of them had been purchased by Mr.
Malters, of Baltimore, and this circumstance—as every
one knew how accomplished a connoisseur Mr. Malters
was—had of itself largely aided in selling other productions of his brush.   The wealthy Mr. Smilax, of Chicago,
had bought one and had given an order for another, the
subject to be the Goddess of Beauty casting pearls before
swine.   Jack had thought long over this order before
deciding to accept it, but at last he had concluded that
something good could be made of the subject, and he
had accordingly gone to work at it with great enthusiasm,
and had produced a picture which the *conoscenti* declared showed real genius in the conception, and that it
was a wonderful piece of composition and coloring.   He
had treated the matter symbolically, the swine being men
and the pearls women.   At first the Chicago gentleman
—who was far more artistic in his tastes than many of
those in the East who make pretensions—looked at the
picture in amazement.   The idea was so entirely different from the one he had formed of feeding swine with
pearls that for a moment he thought there must be some
mistake.

"My dear fellow," he said, "I don't see the hogs."

Jack smiled, but made no reply ; and in a little while
the mental illumination came to his patron with a force
that almost overwhelmed him.

"By thunder !" he exclaimed, wringing Jack's hand
with both of his as though he were squeezing the water
out of a wet cloth.   "You're a genius !   You've produced
the finest thing of the time—one, sir, that will swell your
reputation to such proportions that you'll hardly know

yourself. I wouldn't take five thousand dollars for that picture, and in ten years from now it'll be worth twenty. Give me a pen and ink, please.''

Jack gave him writing materials, and Mr. Smilax, producing a blank check from his pocket, sat down at a table, and in a moment or two handed the young man the product of his penmanship. Jack took it, glanced at it, and handed it back.

"This is for five thousand dollars," he said. "You are only to give me twenty-five hundred for the picture.''

"My dear young friend," said Mr. Smilax, in his most insinuating tones, "it is one of the privileges of wealth to reward talent. When I engaged to give you twenty-five hundred dollars for a picture, I had in my mind one that I thought would be worth the price. This is different, and worth a great deal more than that sum. As I just said, I wouldn't take five thousand for it. I feel that I am getting the best of the bargain when I tender you that amount for it ; but then, you see," he added, smiling, "as a business man I like to come out a little ahead.''

The end of the matter was, that Jack took the check, feeling that in Mr. Smilax he had secured an appreciative patron. And he had ; for the picture, "Casting Pearls before Swine," was the reason of getting him more orders than he could easily attend to. But he was industrious. He worked fast, and when walking or driving, or when at the theatre, or during a lapse in the conversation at a dinner-party, he was thinking of his work, and framing mental images of persons and situations. Many of these, upon reflection, he discarded ; but others were among his best conceptions.

Then the great railway magnate and millionaire, Mr. Van der Linden, had called upon him, and had requested

4*

a picture by him for his magnificent gallery. The gentleman knew a good deal about pictures. It would have been strange if he had not, for his great wealth had enabled him to get together such a collection of the best works of modern painters as was probably unequalled in all the world ; and he had studied them thoroughly, as well as having made himself familiar with the productions of all the schools represented in the galleries of Europe. It was his habit to spend every day an hour in the quiet contemplation of some one picture of his famous collection. At four o'clock punctually he ceased serving mammon for the day, and, entering his coupé, was driven to his house. Then he repaired to his gallery, and, lighting a cigar, seated himself before some noted painting, and resigned himself to its study, endeavoring to obtain some conception of the ideas that had filled the mind of the artist, and that he had transferred to the canvas.

This was the gentleman who, after great deliberation, had given Jack Oldmixon an order. He was accustomed to say that there was not a bad picture in his gallery, and that he did not intend that there should be one. When Jack had asked him for a subject he had answered that he wanted not only a picture, but a subject as well.

" Fix your own price," he had said. " If the picture suits me I shall hang it in my collection ; if it does not, but is good, I'll give it to some friend ; but if it's bad, I'll destroy it. There are enough bad pictures in the world without the number being increased by me."

Jack had accepted the terms, had named his price, and had been assured that it was reasonable and just, large as it was, and had been for a week or more racking his brain for a subject for what he intended should be the great effort of his artistic life.

Thus matters stood with Jack at the time that his uncle was driving up Fifth Avenue on his way to resume relations that had been interrupted for more than a dozen years. The world and he had got along very well with each other. He had shown his independence and his ability to take care of himself. He had rarely met his brother since he had cut loose from his uncle. Mr. Oldmixon had directed Hogarth, on pain of incurring his implacable resentment, to cease all communications with Jack; and Hogarth, being one of those astute youths that are wise in advance of their years, and are at the same time not possessed of principle beyond that of looking out for themselves, had seen on which side of his bread the butter was spread, and had scrupulously obeyed his uncle's commands. At first they had spoken when they had met in the streets; but for the past ten years this formality had been dispensed with, and they passed each other as though they were strangers. Take them all in all, the Oldmixons with which this history has to deal could not be looked upon as being a " happy family."

CHAPTER VI.

"WHAT BROUGHT YOU HERE?"

It was with some degree of trepidation that Mr. Oldmixon got out of his coupé and ascended the staircase of the Vandyke apartment-house to his nephew's rooms. He did not have far to go, for they were on the first floor. In fact, the distance was so short that there was scarcely time for him to compose himself into such a frame of mind as would not reveal itself by his manner. Naturally he was nervous. Little things disturbed his equanimity unduly, and big ones acted with proportionately greater power. The janitor preceded him, and on arriving at the landing was about to usher Mr. Oldmixon into a reception-room while he took his name to the occupant; but to this the gentleman would not listen. "I am his uncle," he said, "and it isn't necessary for me to be announced as though I were his tailor. Show me his door, and I'll manage to get in without your assistance."

The man went along the hall a few steps followed by Mr. Oldmixon, and at last stopped before a door on which was tacked a visiting-card bearing the name of "John Oldmixon." "That's the room," he said. "The gentleman's in"—pointing as he spoke to a little wooden label with the word "In" printed upon it in large letters. "All you've got to do is to knock," with which words he retreated, leaving Mr. Oldmixon to get in through his own devices.

For a moment that gentleman hesitated. He was not quite sure of the character of the reception his nephew would give him. He knew that he had no right to expect any consideration, and he was very certain that had he sent in his name Jack would have peremptorily refused to see him. But he was also aware of the fact that he came strongly armed and with inducements for peace such as few, if any, nephews would care to resist. As he stood before the door he could hear some one, doubtless Jack, moving about the room, and—yes, actually whistling. That was a favorable sign. People don't whistle when they are cross. Jack must be in a good-humor, for not only was he whistling, but he was whistling that classical song "Whoa, Emma!" Nobody, Mr. Oldmixon would have sworn, ever whistled "Whoa, Emma!" when he was in a bad temper.

So far, therefore, the indications for a peaceful interview were favorable.

He knocked, and on hearing a loud "Come in" from the room, opened the door and entered.

Evidently Jack had just been dressing, preparatory probably to going out, for he was in the act of putting his arms into the sleeves of a black frock-coat, when, turning his face to the door, he saw his uncle standing before him.

His countenance changed. Evidently the influence of "Whoa, Emma!" as a factor in causing the evolution of good-humor was not of a permanent character, for the expression upon his face now was not such as, for instance, a book-canvasser or a subscription agent would have preferred to see. There was no element of excitement about it, but it was calmly, darkly, freezingly indignant. It was one that exhibited a potentiality for becoming dangerous, and this idea of its character was increased by the fact that as soon as Jack recognized his visitor he apparently looked behind him involuntarily at the window, as though to ascertain its exact distance and location, with the view of making use of it for a purpose different from that which had led to its construction.

The intrusion was so unexpected to Jack, that it required an instant for him to grasp the situation. But his was a quick-working brain, and generally anticipated what was being submitted to its action before the matter was wholly unfolded. People said that when they talked to Jack Oldmixon he evidently saw the conclusions to which their remarks were leading long before they had fully stated their premises. The situation therefore was not long, so far as its obvious features were concerned, in being thoroughly comprehended, nor was he slow in arriving at a determination as to the action necessary in the premises.

"You!" he exclaimed; "what brought you here?"

Now, Mr. Oldmixon knew that he had every reason to expect a cool, perhaps even an angry, reception. His conscience pricked him not so much for what he had done to the boy, though on that score he did not in his present frame of mind hold himself guiltless, but for the dislike he had unjustly entertained for him, and for the cruel speech that he had made, more than twelve years ago, in regard to the boy's mother. For those sins—sins for which he knew there could be no adequate excuse, he reproached himself bitterly, and for them he had anticipated an unfriendly reception at the hands of his nephew. But to be called on in that abrupt way to tell what had brought him there was not what he had expected. The object of his visit was not to be stated offhand and in a few hasty words spoken on compulsion. On the contrary, it was one that for its exposition would require all his shrewdness and diplomacy and an agreeable frame of mind in him to whom it was to be disclosed. Jack must be placated. That requirement was prominent in Mr. Oldmixon's mind, and how to fulfil it was now the question that absorbed all his powers of attention. Fortunately for his wishes, he was a man of ready resources and prompt action. He had often boasted of never having lost his presence of mind, although it had been his fortune to be placed in many trying situations. Besides that, he knew that Jack was of a generous and forgiving disposition, and he argued from this circumstance strongly for the success of his plans. Jack did not have to wait long for an answer.

"I have come," said Mr. Oldmixon, bending his head in an attitude of humility, and looking down at a figure on the rug about a foot in advance of where he stood—"I have come," he repeated, "in the first place to ask your pardon for my unjust and cruel language of many years ago. I have often thought of it since that time, and I have never failed to censure myself for uttering words that I knew were false and that had no other excuse than my bad temper."

"It seems to me," said Jack, not changing his expression, "that, considering that your insult was uttered more than twelve years ago, you have been a long time in expressing your regret."

"True ; I have been proud and unjust all that time, but I have none the less been aware of my fault. I have come to-day not only to ask your forgiveness, but to show you that I am sincere in my repentance. I wish you to be friends with me once more. I am a changed man, and my vile language, uttered to you a boy, is not the only thing of which I have repented."

Jack felt himself yielding. It was not in his nature to stand out against a repentance and a desire to undo a wrong so sincere as those exhibited by his uncle. Gradually his face cleared up; and before Mr. Oldmixon had done speaking he had resolved to let "bygones be begones" and to resume the relations that the ties of consanguinity justified. He had always regretted the alienation, or, rather, he had regretted that Mr. Oldmixon had spoken as he had, not only because his words were an insult to his mother, but because they required a total severance of all associations with the man that had spoken them. No sooner therefore had his uncle finished his little speech than Jack stepped forward with outstretched hands.

"I am glad you are come," he said, while Mr. Oldmixon grasped the hands held out to him. "You were wrong to say what you did, but it is manly and straightforward for you to express your regret. I suppose we all do and say things when we are angry that we are sorry for afterward."

"Then it is all over between us!" exclaimed Mr. Oldmixon, his countenance expressing the joy he felt at this happy termination in accordance with his desires. "Now, will you let me stay a few minutes and talk over matters with you? Twelve years, Jack, my boy, since we have had a talk! It's a long time for uncle and nephew to be separated."

Before he had finished speaking Jack had rolled a big chair up to him, and Mr. Oldmixon had dropped himself into it.

"I'll talk with you as long as you like," said Jack,

equally pleased with the reconciliation that had taken place. " Some of these days we'll exchange confidences in regard to our experiences during these last twelve years. I've got some interesting things to talk about, and so have you, I'm sure."

" I've kept my eye on you, Jack, and I've been proud of you all the time. You're a great man now. I've gone to the Academy exhibitions every year, and I've looked for your pictures the first thing. You're ahead of them all, Jack. You're the greatest painter in New York, and I'm proud of you just as much as though you were my own son."

" You're very kind, Uncle Victor"—it was the first time Jack had given him the title of relationship. " I've tried to keep up the name."

" God forbid that you should keep up the name as the Oldmixons have kept it up ! We're a bad lot, Jack. You are the only one of us, so far as the family traditions go, that has been any credit to mankind. There's that scoundrel Hogarth—"

" Hogarth ! What has Hogarth done ?"

" What has he done?" almost shrieked Mr. Oldmixon. " What hasn't he done ? Everything but murder, and he isn't too good for that."

" Perhaps I should know more about it if you were a little more specific in your language. I haven't laid eyes on him for a year or more. Of course he has treated me very badly. I'm his only brother, and yet for twelve years he has been a stranger to me. There's something horrible in the idea of passing your own brother in the street and not speaking to him. The fault, however, has not been mine. I always spoke to him, and shook hands with him when we met till he cut

me dead, and then, of course, I took no further notice
of him."

Mr. Oldmixon shifted himself uneasily on his chair
while Jack was speaking, and his face underwent many
changes of expression.

"That was partly my fault, Jack. Indeed, I suppose
I am wholly to blame. Still, he was very willing to do
as I told him. He never remonstrated against my orders.
A true man would never have obeyed them."

"No, I think not," said Jack. "If you had ever
told me not to speak to him, I should have refused to do
your bidding."

"You haven't lost much. Hogarth is one of the most
depraved men in the world. Of course I knew he was
bad when I turned you out of my house. But he was an
Oldmixon, and that idea seduced me. Now I've had
enough of him and of all the brood like him."

"But what new offence has he committed?"

"Haven't you heard?"

"I have heard nothing. I hope it is a small matter."

"Small! he couldn't have done anything much worse.
He was married yesterday." With these words Mr. Oldmixon covered his face with his hands, and his body shook
as though he were convulsed with grief.

"Hogarth married!" said Jack, in some astonishment.
"It's news to me. I suppose," he continued, in a tone
of sympathy, "he's made a bad match."

"No," sobbed Mr. Oldmixon, "he has married the
loveliest girl in New York."

"I don't understand, then, why you should be so distressed over the affair."

"It's very plain," said Mr. Oldmixon, removing his
hands, and exhibiting a face on which traces of tears ap-

peared. "I'm sorry for the poor girl, that she should be mated for life to a blackguard and villain like Hogarth—and—can you keep a secret, Jack?" turning his eyes on his nephew, and speaking quickly.

"I suppose so," answered Jack; "I don't think I'm a babbler; at any rate, I'll keep any secrets of yours as long as you wish me to."

"Well, then, Jack, that wretch has done me the greatest injury one man can do another, for I was deeply attached to the woman that is now his wife. She was so deep in my heart, that although she now belongs to another, I feel as though I could never give her up. Perhaps in time," he continued, with a more cheerful expression of countenance, "I may become reconciled to my loss, but I think not. I do not see that I can ever love again, for I loved her more than I have ever loved any other woman."

"Then," said Jack, with the proper amount of indignation in his voice, "she seems to have behaved very badly."

"Oh dear, no!" exclaimed his uncle; "I don't see how you can think that. Her conduct has been admirable throughout."

"I don't understand," observed Jack, with an expression of hopelessness on his countenance. "If she was engaged to you, and then married another man, it appears to me that most people would regard that as acting badly."

"But she was not engaged to me. Who said she was engaged to me? I've been in love forty-three times, and I have never once been engaged."

"Oh!" exclaimed Jack.

"I don't see any occasion for an expression of astonishment," said Mr. Oldmixon. " I was so unfortunately constituted as to be very susceptible and at the same time to be utterly devoid of confidence in myself. I am the faint heart that never won fair lady. My love has been silent, and I've

‘ Let concealment, like a worm i' the bud,’ etc."

" But," remarked Jack, scarcely able to keep his face from breaking into a smile, " you got over all the other affairs, so that in all probability you'll conquer this one also."

" In time, perhaps, and with your aid. I look to you now, Jack. All my trust is in you, and," he added, after a little hesitation, " one other."

" A lady?" inquired Jack, this time being unable to keep back the smile.

" Yes, a lady, but not, as you appear to suspect, one that I am in love with. She is the very best of her sex, beautiful, intelligent, refined, well educated, good tempered, but not one for *me* "—with a strong accent on the pronoun—" to love. That is all over with me. My regard for her is that of a father for a daughter. With Camilla White — whom that scoundrel Hogarth stole from me—not only was the last spark of the gentle passion extinguished in my breast, but the fuel became exhausted. There is nothing there now but a burnt-out furnace, an extinct volcano, a cinder. What was once the sun is now the moon. I believe the moon is a dead planet or sun, or something of the kind, isn't it, Jack ?"

" Really, uncle, I don't know," answered Jack, scarcely aware whether or not an attempt was being made to perpetrate a joke. " I am not up in astronomy. I have often heard the moon spoken of by young ladies of a sentimental turn of mind as 'cold' and 'pale—'"

"That's it!" interrupted Mr. Oldmixon; "that's exactly the state of my heart, 'cold' and 'pale.'"

"Suppose you tell me all about it, uncle," said Jack, at last, having failed, from Mr. Oldmixon's references, to get a clear idea of the situation, and knowing that it would save time and trouble to be fully enlightened now. "That is," he added, "if the story will not awaken too many painful recollections. You tell me that you have been in love forty-three times. You were joking then, surely."

"No; that is the exact number. When I last talked with you, Jack, you were too young to understand such things, and, besides, I was much more reticent then about myself than I am now. Forty-three times have I given my heart, and forty-three times has something—either death or another man—robbed me of her I loved. Do you wonder, then, that I have determined never again to think of a woman with a view to matrimony? Even if I wished to do so, I could not; for, as I have just said, my heart is burnt out. Now give me your attention for a few minutes, and I will tell you of this last sad affair, and of the vile part played in it by your brother Hogarth."

Then Mr. Oldmixon related the history of his infatuation for Miss Camilla White from first to last, very much in the same words with which he had given it to Barbara.

Jack listened with attention, rarely interrupting him with questions, and gradually, as Mr. Oldmixon went on with the recital, coming to the conclusion that his uncle, if not insane on the subject of his loves, was certainly very near the border line that, in the opinion of some psychologists, separates sanity from insanity. He had long known that the old gentleman was eccentric, and that all his life he had acted in a way different from that in which the average man would have acted under like circumstances. But the present experience was so extraordinary, there was so much earnestness in his uncle's manner, such an evident conviction that he was reasonable and right in his opinions and acts, that Jack could hardly avoid the conviction that eccentricity had become actual insanity. He saw now what had been the exciting cause of the entire change of front that had taken place in his relative's opinions of his two nephews, and he reached the conclusion that but for Hogarth's interference in the way that had so provoked his uncle, the change of front would probably never have ensued. Mr. Oldmixon doubtless perceived what was passing through his nephew's mind, for he hastened to declare, with all the emphasis that he could bring to the assertion, that while it was true that yesterday's acts had capped the climax of Hogarth's misdoings, the rupture must have taken place ere long. It was in vain that Jack endeavored, as had Barbara, to convince Mr. Oldmixon that Hogarth had in all probability been unaware of his uncle's attachment for Miss Camilla White, and that his conduct therefore had no element of disrespect or unkindness in it. The reply was the same as had been given to her—that logic and love had no relation to each other—and he added that there were other crimes than disrespect and unkindness.

"Suppose, for instance," said his uncle, after Jack had put in what by a man capable of reasoning justly would have been considered a strong plea for his brother—

"suppose you are going down the street and a man accidentally strikes you in the face with a whip, when he
had intended to strike his horse, wouldn't you be angry
with that man? Of course you would; and if you were
high-tempered, as I am, you would, if you could, haul off
and give him a good blow in return. It would be wrong
for you to act in such a manner—unreasonably, illogically
wrong. But if you would strike a man who by accident
strikes you, how much more should I strike the wretch
who robs me of my heart's treasure! You can't tell me
anything about its injustice. Justice has nothing to do
with it. I know it's unjust as well as you do. But the
difference between my act and what yours would be
against the man that struck you with his whip, is that
mine is done deliberately and after due reflection, whereas yours would be the result of ill-temper. You would
be sorry for yours almost as soon as you had returned the
blow, whereas I rejoice at mine more and more with
every hour of my life. No, no, Jack; don't interfere
with me in this matter. It's between Hogarth and me,
and I'm going to give him the worst of it, as sure as my
name is Victor Constantine Oldmixon."

"I don't want to see you act unjustly, uncle. Hogarth has been very unbrotherly to me, but that is no
reason why I should, if I can prevent it, allow him to be
treated unfairly."

"Ah, that's it! if you can prevent it! But, my boy,
you can't prevent it. Therefore, say nothing more about
it. Now, shall I tell what is the next most important
thing I have to settle with you?"

"If you please."

"Well, it's this. As you know, when I was such a
blackguard to you twelve years ago I made my will in

favor of Hogarth, giving him everything, and you nothing. I have just given orders for a new will to be
drawn up, and in it for ' Hogarth ' you will read ' Jack '
—that is, my dear boy, I make you my heir, and I am
quite sure that it will not be long before you will come
into your own."

Jack was not unprepared for this announcement ; it was
the legitimate conclusion of what his uncle had been saying for the last half hour ; and though he did not think it
a just act, yet he had no extravagant and transcendental
notions of generosity to his brother that would stand in
the way of his acceptance of the bounty tendered him.
He therefore thanked Mr. Oldmixon for his kindness,
and expressed his intention of doing nothing that could
be regarded as showing a want of appreciation of the
favor shown him.

Mr. Oldmixon deliberated with himself for a while as
to whether he had better tell Jack of the condition contained in the will, or leave that for another time, when he
and his nephew had become better acquainted with each
other, and were on more familiar terms than they were
then. Finally, he concluded to defer it. He reasoned
that Jack would be more likely to accept the condition
after he had fairly grasped the idea of being heir to half
a million dollars, and had sufficiently contemplated the
advantages that the money would give him.

" He'll be less apt to kick," he said to himself, " when
he thinks of what he'll have to give up."

Then after inviting Jack to dine with him at the
Lucullus that evening, he took his departure, and Jack
was left alone to think of the sudden augmentation of his
fortune that had so suddenly come to him. He walked
up and down the floor for fully half an hour, whistling a

variety of popular airs ; and then, having finally settled down into a state of comparative mental repose, went to make a call on Mr. Vander Linden, to communicate to him the perfected views he had formed relative to the subject for the picture he was to paint for that gentleman.

5

CHAPTER VII.

"A FEAST FOR THE GODS."

THERE were few persons in New York that knew as much about gastronomic science as did Mr. Oldmixon. He was familiar with all the noted places in the old world where good dinners were to be got, and he was in the habit of saying that the man that was fond of artistic cookery, as well as of dinner-table æsthetics generally, could have his sense of the fitness of things in these respects more thoroughly satisfied in the city of New York than in any other place on the face of the earth; and not only this, but that there were better wines to be found at the clubs of that metropolis and in the cellars of its famous dinner-givers and hostelries than could be procured in London, Paris, Vienna, or any other European city.

" You see," he said upon one occasion to a group at his club, " an Englishman or a Frenchman is never willing to profit by the experience gained out of his own country till it has been crammed down his throat on the prongs of a fork for half a lifetime, whereas an American picks up good ideas wherever he can find them. Now, here is Lord Glendale, who sets up for knowing something, and who, I know, has lived in Paris two or three months in every year since he became of age, and he's no chicken now, although he tries to make himself look as young as possible. Well, I dined with his lordship last night at Askman's, and after dinner we lit our cigars and walked home together, where we had a little game of poker, of which his lordship is exceedingly fond, but of which, between you and me, he hasn't the faintest scintilla of an idea. He plays it as he would whist. As I was saying, we walked home together, and Lord Glendale began to talk about the dinner. Now, my boys, I think you will all admit that whatever may be our private opinions of Askman, he knows how to give a dinner such as Brillat-Savarin could not have found fault with. And I assure you on my honor as a gentleman and my reputation as a gourmet that that dinner was a gem. There was not a single unartistic feature about it. The *menu* was perfect. The wines were delicious; those that were to be cooled were cooled to exactly the proper temperatures, and his Bordeaux and his Burgundy had that precise difference of five degrees that only the most highly cultivated taste knows ought to exist. Sixty for the Bordeaux; sixty-five for the Burgundy. And, what is of more importance, the wines were served in exactly the proper order. As to the table, it was perfection; and the company—well, I won't say much about the company; but when I tell you that Demne and Bass and Coats were there, and a half a dozen women, the like of whom for beauty and intelligence and *esprit* can't be found throughout the whole extent of the United Kingdom, you'll agree that nothing was wanting on that score."

"Oh, we know all about that," interrupted young Wildmay. "Tell us what his lordship said. Glendale's a good fellow. He's invited me to Glendale Castle for a month's shooting next season. I'd like to have his opinion about dinners, because I'm going to give him one here next week."

Mr. Oldmixon surveyed the young man contemptuously for probably six seconds ; a long time for such a procedure.

" Wildmay," he said at last, " do you ever read the Bible ?"

" Oh, come now, Uncle Victor," exclaimed the young man—" Uncle Victor" being the name generally applied to Mr. Oldmixon by the younger members of the club— " don't begin a theological lecture. Our minds are not set in that direction."

" My dear young friend," said Oldmixon, putting on his most gentle and courteous manner—a sign that he was about to annihilate the person to whom it was addressed —" far be it from me to give you a lecture upon anything, much less upon theology, or to say a word that would tend to set your mind in action. I was simply going to ask your attention to that verse of Scripture that rebukes the tendency of some young men to push themselves to the front before their elders and betters, by advising them to ' tarry in Jericho till their beards be grown.' I know you are one of those gentle youths that do love a lord. You were kind enough, too, to invite me to be one of those that you have selected from among your acquaintances to meet the noble lord ; but I have to request that if the dinner is to be in accordance with his ideas, you will count me out."

" Now, Wildmay," said Mr. Brooks, a man of about forty, " you see what comes of your damned obtrusiveness. Why the devil can't you let Uncle Victor alone ? I may tell you now for your satisfaction that Lord Glendale told me yesterday that the chief object he had in view in accepting your dinner was that of meeting Uncle Victor. The best thing you can do now is to go down on your knees to Uncle Victor and beg his pardon for interrupting him."

"Oh, I'll do that!" said Wildmay. "Consider me on my knees, Uncle Victor, and asking your pardon."

"Go, boy!" said Mr. Oldmixon, magnanimously. "I forgive you; but be more careful in future. Remember, that though the sight of such as you may be refreshing to the eyes, as is the green field to the kine, the ear would fain know you not.

"His lordship," continued Mr. Oldmixon, "had the temerity to find fault, not only with that dinner, but with every other one to which he had been invited in New York. 'Oldmixon,' said he, 'I've dined now with some of your heaviest swells, and not once have I seen a piece of roast beef on the table; and yet I take it that most of your fellows have been in England, and have dined round with some of our people who know what dinners are.' For a moment I was speechless. At last I gasped out: 'Roast beef at a dinner party? If a man were to invite me to dinner—now listen, Wildmay—and were to give me roast beef, while I trust I should have sufficient respect for myself to swallow the vulgar edible, I should make a resolution never again to put my legs under his table.'

"He laughed at this. 'But,' he went on, 'he gave us no champagne till the dessert came. Now in England we always take our champagne—when we have it—with the roast.'

"Well, my dear boys, at this I almost fainted. 'Champagne with the roast,' I muttered; then I roused myself. 'Lord Glendale,' I said, 'champagne is the wine that is to be drank up to. How can a man that has swilled champagne in the early part of his dinner enjoy Château Lafitte and Clos de Vougeot afterward? It is simply impossible. His palate is ruined for that day as soon as the first swallow of champagne goes down his throat.'

"Well—could you believe it?—he said that nothing satisfied his thirst—that's the word he used—like a big goblet of cracked ice and champagne. Now, my dear boys, you all know—unless Wildmay is an exception—that there are two kinds of champagne fiends. The one gives you your wine hot, and the other gives it to you with ice in it. If heaven is open to people belonging to either of these classes, I don't want to go there. I suppose it will be more tolerable for Sodom and Gomorrah in the day of judgment than for one of them; but I am inclined to think that of the two the ice fiend will have a little the better chance. To be sure, he reduces Pommery Sec to the level of ginger-ale or root-beer; but his intentions are good; and though hell is said to be paved with good intentions, he will probably have a comparatively cool place there."

"Yes," said Brooks, laughing, while Mr. Oldmixon looked from one to the other, with an air of satisfaction on his countenance, as though he had demonstrated a most important fact, "his intentions being cool, his place with his Satanic Majesty will be of a like character."

"Yes, that's what I mean. Ha! ha!"

"For my part," said Wildmay, "I like my champagne *frappé*—frozen, you know."

Mr. Oldmixon put on his hat, drew on his gloves, buttoned his coat, and then bowing to each one of the group except Wildmay, turned as though about to leave the room. Suddenly he stopped, and addressing that rather crestfallen individual, said:

"My sweet young friend, I recollect that I have an

engagement for the evening that your dinner comes off, and therefore I shall have to ask you to excuse me. I am very sorry ; for if there is anything that I particularly like it is frozen champagne. It is so nice to have your butler going round the table and slapping his hand on the bottom of the bottle in order to get the congealed liquid to flow through the narrow neck. The noise is an agreeable diversion, and the act attracts the attention of the company, and saves them the necessity of listening to some bore who may be telling a long story. Besides, there is always a fine chance of the contents of the bottle —not wine, it is no longer wine—under the influence of some more than usually strong thump, coming out with a gush and spattering the table-cloth or the ladies' dresses. Such a timely accident always causes a laugh, and therefore interrupts the monotony that otherwise would be tiresome. Then—and this is the chief advantage—it is so much more convenient to eat your wine than to drink it. I would suggest that you serve it as a sorbet with spoons. Yes, I am extremely sorry that I shall not be able to assist at so delectable a feast as yours will be ;" and with a profound bow to the extinguished Wildmay, Mr. Oldmixon left the room.

"Run after him, Wildmay !" exclaimed Brooks. "You can't get along without Uncle Victor, and Glendale won't come if he doesn't. Tell him he may order the dinner. That's what he wants. It will cost you twice as much as if you ordered it, but then it will be perfect."

"I'll be hanged if I do !" said Wildmay. "He may go to the devil ! By George ! he's getting to think that nobody but himself knows anything, and you fellows all help him to keep up that delusion. Besides, I think he's as mad as a March hare on some things. See how he treats Jack Oldmixon and cuddles that scamp Hogarth. I know lots of people who think he's a lunatic."

"Just as you please," rejoined Brooks, while the others intimated by a few words that they thought Wildmay had better catch Uncle Victor before he got out of the club house. "It's your dinner, you know. But I can tell you, my dear boy, that if you don't propitiate that great man you'll rue it to the last day of your life. Another thing, too, you'd better bear in mind : don't act on the assumption that Uncle Victor's crazy. He's queer sometimes, I admit, and he's done some of the most preposterous things that a man ever did ; but for all that he's got a head on his shoulders, dear boy, that it would be dangerous for you to trifle with. You'd better overhaul him before he get's away."

"Confound it all !" exclaimed Wildmay ; "with every one of you against me, I suppose there's nothing else for me to do. You'd better call this Oldmixon's Club, for hang me if he doesn't run the whole establishment."

He left the room, and it's needless to add succeeded in placating Mr. Oldmixon by giving him *carte blanche* to arrange not only the *menu*, but the decorations also.

From all of which it will be sufficiently apparent to the reader—if he or she has not already acquired that idea—that Mr. Oldmixon was a power, and a despotic one at that, in more than one circle in the city of New York.

Jack was at the Lucullus at seven o'clock precisely, and his punctuality elicited the warmest encomiums from his uncle, who was on hand in the reception-room.

"I've invited Brooks and a Mr. Partridge of St. Louis to join us," he said. "Brooks you know, of course, and

Partridge is a picture-collector. He's just got back from Paris with the last picture of some great painter."

"Yes, I know Brooks, and I know Mr. Partridge also. He gave me an order yesterday."

"The devil he did! Well, Jack, you seem to have got to about the top of the ladder. I hope you won't be spoiled, my boy."

"I don't think there's any danger of that," answered Jack, laughing. "What success I have had has come from hard work, and therefore I am not likely to estimate it at more than it's worth."

"I'm proud of you, my boy; and to think that I should have cut myself off from a man like you to take up with one like that blackguard Hogarth! The snake in the grass! He has bitten the bosom that warmed him! That's it! That's just what he's done, the ungrateful serpent!"

"Well, uncle," said Jack, "as I said to you this morning, I can't agree with you in this matter. Hogarth may be a bad fellow. I have no reason to praise him; but common justice, I think, requires that he should not be blamed for marrying a woman who he had no idea was beloved by you."

"We won't talk about it, Jack, especially as here are our friends," as two gentlemen approached; "but I must say once and for all, as I've already said a dozen times, that 'common justice' may go to the devil. It has nothing to do with the case. How are you, Brooks? Good-evening, Mr. Partridge. You both know my nephew, Mr. John Oldmixon, I believe. Come! We'll take the elevator. We'll make a nice little *partie carrée*. I wouldn't take a thousand dollars for the enjoyment I expect to get out of this dinner and your society for the next three hours or more."

5*

"I think," said Mr. Brooks to Jack, as they were going up in the elevator, "that there isn't a living man that enjoys a good dinner more than does your uncle, and, I may add, knows better how to give one."

"That is no small praise, Brooks," said Mr. Oldmixon, "for I look upon you as one of the few men now living whose opinion on the subject is worth anything. As for me, dinner-giving stands at the head of the arts and sciences. I came across an old book a few days ago," he continued, as he took Mr. Partridge's arm on getting out of the elevator, while the party crossed the hall to the room in which they were to dine, "that contains a sentence that embodies my idea exactly. It is to the effect that no man is fit to govern an empire who does not know how to give a dinner to his friends."

"I think there is some truth in that," said Mr. Partridge, laughing. "Certainly, the best Presidents we have had have been those that gave the best dinners."

"Yes; the qualities necessary in a giver of good dinners do not differ from those requisite in a great and good ruler," said Mr. Oldmixon, after his guests had taken their seats and he was unfolding his napkin. "If ever I am a candidate for a high office, I want only one war-cry to be sounded in my behalf—'He gives good dinners.'"

"I am afraid," rejoined Mr. Partridge, raising a Blue Point oyster scarcely larger than the end of his thumb to his lips, "that in this selfish age the announcement would not do you much good unless you added the words, 'and you are all invited to them.' Then you'd get votes."

"I shouldn't object to the number so much as I should to the kind of people I should have to invite," said Mr. Oldmixon, who was now in his element. " Big dinners, however, are generally dreary affairs. Think of that one given to the Goddess Bubastis, on the banks of the Nile, at which seventy thousand sat down at the table and seven hundred thousand looked on, and at which more wine was drunk than in all Egypt during the rest of the year ! Jack, my boy, what do you think of that Montrachet ? Don't mind my asking such questions, my friends," he continued, addressing his other guests. " This is a little family affair, at which we are at liberty to criticise the wines and the dishes. I've got a surprise for you in the next course after the soup, in regard to which I shall want your individual opinions. It's a new dish, an original one—one of my own devising ; and if it's successful, I would rather be the inventor or the discoverer of it than to be the first man to reach the North Pole."

Jack gave it as his opinion that the Montrachet was excellent.

" It's so much better," he ventured to say, " to drink white Burgundy with your oysters than that sweet Yquem, which is certain to deaden your taste."

" That's right, my boy !" exclaimed Mr. Oldmixon. " Good Heavens ! how delighted I am to hear you enunciate an opinion like that. The only wines fit to drink with your oysters are Chablis and Montrachet. Yquem is a dessert wine, and only fit for women at that ; and yet there are people pretending to a knowledge of oinology who hand it to you as soon as your legs are under their table. Faugh !"

" I see you had a nephew married yesterday," said Brooks, changing the conversation. " Hogarth ; I don't know him. He's been away, hasn't he ?"

Nothing could better show the difference between insanity and eccentricity than Mr. Oldmixon's ability to restrain the manifestation of any of his peculiarities whenever he thought it advisable to do so. He had no intention of opening his family closets, and of displaying the skeletons therein contained either to Mr. Brooks or Mr. Partridge. He did not, as may be supposed by some persons, bearing in mind the anxiety he showed to unbosom himself to Barbara Henschel, go about talking in clubs and other places of social resort of his loves and of his intentions toward his nephews. He was prone to form sudden intimacies with people that impressed him by their possessing some agreeable feature of mind or of person, and he was equally disposed to contract dislikes from the opposite influences. The difference between him and most persons in these respects was that his likes and dislikes were often—not always by any means—of so preposterous a character as to be altogether unexplainable upon any theory based upon normal human experience. Such, for instance, had been his affection for his nephew Hogarth, a person who, as boy and man, had scarcely a redeeming quality, but who would probably, nevertheless, have remained his favorite had he not unconsciously interfered with his uncle's love-affair. The immediate inclination that he had manifested for Barbara Henschel was probably only a caprice, that he himself would not have been able to explain. He had placed it to her display of philosophy at his first interview with her; but as we have seen, she had not shown any evidence of an acquaintance with the subject, and it is probable, therefore, that he deceived himself on this point. That he should have been attracted by that indescribable charm that she possessed—a charm that was not exactly beauty, but rather a potentiality for beauty, as well as by the sweetness of her manners, was not surprising ; but that he should have carried it to the extent of making her his confidante and the arbiter between him and his nephews was certainly not an act compatible with the idea that his mind was a normal one, acting within the limits of perfect mental health. Most people, no matter how regularly acting are their brains, perpetrate acts that are essentially insane —acts, in fact, that if committed by a lunatic having the freedom of the asylum ward, would certainly lead to his being put in a strait-jacket, or some other kind of durance, or to a further extension of the period of his sequestration. Mr. Oldmixon appeared to be especially liable to say or do something that would be called insane by any competent alienist, and yet in the generality of his acts to exhibit a strength of purpose and of will and a capacity for thought of a robust character that the most intellectual man alive might have envied. In the matter of his love-affairs he had come very near to positive lunacy, if he had not actually crossed the line ; but he had shown an ability to get out of them with as great a degree of facility as to enter into them, and had finally announced that never again would he entertain the emotion of love in his heart. This power was one that no lunatic could have possessed. It really seemed as though he had the ability to become sane or insane at will. He had frequently reasoned with himself on this point, and had arrived at the conviction that he really did possess this somewhat dangerous power.

While Brooks was referring to Hogarth's marriage, Mr. Oldmixon was determining what answer he should give. Before the speaker had finished, he had fully resolved upon the reply to make. He knew that his change of affection from one nephew to the other would sooner or later become known, and he very shrewdly resolved that the announcement should come from himself. Brooks was something of a gossip, as are most club men, and Mr. Oldmixon knew that before twenty-four hours had expired the story, as he was now about to give it, would be all over New York.

"Yes," he answered; "my nephew Hogarth was married yesterday to a lady who is, I understand, one of the worthiest of her sex. She is entirely too good for him. Henceforth I do not expect to have any friendly relations with my nephew Hogarth. I hope never to see him or even to hear of him again. My nephew Jack, from whom for many years I have unfortunately, through my own acts, been estranged, has been good enough to forgive me, and henceforth will be my adopted son. It would be unbecoming in me on this occasion to express my opinion of either of my nephews; but it can readily be inferred from what I have said. Now, gentlemen, that I have discharged an unpleasant, though an imperative, duty, let us change the subject."

"By George, Uncle Victor!" exclaimed Mr. Brooks, who with the other two gentlemen had listened with the greatest attention to Mr. Oldmixon's remarks, "that is the manliest and most straightforward speech I ever heard. You're a trump!"

"Allow me to shake you by the hand, Mr. Oldmixon," said Mr. Partridge, with equal warmth, but, as was natural in a stranger, with more dignity. "Your nephew is certainly to be congratulated on having an uncle not ashamed to admit his fault; and I have no doubt you are equally to be congratulated on your nephew."

As to Jack, his heart was too full to speak. He had

appreciated at its real value every word his uncle had said, and he began to think that a total revolution had taken place in his character. And he admired above all else the decision and strength of mind that had been exhibited in seizing the opportunity that had been offered for making an explanation, thus forestalling preposterous rumors that would otherwise be sure to arise, as well as the relation that might be set afloat by what was now the other side of the house. Finally he managed to stammer out his thanks to his uncle, and then the dinner proceeded.

CHAPTER VIII.

A HORRIBLE DEED.

"My friends," said Mr. Oldmixon, after they had finished their soup and were scanning their *menus* with a view of forming pleasant anticipations of the next course, "I have taken the liberty of asking you to assist in the inauguration of a new dish. It is one that I have myself, after much thought and no little labor, discovered and invented. It is the one that I am now about to refer to your critical judgments, and this will be the first time that any one save your humble servant will have submitted it to the action of his gustatory nerves. I have named it, in honor of myself, *Petites croustades à la Oldmixon*."

As Mr. Oldmixon finished speaking, a servant entered with a dish elaborately garnished, which he placed on the table before that gentleman, and after leaving it there a few moments for the admiration of the company, proceeded to hand it round, while Mr. Oldmixon went on with an account of the wonderful delicacy.

"I shall not tell you what it is," he said, "till you have eaten it and given me your honest opinions of it. And mind, I want your real, honor-bright opinions; for if this production is bad or indifferent I want to know the fact just as certainly as though it were good. Such palates as you gentlemen possess are of infinite use to the gastronomist, especially to me; for as I get older I fear I am losing that dainty, discriminating, and penetrating sense of taste for which I used to be distinguished. Now, my friends, let us in silence concentrate our attention on what the gods have given us."

Brooks was the first to speak. "By all the deities that ever feasted on Mount Olympus," he exclaimed, shaking hands across the table with Mr. Oldmixon, "I can keep silent no longer. That is, without exception, the most delectable morsel that ever went down my throat. You ought to be crowned king of the gastronomes."

"Yes," said Mr. Partridge; "you have capped the climax of a long and honorable life with a performance that of itself will hand down your name to posterity as one of the greatest benefactors of mankind. Dainties like this cause us to think that there is, after all, something godlike in the human mind."

Mr. Oldmixon was delighted. He bowed and smiled and rubbed his hands together, and uttered many little deprecatory speeches, which, however, deceived no one.

"Now, Jack, my boy," he said, addressing his nephew, who had already, with the others, been helped a second time, "you are an artist, and can therefore sympathize with a brother artist, even if he does work in a different and perhaps a humbler field. What do you think of my new dish?"

"What I could say," replied Jack, "would be commonplace after the encomiums of Mr. Brooks and Mr. Partridge, who are both such consummate gourmands; but I think I detect in this most exquisite compound a quality that will commend it to those who are in search of new sensations. You know, doubtless, that physiologists have discovered that there are nerve papillæ that only react to certain stimuli, or perhaps I should be more correct were I to say that there are certain nerve-centres that only respond to particular excitations. These *petites croustades*, to which you have appropriately given your name, appear to me to have the power of rousing into action that part of the brain that presides over the imagination. I have been trying, as you know, to get a subject for Mr. Vander Linden's picture. I have read book after book in search of an idea ; I have studied a dozen different systems of religion ; I have drank champagne, sherry and egg, milk-punch, and, what was specially recommended, arrack, but all to no effect. Then I have sat with a cigar in my mouth for hours at a time, trying my utmost. I might as well have ducked my head in a horse-pond for all the good I received. But hardly had I eaten a mouthful of this brain-tickling compound than the conception began to come ; and ere I had finished one *croustade* it was before me in all its completeness. I am eating another now to fix it indelibly on my mind, just as the photographer fixes the image on his sensitive plate.

"Bravo ! Mr. Oldmixon," exclaimed Brooks, " you are the most appreciative of us all. No wonder your uncle is proud of you. If I had a nephew who could talk that way about any dish I might discover, I'd cherish him as the apple of my eye, whatever that may be."

"Jack, my boy," said Mr. Oldmixon, much moved, "you are a gentleman and a scholar. More than that I cannot say, except that I am grateful. We'll not ask you to tell us what subject the *petites croustades* have evolved out of your brain, but you must promise to give us a first look at your picture. Now, my friends, tell me what constitutes the chief constituent of this dish ?"

One guessed one thing, and one another—no two agreeing, however. Brooks thought it was Strasburg goose liver, but admitted that it had a much more delectable flavor than that famous edible. Mr. Partridge at first frankly confessed that he did not know what it was, but afterward thought there was something about it that reminded him of a dish he had eaten in Japan, which was composed mainly of a vegetable, the name of which he had forgotten ; and Jack gave it as his opinion that it consisted essentially of the concentrated essence of the flesh of the green turtle mingled with cocks' combs cut into dice.

Then Mr. Oldmixon, after drinking another glass of old Madeira—the wine that had been served with his culinary triumph—related the history that all were anxiously waiting to hear.

"I have a young medical friend," he said, "who is an assiduous student of physiology. He performs a great many original experiments, and sacrifices numbers of all kinds of animals. He was kind enough, about a month ago, to invite me to witness some of his investigations, and I accordingly went to his laboratory for that purpose. In the course of his procedures he killed a dozen or more splendid frogs, and I saw then—what was a revelation to me—that that animal has a remarkably large liver. At once the idea occurred to me that something very wonderful in the gastronomic art might be made out of frogs' livers. He gave me all I wanted, and I took them home with me, and that very night made my first experiment with them. The result, although not entirely satisfactory, was nevertheless enough to show me that I had made a discovery that ought to immortalize me, if I met with the appreciation to which I felt I was fairly entitled. Of course I got more livers from my friend, and also from several small boys that I employed to visit the swamps along the north side of Long Island Sound, and to capture

the reptile. As you know, the only parts brought to our
markets are the hind legs, which, though good enough
in their way, are in nowise comparable to the liver. I
may say, *en parenthèse*, that I have made arrangements
with a frog-catcher in Canada to send me every week
six dozen frogs' livers. Well, I made numerous essays
to perfect the modes of cooking the delicacy I had discovered, and now I have definitely decided upon ten different methods. The compound you have eaten to-night
is one of the best. Of course it requires an artist to cook
it—a male artist. It appears to be altogether beyond
the power of a woman-cook. Now, I'll tell you in general terms how this particular dish is prepared."

At this Brooks got out his pencil, and proceeded to
take notes on the back of his *menu* of the details given
by Mr. Oldmixon.

"First," said that gentleman, "you cut the livers
into dice, then you take a sufficiency of truffles and fresh
mushrooms—fresh, mind you, Brooks, not those horrid
little buttons that come from France—which you also cut
up, but into very fine pieces—not much bigger, in fact,
than the head of a pin ; next you add a little rice-flour,
then your seasoning—salt, pepper, butter—a few drops
of lemon-juice, and several yolks of eggs. Now, the next
stage is very important, and I worked at this a long time
and experimented with many things before I got the
right one. Nothing can take the place of the substance
next to be added. It seems to be the only thing capable
of bringing out, in all its ethereal delicacy, the full flavor
of the livers ; it is *purée* of pheasant. Add enough of
this to make the consistency of the mass about that of a
rather thin mush. Then have your croustades ready.
They should be made either of rice, or what is, I think,

a little better—and to this point I have directed hours of
anxious thought—of powdered maccaroni. These, as
you have doubtless perceived, are of rice; and the fact
is owing to the obstinancy of the great man who presides
over the kitchen of this club, and who had the impertinence to tell me that maccaroni couldn't be powdered
fine enough; they are to be cooked in a *bain-marie*, and
when they are nearly done a little silver funnel should
be inserted into each down to the bottom, and a tea-
spoonful of old and very dry Madeira poured in. By
this arrangement, which is original with me, the wine
goes to the bottom, where it is heated, and the ethereal
vapors, instead of being dissipated in the air, permeate
the mass, and give it their delicious odors and flavors."

"You are a wonderful man, Mr. Oldmixon," said Mr.
Partridge; "I think I recollect your directions suf-
ficiently to try this dish when I get back to St. Louis.
We are famous for our frogs there."

"I shall try it to-morrow if I can get the livers," said
Brooks; "and I agree with Mr. Partridge in saying that
you are a wonderful man."

"I ought to have been educated as a cook, I suppose,"
rejoined Mr. Oldmixon, with great complacency. "I
have more respect for a *cordon bleu* than I have for a
bishop."

As to Jack, he could not conceal his astonishment.
His uncle was altogether a different kind of a man from
what he had anticipated. He remembered him twelve
years ago as irritable, fretful, prone to say disagreeable
things, even to those he liked, ready to take offence at
trifles or when no offence was intended, and then cruel
both in language and acts. Now he was good-tempered,
anxious to please, considerate—in fact, the reverse in

almost every mental characteristic. "Age," thought Jack, "sits well on him. Some persons become disagreeable as they get old, but Uncle Victor is certainly an exception."

The dinner proceeded to the entire satisfaction of Mr. Oldmixon and his guests, and the conversation, under the influence of the associations and, perhaps, in no small degree to the wines, not one of which was commonplace, became more than usually brilliant when compared with the talk that is ordinarily indulged in at New York club dinners. The host interfered no further with the *menu* till a little while before the canvas-backs were reached. Then he called a servant to him:

"Go down to the kitchen," he whispered, but loud enough for all at the table to hear him, as he intended they should, "and bring me word from M. David what temperature exists at a point ten inches distant from the front of his fire. I can't trust these Frenchmen," he continued aloud, after the man had gone, "to cook canvas-backs, so I prefer to direct the operation myself. A fire too hot or a half minute too long in the roasting spoils the ducks. The heat and the time should be exquisitely proportioned to each other, and then you have a bird that ought to be held up as the reward for us in the next world, if we do our duty in this."

Here the servant that he had sent to the kitchen returned, and handed Mr. Oldmixon a card.

"Sixty-seven and five tenths," he read. "That won't do. It must be twice as hot. Go down and tell him. Hello! Stop! He's a Frenchman, and uses a centigrade thermometer. Wait a moment."

He took a pencil from his pocket, and made a little calculation on the back of the card.

" It would be 153½° Fahrenheit," he resumed. " That will do nicely. Now, are the ducks ready ?"

" Yes, sir ; everything is in readiness."

" Very well. Now, go down and give my compliments to M. David, and request him to be kind enough to observe these directions : place the ducks in front of the fire, with the screen before them, when I ring the bell. Then when I ring it a second time remove the screen ; and when I ring it a third time replace the screen and bring the ducks here as fast as the dumb-waiter and your legs can carry them. Now, are you sure you understand ?"

" Oh, yes, sir ; perfectly sure."

" Then go, and may the Lord have mercy on your soul if you make any mistake, for I shall have none on your body !"

As soon as the man disappeared, Mr. Oldmixon rose from the table and went to the end of the room, where a little button projected from the wall, showing the existence of communication with an electrical bell. He waited till he thought the man had had time to reach the kitchen, and then he pressed the button.

" Now," he said, " the screen is being placed in front of the fire and the ducks on the spit behind the screen and ten inches from the fire." After a little time, with his watch in his hand, he again pressed the button.

" With that," he remarked, as he walked up and down the floor, still holding his watch in his hand, " the screen is removed and the cooking begins. Exactly sixteen minutes and a half will be required to accomplish the act to perfection. A half minute more or less will certainly spoil the ducks."

" Let him alone," said Brooks, in a whisper to the

other gentlemen. "He'll walk the floor and talk, and you'll certainly get some valuable hints from what he says. I've seen him at this before. How much humbug there is in it I don't know. Perhaps all this care is necessary. I do know, however, that no canvas-backs in New York or anywhere else are as good as those he cooks."

"You are men after my own heart," continued Mr. Oldmixon. "Many persons I know would have been disgusted on being told that they had eaten frogs' livers. But you were all as pleased over the information as though I had told you that the dish was made of pork and beans. Ha! ha! pork and beans! Well, I should think so! The Lord deliver me from pork and beans! Now, I've no prejudices; I can eat anything that's good; I've eaten rattlesnake, and it's good. I've eaten crow, and when properly cooked--not 'b'iled'—it's good. I've eaten shark's fins, and they're as good as the green fat of the turtle. Only one thing was rather disappointing, and that was wolf-steak; I tried that once in the Rocky Mountains, and it was simply damnable. It tasted as though it might be cloth woven of leather shoe-strings. But the fat of the wolf, when he has any, isn't a bad substitute for butter.

"I say, Partridge," he continued, addressing that gentleman after looking at the watch in his hand, while he continued to pace the floor, "did you ever eat a peacock?"

"No," answered that gentleman; "I can't say that I've been very venturesome in dietetics. You have given me a lesson, however, that I shall not fail to improve."

"What about the peacock, Uncle Victor?" said

Brooks, winking at the others, as much as to say, " Now, we'll draw him out."

" What about the peacock ? Oh, nothing, except that it's had its day, and will probably never regain its former position in gastronomy. Formerly it was food for kings and princes. Hortensius introduced it to the Romans in a magnificent feast that he gave when he was made augur. The price of a peacock in his day was about ten dollars of our money, which, allowing for the depreciation of gold and silver, would make about fifty dollars now. Florentius says it is a noble bird, whose flesh should only be served to lovers and heroes ; and Donatus says women should not be allowed to eat its flesh, for that it predisposes to vanity, and they are vain enough already ; and Du Boisé declares that only men of gentle blood should be permitted to have it on their tables. They roasted it on a spit, and it was always served with its feathers on. Just before cooking it, it was skinned very carefully, and then before sending it to table the skin and feathers were replaced, the crest and tail spread out, and in this gorgeous fashion it made its appearance before the guests.

" Sixteen minutes," he continued, going to the bell-knob and resting a finger gently on it. " In half a minute our ducks will be done. Excuse me a moment, my friends. This requires all the attention that can be given to it. At another time I'll tell—there !" as he pressed strongly on the button. " To the very second. Joseph," to a servant who stood by with a decanter full of ruby wine, waiting for orders, " have you taken the temperature ?"

" Yes, sir."

" What was it ?"

G

"Sixty-four and a half, sir; I thought that was near enough."

"I told you sixty-five, didn't I?"

"Yes, sir."

"Then it was a great piece of impertinence for you to put your opinion against mine. I shall report your conduct to the house committee. Bring me the thermometer," he continued, taking the decanter from the man. The instrument which was passed through a cork was handed to him. He inserted the cork into the decanter, and slowly pushed the thermometer through the wine, reading off the temperatures as he did so: "Sixty-eight, sixty-seven, sixty-six, sixty-five, sixty-four, sixty-three. From sixty-eight to sixty-three. Now, don't you see," addressing the man, "that this wine ranges from sixty-eight at the top to sixty-three at the bottom? Now, I turn the decanter upside down two or three times, and now, as you see, the temperature is a uniform sixty-five. Keep it so. Ah, here are our ducks!" as another man entered with four splendid-looking birds on a dish. "Now, my friends, I wouldn't exchange the next half hour of my life for the same length of time in the existence of any man on earth."

He seated himself at the table, and the ducks being passed round, each gentleman took a whole one and proceeded to cut off the breast on each side with a knife as sharp as a razor. Then the carcasses were removed, and in silence the delicious morsels were eaten. Only once was a word spoken, and that was when Mr. Partridge asked a servant for some currant jelly. Mr. Oldmixon raised his eyes for a moment, but was too polite to make any remark. From that time on, however, his spirits seemed to have declined. He made no more speeches, and answered only in monosyllables. His countenance wore a dejected air that was totally at variance with the jovial expression it had borne during the early part of the dinner. Brooks understood the matter, but Jack was unable to account for a change so radical as to be almost alarming. He was apprehensive that something serious—an apoplectic attack, for instance—might be about to occur. While he was trying to find a solution of the circumstance, Mr. Oldmixon took a little vial from his pocket, and removing the cork held the open mouth to his nose.

"A little faint," he said, "that is all. I suppose it's the heat. The room is hot, isn't it?"

"Yes," answered Jack; "it is warmer than it need be. Shall I open the window, uncle?" rising as he spoke.

"No, no; it's over now. My heart is a little weak, so I'm told, and occasionally I have to take a sniff of nitrite of amyl. It acts at once like a charm."

But although Mr. Oldmixon declared that he was all right, it was evident that there was going to be no more hilarity that night. The rest of the dinner was eaten almost in silence; and at its close, Mr. Partridge, looking at his watch, pleaded another engagement; and after a few polite speeches on both sides took his departure. No sooner had the door closed upon him than Mr. Oldmixon broke forth:

"This is the last time that fellow dines with me. Great heavens! to think that I should have been so imposed upon. I took him for a man of gentlemanly instincts, of fine perceptions, of delicate taste, and I find him to be a boorish, uncouth cad, that it is contamination to have at my table. Brooks, Jack—I ask pardon of both of you for asking you to meet a low-strung, coarse-minded lout."

Brooks smiled knowingly, but Jack was astonished at his uncle's vehement abuse of a man for whom all through the early part of the dinner he had shown great respect.

"What did he do?" he at least managed to inquire, though he was somewhat apprehensive that in the attempt to answer his uncle might again experience the inconvenience of having a weak heart. "He seemed to me to be a gentleman."

Mr. Oldmixon was overcome, and was obliged again to have recourse to his vial.

"What did he do?" he shrieked rather than spoke, after he had refreshed himself with a couple of inhalations. "Didn't you hear him ask for currant jelly? Didn't you see him spread it over the noble flesh on his plate, as though he were daubing a piece of bread with molasses? Didn't you see him treat the glorious bird as though it were a muscovy? O Jack, Jack, that *you* of all men should ask me what he did!" And Mr. Oldmixon buried his face in his hands and trembled as though he were seized with a fit of the ague.

"I didn't observe him," said Jack, apologetically. "I was so busy with the contemplation and the disposition of what I had on my own plate that I neither heard nor saw Mr. Partridge. But come, uncle; we three can afford to forgive him. Evidently he was unconscious of his crime."

"Yes, that's the worst of it. If he had done it through spite or bravado, or because the duck was badly cooked, I could forgive him; but to do such a thing as that through ignorance or because he liked it puts a wall between him and me that can never come down. Henceforth our paths through life are as divergent as north and south. The man that puts currant jelly on a canvasback can never be the associate, much less the friend, of Victor Constantine Oldmixon. I have seen the crime committed before, and it has always made me shudder; but this is the first time, and it shall be the last, that such an outrage has occurred at my table."

Nothing that either Brooks or Jack could say had the least effect in pacifying Mr. Oldmixon. "It's worse than that other thing," he whispered to Jack as they stood on the porch of the Lucullus Club House while his coupé was driving up. I thought nothing could touch me like that; but this has sounded a lower depth. Goodnight. I intended to have taken you home with me and to have talked over some matters of great importance, but this has unfitted me for all mental exertion. I'll call for you to-morrow or next day, and bring you down to my house. If I don't, come and see me; and in the mean time, my boy, think whether it wouldn't be pleasant for you to live with me. I'll give you a whole floor to yourself, and there's a splendid room that will do for your studio. I'm getting old, Jack. Such a thing as this to-night tells on me, and I may go now any day. Good-night again," as Jack, with a few consolatory words, helped him into his carriage. "I'll see you to-morrow, or next day at farthest."

Jack stood on the steps for a moment, thinking of the singular behavior of his uncle. Many circumstances in his conduct, as he had observed it during the twelve hours that had elapsed since the reconciliation, appeared to him to be incompatible with the existence of a sound state of mind. The statement of his love affairs, and es-

pecially of the last one ; the unreasonable prejudice that
had been suddenly formed against Hogarth, to the entire
disregard of acts on the part of the young man that
would, at any time during the last twelve years, have
justified renunciation by his uncle ; the intense affection
that had sprung up within a few hours for him, Jack ;
the excessive interest he had shown in the new dish he
had compounded out of frogs' livers ; the excessive degree
of irritation he had shown at Mr. Partridge's act of putting currant jelly on the canvas-back ; and last, but certainly not least, the existence of a peculiar excitability
that Jack could not describe to himself, but which he
clearly saw was unnatural, and which had marked his
uncle's manner during the dinner, until with Mr. Partridge's *lapsus* it had disappeared, to be succeeded by an
equally abnormal mental inertia — all these facts had
made a deep impression upon him, and had kept him
through the dinner wondering whether or not his uncle
was a lunatic.   Several times, just as he had arrived at
the conclusion that he certainly was of unsound mind, he
would say something that indicated the existence of a
force of intellect and a degree of mental equanimity
such as Jack could not conceive could be possessed by an
insane person.   Of course Jack had never given any
time to the study of insanity.   All he knew of mental
aberration he had got from reading accounts of murders
and other acts of violence, and of will-trials in the newspapers, and from a couple of visits he had paid to a lunatic
asylum with a young medical friend when he was studying types for a picture of Ophelia he was painting.   He
had observed that at one time his uncle had looked at
Mr. Partridge with such a diabolical expression on his face
that Jack had, for a moment, feared that he intended to

throttle the unfortunate gentleman. He had seen just such a look on the countenance of a lunatic, who the next day had killed his keeper by striking him over the head with a wash-tub. Still, he had noticed that Mr. Brooks, who had known Mr. Oldmixon very intimately for many years, did not appear to be astonished at anything that had occurred. Perhaps, after all, it was only an eccentric manner, showing that his uncle, instead of differing a little from other people, differed a great deal. And with this comforting doubt Jack took a cab that was standing in front of the club house, and was driven to the Vandyke.

CHAPTER IX.

At the two windows of a room in an old and straggling hotel in the ancient city of Annapolis sat Mr. and Mrs. Hogarth Oldmixon. Mr. Hogarth Oldmixon was seated at one window and Mrs. Hogarth Oldmixon at the other, and each was looking eagerly into the deserted street, as though trying to discover something that might relieve the distressing monotony of the situation. There did not appear to be, if this was their object, much chance of a successful result, for the rain was pouring down in torrents, and not a creature of any kind was visible save the old negro man at the corner who sold crabs, and who gallantly continued to fly his flag, regardless of the unfavorable state of the atmosphere. Every now and then a crab would crawl over the edge of the basket in which it, with its companions in captivity, was confined, and endeavor to make its way to the torrent of water that flowed down the gutter; but the old man was always too quick for it, and with a word and a blow tossed it into the receptacle whence it had come. Mr. and Mrs. Hogarth Oldmixon had watched the old man for considerably over an hour, and had extracted from his actions all the amusement that it was possible to get. At first they had laughed inordinately at the antics of the venerable negro, most of whose joints appeared to be stiff with rheumatism; but eventually, as nearly always happens in such cases, the most eccentric contortions that he made failed to excite their risible faculties. All mental impressions and all sensations, however pleasant they may be at first, become wearisome or painful by their continuance or frequent repetition. The perfection of physical comfort is the absence of any feeling in any part of the body ; and, strange as it may seem, the persistence of a sensorial impression leads to the abolition of sensibility for all other impressions that can be made on the organ receiving them. If a person could be caused to restrict his vision to the sight of one single object, he would become blind so far as all other objects are concerned ; the hearing of one unvarying sound would cause deafness to all other sounds ; a single sapid substance held in the mouth destroys the perception of taste for other substances ; and the mind running constantly on one subject becomes incapable of appreciating others.

But before this stage is reached a state of the most intense weariness is experienced. The period required, however, to bring about this condition varies in different persons. In the cases of Mr. and Mrs. Hogarth Oldmixon an hour had been sufficient. I have known instances in which, through some peculiar unimpressibility of the brain, the same excitation produced pleasure after hundreds of repetitions. Thus at the theatre one evening I witnessed the three hundred and seventy-eighth representation of the grand spectacular piece entitled the "Ice Demon of the Frozen Caves." It was full of stupid jokes, and I observed that no one among the audience laughed so long or so loud over each attempted witticism or ludicrous situation as did a member of the orchestra who played the violoncello. So extraordinary apparently was the fact, that during an *entr'act* I sought out the

6*

leader of the band. I found him imbibing lager beer in
the cellar, and nothing loath to drink a couple of glasses
with me.

" Who is the man," I asked, " that plays the violoncello ?"

" Oh, dot's Mr. Schunemann."

" A new member of your splendid orchestra ?" I said,
insidiously and interrogatively.

" Gott in Himmel, no ! I dinks I have Schunemann
seven year."

" And does he play every night ?"

" I should dink so, and two matinées extra."

" Then he has played in the orchestra during the
three hundred and seventy-eight times that the ' Ice
Demon of the Frozen Caves ' has been performed ?"

" Zurely. If he didn't, don't you thought I would
knew it ?"

" I saw him laughing at the fun of the piece," I said,
humbly.

" Laugh ! I should dink so ! I laugh at him myself
two hundred times. Den I laugh no more. But Schunemann is joost de most—*schwermüthig*—saddest man
dot lives in New York, and he never laughs only when
he sees dot performance, and den he laughs all de while."

It was the dreariest of dreary spectacles to me after I
had seen it once, and yet these men could laugh over it
hundreds of times !

But Mr. and Mrs. Hogarth Oldmixon were differently
constituted. For them—especially for Mr. Hogarth Oldmixon—variety was the spice of life, and just at this
time their life was absolutely free from spice. What
was to be done ? Mr. Hogarth had never cultivated the
little conversational power that he once had, but had de-

veloped a kind that was scarcely adapted to the society to which he was now condemned ; and Mrs. Hogarth, who could talk enough when the conditions were favorable, found it impossible to keep up a conversation with a man who only answered, when he answered at all, with a " yes " or a " no."

They had been married five days, and this was their wedding-journey. The prospect for a cheerful and a happy married life was certainly not bright, and Mrs. Hogarth felt her heart sink within her as she thought of what was probably before her in the long future. She was not a particularly intelligent woman. She had managed thus far to get through life without any special mental exertion. To be sure, she had thought, when occasion had seemed to require her to think ; but the effort to concentrate her attention upon any subjects but dress and the pleasures of society had been so unpleasant, that for several years past she had allowed her mother to do for her such thinking as was absolutely necessary should be done by some one in her behalf. When, therefore, Mr. Hogarth Oldmixon, after having seen her at the opera, and being introduced to her under the impression that she was a rich plum worthy of his gathering, had asked her to be his wife, she had answered that she had no objections if mamma approved ; that she had not considered the matter herself, and did not see that it would do any good for her to bother over it ; that mamma knew what was best for her, and that—yes, he might kiss her if he cared to, but that for her part she thought such things were very vulgar ; and much else to the same effect.

Then Mr. Hogarth had sought an interview with Mrs. White, and in the best language at his command had opened his heart to that lady regnant in the White family.

"We have seen very little of you, Mr. Oldmixon," she had replied, smoothing the front of her dress with her fat hands, and settling herself into her chair, as though getting ready for a long conversation. "Our sets are different. Society in New York is so large, that it is impossible to know everybody worth knowing. You are the son of Mr. Victor Oldmixon, I believe?"

"No, madam, I am his nephew."

"I thought you were his son. Mr. Condor, who assumes to know everything, certainly told me that you were his son."

"I am only his nephew."

"Of course I am obliged to consider the future of my dear child. She is so inexperienced and so far removed from all mercenary motives that she would never think of such a thing herself. She would give her heart, and then she would think nothing more was required. But we mothers, Mr. Oldmixon, must look farther. I thought you were Mr. Oldmixon's son, and that you would, therefore, be the heir to his estate, which, though I understand it is not very large as these things are considered in our day, is ample enough for all practical purposes. As you are not his son, I am obliged, in the interests of my sweet child, to ask you what are your present means of support, and what are your prospects for the future?"

Hogarth was not a diplomatist, nor skilled in didactic fence, especially when his antagonist was a woman. He knew very little of refined and educated women, though his acquaintance with certain representatives of a large class of the sex was not restricted to narrow limits. He had seen Camilla White at the opera, and he had fallen in love with her at first sight, for reasons that must have been fully as inexplicable to himself as they were to others. To be sure, her father was supposed to have money; but though this fact may have had some influence in causing him to continue his addresses, it could have had none in the origination of his passion. She was not pretty, she was not distinguished-looking, she was not, as a rule, even well dressed, though doubtless her clothing was expensive; and yet two Oldmixons—uncle and nephew—had fallen violently in love with her, and she had been the innocent cause of their estrangement.

Now, Hogarth never told the truth when a lie would better or even equally serve his purpose. His uncle made him an allowance of three thousand dollars a year, and had told him that he might consider himself his heir. Over and over again he had said to him : " Hogarth, my boy, all that I have in the world will be yours when I die. That milksop Jack, who I don't believe has a drop of Oldmixon blood in his veins, shall never have a cent of my money ;" and Hogarth had duly said, " Thank you, Uncle Victor," without appearing to notice the insult to his mother, which, as the reader knows, was the same that Jack had resented so energetically while only a boy.

He might, therefore, with perfect truth have declared that, although only a nephew, he was Mr. Oldmixon's sole heir ; but this of itself would not altogether have answered his purpose ; so instead of adding, as was the fact, that his uncle allowed him three thousand a year, he told Mrs. White, apprehensive doubtless that she would deem this sum insufficient to maintain her daughter in the condition to which she was accustomed, that his allowance was ten thousand, and that doubtless this would be increased on his marriage.

"My uncle is seventy-five years of age," he said. "He does not spend more than five or six thousand a year, for he lives in one of his own houses, and takes his meals at his club. His income is certainly at least thirty thousand a year, and I am confident that when I marry he will make mine fifteen thousand."

All this looked very promising to Mrs. White. She saw already her daughter well settled in life as the wife of a man of ample income and of great expectations.

"I will be equally frank with you, Mr. Oldmixon," she said, relaxing greatly in the frigidity of manner that had characterized the early part of the interview. "Mr. White is what is generally called ' rich,' but he has eleven children, and when my ' thirds ' come out of his estates there will not be over two hundred and fifty thousand for each. He has authorized me to say that the allowance of three thousand dollars that he now gives Camilla will be continued after her marriage, but that she will get nothing more till his death. To be sure, he is seventy-two, but he is hale and hearty for his age."

This information had a somewhat depressing influence on Mr. Hogarth; but he reflected that with an uncle, whose heir he was, seventy-five years old and a father-in-law seventy-two, it could not be very long before one or the other or both would ' shuffle off this mortal coil,' and leave him in comparative affluence. His own three thousand and Camilla's like amount would do very well for the present, and besides he was really confident that his uncle would at least double his allowance, so he made a magnanimous answer to the effect that it was Camilla, not money, that he wanted, and Mrs. White had thereupon graciously given her consent, remarking as she did so that this at least was an instance of that perfect disinterestedness as regarded pecuniary matters that ought to attend in all affairs of the heart, "except, Mr. Oldmixon," she added, "that every mother is bound to see that her daughter shall not want for the comforts of life." So the matter was settled, and Camilla White in due time became the wife of Hogarth Oldmixon.

Immediately before his marriage he had written a letter to his uncle, informing him that he was going to Washington and Annapolis on his wedding tour, that he expected to be absent about ten days, and that on his return he should be very happy to present Mrs. Hogarth Oldmixon to her respected relative.

"She seems almost to know you," he added. "She has seen you so often from her windows, which are just opposite yours, that she has formed quite an affection for you, and she wonders why, since our engagement, you have not called on her."

This letter lay on Mr. Oldmixon's desk for several hours unopened, as was often the case with the communications of his dutiful nephew, and when read, as it was the next day, had not added to Mr. Oldmixon's peace of mind. On the contrary, it had made him distinctly uncomfortable.

"I knew she loved me," he said, mournfully, "and now that scoundrel has carried her off. Bitterly shall he rue his cruelty before I've done with him."

Mr. Hogarth looked up and down the street, and then at the sky for the twentieth time at least.

"I believe it's going to rain all day," he said, at last. "If it would only stop now we might go and see the

Naval Academy. That's what we came here for, was it not?"

"Indeed, I don't know," answered his wife, with her accustomed indifference. "I left it all to you. I supposed there was some reason for your wanting to come here."

"So there was a reason, but I've been disappointed. I expected to meet a friend here, and now I find I've got to stay here three days before she comes."

"A lady!" exclaimed Camilla, roused into something like interest by her husband's speech.

"Yes, a lady," he answered, with something like a sneering tone in his voice. "Oh, you needn't be jealous," he continued, with a laugh. "She's sixty years old, and she owes me two thousand dollars. She's going to pay it, and that's why I want to see her. It's money I won from her son at a little game of draw poker a year ago. Now, Mrs. Oldmixon, are you satisfied?"

"I wasn't dissatisfied. You can have as many friends as you like, men or women."

"Well, you *are* a cool one, I must say," he observed, after looking at her somewhat contemptuously for a moment. "You mean to say you don't care how many lady friends I have?"

"Whatever suits you will suit me. I suppose we'll get tired of each other after a while, as married people generally do."

"Well, for my part," said Hogarth, not to be outdone in nonchalance, "I'm tired already."

Mr. Hogarth was a pretty bad fellow, though not quite so desperately wicked as his uncle had made him out to be in his conversation with Barbara Henschel.

He was a drunkard, a gambler, a liar, a consorter with vile people of both sexes, and he had probably, without having formed any distinct intention of doing such a thing, somewhat hastened his mother's death. But he had not stolen money from Mr. Oldmixon, as that gentleman had alleged, nor had he perpetrated any other crime that would render him amenable to the law. There are many offences which, though they do not consign the perpetrator to the penitentiary, place him outside the pale of respectable society; and of these Hogarth Oldmixon had committed more than the share that ordinarily falls to the lot of the social outcast. Indeed, the total would, had it been known, have been sufficiently appalling to any one with a spark of decency in his composition. As it was, no one person knew the extent of Hogarth Oldmixon's wickedness so well as he knew it himself, and hence his reputation was better than he deserved. If all those that were acquainted with his conduct could have come together and have compared notes, each one of them would have been astonished at the revelations of the others. As the knowing ones, however, were to a greater or less extent participators in his lapses against the laws of decency and morality, it was not very likely that he incurred any great risk of exposure. He was very reticent even with his intimate companions in regard to conduct of his with which they were not particularly concerned, and he had the reputation of being a remarkably shrewd, sharp, self-reliant, secretive, and, to a certain extent, unscrupulous man. The limit to his scrupulousness was his uncle. Whether he really was attached to the old gentleman or not was known to no one but himself. He always, so far as externals went, treated him with respect, but this was with such a man much more likely to be based on policy than on affection. He had several times, however, been strongly tempted by himself and others to perpetrate some act of fraud on his uncle, but he had never yet been able to reconcile conduct of the kind with his conscience.

He was three years younger than Jack, and, as the reader already knows, had taken sides with his uncle in the quarrel into which his brother had been forced. Since the rupture he had had nothing to do with him, though once or twice, when his funds had been low, and he had heard how well Jack was getting on in the world, he had thought of applying to him for pecuniary assistance. Reflection, however, had tended to convince him both of the impropriety and the uselessness of such an appeal.

It was, perhaps, all things considered, fortunate that his wife was not possessed of any great degree of refined sensibility or was deeply attached to him. She therefore smiled when he remarked that he was already on the stool of repentance, but made no other answer, doubtless for the reason that it was entirely useless for her to express a concurrence that it was quite obvious she felt.

"I say, Milly," he remarked, after a few minutes' silence, during which he had, what was an unusual thing for him, read a few pages in a recently published novel, "I shouldn't be surprised if we've made a big mistake. I don't see though how matters are going to be helped. We're tied together for life, I suppose, and we've got to make the best of a bad bargain. The hero in this book, when he found out that he had married the wrong woman, blew his brains out; but I'm not fool enough to do that."

" I might go home, and then you could get a divorce on the ground of desertion."

" That's so ! You seem to have been thinking the matter over. By George ! To think of a girl of your age and brought up as strictly as you've been brought up, knowing so much about divorce !"

A knock at the door interrupted Mrs. Oldmixon in any reply she might have been about to make, and a servant entering with a letter still further indisposed her to give any answer. She always got rid of discussions when there was the least show of an excuse for so doing. There was ample reason, as she soon discovered, for deferring the further discussion of the subject to a time sufficiently remote for her to allow of her giving it ample consideration.

" A letter from Ridley," said Mr. Hogarth, reading the name printed in one corner of the envelope, " and it's forwarded from Washington. I don't see what reason he has for writing to me, unless it's to tell me that the old gentleman has seen the propriety of increasing my allowance without waiting for the suggestion to come from his dutiful nephew."

He tore open the envelope and read the letter. It was short, and, to judge by the expression of his face, the contents were not of a character to cause pleasure, and this impression was heightened by the remarks that fell from his lips as he finished the perusal, and sat apparently for the moment half stupefied with astonishment and anger.

" Well," he said, when he had in a measure recovered from the immediate effects that the information had produced. " This is the very devil ! I don't understand it at all. Something's gone wrong that's certain."

Mrs. Hogarth raised her eyes at these words, and looked at her husband as though she had some half-formed expectation that he would enlighten her; but she did not intimate by words that she entertained such an idea.

"If you knew what was in this letter, Mrs. Oldmixon," continued her husband, rising as he spoke, and walking up and down the floor with the letter still in his hand, "you wouldn't take the matter so devilish quietly, for you'd discover another cause for disappointment in me. You'd find out that you'd married a beggar."

At this Mrs. Oldmixon roused herself sufficiently to ask what was the matter.

"Just about the worst thing that could happen. Listen to this, and if you've got a heart I rather think the strings will be stretched a little when you get the news through your head:

"DEAR SIR: I am instructed by Mr. Victor Oldmixon to notify you, that the allowance of three thousand dollars that he has hitherto made you will cease with the current month.

"I am also instructed to say that any expectations you may have entertained relative to being Mr. Oldmixon's heir may as well be abandoned, as he has formed views in regard to the disposition of his property into which you do not enter.

"And I am further desired by Mr. Oldmixon to inform you that the relation of uncle and nephew between him and you exists now, and will exist in the future, only in name, and that it will be quite useless for you to seek personally, or by letter, or by other means for a revocation of his action in any of the points referred to in this

letter.   Henceforth you and he are strangers to each
other.

" Your obedient servant,

" THEOBALD RIDLEY."

" I'd give all I am worth," he continued, excitedly,
" to know what it all means.   He must be crazy.   I've
done nothing to put him into such a passion with me,
for he is furiously angry, just as he was with Jack a
dozen or more years ago.   By G—d ! I believe *he's* at
the bottom of it all.   He's got hold of the old fool and
has cut me out."

Another knock at the door was followed by the
entrance of the servant with a second letter which he
apologized for having overlooked, though it had come
in the same mail as the first.

" Ah !" exclaimed Mr. Hogarth, opening it after the
man had left the room, " this is from Masters.   Now I
shall know the ins and outs of the business.   He's Ridley's clerk you know, and a friend of mine.   He'd better
be.   I could— Well, never mind what I could do.
Let's see what he has to say :

" MY DEAR MR. HOGARTH : Mr. Victor Oldmixon was
down a couple of days ago, and from some cause or other,
the nature of which I could not ascertain, is very indignant against you.   He has directed that your allowance
be stopped, and has made a new will, giving the whole
of his estate to your brother John, on condition that he
marries somebody whose name was left blank in the draft
of the will for him to fill up.   Mr. Ridley knows who,
but, of course, it's no use trying to get it out of him.   If
your brother does not marry this woman within a year

after your uncle's decease, the whole estate goes to her. The idea appears to be to force Mr. John into marrying her. For what reason you may be able to tell—I can't even guess. The whole scheme appears to me to look very much as though it was the offspring of an insane mind, and if such is the case, you would probably, from your intimate acquaintance with Mr. Victor, be able to furnish proof that would satisfy the surrogate or a jury. He can't live much longer, and, although you can't attack the will till it is offered for probate, you might very readily begin now to gather evidence and to talk the matter up. If you can manage to give him a reputation for insanity before his death, you will have done a great deal.

" I take this occasion to inform you that I am about setting up for myself, and that I shall make a specialty of practising in the surrogate's court. It will give me great pleasure to look after your interests in this or in any other connection.

" Very respectfully,

" Your obedient servant,

" Jeremiah Masters."

Mrs. Oldmixon had listened with all the attention of which she was capable to the reading of these letters. The effect upon her was not, on the whole, inspiriting, though a hot—hot for her—feeling of anger was engendered within her breast. She was quick enough to perceive that the means for a comfortable support had been suddenly taken away, and that they would have in future to depend upon the three thousand dollars allowed her by her father. She saw, also, that the hopes of wealth that had been developed in her by a consideration of the relation of heir that her husband had borne to his uncle, were also dashed to the ground. All this was bad enough, but it was as nothing compared to the indignation she felt against him for the fraud that his reading of Mr. Ridley's letter showed he had practised upon her and her mother. It was not often that she got angry, for anger was not only troublesome in itself, but was likely to lead to complications that were themselves sources of discomfort, and the chief object that Camilla Oldmixon née White had in continuing to exist was her own personal comfort, to the exclusion, if necessary, of the personal comfort of every other person in the world. Now, her comfort had been ruthlessly interfered with. This man had come to her mother with a lie. He had told her that his allowance was ten thousand a year, and this letter that had just been read showed that it had never been over three thousand. He had, therefore, cheated her out of seven thousand a year—ten thousand in fact, for now he had nothing, and all his magnificent prospects had gone, doubtless through some act of his own, that he was now ashamed or afraid to confess.

She had kept silent during the reading of the letters, but her anger was accumulating in force, as fact after fact was forced upon her attention. She would have broken out when Hogarth had finished with the first letter, but the entrance of the servant with another had had the effect of calming her for the time being. For, she argued, it might be that this second communication was a reversal of the first, and, in that case, rage would have been an exertion that she might have spared herself. When, however, she learned that instead of being a contradiction of the other letter, it was a full and detailed confirmation, she could restrain herself no longer.

" You have committed a fraud," she exclaimed.
" You told my mother that your allowance was ten
thousand a year. I say nothing of what you declared
relative to your expectations. You may honestly have
had them, but this other was a deception in regard to a
matter of fact about which there could have been no
mistake. You told a lie, a deliberate, wilful lie, for the
purpose of entrapping me into a marriage with you. If
I had not believed what you said, I should have let you
rot in the street before I'd have married you." With
which words Mrs. Oldmixon left the window and sat
down in a rocking-chair near the centre of the room,
and in her excitement rocked herself vigorously.

Mr. Hogarth was astonished. This exhibition of rage
on the part of his wife was a revelation of possibilities
of character that he had not hitherto supposed her to
possess. She had taken everything thus far with such a
degree of indifference, had scarcely ever replied otherwise than by an expressionless smile to his most cutting
observations, and had evinced so little interest in him or
his fortunes, or, for the matter of that, in their combined
fortunes, that he had supposed her to be one of those
women that take what comes to them, whether good or
bad, with equal equanimity. This outburst was, therefore, something for which he was altogether unprepared,
and for a moment he was in doubt what kind of a
reply to make. The fact that he *had* deceived her and
her mother never entered as a disturbing factor into his
reflections on the subject. He had deceived so many
persons in ways much worse than that that he had adopted
on this occasion, that it failed altogether to touch his conscience. That he had said " ten " when he ought to
have said " three" was, in his estimation, a small mat-

ter. He certainly did not intend to descend to the humiliation of asking her forgiveness. On the contrary, after a very little thought, he resolved that he would brave it out, and his wife might do what she pleased. He did not see what she could do. She could use her tongue on him, it was true, but he could, he rather thought, beat her at that game, skilful and reckless as she might be in its exercise. And then he would always have the alternative of getting out of her presence if the fire became too hot. He had subdued women before in his day—women much more formidable than this one, he thought, and he had invariably found that it was best in all contests with them not to fire blank cartridges, but to open ruthlessly at point-blank range with all the artillery he could bring to war. Yes, he would give her a lesson at once. He would show her just what kind of a man she had to deal with, and he flattered himself that she would be as much astonished at the knowledge she would obtain as he had been with the demonstration she had given him. It would be an immense saving of trouble, and he thought would be far more efficacious in the long run. One crushing victory would be better than even a long and uninterrupted series of small ones. Besides, he was in the humor for crushing somebody, and that somebody might as well be a woman, though the woman was his wife. He was not afraid of women.

7

CHAPTER X.

BARBARA WORKS AND THINKS.

Mr. Oldmixon and his remarkable story were in Barbara's thoughts for several days after his visit. Time and again the idea occurred to her that he was insane, and that the whole account that he had given of his loves and his nephews was a figment of his imagination. Her father encouraged her in this opinion. The old man was of a practical turn of mind, and frequently saw mental derangement in the conduct of people that was not in accordance with his conceptions of healthy mental action. "There are more lunatics out of the asylums than in them," he was accustomed to say when some particularly erratic performance was brought to his knowledge.

"Half the world's insane, in my opinion. You've only to read the newspapers to discover that fact. Indeed, you needn't even do that. Only go into the business of taxidermy and you'll find it out quickly enough. Why, half the people that I do work for are as mad as March hares. I don't suppose, however, that we've got a monopoly of the cranks ;" and then he would laugh heartily, doubtless as much from the consciousness that *he*, at any rate, was in his sound mind, as from the conviction that half the rest of mankind was not.

"But as to this Mr. Oldmixon, my dear," he said to Barbara, "whether he's crazy or not need not concern us. We're not likely to see him again. So, we'd better go our own way and let him go his, whether it's a crazy one or not."

"I'm sure he's not crazy, father," answered Barbara. "He may be different from other men in many things, but I don't think you should find fault with him for that, for you've often said that the tendency of civilization was to destroy the individual differences that gave interest to life up to a hundred years or so ago."

"Yes, yes. I said that, and I say it now. Machinery and steam and electricity and travel, and, above all, printing—newspapers and books—are gradually reducing mankind to a state of uniformity. Look at the mere matter of dress! Why, the last time I was in Denmark, the men and women of my native village looked as though they had just come from a New England town. All through Europe you see the same thing. It's getting to be the same with their thoughts too. Take out politics, and all the civilized nations think alike."

"And then when a man comes who is different from the others and thinks for himself, you call him a lunatic."

"I'm afraid you're right, my girl."

"Well, if that's the sort of a lunatic Mr. Oldmixon is, I've no objection to your calling him one."

"Let him drop, my dear," persisted the old man, from some vague idea of jealousy, which was very apt to arise in his breast when Barbara evinced any particular interest in any one—man or woman. "If he ever comes in our way again it will be time enough to talk about him. Now tell me about this silver fox," going, as he spoke, to the glass case in which the partially mounted skin lay. "The gentleman that brought it here was very particular in his directions about expression. As you know, it is the most difficult of all animals to approach, or to

trap, or to catch in any other way, and I want you, my
dear, to bring all your knowledge and skill to bear on the
matter of indicating the shrewdness of the animal.   It
is all ready now for your work.   I'll just moisten it a
little, and then you can take it in hand."

Barbara looked at the animal reflectively for several
minutes, apparently considering how she could best bring
out in her work the characteristic qualities of the silver
fox.

"We've only mounted ten silver foxes since you began
the business," she said, after looking over a large book
that she took from a shelf near by, "and seven of these
were during the first twenty years after you came here.
That would seem to show that the animal is getting
scarcer."

"Yes, or that it is now so valuable that people would
rather have the two or three hundred dollars each skin
will fetch than to have it stuffed and set up in their
houses."

"I've never mounted a silver fox, father.   Don't you
think you had better do this one?"

"No, Barbara, I don't think anything of the kind.
You know the habits of the animal better than I do, and
you know how to mould the face into the proper expression infinitely better than I, or, indeed, any one I know
of.   The gentleman could have had it mounted for ten
dollars, but he chose to come here and pay fifty—for
Mr. Maurice told him he would get a work of art here."

"Did he tell you how he got the fox, or give you an
account of his hunt for it?   Any information on these
points would be of great assistance in mounting the
specimen."

"No; he only told me that last winter he visited a

friend at Fort Resolution, on Great Slave Lake. This gentleman was a high official in the service of the Hudson's Bay Company, and gave his visitor the opportunity for many stirring adventures in the pursuit of skins, of which he was not slow to avail himself."

"Then he's a great traveller, I suppose?"

"I don't know about that. He must be fond of adventure, or he wouldn't fancy spending a winter at Fort Resolution."

"He didn't shoot the fox. There were no bulletholes in the skin."

"No; he either caught it in a trap or poisoned it."

"I hope he didn't poison it," said Barbara; "that is such a mean way of killing an animal."

Then again, after a few minutes, during which she had examined the stuffed skin, and which was ready to be placed in position on its temporary platform: "I wish I knew how he caught it. There must be a story about the adventure, and if I knew it I could make use of it in getting ideas for setting the animal up."

"Well, my dear, you can ask the owner to tell you all about it, for he's coming here this morning to get his treasure. He insisted on calling for it. He'll be disappointed, I'm afraid, unless you work pretty hard for the next hour."

"Oh, he's coming for it this morning! Then I think I'll wait till he can tell me something about how he caught it. I'm sorry to disappoint him, but I think he will be pleased if I can carry out a plan I have for giving him a good piece of work. So, if you've no objections, I'll finish that apteryx that Mr. Balman sent here."

"Very well, my dear; you can do as you please."

"What an uninteresting bird an apteryx is!" she said,

after she had spent a few minutes in getting its legs into proper shape and setting its head in the most advantageous position. " There is so little opportunity for making a striking form. It's about equal, I suppose, to making a statue of an armless man. I can never quite get over the idea that the apteryx is a monstrosity, like the man without arms who plays the violin and writes letters and cuts silhouettes with his toes."

" Ay, ay ; and it isn't remarkable for sense either. I had a live one once, and every time any one came near its cage it rammed its head into the sand."

" It isn't the only animal that thinks it can escape danger by shutting its eyes to it. Man does the same thing. What time is the owner of the silver fox coming ?"

" I suppose he'll call at about twelve o'clock. These fine fellows don't get out much before that time in the morning."

" Is he a fine fellow ? I thought you said the other day that he didn't look as though he had more money than he wanted."

" Ha, ha, ha !" laughed the old man ; " that was only my clumsy attempt at a joke. Did you ever, my Barbara, see a man, or a woman either, that looked as if they had more money than they wanted ? There may be such people, but I don't think you or I have ever seen them."

" Did he seem to care much how the mounting was done—I mean," she added, " did he appear to know what he wanted ?"

" Ay, did he !" exclaimed the old man. " He knows what's what, that you may depend upon. Do you think he'd have come here if he didn't, and pay fifty dollars for what Bangs would charge him ten for ? That looks, too, as if he had money enough, doesn't it ?"

The question was hardly one that required an answer, and Barbara went on with her work, wondering, however, what kind of a man he could be that had such a high appreciation of their art as to pay five times as much for the mounting of his silver fox as he could get it done for by another taxidermist. Then, after a little cogitation over this enlightened and doubtless accomplished person, and speculations as to his occupation and appearance, her thoughts reverted to Mr. Oldmixon, and especially to what he had told her relative to his two nephews. She could not help feeling an interest in them, for had she not decided their fate? How strange it was that she should have been thus powerful in determining a question of such vast importance as the one Mr. Oldmixon had submitted to her, and one that concerned so nearly two men that she had yet never seen, and until a few days since had never even heard of! She hoped she had done right. And yet, situated as she was, with scarcely a probability that she would even become acquainted with either one of the brothers, she felt that, in regard to this point, there would always be some doubt in her mind. One had, through her, been reduced from a position of wealth to what she had understood from Mr. Oldmixon was one of destitution. He had been the favored one, and had been brought up in luxury, with all his wants supplied as soon as they were formed, and with expectations of succeeding, in the course of nature, to a large fortune. What would be his feelings toward her, she thought, if he knew of the agency she had had in reducing him to a penniless condition? She had been told that he was bad past belief, but there must be some good in him. Everybody had that. Even Satan, as described by Milton, was brave and free from sycophancy.

There must be something in this young man that should have plead with her for a less condign punishment than that of taking all from him. He too might be brave and free from servility ; and if so, was not his punishment too great ?

And as to the other : was it quite certain that he was as worthy as his uncle, with his heart embittered against the one whom he supposed had injured him, thought him to be ? Assuredly, there had not been that frame of mind present in Mr. Oldmixon that it was desirable should exist when a matter so important as the one in question was to be decided. If this new favorite were so good and noble as his uncle now represented him to be, why had he been neglected for all these years, and his unworthy brother exalted over him ? Mr. Oldmixon, though certainly eccentric, was, as she plainly saw, no fool. Was it within the limits of possibility that, knowing these two as well as he did, he would have shamefully oppressed the one, and, with an equal disregard of justice, have exalted the other above his merits during a dozen years, and then only have been prompted by an unforeseen occurrence to act righteously ? It was hard for her to believe this, and yet she did believe it. There had been something that she could not quite understand about Mr. Oldmixon's manner that had carried conviction with it. Perhaps it was his earnestness, perhaps his unconscious nervousness, perhaps something in the expression of his countenance that he had not intended should appear, but that, nevertheless, told her he was speaking the truth. No, he had not lied. He might be insane—of that she was not altogether sure—but he had been honest with her. Was a lunatic, she asked herself, necessarily a liar or always incapable of perceiving matters correctly ?

Then suddenly an idea occurred to her that filled her with delight, and which, if it could be carried out, would, she believed, lead to a satisfactory settlement of the whole affair, so far as the money involved was concerned. It was this: If the elder brother were the good and magnanimous man that his uncle represented him to be, he would very willingly divide with the unfortunate one, who had so suddenly, and without any special fault of his own, so far as she could see, fallen from grace. It might safely be left in his hands with the confidence that he would act justly and kindly. She was afraid that she was prevented by her implied promise from revealing to him any part of the story told her by Mr. Oldmixon so long as he lived. Well, there would be no occasion for her to open her mouth now. He had not yet come into possession of the estate. When it was his, she could speak, and doubtless he would heed what she said, and do what was right.

"There, father," she said, after all this and much more to a like effect had passed through her mind, "I have done the best I could with the apteryx."

"Why, Miss Barbara," said Peter, who at that moment entered the workshop from the office, "you've made that bird so beautiful that if he could see out of those glass eyes, and look at himself in the glass, he wouldn't know himself."

"Do you think so, Peter?" replied Barbara, smiling. "If you are right, the best thing I can do is to remount the wretch. If one apteryx doesn't know another apteryx when he sees him, something is wrong with one of them. Either the apteryx that looks is incapable of seeing things properly, or the apteryx that is looked at is not as he should be. Now, if this apteryx were to be endowed with

7*

the sense of sight, and were to be incapable of recognizing his own image in a glass—"

"O Miss Barbara, you are laughing at me!" exclaimed Peter; "you always make fun of me when I pay a compliment to your work. What I meant was, that that is the most beautifully mounted apteryx that was ever set up in New York. I saw one the other day that had been mounted in Paris, and it wouldn't compare with this. The eyes were as big as a ten-cent piece, while you have made these almost as small as the head of a pin. That's the way they ought to be. I heard Professor Laird say so, and this apteryx looks as if he was just about to pick up a worm."

"Well, Peter, worms are what they feed on. I tried to make him appear to be viewing with a critical eye a worm, as though he might be trying to decide whether or not it was sufficiently inviting to warrant him in making the necessary exertion for seizing it."

"And you've hit it exactly. He's got his head turned a little to one side, and his right eye is studying that worm with great deliberation. What life you do put into all your work, Miss Barbara!"

The idea flashed through Peter's mind, that with her as his wife he could keep up the reputation of the place. He had thought before of the advantages of marrying Barbara, but he was rather inclined to be dull, and her skill and knowledge as a taxidermist had not previously entered into his calculations. Now, however, he saw how doubly desirable it was to get her for a wife.

"I'm glad you admire the mounting," she said, after giving the least possible touch to one of the legs of the bird. "It won't be many years before, like the dodo, the apteryx will become extinct. Then we shall value these mounted specimens more than we do now."

"I almost forgot what I came for," resumed Peter, with a laugh, having settled the matrimonial idea to his satisfaction. "The gentleman is here for his silver fox, which he said was promised for to-day. I didn't like to tell him that it wasn't done, for he seems so anxious to get it."

"Oh, has he come!" exclaimed Barbara; "I'll see him about it."

She was not vain, but she was a very woman, so she gave a little glance into the old mirror, just so as to convince herself that there was nothing radically wrong about her appearance—no unbecoming disarrangement of her hair or of the pretty dark blue ribbon that she wore at her throat—and then she passed into the front room.

She saw before her a tall, handsome, well-dressed man, with a face that had an evident unfamiliarity with the razor, for it was covered with the beard over the whole surface upon which nature intended it to grow, and who had, what she was quick to recognize, although not a fashionable young woman, the unmistakable air of a gentleman. That was about as much as she could ascertain from the rapid glance only that she could then give.

He was standing with his hat on, but on her entrance he took it off at once, and made her a slight bow. This impressed her favorably, for very few of the men that came there, whether they pretended to be gentlemen or not, took off their hats in her presence, or smiled so graciously as did this visitor.

"I have come for my silver fox," he said, still smiling, and looking at Barbara with an expression of respectful admiration, that she was not slow to observe. "It was to be done to-day, I believe."

"Yes," she answered; "father promised to have it finished to-day, but we have been unable to get it ready, owing to the want of certain information that we thought might enable us to do a better piece of work than if we went at it ignorantly."

"Then you are Miss Henschel!" he said, a still more pleased expression passing over his face. "I have often heard of you as taking such a great artistic interest in your work. In fact, it was my friend Professor Laird, of the Smithsonian Institution, who told me to come to you with my fox. He said you were the only person in the country that could set it up as a work of art—the art that interprets nature correctly."

"Professor Laird is a good friend of ours, and is very kind." She was dying to know who this gentleman was who talked of art, and whose prepossessions were so greatly in her favor; but she thought it would never do to ask the question directly. Doubtless she would find out before he left. "I am very willing, Miss Henschel, to give you any information that will enable you to mount my fox in the most artistic manner. It is such a beautiful specimen of a rare animal, that I want the most made of it that is possible. You see, I'm an artist myself."

An artist! She might have known it, she thought, for who but an artist would talk as he had talked about "artistic interest" and "art interpreting nature!" The people generally that came there, except, of course, the scientific ones, were such commonplace beings! This one was very different.

"I should like to know how you caught it?"

"After two weeks of incessant labor and vigilance, in

which the fox's wits were pitted against mine, and in which he always won till the last night, I succeeded in catching him in a trap."

"I'm glad you did not poison it. I knew you had not shot it, for there were no holes in the skin, and I thought the silver fox was too cunning to be caught in traps."

"I did not like to poison him, but I wanted his skin very badly, and I think if I had not caught him at last, I should have been mean enough to poison him. You would not have liked that, would you?"

"No," answered Barbara, frankly; "I have a horror of poison. I might excuse its use against savage animals that we might wish to kill for our protection, but as a means of destroying them for their skins, I wouldn't use it."

"Hunters have not your nice discrimination," said the gentleman. "They are making their living by getting skins—and a hard living it is, too—and they are not likely to stand on ceremony with the animal that has a skin they want. However, I am happy to say that to some extent I share your feelings, Miss Henschel; and, at any rate, this fox was not poisoned. I suppose I could have had him a great deal sooner if I had put some strychnine in a piece of dried beef and laid it on the snow near some one of his haunts, but I could not quite make up my mind to treat him so treacherously. Besides, he had a reputation for knowing poisoned meat."

"That was right!" said Barbara, emphatically. "Now, please tell me exactly how you caught him, because I propose to mount him in as nearly as possible the attitude he took just before he was captured."

"You must know, Miss Henschel, that the cold at Fort

Resolution—where I was staying with a friend—is, during the winter months, so intense that for weeks together the mercury is frozen in the thermometer bulbs. I liked it, however, and when well protected the sensation on going out in the morning is delightful. The effect on the circulation of a man—he has to be a strong one, though—is not unlike that of a glass or two of champagne.

"I wanted a silver fox, and I determined to get one. The animal is becoming scarcer every year, and will soon be extinct; and that made me all the more anxious to succeed."

"Won't you walk into the next room?" interrupted Barbara, perceiving that the story would take some little time to tell. "It is our workshop, and, though I shall not show you your fox—I don't want you to see him till he is finished—you will be less likely to be interrupted there."

"I regard this as a great compliment, Miss Henschel," he continued, sitting down in a big Shaker rocking-chair that Barbara pushed toward him, while she sat on a stool in front of her work-bench. "This is your studio," looking around him as he spoke. "Ah, here are many of your works! An apteryx! I could swear that fellow is alive! He looks exactly like one that I saw in the Jardin des Plantes picking up worms that had been put into a mass of earth for his delectation. You know—of course you do, or you would never have put such an expression into his right eye and his head—that he is a very dainty bird, and the worm must be a first-class one, or else he will not eat it. This particular apteryx looks as though he was working every bit of brain he has in the effort to determine whether or not he shall gobble up the worm that is lying on the ground before him. There must be a worm there," he continued, getting up and pretending to look for one on the imitation moss on which the specimen stood. "No, there is none. It has probably crawled away while Master Apteryx was deliberating."

Barbara laughed. "I didn't think I could make much of the apteryx," she said; "it has no wings, or at least only little stumps, and no tail, either."

"But you have done all with it that was possible. The truest artist is the one that makes the most of his subject, without passing the limits of truth; and this you have done."

"Thanks; you are very kind to say all that. I'd rather please an artist than a king."

"Who told you I was an artist?"

"You did just now."

"Did I? I had forgotten. I ought to have told you my name too, oughtn't I?" Then, without waiting for an answer, he handed her a visiting card.

"I don't suppose you have ever heard of me," he went on; "but as we are likely to have sundry conferences about that silver fox that you are going to mount so artistically for me, you should know what to call me."

Barbara took the little piece of pasteboard and read:

Mr. John Oldmixon,
The Vandyke,
61 West —th Street.

CHAPTER XI

BARBARA was overwhelmed with astonishment to find that her visitor was no less a person than that nephew of Mr. Oldmixon that had been so badly treated, and that now, after years of neglect, had come, or was about to come, through her decision, more than ever into his uncle's favor. Surely, he must see the look of surprise on her countenance, and wonder why the announcement of his name had caused so great a degree of facial disturbance. She dreaded to look, but yet, like a bird drawn irresistibly into the snake's jaws, she felt that she must look. She raised her eyes. No; he had not observed her. He was studying the apteryx.

" Ah, young man !" she thought to herself, " little do you know what I've done for you. I'm glad I did it. I like him. I'm sure he's ever so much better than the other. He isn't a bit like his uncle. No wonder he said this one didn't look like an Oldmixon, and had none of their bad traits."

" Now, Mr. Oldmixon," she said, " won't you tell me something more about the silver fox ?"

" Oh, yes ! I was so busy looking around at your work, that I forgot all about the fox. Well, I used to go out every morning with my gun, looking for a silver fox, and one very cold day, and when the snow was falling, I saw the track of one in the new snow. Of course I followed it. It led me several miles to a thick pine forest, and here I lost it. I went home, got my trap, and at once started out to set it before night. I placed it, nicely baited, just at the edge of the wood, and then started for the fort, which I did not reach, however, till long after dark.

"The next morning, early, I was off to inspect my trap. What was my surprise to find that the fox had been there, and had taken the bait without disturbing the underpinning of the fall, and had thus gotten off. I knew it was the fox, for I saw his tracks around the spot. I made use of some words very derogatory to my good sense in not fastening the bait more securely, and then I set the trap again.

"When I got home and told my story at dinner, I was greeted with a hearty laugh by the assembled wisdom at the table. Somers, my friend, was particularly disposed to make fun of me. 'You've got hold of "old Machiavelli,"' he said, 'and you've tried to catch him by putting salt on his tail. That's what it amounts to. Why, my dear fellow, every man, woman, and child at Fort Resolution has made an attempt to catch "old Machiavelli"; but he roams the forest and the plain, as sound in mind and body as he was three years ago, when we first made his acquaintance.'

"'Has anybody ever seen him?' I ventured to ask, with all due humility.

"At this every one burst into a loud laugh.

"'Seen him!' shouted Somers—'seen old Machiavelli! Do you take him for a fool, that he'd let any one see him?'

"'I don't know what he is,' I answered, somewhat put out by the manner in which I was treated; 'he may be the devil, for all I know. Probably he is, as you seem to know so much about him.'

"'My dear Oldmixon,' said Somers, still laughing, '"old Machiavelli" is the name given to a silver fox that is the cunningest of all his kind. He first made this region his dwelling-place about three years ago. Where he came from no one knows, but he was full-grown in mind and body when he arrived. No one has ever laid eyes on him, but by his tracks he is known to be a very large animal. I say no one has ever seen him, but that may be an error. Kashacogno, an Indian buck, declares he saw him one evening, just as the sun was going down, and that he was as large as a wolf ; but as Kashacogno had been drinking of fire-water pretty heavily that afternoon, his testimony is to be taken with some grains of allowance.

"'Then we tried to capture him, dead or alive. Traps of all kinds were made use of ; but if they were very delicately set, he would either not go near them, or would manage to knock the arrangement down and to drag out the bait at his leisure. If they were coarsely set, as yours was last night, he would go in and deliberately take off the bait, without bringing down the trap. Then strychnine was tried, but never once would he eat a piece of poisoned meat. He'd turn it over and over, and once carried a piece a mile away from the place where it was laid ; but then he had dropped it, having apparently, in some way or other, discovered that it was poisoned.'

"'Why didn't you watch the traps and shoot him ?' I inquired.

"'We watched the traps day after day and night after night, but never once did he make his appearance. He has the keenest eyesight and hearing and the best brain of any fox that ever lived in these parts. Finally we gave up trying to catch him, and named him " old Machiavelli," as a compliment to his astuteness.'

" All this sank deeply into my heart, and I resolved that I would have that fox, if I had to devote a whole winter to the work of capturing him. I set a trap, and finding that he gnawed away the string with which the bait was fastened so delicately that he did not disturb the underpinning, I fastened the meat with wire, so that he would have to make more disturbance than if a piece of deer-skin or a cord was used ; but then he would not touch it. I tried this several times, and always with the same result. Once I saw him. I had set my trap, and had retired to a clump of underbrush about a hundred yards to leeward, and then secreting myself, resolved to wait there, if I had to stay till dark. I waited, and not only till dark, but far into the night. Fortunately, there was a full moon, and this, with the bright stars and a wonderful aurora, that lit up the sky and the snow, made it almost as light as day. I sat on a log and watched my trap ; but I was hungry, and it was after nine o'clock, and I had at least five miles to go to reach Fort Resolution. I was just getting ready to go home when I thought I saw something moving stealthily toward the trap. The night was cold and the light wind was blowing from the trap toward me, so that I knew the animal, whatever it was, could not detect me by the scent. I rose to my feet, and strained my eyes to their utmost. Yes, it was ' old Machiavelli' undoubtedly—the biggest silver fox I had ever seen, and with head thrust forward and ears erect, moving slowly toward the trap. I could have killed him with my rifle, perhaps, but I had vowed to catch him with a whole skin, so I would not fire, though strongly tempted to do so. So slowly that I could barely see that he moved, he approached the trap, to a distance, as nearly as I could judge, of three feet from it, and there he stood, surveying it, and doubtless bringing to bear upon it all the acumen with which a wise Providence had endowed him."

Barbara had been deeply absorbed throughout the whole of Jack's recital; but as he told her how the fox had stood and looked at the trap, her interest became still greater. She left the bench on which she was sitting, and going to a corner of the room, stood there before something that was on a table, and at which she began to busy her delicately formed fingers.

"Now, Mr. Oldmixon," she said, "don't look at me, please. No," as Jack turned his face toward her, "you must look the other way. Yes, that will do," as he wheeled round his chair, so that the back was toward her. "Now, tell me just exactly how the fox stood and looked at that trap."

"Well," said Jack, obediently—he rather liked being ordered about by Barbara, and he must paint her if he died for it—"he stood as motionless as a statue, his head projected forward—"

"Yes," interrupted Barbara, pulling the head of the silver fox first one way and then the other, while she slowly repeated his words, "his head projected forward."

"In a straight line with the rest of his body," continued Jack.

"Yes," as she worked deftly at the specimen.

"His ears thrown in the same direction so strongly that they were almost on a line with the top of his head."

"Ears almost on a line with the top of his head—wait a moment, Mr. Oldmixon, please."

"O Miss Henschel!" exclaimed Jack, who up to this time appeared to have been under the impression that she was writing out his description for future use, "are you mounting my fox now?"

"You mustn't ask any questions, and you mustn't look. If you do either, you will break the charm."

"I'll do just as you say."

"Now," said Barbara, after she had moulded the ears into the position in which she wanted them, and had stuffed them with a little cotton wool, "go on, please."

"His left foot raised from the ground in the attitude that a pointer takes when he comes on a covey of partridges, and his brush as straight a continuation of the line of his spine as though it had been laid out with rule and compass."

Barbara worked on in silence for a minute or two, and then,

"What was that you said about something being on a line with his spine?"

"I said his brush was—"

"His brush! Oh, yes, I know now. You are giving it the huntsman's designation. We taxidermists call it a tail."

Jack laughed at this, and then Barbara laughed, going on with her work, all the time sponging the skin, so as to moisten it, and then moulding it with her hands into the shape she wanted. Finally she appeared to have finished. She looked at her work from several points of view, giving it a few touches here and there, and then covering it with a cloth, washed her hands. "Now, Mr. Oldmixon," she said, "was the fox, as he was looking at the trap, anything like this?"

He came toward where she was standing, and she raised

the cloth, revealing to him his fox in the attitude of attention and inquiry that he had described. He was delighted.

"I have never seen anything in the way of taxidermy as good as this," he said, while his face expressed the pleasure and astonishment he felt. "You have got the position of the animal exactly as I saw it, and you have done it with a degree of ease and celerity that I could not have believed possible. You did not acquire your art, Miss Henschel. It was born in you. No wonder everybody praises your work, when you turn out such specimens of it as this."

"I am glad you like it. I felt the impulse to do it while you were describing the scene to me. One can work so much better when the inspiration is present than when one has to work because one must."

"Yes, I feel the truth of that constantly. I think, when I complete a picture that I am under an engagement to paint for Mr. Van der Linden, I shall do no more work to order. You ought to model in clay, Miss Henschel; that is your vocation."

"Do you think so?"

"I know it. You are a genius. You will never get credit for your artistic inspiration while you confine your work, beautiful as it is, to mounting animals. You should attempt the human form. You should become a sculptor, and, my word for it, ere many years have passed you will make the world ring with your praises."

She was silent, but his words fell on willing ears—ears that were much more ready to hear than they were when her father had said almost the same things to her only a few days previously. For, in the mean time, she had thought much of what the old man had said, and the spirit of ambition was beginning to be developed within her. And now an artist—one who must be distinguished, for he was painting a picture for the rich Mr. Van der Linden, who had the grand gallery that she had already visited twice on days on which he threw it open to the public—had praised her work. Her revery was broken in upon by Jack.

"Will you allow me to take this home with me now, Miss Henschel? I have a few friends coming to visit me to-night, and I should be delighted to show it to them."

"But it is not quite finished. It is to have a board yet to stand on—a board covered with artificial snow."

"I'll get the board and the artificial snow. I'll also have a trap made and placed right in front of him, and then I shall have the scene before me in all its exactness, whenever I look at it."

"But it is wet; it will take several hours yet for it to dry."

"I'll carry it with the utmost care. I'll get a cab from a livery stable around the corner, and that will insure my getting it home in safety."

"Well," said Barbara, laughing, "if you want it so badly as all that, I suppose you can take it."

"Thanks! I'm ever so much obliged to you. Now, I'll get a carriage, and then I'll rid you of the fox and myself at the same time."

He went out, but was back before Barbara had had time to tell much of the incident to her father, who had in the mean time returned from a visit he had been making to the American Museum of Natural History.

Jack had met Mr. Henschel before, and he was glad to meet him again, in order to discharge with more ease to himself an important duty that still remained to be performed, and that was, paying for the mounting of his specimen of the silver fox. It would have been unpleasant to him, after his conversation with Barbara and his references to " high art," and, above all, after the impression that her beauty and sweetness had made on him, to spoil all by tendering her the fifty dollars he had agreed to give for the work. It would have caused a jar to his feelings to have them mixed up with a pecuniary transaction. But with Mr. Henschel no such delicacy would be experienced, so he opened his pocketbook, and placed five crisp ten-dollar notes in the old man's hand, much to the latter's satisfaction, for he loved money as fondly as do most people, whether they be rich or poor, grand or humble.

While Mr. Henschel went into the office to make out a bill and receipt, Jack thought it a good chance to give expression to an idea that had occurred to him with more or less distinctness soon after he first saw Barbara, and that had now become perfected to his satisfaction.

" I told you, Miss Henschel," he said, " that I had accepted an order from Mr. Van der Linden for a picture. He has very intelligently left the subject to me, and I think I have at last settled upon one that I may be able to develop into something ; but I want your assistance."

" My assistance, Mr. Oldmixon !" exclaimed Barbara.

" Yes, yours ;" and his voice became lower and more earnest. " I have been in doubt in regard to my ability to carry out the conception, for I lack imagination ; but since I have seen you I am reassured. Miss Henschel, I want you to sit for the principal figure in my composition."

Barbara was frankness itself, and altogether **free from**

that species of vanity that causes some people to seem to avoid or to refuse what they are especially anxious to receive or grant. She answered at once, "I should be very glad to do so, Mr. Oldmixon, but I am afraid I have no time, and besides," she added, "I have no one to go with me to your studio."

"Oh, I shall not ask you to put yourself to such an inconvenience! Although I am deficient in imagination, I have a wonderful memory. All I ask is, that you will allow me to come here for an hour every day for a week, and look at you, and perhaps I may ask you to let me set up my easel here for a few days."

"I don't think there would be the least objection to that, but I will ask father. What is the subject that you have determined upon, Mr. Oldmixon?"

"I had determined to paint Queen Alfgive pleading with her husband, King Knut, for the life of an Anglo-Saxon earl who would not give his allegiance to the Danes; but I have, since I came here, given that up. I shall now, if you let me, paint 'The Taxidermists'— you and your father at work in this room."

"But, Mr. Oldmixon, the other is a much more noble subject, I should think."

"I don't know anything about its nobility, and I don't know anything, either, about Queen Alfgive or King Knut or the Anglo-Saxon earl—the subject came into my mind at dinner a night or two ago—but this place I know, and you and your father I know. You are flesh and blood of our own day; and if I do not mistake Mr. Van der Linden, he would infinitely prefer this subject to the other. What does he care about Danish kings and queens and Anglo-Saxon earls? All those historical subjects run in one rut. I should look through some illu-

8

minated manuscripts to get the costumes and architect-
ure, and then I should place the king on his throne, and
the earl held by two soldiers, and the queen on her knees
supplicating her lord, and that would be all.   But here I
should have your father, with his fine old face, and you,
with your—your—looking, you know, at a bird or something, and the silver gray fox—yes, working at the silver
gray fox, with other animals standing around, just as they
are here.   Oh, I could make a glorious picture of all
that !''

Ile spoke with an enthusiasm that delighted Barbara,
and she looked at him with undisguised admiration.
Ilere was an artist—one who felt all that he expressed,
and one, moreover, who had received an inspiration from
her and her associations.   All this was very pleasant to
her, for nothing so rouses the sympathy of a woman as
to discover that she is a power and exerting an influence
over some one she likes or, still more, loves.   Of course
Barbara did not love Jack Oldmixon.   She was not a
woman, sensitive though she was, to lose her heart on a
first acquaintance.   She could very readily have dispensed with his society from that time on to the end of
her days, without experiencing more than a transient regret that one who was agreeable to her had passed out
of her life.   But he was interesting, and there was not
so much variety in her existence that she could view
with indifference the advent of a handsome, intelligent,
sympathizing, and, above all, art-loving young man like
Jack into the course of her life, without there being
more or less emotional disturbance of a pleasant character.   This proposition of his, to make her and her father
the subject of his picture, was one, however, to which she
was not able to give her consent without the concurrence

of her father ; but she did not anticipate any difficulty
on that score. He generally allowed her to have her
own way, for her way was a good one, and no one knew
it better than Mr. Henschel.

Jack intuitively divined what was passing in her mind.
" Of course," he said, " I shall ask your father's consent. I only wanted to get yours first, for if it is not
agreeable to you, that's the end of it. I hope you approve, Miss Henschel ?"

" If the subject is one that you think you could make
interesting, you are at perfect liberty to paint it, so far
as I am concerned. I don't think my father will object.
He is very proud of his art, and so am I."

" Well, here he is, and I will ask him now."

Jack then laid the subject before Mr. Henschel, and
was happy to find that the old man entered with great
enthusiasm into the idea. That he should see his Barbara in a picture that would probably become famous—
one that, at any rate, would hang in a famous collection,
and be seen by many people, was a thought that gave
him great satisfaction. He had a very keen appreciation
of his daughter's peculiar style of beauty, and when he
encountered a person that saw it as he saw it, his heart
expanded with that phase of self-complacency that most
of us feel when others approve of our thoughts or acts.
It did not take long to arrange the matter, so it was settled that Jack should begin the next day by bringing his
easel and all his other paraphernalia to the shop, and that
he should then study the interior, so as to form a clear
conception of what he wanted. " I shall not be surprised," he said, " if I shall have to spend the first two
or three days in making up my mind how to arrange you,
so as to get the best effect. Yes," looking around as he

spoke, " I shall have to change your position, Miss Henschel, so as to get you more in the light of that window.
However, we'll arrange all that to-morrow. Good-by,"
he continued, holding out his hand, and smiling, while
in the other he held his silver fox. " I shall bring
this back to-morrow, and place it where it will be well
seen in my picture. I am greatly obliged to you, Miss
Henschel. I hope I have not stayed too long, and tired
you out with my loquacity ; but the time was passing so
pleasantly that I forgot myself."

" But," said Barbara, laughing, " you have not yet
told me how you caught the silver fox."

" No ; and therefore there is another reason why I
should return. It's a very interesting story, Miss Henschel. Again, good-by !"

His carriage was at the door, and entering it, he was
driven away in the direction of his residence. But he
had not gone more than a block when, putting his head
out of the window, he called to the driver.

" Go to No. 73 Lake Street," he said ; " I like com-
parisons," he continued to himself. " I'll take a look
at that other girl who is a taxidermist, and who Sliven
told me was so expert at the art as to have no rival in
this or any other country. I'll see if it's taxidermy that
makes angels out of women." In a few minutes the
carriage stopped in front of a respectable-looking house,
and Jack got out. On the door was a sign, " Thomas
Bangs & Co., Taxidermists." In a large bay-window
were several specimens of the taxidermist's art. A bell
on a spring rang as he opened the door, and then he
found himself in an apartment the walls of which
were lined with cases containing stuffed animals of various kinds. From an inner room, doubtless brought out

by the sound of the bell, came a young woman dressed
in tawdry finery, a heavy gold chain—or of what looked
like gold—around her neck, her hair frizzled all over her
head, and her face and hands showing evident marks
of unfamiliarity with soap and water. He looked specially at her hands. He had observed that Barbara,
after completing the mounting of his silver fox, had
washed her hands before joining him again. This girl's
were dirty, and her nails were uncared for. He had
seen enough, but he thought a little further exploration
would be gratifying.

"Is Mr. Bangs in ?" he inquired.

"No, he ain't in ; but if you want to see him on business, I guess I can attend to it."

"I have a wolverine that I would like to have
mounted."

"A what ?"

"A wolverine—one that I captured in Canada last
winter, and that I would like to have mounted. I will
send the skin and the skull to you to-morrow."

The girl seemed confused. She was not a bad-looking girl, or rather she would not have been bad-looking
had she been clean and kempt. She had a bright pair of
eyes, a good mouth and teeth, a naturally clear complexion, and by the great majority of people—men
or women—would have been considered a far more
beautiful girl than was Barbara Henschel. Soap and
water and care, of which Barbara had no stint, would
have made this girl still more attractive, and not one in
a hundred would have passed her by for the red-haired
girl, with the glorious smile, whose beauty required to
be looked for and thought of in order to be recognized.

Then, undeniably, this girl was ignorant. She did

not know what a wolverine was, and her speech was like that of a New York shop girl of the lowest grade.

"Pa's not in, as I said," she observed, after she had apparently made up her mind in regard to the kind of animal under consideration, "but we can do it, I guess. We've stuffed a good many wolves in our time. I'm Miss Bangs, and I do the finishing. Them wolves requires a good deal of life to be put into them. I done one for Mr. Jacobs, in Fifth Avenue, and he said it was just splendid."

"But the wolverine is not a wolf. It is altogether a different kind of an animal. It's sometimes called the glutton, and it is the pest of the hunters in the north, for it steals the bait out of their traps."

"I guess there's a picture of it in 'The Quadrupeds of North America.' I'll mount it after that pattern, if there is one. Stop a minute! We ain't got that book, but when we want to use it I go over to the Astor Library, and I copy the pictures we want on a piece of tracing paper. But there's a 'Webster's Unabridged' here, and I'll look it up if you'll wait a little."

She took down the large quarto volume, and began to turn over the leaves. After she had done so, much to Jack's amusement, for several minutes, she exclaimed:

"No, it ain't here. You never can find the thing you want in them dictionaries."

"Let me look, please," said Jack. She handed him the book.

"Here's 'wolf,'" she said, "and—oh, yes, here it is in the next column, and I never seen it! And a picture of it, too! We might set yours up just like that."

Jack had seen and heard enough.

"I'll send you the skin and skull to-morrow, Miss

Bangs," he said, "and you can mount it in your own way. Doubtless," he added—Jack was always polite—"you will succeed admirably."

"Oh, we never make no failures! Do you want a glass case for it?"

"No, I have not yet made up my mind what to do with it."

"Name, please."

"John Oldmixon," giving her his card as he spoke.

"We generally require a deposit, unless the skin's valuable."

"Well, as this skin isn't worth much, I come under the rule. How much shall I leave you?"

"It will cost eight dollars to mount it. I guess five dollars will do. You can send the money down with the skin."

"No, I'll leave it now. It will save trouble to do so."

He laid a five-dollar note on the counter, took the receipt she handed him, and with a bow left the house.

"That girl's a tradeswoman—a shop girl," he said, as he got into the carriage. "The other one's a lady and an artist. Dress the Bangs girl up, and she'd stand a good chance of getting the prize for beauty at a dime museum or an agricultural fair, while the other requires a gentleman and an artist to see her beauty. The one scarcely varied the expression of her countenance the whole time she was talking; the other's face is a study; it changes with every thought she conceives and every emotion she feels, and when she smiles—well, I never saw anything like her smile, and I haven't been blind to female beauty, either. Two taxidermists! They're as different as night and day. The one practises it as a trade, the other studies it as an art. The one is a coarse, ignorant, vulgar woman, with no soul above the shop ; the other's an angel.''

And with this conclusion, the final word of which seemed to him to embody in its meaning all the virtues and perfections that are ever bestowed on womankind, Jack's thoughts became less coherent, though they were still concerned with Barbara Henschel.

CHAPTER XII.

A PAIR OF DOCTORS.

Mr. Oldmixon was so overcome by the nefariousness of Mr. Partridge in putting currant jelly on canvas-back duck, and by the excitement that had been developed, followed as it was by a severe degree of reaction, that he was not able to leave his room for several days. Jack saw him every morning for half an hour or so, but his uncle was at no time in a fit condition to disclose his intentions relative to his nephew's future life that he had incorporated into his will. Finally, it was deemed advisable to call in a physician. The gentleman came, asked a few questions, felt his patient's pulse, looked at his tongue, listened at his chest.

"Weak heart," he said under his breath. Then to the patient: "My dear sir, it appears to me that you have received a severe shock of some kind. Your nervous system is all unstrung, and your heart feels it very evidently. Am I correct in my suspicions?"

"Two shocks, doctor," said Mr. Oldmixon, feebly —"two, one after the other, and both severe. The nature of the first I prefer not to communicate to you; but the second is the result of a man—a fellow that I took to be a gentleman, and that I invited to my table —an æsthetic table—at which all the appointments, from the salt-cellars to the guests, were in keeping, and of which the *menu* was the result of days of anxious study.

8*

The ducks—canvas-backs—were cooked according to the principles of physical and gastronomic science. There was one apiece, and the rich, fragrant, crimson-streaked juice flowed gently from their pectoral muscles when the knives—silver-plated—coursed through them like the sharp-cut bow of a gondola through the bosom of the Adriatic."

Mr. Oldmixon stopped to take breath, and the doctor, not quite sure, perhaps, that the metaphor was correct, and that his patient might not be the subject of a little mental confusion, looked as much surprised as his expressionless face permitted. Certainly the prelude to Mr. Oldmixon's account of his shock was altogether different from any that he had ever heard before, and he could not imagine to what it tended. He was not a club-man, or one accustomed to good dinners, and hence his patient's language was almost unintelligible.

"Well, doctor, would you believe it," resumed Mr. Oldmixon—after having mixed the yolk of an egg with a glass of sherry and swallowed the compound—"one of my guests, a man who, as I have just said, I thought was a gentleman—one who, at any rate, if he did have depraved tastes, would not seek to gratify them at my table—this man having cut off a slice of duck that would have tempted the Pope in the middle of Lent, orders some currant jelly to be brought to him—he wouldn't have got it in my house, and I think I shall resign from the Lucullus for keeping such a vile mixture—and having got it, deliberately spreads it over the luscious-looking morsel that lay on his plate waiting for proper appreciation, as if he was lathering his nasty face with soap-suds, and then proceeds to eat the horrid *mélange*. I restrained myself as well as I could—being at my own table—but the effort was a task such as I have never performed before, and was, as you see, sufficient to precipitate me into this dreadful state.

> ' If I had a thunderbolt in my eye,
> I can tell who should down ;
> It would be that wretch.' "

"You don't mean to say," said Dr. Jimnay, who probably had never eaten canvas-back duck in his life, with or without jelly, " that the state in which I find you has been induced by one of your friends putting currant jelly on duck !"

"Canvas-back, doctor ! Jelly is good enough on a barnyard duck, for you want something to give it a flavor ; but on a canvas-back ! O Lord, the very thought makes me faint !" Then calling to Jack, he whispered to him, " Pay that man his fee and send him off. He's not a gentleman ; he doesn't know a canvas-back from a scoot, whose flesh tastes like a Dutch herring. Get me a gentleman, and get this man out of the room ; the very sight of him makes me sick. He has a bad countenance ; I wouldn't like to meet him at night in a dark alley if he had a grudge against me and he was armed with a box of pills. He'd seize me and make me swallow the lot. Get him out and send for Milledge ; he knows what's what, and he's a gentleman, besides."

Jack discharged the rather unpleasant duty put upon him by his uncle with all the tact and discretion of which he was capable, and the obnoxious son of Galen took his departure, with his fee in his pocket.

"How much did you give him, Jack ?" asked Mr. Oldmixon, in a feeble voice, as the door closed.

" Five dollars."

" What !" exclaimed Mr. Oldmixon, rising up in his
bed and resting on one elbow, while he gazed at Jack
with an expression of the utmost surprise on his face,
" did you say five dollars ?"

" Yes ; I gave him what he asked, of course."

" Five dollars !" groaned Mr. Oldmixon, sinking back
on the mass of pillows behind him.   " No wonder !
What can you expect from a doctor that charges five
dollars for a first visit to a case like this ?   A case of
nervous prostration, that requires the skill and tact of a
first-class man for its elucidation, to be attended to by a
fellow that values his opinion at five dollars !   Have
you sent for Milledge ?   Get him at once, and let me
forget all about that little beast.

  ' Learn from the beast the physic of the field.'

Ha, ha ! that's a somewhat different meaning from what
Pope intended, but it suits the emergency.   I've had
my beast, and I've learnt my physic."

" Yes, uncle, I've sent for him," said Jack, with a
smile that he could not repress.   " You won't get off
with five dollars from him.   It will be twenty-five, at
least."

" All right, and I shall have the consolation of knowing that my medical attendant is a gentleman that doesn't
put currant jelly on canvas-back duck."

The great man came, saw his patient, treated him with
the most sympathizing *hauteur* and autocratic kindness,
smiled incredulously when told that a guest at the Lucullus had put currant jelly on a canvas-back, threw up his
hands in a deprecatory manner when told that the man

lived west of the Alleghanies, prescribed Vichy with Lithia, ordered a month at Saratoga, although it was a little late in the season, and then taking his twenty-five dollars with a slightly wearied air, as though he had pocketed a dozen or more like it that morning, and was tired of the process, prepared to take his leave.

" You'll get over it, Mr. Oldmixon ; the provocation was great, I admit ; but a man of your strength of will generally masters these *désagréments.*"

" Yes, doctor, I suppose so ; but I never before felt so strong a desire to kill a man as I did to kill that wretch. If it had not been for the law and the personal inconvenience to myself of a trial, as well as the disgrace to my nephew to have his uncle hanged, I should have poisoned his wine on the spot. I had no conscientious scruples on the subject—none whatever. Besides, I'm born with it in me. Lewes says, and he isn't the only one that's said the same thing, that murder, like talent, seems occasionally to run in families. It runs in ours, though we haven't always got our deserts for yielding to the inclination."

The doctor laughed, said he didn't think it necessary to call again, and then, after a few words of gossip, took his leave.

" Now, he's something like a physician !" exclaimed Mr. Oldmixon. " What confidence in himself ! What *aplomb !* Did you ever see anything grander than the poise of his head ! To compare Milledge and Jimnay is worse than comparing Hyperion to a Satyr. It's more like pitting Apollo against a sanctified but dilapidated ghoul. I suppose I'll either die now or get well. I have had my due allowance of doctors.

'See one physician, like a sculler plies,
　　The patient lingers and by inches dies,
　　But two physicians, like a pair of oars,
　　Waft him more swiftly to the Stygian shores.'

" How much did you give him, Jack ?"

" Twenty-five dollars."

" And cheap at the money. I feel better already.
Won't you be kind enough to ring that bell for my man ;
I think I'll get up, and to-morrow I'll go to Saratoga.
I'm sorry I didn't kill that fellow Partridge," he added,
after a few minutes' silence. " So many of my ancestors
were hanged, or otherwise executed, that I ought to have
done it, if only for the sake of the family. There hasn't
been an Oldmixon killed now for nearly a hundred years,
and you and that rascal Hogarth and myself are the only
ones left to maintain the honor of the race. I don't
suppose you'll be hanged. I've missed the best chance
I ever had in my life, and shall probably never get
another, so that the only one left to preserve the family
from sinking into oblivion is Hogarth. Well, I'm inclined to think he'll do his duty in this respect."

Mr. Oldmixon went to Saratoga, and was absent during the whole period that Jack was painting his picture
of the taxidermists in Mr. Henschel's back room. He
could not make up his mind to stay longer than ten
days, notwithstanding Dr. Milledge had so strenuously
insisted upon a month. At that season of the year
Saratoga was not a desirable residence for anybody, much
less for a man like Mr. Oldmixon, who consulted his
comfort in everything he did, and who could find few
of the, to him, necessaries of life in the plain boarding-
house at which he put up at the Springs. But he walked
out to the Geyser every morning, and drank a half a

dozen tumblers of the water of that remarkable spring during each day. And then, having imbibed sixty glasses of the health-giving liquid, he came to the conclusion that the latent gout, to which Dr. Milledge had ascribed his symptoms, was thoroughly washed out of his blood, and that it would be a very proper thing for him to return to New York, and begin over again. Besides, he must tell Jack about the will and the conditions he had imposed.

In the mean time Jack had had his easel carried to Mr. Henschel's house and set up in the workshop, and here he spent an hour every day at work on the picture, which he had determined should, more than any other, be representative of his peculiar style. He had no difficulty in arranging the living and inert *materiel* to the best advantage, and in this was glad enough to avail himself of Barbara's artistic instinct and keen sense of color and form. These hours had been the pleasantest of his life, and each one had passed with the girl more firmly placed in his heart than before, so that when they had come to an end, he was over head and ears in love, and ready to sacrifice all his prospects in life for the sake of Barbara Henschel.

Before meeting with her, Jack had always declared, when questioned on the subject, that he should never marry, and had insisted, with great vehemence, that matrimony and art in its highest regions were absolutely incompatible. "It's a difficult thing for a man to become a great artist," he said one night to half a dozen congenial companions, sitting with him on the piazza at the Long Beach Hotel, "with everything in his favor, and when he can entirely abstract himself, as occasion requires, from all the little wearying affairs of life. But for a married man I look upon the thing as almost an impossibility. The great artists that have been married are few, and they were such geniuses that no antagonistic circumstances could have kept them from rising. What I say, however, doesn't apply to geniuses. They are quite an exceptional class ; but no one, I think, will contend that a genius makes a good husband. He'll stick to his art, and let his wife and children go. An ordinary fellow, however, like any of us, with a moderate talent for art and sufficient love for it to cause him to devote himself to it assiduously enough to make himself a good reputation, when he marries is going to give it up, and tag on to the petticoats. He can't help himself. His heart isn't big enough for both, and the woman wins.

"That's all humbug !" said Danforth, a promising young painter, who was known to be on the eve of marriage with a very beautiful girl. Look at Rubens, and Murillo, and Titian, and Tintoretto, and—"

"And look at Michael Angelo, Leonardo, Raphael, and a dozen others I might mention," interrupted Jack. "Besides, the men you mention were geniuses, and they all made bad husbands."

"How do you know they did?" demanded Danforth. "That's an assumption on your part for which there's no warrant."

"Read their lives, my boy, and you'll find out. Now, to come nearer home, there's Pickett. Two years ago no one in this country bid fairer to reach the top of the ladder of fame than Pickett. He had done some of the best work that's been done in twenty years anywhere. Well, he got married, and what is he now ? He sent a picture to the *Salon* last year, and they wouldn't hang it ;

and he sent one to the Academy this year, and they declined to put it on the walls. I met him driving in the Park a few days ago with his wife, two babies, and a nurse, actually looking idiotically happy. It's all very well for a fellow that goes in for that sort of thing, but you can't serve God and Mammon, and I don't propose to try."

They all laughed at this tirade, and Jack felt that degree of elation that every man feels when he has made a point and subdued his polemical adversaries.

But after once seeing Barbara Henschel, his opinions began to waver, and before he had finished his sittings in the workshop they had undergone a complete change, and he would have been willing to renounce art forever, had the sacrifice been necessary to gain her love. He had discovered not only that she was beautiful—he had found that out on the first day he had met her—but he saw every hour that he passed in her presence some new facial expression or mental characteristic that he had not noticed before, and that enraptured him to a degree that when he got home made him feel ashamed of himself for his susceptibility. Finally the picture was done, so far as it could be completed there, though there were still many days of delicate touchings and re-touchings necessary before it would be fit to go out of his hands, and there would no longer be any excuse for making the daily visits that had been a source of pleasure beyond any that he had yet experienced.

Nevertheless, when he came nearly to the end of the last sitting that Barbara was giving him, and looked back over the past week, he could not conscientiously say that he had any cause for self-congratulation. She had always treated him with civility—indeed, even with friendliness, but she had never shown the least sign of any particular feeling for him, although she must have noticed from his looks, his manner, his speech, that she was fast becoming of more than passing interest to him. Women have it in their power, as Jack very well knew, though he had never had an affair of the heart before, to let a man see whether they care for him or not, and that without compromising themselves in the slightest degree. There are a thousand ways of doing this. It may be a look, an action, a phase of manner, a word, even an accent, a little thing of no consequence in itself, one that may, without reproach, be disavowed should occasion require, and that is of pregnant meaning when spoken by a woman to the man she loves. Jack had looked for some such token from Barbara, but he had looked in vain. There had been nothing—absolutely nothing—that he could bring back as a *point d'appui* for the love that had taken him captive.

This was his last day, and what excuse could he make for coming again? That was the question that occupied his mind just then. Barbara was sitting at her work-bench in the attitude in which he had placed her in his picture, and he was trying to improve the conception of her face that he had transferred to the canvas. He soon found, however, that his first idea—the one that had come from the inspiration of the moment—was more truthful than any he could elaborate by subsequent study, and that there was really nothing more to do.

" I won't keep you any longer, Miss Henschel," he said ; " by this, as it now is, I'll stand or fall. You have been very good to me and very patient, and I thank you from the bottom of my heart. I'll send for these things to-morrow morning, and I'll put on the finishing touches at my leisure."

Barbara had not yet seen the picture. Jack had begged her not to look at it till he gave her leave, and she had scrupulously respected his wish. Every day when he went away he had covered the canvas with a thick linen cloth, and she had never once raised even a corner, though she had felt no small degree of curiosity to see what had been made of her.

But now she thought the time had come for her to take a look, even if work still remained to be done on it; so after telling Jack that it had been no trouble to her to sit for him, and that she was glad to have been the means of helping him to a subject, she ventured to ask if she might see the picture before it was taken away.

"I don't see why you shouldn't do anything you like with it," responded Jack, magnanimously. "If it hadn't been for you there would have been no picture, and all there is in it that's worth looking at is your image and—and—your father's, of course. He has a grand old face, and I've given special attention to bringing out all its strong points. Certainly you shall see it, Miss Henschel. Come round here. Wait a moment till I get it in a little better light. That's it; now stand right here."

Barbara moved round to the front, after Jack had adjusted the easel according to his notion, and looked at the picture. It represented the workshop with entire fidelity; somewhat in the background sat Mr. Henschel, at work at a magnificent specimen of the mountain-sheep, which looked as though it were standing on one of its native Rocky Mountain crags. All the details of the old man's face and figure had been elaborated with the

utmost minuteness, and Barbara gazed at the portrait
without seeing more than the dim outline of her own,
so thoroughly impressed was she with the life-like representation that the painter had made of her father.   Then
she slowly turned her eyes to what Jack had intended
should be the chief feature of his picture—the likeness
of herself.   He had painted her sitting at the work-bench
and moulding into form the ears of the silver fox which
stood before her.   The attitude was full of grace ; her
fingers seemed to play about the delicate ears of the
animal, touching them as airily, as discriminatingly, and
yet as firmly as though the task were one of loving care,
requiring all the skill and attention of the worker.   The
head was thrown slightly back, and as the work-bench
was rather low, the eyes were a little cast down ; but
their expression was one of infinite softness, almost tenderness, and there was just the least gleam of a smile
around the corners of the mouth, that appeared to show
that she was well pleased with what she had accomplished, and that gave an aspect of surpassing beauty to
the face.

Barbara looked at it in silence ; she had never thought
herself beautiful ; but this girl in the picture was lovely
beyond any woman she had ever seen before.   She could
not believe it resembled her, and hence she was disposed
at first to think that the artist had flattered her, or else
that he had altogether failed to catch the likeness.

But as she contemplated the painting more attentively,
and studied the portrait with greater thoroughness, she
began to recognize the fact that it was like her, that the
artist had caught an expression that she had at times seen
on her face, and that he had succeeded in transferring it to
the canvas with a truthfulness and a skill that struck her

as being marvellous, while, at the same time, it gave her
infinite pleasure. Surprise and delight were on her face
as she turned to Jack, who had all the time been waiting
and wishing that by some supernatural power, as there
was no other way of doing it, he could, at once, paint
her as she then looked.

"O Mr. Oldmixon!" she exclaimed, "is it possible
I look like that?"

"Not always, Miss Henschel," replied Jack, laughing; "but sometimes you do. "I tried to get you at
your best, and I thought till just now that I had succeeded; but now I know that your face is capable of
lovelier expressions than the one I captured. I beg
your pardon," he continued, seeing that Barbara was
blushing deeply; "I did not intend to descend to the
triviality of paying you a compliment on your personal
appearance; I would have no right to take such a liberty.
I was speaking altogether from an artistic standpoint,
and was thinking of you, not as Miss Barbara Henschel,
who has been kind enough to do me the greatest favor I
have ever received, but as the model from whom I have
derived whatever inspiration guided my brain and hand."

"And father," said Barbara, shifting the subject of
conversation as soon as she could; "you have made
an admirable likeness of him. There is not a feature of
his face that is not truthfully brought out, and the expression is exactly that that is always present when he is
greatly interested. Oh, yes, you have made an admirable likeness of him! He will be delighted, I know. I
had no idea that you would succeed so well with the
animals," she continued, after she had minutely examined the representations of the silver fox, the mountain
sheep, and two or three others of less importance that Jack

had introduced. "I think you have had the exact idea in regard to them that you ought to have had. I was afraid that you would make them too life-like, and that, therefore, it might be thought that you were painting them from nature ; but every person can see that these are mounted specimens."

"You have hit upon the one point, after that of getting your likeness, that gave me the most trouble, and my difficulty came from the fact that your mounting is so perfect, that it is almost the exact counterpart of nature. Of course I had to represent the work of the taxidermists, and not live animals, and I found it a tough piece of work to steer so as to avoid the Scylla of naturalism, and yet not run into the Charybdis of artificiality. Your opinion that I have succeeded gives me every assurance I could desire. Here, at least, Miss Henschel, I may compliment you, and say, that there is no one I know whose judgment in such a matter is as good as yours."

So they talked, and finally Mr. Henschel came in ; and Jack, declaring that at last there was an opportunity for him to get an unbiassed judgment of his portrait of Barbara, called upon the old man for his opinion.

Mr. Henschel was no mean judge of such matters. He had seen nearly all the famous pictures of Europe, and had formed ideas of composition and coloring that were based upon a knowledge of the manner in which they had been treated by the greatest masters that the world had known. One glance at Jack's picture was sufficient to engage his attention, and to keep it engaged till he had carefully studied it in all its details.

"It's a fine picture, Mr. Oldmixon," he said, at last ; "it's enough to make the reputation of any painter. It puts me in mind of one of those Flemish interiors, of which Teniers has given us so many striking examples. And you've got the very look on Barbara's face that I would rather see there than any other. It's the best you've got, my dear," turning to address his daughter, and finding, to his surprise, that she had disappeared. "Ah well! it's perhaps better that she should not hear too many praiseful speeches," he continued. "You've never painted as beautiful a face as that before, have you, Mr. Oldmixon?"

"Never!" exclaimed Jack, enthusiastically. "I can say to you, Mr. Henschel, what I could not say to her—it's the loveliest face I ever saw."

"Ay, and not only her face! Look at the sheen on that hair. Isn't it what you might think molten gold would look like with the sunlight gleaming on it? And the poise of the head! How gracefully she has thrown it back, and turned it a little to one side, while she looks critically at the work she is doing, and the hands and the arms from which the loose sleeves have fallen back, just far enough to show the delicate wrists passing almost imperceptibly into the fulness that marks where the muscles are that move her slender fingers. But," he continued, with a smile, "I am talking like an old man, and I'm afraid a little too much like an anatomist. I don't think I ever talked that way about my girl before, and, in fact, I forgot in my admiration of the picture that it was my daughter I was speaking of. Set it down to the picture, not to her; but it's wonderfully like her, Mr. Oldmixon."

Jack was now satisfied; so throwing the cover over the picture, he began gathering his property together into one place.

" I shall send for all this to-morrow, Mr. Henschel,"
he said, " and then I shall cease to trouble you."

" Oh, it's been no trouble ! You've done us a great
honor in making us the subject of your picture, and if
there's anything I can do for you, I hope you'll let me
know. Some time or other you might want a rare animal
for a model, and I am in the way of getting such things."

" Thanks ; I shall certainly avail myself of your kindness should occasion require, and in the mean time I
have a favor to ask of you."

" You've only to mention it."

" Let me come here occasionally to talk to you and
your daughter while you are at your work. You both
know so much more than I do of many things that I
want to know, that I trust you will not refuse me the
opportunity of learning them."

" Ay, ay, we'll both be glad to see you. But we'll
not be here long now ; I have nearly completed all the
arrangements for selling the business and moving to a
little farm I've just bought near New Rochelle and
Mamaroneck."

" You are going away ?"

" Yes ; but not far. I gave Barbara a month to think
of it, but she only took a week, and then she told me
she was ready to go."

" And you will no longer be taxidermists ?"

" Not for more than a week or so longer ; but my
daughter is going to become a sculptor. Mr. Maurice
is to be her instructor. Do you know him ?"

" Oh, yes ; every one knows Maurice ; he is the most
competent man for the work of an instructor in sculpture
that there is in the city."

" Then you can, perhaps, come out to see us some

day, and look around our little place, or take a sail on the Sound."

" I should be delighted."

" Yes," said Barbara, entering the room at the moment, " you will have to come, if it's only to tell us how you caught the silver fox."

9

CHAPTER XIII.

A TENDER-HEARTED HUSBAND.

Mr. Hogarth Oldmixon, whom we left reflecting upon a few plain-spoken words from his wife, was not one of those exceptional persons that believe in the efficacy of soft answers in turning away wrath. It was his system not so much to divert angry feelings as to subdue them, and he effected his purpose, not only by the use of significant and energetically expressed language, but by the employment of such additional measures in the way of physical force as his experience had taught him were likely to promote peace by silencing his adversaries.

After Mrs. Hogarth Oldmixon had delivered herself of the sharp little speech recorded in a previous chapter, her husband sat for a moment or two without making any response, either by word or deed. Then he very deliberately got up, locked the door, and put the key into his pocket. Then he came to where his wife was sitting rocking herself with great energy backward and forward in a chair, that, every time it reached its full extent of inclination in either direction, looked as though it would topple over and land its occupant on the floor. He stood before her with his legs wide apart and his hands rammed down into the depths of his trousers pockets, and having regarded her with a look of which low cunning and superciliousness were strong features, as long as he thought desirable under the circumstances, he reached out both hands as though to seize her by the neck and shoulders as the initial step of his active proceedings. Suddenly, however, as if influenced by some other thought, he dropped his arms, and turning away, strode to one of the windows and looked out on the deserted street, down which torrents of water were still rushing.

While Mr. Hogarth was looking at her with his mixed expressions of malicious astuteness and contempt, Mrs. Hogarth continued to rock herself violently, as though the chief object of her life was to get through a certain amount of the oscillatory exercise in a certain time. She never raised her eyes to her husband's face, though it cannot be said that she quailed before him. If she had seen the look of devilish malice on his countenance she might have felt some qualms of fear, and have kept a silent tongue in her head during the rest of the interview. But she was one of those women that never know when they are well off, and who, moreover, know so little of the male part of the human race that they are sure to misinterpret any action not of the most positively demonstrative character. They are like the woman who told me upon one occasion that she never knew her husband was in earnest about anything till he had kicked her two or three times, to prove his sincerity.

As Mr. Hogarth went toward the window, Mrs. Hogarth raised her eyes, and gave a withering glance at his retreating form. Then the word "coward" came hissingly from her lips; and as this met with no response she repeated it, with the addition of the word "bully!" Still meeting with no reciprocity, she went still farther. "Coward, bully, and liar!" she said, and then apparently reaching the conclusion that she had, for that occasion at least, exhausted her powers of invective, she threw herself back in her chair, and resumed the rocking process, which had been temporarily interrupted.

But she was not to be left to pursue this innocent, if ungraceful exercise without interruption. Whether or not the word "liar" is more aggravating when applied to a person than "coward" or "bully," or both combined, may never be definitely determined for mankind at large; but it certainly appeared to be the case, either that Mr. Hogarth regarded it as more vituperative in itself, or, like the last straw that broke the camel's back, it was cumulative, and hence added just the necessary force required to convert the gentleman to whom it was addressed from a comparatively peaceable man into one in whom rage had taken the place of reason. At the word "coward" his fingers had moved spasmodically; at "bully" his face had twitched and his eyes had glared; but there did not appear to be any indication that Mr. Hogarth's emotional disturbance would carry him beyond the point of manifesting these, in themselves harmless muscular motions. But at the word "liar" he started, turned, and with one bound reached the chair in which his wife was rocking herself. To seize her around the waist and to carry her to the bed in the next room were acts that were done in an instant. She had at first been too much astonished to cry out; but now she began to make attempts to shout, which, however, were promptly rendered abortive by her husband cramming his handkerchief into her mouth. He threw her on the bed with all the strength of which he was master, and then taking the pillow, was proceeding to press it on her face, but her struggles were of so violent a character that he could not succeed all at once in accomplishing his object. She fought with her hands; she fought with her feet; and she twisted her body in all directions with such a degree of agility that he was for a time baffled. She saw that he meant to kill her. His eyes were bloodshot and staring, his face was of a livid hue, his lips were retracted so as to show his teeth, and he uttered threats and denunciations—incoherently, it is true, but, nevertheless, with sufficient distinctness for her to understand that he intended to take her life. He was a man of great physical strength, and the contest, with everything in her favor, would have been only a question of time. As it was, with her on the bed and he standing over her and bringing the weight of his body to act in conjunction with his strong arms, her chance was slim. Gradually he obtained more fixedness for the pillow, and at last he got it over her face, and held it there, while her arms and legs twitched convulsively and her breast heaved in the ineffectual effort to get a breath of air. Then all was still—all except his own hurried breathing and the pulsation of his heart, the sound of which organ struck with a dull, muffled thump upon his ears, and jarred his body as a laboriously-working machine jars the house in which it is lodged.

He stood by the side of the bed for a few moments, as if endeavoring to collect his thoughts. Then he took away the pillow from the face of his wife, and minutely inspected her countenance. There was no distortion of the features, and after he had adjusted the limbs and smoothed her clothing and the bed, she looked for all the world as though she were asleep. He felt her pulse, then placed his hand over her heart, then watched closely for the slightest motion of her chest. Yes, she might look as though she were asleep, but for all that she was dead, and he had killed her.

Now, strange as it may seem, he had not at first intended to kill her. He had been irritated beyond measure by her taunts and abuse, and he had purposed giving her a taste of his power by carrying her to the bed, and then, tying her hand and foot, to leave her there till it should suit his pleasure to release her. But her attempts to scream and her sturdy resistance had still further developed the diabolical spirit that he possessed, and then he had been carried far beyond his original design. As she resisted, he attacked; as she endeavored to escape, he made more determined efforts to subdue her, until finally the distinct purpose of ridding himself of what he considered was a bad bargain came suddenly into his mind.

It was not a spontaneous thought, neither was it one developed by the opposition he had met from her struggle for life; but it was evolved out of the idea that she was in some way or other the cause of his uncle's displeasure with him. At first this was only the dimmest kind of an impression, but in a few seconds—the brain works with wonderful celerity at such times—it had become an overwhelming conception of such intense distinctness that he imagined that he could see and hear his uncle denouncing him for having married Camilla White. Then his resolution was taken. He would kill her now that he had the chance, and rid himself forever of the one that stood between him and wealth.

He was not the man to feel remorse for any act that he might commit, especially when it was one like this, that apparently was going to work to his advantage; but he none the less felt the danger that he had incurred and the necessity that existed for making such an arrangement of matters as would divert all shadow of suspicion from himself. He had already put the corpse and its surround-

ings into a state of order ; to wash his face and hands,
to brush his hair, and to set his clothing to rights were
small matters, but they had a great effect in causing him
to look calm and comfortable. Indeed, as he glanced at
himself in the glass, he could not discover a trace of the
severe contest through which he had just passed ; and certainly no one examining his countenance, with all the
trained skill of a physiognomical expert, would have suspected that he had, not half an hour before, killed his
wife.

Hogarth Oldmixon was a man of ample resources, especially when they were to be exercised for his own protection. In the first place, he had that command of himself
so long as his reason was not obscured or overwhelmed
by furious rage, as it had been just now, that enabled
him to preserve a calm exterior under all kinds of trying
circumstances ; and in the next, he was ready, with well-
constructed stories that were amply sufficient to explain
any incongruous acts that he might have committed, and
that were so plausible, coherent, and systematic in all their
details, that no one hearing them was likely to suspect
that he had done anything that he ought not to have done.
His great danger was his ungovernable temper ; for
when that was excited he was apt to talk with an utter disregard to his own welfare and with a tendency to reveal circumstances that in his rational state he would have
died rather than confess.

He knew the advantage in circumstances such as those
that now surrounded him of attention to what were apparently small things ; so, after taking another look at the
corpse, to see that everything connected with it was exactly as he intended it to be, he drew on his gloves, brushed
his hat, put a clean white linen handkerchief into the

breast-pocket of his coat, and then taking his cane, unlocked the door, leaving the key on the inside, and then proceeded down-stairs to the office. He went to the door, and looking out, pretended to be inspecting the state of the weather.

"I think it is going to clear," he said to the clerk behind the counter. "Mrs. Oldmixon is very anxious to visit the Naval School, and to see something of the city. Will you be kind enough to order a carriage for five o'clock? It is now just four," looking at his watch as he spoke the last words.

"Will you have a close or an open carriage?" said the clerk.

"Which do you think would be best? Suppose you send up and ask Mrs. Oldmixon which she would prefer."

"It is certainly going to clear," said the clerk; "the blue sky is showing itself now off there in the west, and in an hour it will be as bright as can be."

"Well then, never mind sending to Mrs. Oldmixon. I'll take the responsibility of ordering an open carriage. In the mean time I'll take a walk. Which is the way to the State House?"

The clerk pointed out the direction, and Hogarth was soon walking around the State House circle, and thinking to himself what a bold stroke that was to invite the clerk to send up to Mrs. Oldmixon, when, if he had done so, the fact of her death would have been at once discovered. He smiled as he thought of the occurrence. "I saw there was no servant about," he said, "and that it would be some trouble for him to get one. Besides, they charge more for open carriages than they do for close ones. It was a pretty safe move, and it will do me an infinite degree of good in about an hour from now."

Having gone around the circle, he walked down a street that led to the water, and then across to the main street, upon which the hotel stood. His chief object now was to occupy the time till the carriage arrived at the door, and it became necessary to notify his wife to get ready for her drive. He was aware that many persons in situations similar to his betray themselves by their excessive anxiety not to appear discomposed, and by a meddlesomeness with matters that are working well, and that should therefore be let alone. He was not one to wreck himself on any such shoals as these. He had, ever since he had left the hotel, been thinking over the probable course that an average man would pursue if he had ordered a carriage for a live wife, as he had ordered one for a dead wife. He was trying to find out exactly what the boldness of innocence would prompt a man to do, and having, without much difficulty—for his knowledge of human nature was great—arrived at a definite conclusion on this point, he had nothing further to accomplish than to walk about the place as openly as possible till the hour for returning to the hotel came round. While it was no part of his plan to do things for the purpose of disarming suspicion, he thought it would not be amiss for him to enter one or two shops and to purchase some trifling article in each. It would give the occupants an opportunity for noting his calm and equable manner, and that might be of importance to him. He could imagine them saying to each other,

"Just think, that while he was in here buying that tooth-brush—and as pleasant a man as ever came into the store—his poor wife was lying dead in her bed at the City Hotel. He would have looked very differently, I guess,

9*

if he could have known that his bride had gone to another world ;" or,

" Poor fellow ! little did he know when he was picking out that soap for her that she was gone to where the soul is cleansed [the Annapolitans are a pious people] of all its impurities by the blood of the Lamb, that washes whiter than soap. How particular he was to get violet ! It was her favorite perfume, he said."

That was about the way they would talk, he supposed, and the result showed how profound was his knowledge of the way of the world.

He walked around the church circle, and then out toward St. John's College, and then turning to the east, reached a street that took him to the State House Circle again. He looked at his watch. It was a quarter of five. It was time for him to return and face the terrible ordeal that had within it perhaps the potentiality of sending him to the gallows. Pshaw ! That was impossible !

As he entered the hotel he saw that a carriage, presumably the one he had ordered, was at the door. He crossed the hall on his way to the staircase in full view of the clerk, who was standing behind the counter talking to one of the servants of the house.

" Is that my carriage ?" he inquired.

" Yes, sir," answered the clerk ; " shall I send up for Mrs. Oldmixon ?"

There was a hesitation of the fraction of a second before Hogarth answered. A less bold or a less shrewd man would have jumped at the chance offered of having the awful discovery made for him that a visit to the room above must necessarily reveal. But Hogarth was bold and he was shrewd. He reflected that it would be more in accordance with the fitness of things that a newly married man would, under the circumstances, after having been absent an hour, go himself to inform his wife that he had arranged for a drive, and that the carriage was at the door. At the same time, he thought that it would be well that some one should be present when the discovery of the dead body was made, and it took only an instant for him to arrange in his mind for that object.

"No," he replied ; "I will go up for her myself. I wish, however, you would send a man to unstrap a trunk that I want to get at."

"Go with the gentleman, Tom."

Hogarth ascended the steps, followed by Tom, a big, good-natured negro, who, like his people generally, was ready to enter into conversation with strangers.

"I guess 'Naplis' ain't as big as New York," he said. "It's growed a heap, though, since they brought 'the Yard' here."

"No, it's not so large as New York," answered Hogarth, in his suavest tones. "What's the best drive about here, Tom?" he inquired, determining to make friends with the man.

"Well, everybody goes down to 'the Yard.' And then there's the hay-scales—'most everybody goes to see them scales."

By this time they were at the door of Hogarth's room— the one that he and his wife had used as a sitting-room. He turned the knob and entered, followed by Tom. The door between the two rooms was closed.

"There's the trunk, Tom," he said, pointing to it. "The tongue of one of the buckles seems to have got bent in some way or other, and as you're stronger than I am, perhaps you can straighten it."

"I never seen the trunk yet dis chile couldn't open.

Dat is, of course," he added, laughing, "if I had the key."

He bent over it, and while he was busy fumbling at the strap, Hogarth opened the door between that room and the one in which lay the corpse of his wife. Yes, there it was, just as he had left it. He stood for a moment looking at it, and then he hurriedly crossed the floor to the bed. The man in the next room could have seen every action, had he turned around. Hogarth did not know whether he was looking or not, but he hoped he was, and he felt quite sure that he was, knowing, as he did, the curiosity of the negro. At any rate, his actions were all based upon the presumption that he was observed, and hence he intended that they should be as nearly as possible such as his knowledge of human nature had taught him would be natural under the circumstances in which he was apparently placed.

"Milly!" he said, as though addressing his sleeping wife. "Milly!" he repeated, in a somewhat louder voice. "Milly!" again, still louder, accompanied with a gentle shake of the shoulders of the dead woman.

Then he placed his arms under the body and raised it up in the bed. "Milly! Milly!" he cried. Then to the man who had been looking and listening all the time: "My God, something has happened! Run at once, and tell them to send for a doctor!"

Tom gave one good look in through the door. He saw Hogarth supporting the form of his wife with one hand, while he rubbed her forehead with the other, and spoke to her in the tenderest words a man can use. Then he rushed down-stairs at full speed, telling a couple of chambermaids he met on the way to go in there to No. 22, and help the gentleman. "His wife's fainted, I guess, or somethin' o' that sort's happened." Then shouting out to the clerk that something was the matter in No. 22, he dashed across the street to summon Dr. Ridings.

The clerk was as dignified an individual as a hotel-clerk ought to be. It was against his principles to show haste, or even undue interest, in anything that he did; but Tom's manner, as well as his words and the screams that reached his ears from up-stairs, told him that something serious had occurred, and that the honor of the house required that he should make himself personally acquainted with the circumstances. He therefore—and he could not recall that he had ever done the like before in all his life—mounted the stairs two at a time, and at the door of No. 22 was met by Mr. Hogarth Oldmixon, who, as pale as death, gasped out:

"A doctor! for God's sake, a doctor! Is there no physician to be had for love or money?"

"What's the matter?" said the clerk. "I've sent for a doctor." He entered the room as he spoke. The women in the next apartment had ceased screaming, but they were busy rubbing the hands of the limp body that lay on the bed.

"O Mr. Campbell!" said one of them, "she's quite dead. She must have been dead an hour, for she's getting cold."

All this time Hogarth was walking the room wringing his hands, and ejaculating every moment expressions that were well calculated to show the depth of his grief.

"So young," he said, approaching the bed, while tears —real tears—ran down his cheeks, "and so happy, and to be taken off in this way! My God, I do not understand it. I left her an hour ago well and joyous. I return to find her dead. Oh, it is hard, very hard!"

"Calm yourself, Mr. Oldmixon," said the clerk, who had satisfied himself that Mrs. Oldmixon was really dead. "These things are hard to bear, but—"

"Hard to bear!" exclaimed Hogarth, passionately, throwing himself across the dead body of his wife—"*this* is impossible to be borne. Oh, why was I not also taken? Milly, my darling! are you really dead? So young! so lovely! My wife! my wife! come back to me! oh, come back!"

"Mr. Oldmixon," said the clerk, moved to tears by the unrestrained grief of the afflicted husband, "there is the doctor"—as that gentleman entered the room, followed by Tom—"perhaps there may still be a spark of life, and it may not yet be too late to revive her."

The doctor, without speaking, approached the bed, while Mr. Campbell gently raised Hogarth from the dead body that he was passionately embracing, and led him into the next room.

It did not take the physician long to arrive at an opinion relative to the case to which he had been called, although Tom's information had not led him to expect one of such great gravity. Mrs. Oldmixon was dead. The only thing he had to do was to ascertain, if possible, the cause of her death, and then to give the certificate for burial or removal from the city, as might be desired. The authorities in small towns, where crimes of violence are less common than they are in the large cities, are not so strict in such matters as they ought to be, and the doctor, who disliked making a fuss when it could be avoided, hoped that there would be enough of a history of the case for him to base an opinion on without his being obliged to resort to a post-mortem examination or a coroner's inquest.

"This is a very sad event," he said, going over to where Hogarth sat, under the soothing admonitions of Mr. Campbell, "and a very sudden one, too. Will you try and calm yourself, Mr. Oldmixon, sufficiently to give me an account of the event, so far as your knowledge extends?"

Hogarth at these words looked wildly around him for a moment, as though endeavoring to ascertain where he was, and then having apparently settled his mind on the point, said :

" I left her at four o'clock in perfect health ; I returned at five to find her dead. That is all I know." He buried his face in his hands when he had said these words, and sobbed as though his heart were broken.

" Had she been complaining of pain in her head or chest?" inquired the doctor, whose thoughts were running in the direction of brain or heart disease.

Hogarth shook his head. " No," he said, after waiting a moment, as though to give effect to the double denial, " she complained of no pain anywhere. She said she felt a little tired, and would lie down while I was out."

" Was that all she said?" continued the doctor, anxious to find some symptom that would lead to further inquiry, and thus do away with the necessity of a post-mortem examination.

" She asked me to purchase one or two toilet articles for her. I have them here." He took from his pocket the tooth-brush and soap he had bought, and laid them on the table. " Yes," he continued, with more animation than had yet characterized his remarks, " she said she felt faint, and I sprinkled a little *eau de cologne* on her handkerchief, and held it to her face for a moment. That seemed to revive her."

"Were there no nausea, feeling of suffocation, dizziness, or sense of constriction about the head or chest? No pain—nothing but what you have mentioned?"

"No; there was nothing. I attached no importance to the faintness, as she had several times experienced it. I supposed it was the result of slight dyspepsia."

Now, strange as it may seem—though it is only another instance of the boldness with which Hogarth Oldmixon was endowed—he desired that there should be a post-mortem examination of his wife's remains, and a regular certificate of the cause of death given. He knew that such a certificate, followed as he desired it to be by a coroner's inquest, would be the most effectual confutation that could be had of any hints or suspicions that there had been foul play. He had heard it said that not one person in a hundred has a perfectly healthy heart. His wife had once or twice complained of feeling a little oppression after climbing many steps. She was slightly inclined to stoutness, and he had understood that one of her sisters had several years previously died of heart disease.

Besides these points, there were two others that he deemed of great importance. He saw that the doctor was an old-fashioned practitioner, who probably had not made a post-mortem examination since he had been a medical student, and he knew enough of the human body to be aware of the fact that he had, by suffocating his wife, produced a congestion of the lungs, such as would have resulted from a failure of the heart to send the blood through them, and that this organ would be found gorged with the fluid that it could not propel into lungs that could not expand. He was quite sure that a post-mortem examination would convince the doctor that death had been due either to congestion of the lungs or heart-disease. Armed with his certificate to this effect, and the verdict of a coroner's jury based upon it, and his wife's dead body in the ground, he would be absolutely safe, not only so far as his neck was concerned, but even from the suspicion that he had committed murder.

"My dear friend," he said, taking hold of the doctor's hand, "you are very kind, and I see that you wish to spare me the pain of a post-mortem examination of the remains of my dear wife. But, however terrible the idea may be, I desire that nothing shall be omitted that can throw light on the cause of her death. I hope, Mr. Campbell," he continued, turning to the clerk, and speaking with more firmness, "that you will at once notify the coroner that a sudden and altogether unexplainable death has taken place, and request him as a favor to a wretched man, too much disturbed to write for himself, to make his examination as soon as possible—this evening, if it is within his power."

"I will go to him myself," answered the clerk, "and I will engage to have him here in half an hour."

"At the same time," continued Hogarth, "be kind enough to send this message by telegraph to her poor father." He tore a blank leaf out of a book and wrote:

"Camilla died suddenly between four and five o'clock this afternoon. Further particulars will be sent in an hour. If you leave to night, you can be here to-morrow morning. I am wild with grief. Come.

"HOGARTH OLDMIXON."

Within the half hour the coroner arrived, and at once directed that a post-mortem examination should be made. Dr. Ridings performed it, and unhesitatingly gave his evidence to the effect that death had ensued from congestion of the lungs, probably due to a feeble heart, and the coroner's jury returned their verdict in accordance with the physician's dictum. And all the medical wisdom of the world, with nothing but the corpse before it, unacquainted with the facts, and with no ground for suspicion, could not have arrived at any other opinion than that the death was due to natural causes, inherent in her organism.

CHAPTER XIV.

A VISION, OR WHAT?

A FEW days after Jack had finished his picture Mr. Oldmixon returned to New York, feeling, as he declared, as well as he ever had felt in his life, so far as his body was concerned, but stupid and indolent to an extreme degree in everything that related to mental activity. He had invited Jack by letter from Saratoga to breakfast with him at the Lucullus, and the two were sitting at the table enjoying that delightful meal, the ability to appreciate which is one of the surest evidences of good health. He had heard nothing of the sudden death of Mrs. Hogarth Oldmixon at Annapolis, having while at Saratoga been shut off from all newspaper facilities for getting a knowledge of what was going on in the world at large, or, rather, having shut himself off purposely from such means of communication. The large hotels were all closed, he saw nobody that he knew, and it was too much trouble for him to get a New York paper. He had come there for the benefit of his health, and he did not want to have the restorative processes that had been set in action disturbed by reading of the murders, arsons, robberies, embezzlements, and other crimes that constitute the staple items of intelligence furnished by most of the newspapers.

But Jack had read of the sad event in the papers of the following morning, and had attended the funeral of the young wife at the church and at the cemetery. He had seen Hogarth there, but Hogarth had not seen him, being apparently so much overcome with grief that he had kept his face buried in a handkerchief all the time that the services were going on in the church and at the grave.

He saw as soon as he and his uncle came together that the old gentleman knew nothing of the catastrophe, and he was deliberating with himself whether or not he should tell him of what had occurred. "Perhaps," he thought, "it will be better for me to let him find it out for himself."

But a little reflection brought him to the conclusion that this would be neither wise nor kind, and he perceived that such a course would justly lay him open to rebuke from his uncle. He resolved, therefore, that as soon as the breakfast was over he would enlighten him, and he concluded that the best way to do this would be to give him the newspaper to read that contained a full account of the affair as known to the public, and which he had at that moment in his pocket.

"I feel particularly charitable this morning, my dear boy," said Mr. Oldmixon, after he had swallowed the last glass of Chablis—a wine he always drank for his breakfast—"I feel at peace with all the world, always saving and excepting that rascal Hogarth. I even think I could forgive Partridge for putting that vile jam, or whatever it was, on canvas-back. I've been thinking it over. You know they don't know much about canvas-backs in St. Louis. How the devil should they, when they are two thousand miles west of the Chesapeake?"

Jack laughed; "I don't think you can fairly let him off on that score," he said. "They get the canvas-back now about as promptly in St. Louis as they do in New York, and they know how to cook and eat it there, too."

" Now, Jack, you're determined to outdo me in generosity. No one knows how to cook and eat a canvas-back unless he's been born and brought up on the Chesapeake, or very near it. Why, they don't even know in New York, unless it is the few choice spirits, like myself, who have been lucky enough to come from where the ducks come from, and the still fewer people we've taught. I've eaten canvas-backs in this very town at the tables of people that ought to know better, and they tasted as though they had but one hour before been puddling in a mud-paddle—I mean paddling in a mud-puddle," he continued, hastily correcting himself.

" I'm sorry, Uncle Victor," said Jack, who judged that his time had now come, " that you still feel so hardly toward poor Hogarth."

" Now, Jack, none of that ! I've had enough of ' poor Hogarth ! ' and I propose to drop him altogether out of my recollection, if I can. He never did you a good turn in all his life, yet here you are eternally bringing the fellow up, as though he were the best friend you had on the earth."

" He is my brother," said Jack, with some feeling.

" Yes, and much good the relationship has done you. No more of ' poor Hogarth.' You'll make me think that you're the

> ' —— sweet little cherub that sits up aloft,
> To keep watch for the life of poor Jack— '

Hogarth, I mean."

" I didn't know, Uncle Victor, but that since Hogarth has met with such an awful misfortune, you might be a little more kindly disposed toward him, that's all."

" Misfortune ! What misfortune ? Has he been sent

to the penitentiary, or'' (with an utter disregard of the possibilities) "been hanged, or has he blown his brains out?''

"No," answered Jack, "it is none of these. Haven't you heard?''

"Hear! How the devil could I hear, shut up in that damned hole, with no one to talk to but a freckled and toothless old woman, who wanted to cure my gout with hard cider? What *has* happened to the fellow?''

"His wife is dead.''

"What! Camilla! Dead!''

Mr. Oldmixon uttered these three words with a long interval after each, and then his jaw fell, his eyes glared vacantly at nothing, his hands dropped to his side, and he appeared to have lost consciousness.

Jack sprang to his uncle's side, and soon discovered that the condition of collapse, though severe, was not likely to be of long duration. In a few moments he asked for a glass of wine, and having drunk it, expressed himself as feeling better.

"It was a great shock to me, my dear boy. These things seem to be coming in battalions. Give me my nitrite of amyl. I shall be all right physically if I can get a few whiffs of that; but my mind, Jack, is getting to be hopelessly shattered; it will never be what it once was.''

Jack put his hands into his uncle's waistcoat pocket and took out a small vial. A few whiffs of the contents seemed to act as a restorative to the old man, and to enable him to talk with greater ease.

"Tell me all about it," he continued; "I think I can stand it now.''

Jack got out the newspaper. "Her death was very sudden. There is a full account of it here, and I'll read it to you. It's a telegraphic despatch from Annapolis, and was published in all the papers on the morning after the occurrence."

Mr. Oldmixon closed his eyes, and lay back in his chair while Jack read :

" ' Sudden Death of a New York Lady.

" ' Annapolis, Maryland, *Nov.* 24, 1881.—Mrs. Hogarth Oldmixon, a bride of only a few days, died here very suddenly at the City Hotel this afternoon, between four and five o'clock. Her husband left the hotel for a walk at four o'clock, and when he returned, at five, found his wife a corpse. Life had probably been extinct for nearly an hour.

" ' A post-mortem examination was made by Dr. Ridings, with the result of ascertaining that death had ensued from congestion of the lungs, the consequence, probably, of fatty degeneration of the heart, or some other form of cardiac weakness. The coroner's jury returned a verdict to that effect.

" ' Mrs. Oldmixon's father is expected here to-morrow morning, when the body will be taken to New York for burial. Mr. Oldmixon is almost distracted with grief.'

" In this other paper," continued Jack, " there is an account of the funeral. I thought it an act of respect to go to it, and—"

" Did you go to her funeral, my boy?" interrupted Mr. Oldmixon. " God bless you for that !"

" Hogarth appeared to be in great grief," resumed Jack. " I would have spoken to him, only I did not like to intrude upon him at such a time, and besides—"

"No," exclaimed Mr. Oldmixon, jumping from his chair; "never speak to the wretch if you live a thousand years! He is a murderer! I tell you, Jack, he killed his wife. I saw him do it! Yes, I saw him do it! He murdered her, cruelly murdered her, and I—I—saw him do it."

The last words were spoken very feebly, as Mr. Oldmixon, unable to stand any longer, fell back into Jack's arms, and was by his nephew carried, or rather dragged, to a sofa, where he lay down at full length, inhaling the nitrite of amyl that was held to his nostrils.

Jack's first idea was, that his uncle had suddenly become insane; and the persistency with which he reiterated the assertion that he had seen Hogarth kill his wife did not tend to lessen this impression. Indeed, he had, ever since the renewal of pleasant relations with Mr. Oldmixon, been disposed to think that he was subject to periodical attacks of lunacy, and he was convinced that he was suffering from a paroxysm now of as well-marked a character as had ever been witnessed inside or outside of an asylum. He therefore made no reply to the assertions of his uncle, hoping that in a short time the delusion would disappear.

"Jack," at last said the old gentleman, "doubtless you think I'm a lunatic, and I should not blame you if you did, for the Oldmixons, as you know, are a queer lot, and there's been insanity in the family, as well as worse things, for many generations back. I may be insane, sometimes I think I am, for I am conscious often of saying and doing things that sane men don't say or do. I think I told you some time ago that I thought I possessed the power to become sane or insane at will. But if you were to think that I'm insane from what I said just now, you'd make a great mistake. I never was more in earnest in my life, and never more fully in possession of my mental faculties. Jack, I tell you I saw him murder her!"

"I don't understand, Uncle Victor," said Jack; "you were at Saratoga at the time. At least, I suppose so, and Hogarth and his wife were in Annapolis, three hundred miles distant. It seems scarcely necessary for me to ask you how, under these circumstances, you could see such an act as that you speak of, for of course you could not. Your prejudice against Hogarth has distorted your mind to such an extent that you deceive yourself, and you are ready to believe any absurd fancy to his disadvantage that comes into your head."

Jack spoke decisively, and with a good deal of feeling. He was determined not to countenance his uncle in the outrageously unreasonable notions that he was disposed to entertain relative to Hogarth, and this, the most preposterous of them all, he resolved to crush at once.

"I don't wonder to hear you talk that way, my boy," said Mr. Oldmixon, feebly; "you're such a good fellow yourself, that you can't suspect evil in others. As to my knowledge of the fact that Hogarth murdered his wife, I am as much surprised at it as you can be, and I did not accept my information as being true till you told me that my Camilla was really dead. Then it all flashed upon me in an instant, and now I know him to be a murderer."

"I was not aware that you had any information on the subject," observed Jack, apologetically, "or I should not have spoken so positively. Pray, forgive me. As to what you tell me about Hogarth, it is wonderful. I only hope that you have been misinformed. I think you

10

ought to put me, his brother, in possession of all that
you know on the subject."

"I intend to do so, Jack, just as soon as I get a little
more composed. I suppose I might as well do it now,"
he continued, as he sat upon the sofa. "Ring the bell,
Jack, and ask the fellow to bring me some brandy and
soda."

Jack did as requested, and his uncle, after having
mixed and drunk the liquids he had ordered, began :

"I wouldn't expect you to believe what I am going to
say, if I didn't have the proof in my pocket, and which
I'll show you when I get through. I was sitting on the
lawn in front of my boarding-house at Saratoga on the
afternoon of the 24th of last month ; I had just finished
reading a chapter of Silberhausen's great work on wines,
and was thinking of what he said about the prospects of
producing wines in this country that would excel those
of France and Germany, when suddenly I saw a scene,
apparently enacted before my very eyes, that filled me
with horror. And yet, when I say that I *saw* it, I am
not quite sure that I am correct. I certainly *perceived*
it, but I think I saw it just as distinctly when I closed
my eyes as I did when they were open. Indeed, I am
sure I did. By whatever means the images got to my
perceptive faculties, this is what I perceived :

"A man was standing by a window looking out into
the street ; a woman sat in a rocking-chair behind him
rocking herself violently. The man was Hogarth, the
woman was Camilla. It was a clear and delightful day
where I was ; it was raining furiously at the place where
these two were. Bear that point in mind, please.

"A horrid scowl was on Hogarth's face, and his hands
were twitching convulsively, as though itching to get hold

of something or somebody. Camilla looked dignified and calm, though at the same time angry. I could not hear a word, and therefore had no knowledge of what they had said, or were saying to each other; but their actions were as clear to me as yours are now."

Mr. Oldmixon took another potion of the brandy and soda, and then resumed his relation.

"Suddenly the scowl on Hogarth's face deepened; his countenance flashed with rage; he turned, and with one great bound seized Camilla, and lifting her from the chair, bore her rapidly into the next room. Here he threw her on the bed and stuffed a handkerchief into her mouth, while she struggled violently to free herself from his grasp. But it was no use; he held her down on the bed, and then he took the pillow and pressed it over her face, so that I could no longer see it.

"All this was so real to me, that I screamed out aloud for help, but I was powerless to rise from the chair, and in the mean time the horrible drama was being enacted before my mental vision.

"He forced the pillow against her face, and then leaned over it with the whole weight of his body. She had not ceased to struggle, but I could see that her movements were those involuntary, spasmodic ones that are performed without consciousness. Gradually they became less violent, and at last ceased altogether. Still Hogarth continued to lie with his whole weight on the pillow. He was determined to make a sure thing of it.

"Again I screamed, 'He is murdering her! He is murdering her!' But no one answered, and all my efforts to get up and run for assistance—for so real was the whole scene to me that I could not rid myself of the idea that it was taking place right there—were in vain. I seemed to be like lead; I could not move a limb.

"Finally Hogarth raised himself from the bed, and then, after a moment's pause, removed the pillow from Camilla's face. She lay there perfectly motionless, and as peaceful-looking as though she were asleep. He put the bed-clothes in order, folded her hands across her chest, smoothed her dress, and then turned to leave the room. At that instant I caught a last sight of his face. If I live a thousand years, God save me from ever beholding such another face as that! It contained in its expression all the concentrated rage and wickedness of a lifetime. And fear! Ah! yes, there was fear there. The wretch was already bleached with terror. Large drops of sweat—cold sweat, I do not doubt—stood out on his face. He seemed to be about to run away, panic-stricken, from the body that he had made a corpse. Yes, he saw the gallows looming up in awful distinctness before him, but in a moment he became calm, and then I saw nothing more. A half a dozen women came running toward me from various parts of the house, asking what was the matter, and insisting that they had heard cries for assistance that seemed to come from me."

"You fell asleep, uncle, and dreamed all that. It is very clear. You had been thinking of Hogarth and his wife, and fearing that he would not treat her well; and that idea directed the cause of your dream. Doubtless you also called out in your sleep. People often do that."

"Yes, I know. That's what the women said when I denied having called out; for you see I didn't care, of course, to tell them what I had perceived. But it was no dream; I was not asleep for a single instant."

"Well, uncle, what was it? You surely don't mean

to say that while you were at Saratoga, and Hogarth in Annapolis, you saw him kill his wife?"

"Yes, I do!" exclaimed Mr. Oldmixon, jumping up and bringing his fist down on the table, till the glasses jingled. "That's exactly what I mean to say. Explain it I cannot. But I know that I saw what was real, and by the living God I'll bring him to the gallows for his crime! There hasn't been an Oldmixon hanged for many years, but many months will not elapse before he'll dance on nothing!"

Jack saw that it was useless to attempt to argue the matter. His uncle's convictions were as strong as it was possible for them to be, and nothing but time could be expected to act as an effectual antidote to them. It was not likely that they would lead to anything further.

"I wrote it all down," continued Mr. Oldmixon, after he had refreshed himself with a few whiffs of the nitrite of amyl, and another glass of brandy and soda, "and I have the record here."

He took out his pocketbook, and from one of the compartments extracted a sheet of paper folded like a letter. This he handed to Jack.

"Read it," he said, "and see if it accords with what I have just told you."

Jack did as requested, and having finished reading it, gave it back to his uncle.

"It is almost word for word with what you have stated," he said.

"Very well! Now look at the date here on the back."

Jack again took the paper and read:

"*Thursday, November* 24, 1881, 3.35 P.M."

"I took out my watch at the moment I ceased to see anything," resumed Mr. Oldmixon, "and that was the exact time. Now," he continued, bending toward Jack, and speaking with a degree of concentrated energy, "*I solemnly declare that at that very hour, allowing for the difference of time, Hogarth Oldmixon murdered his wife.* My bird," he sobbed—his voice losing its force and relapsing into a weakness that rendered the words uttered almost indistinguishable—"killed her bird, my nephew killed her. A truly sad experience she has had of the Oldmixon family. There's only one event wanting to make the group perfect, and that is the hanging of her husband. That shall be my life-work till it is accomplished or I have driven him to suicide."

"Why, what a sanguinary old uncle he's getting to be!" said Brooks, entering the room at the moment. "They told me down-stairs that you were here, and that I could come right up for all they knew to the contrary. Who's that you're going to drive to suicide? Some one, I'll bet, that's given you warm champagne. How are you, Uncle Victor? How are *you*, Mr. Oldmixon?"

"Yes," said the old gentleman, never for an instant losing his presence of mind, "I was alluding to a fellow who did that very thing; curious coincidence, isn't it? I've been away, you know. Spent ten days at Saratoga, drinking the Geyser water and gaining wisdom from my books and the contemplation of nature. Happy is the man who can be his own companion!"

"Why, Uncle Victor, you have come back more of a philosopher than ever. You've been absorbing knowledge and wisdom, as this new luminous paint absorbs light, and you're giving them out to us as it emits in the darkness the rays it has received from the sun."

"Yes, yes," answered Mr. Oldmixon, complacently, "something of that sort, I suppose. Let us hope that, unlike the luminous paint, I shall not confine my illuminations to the dark.''

'' Ha ! ha ! very good ! But,'' assuming a serious air, '' I beg to offer my condolences on the death of Mrs. Hogarth Oldmixon. Very sudden, wasn't it ? I saw your nephew yesterday. He was looking as though he had suffered greatly. Poor fellow ! A widower in five days ! That's what I call hard luck.''

'' Yes,'' answered Mr. Oldmixon, with a degree of composure that fairly astonished Jack, '' Hogarth has been unfortunate. I did not know the lady he married except by sight, but I understand she was a very estimable woman.''

Truly his uncle was a remarkable man, and Jack no longer had any fear that he would make use of the '' information'' he had received in a way to create a scandal. He would probably go to work secretly to inquire into the matter of the truth of what had so vividly been impressed on his mind, but there would be no public denunciation of Hogarth. Indeed, any such course now, with no other evidence than his vision or whatever else it might have been, would only recoil upon himself, without doing the least harm to the object of his attack. The whole matter would be regarded by the public as an act of persecution against a nephew who had offended him. No ; Jack felt sure now that his uncle would do nothing of the kind unless he should succeed in obtaining more tangible proof of Hogarth's criminality than that in his possession. He was not to be long without other evidences of Mr. Oldmixon's sagacity and at the same time of his perseverance ; for in a few minutes Mr. Brooks, discovering, probably, that he had broken in on a party that wished to be in privacy, took his departure. No sooner had the door closed behind him than Mr. Old-mixon began :

"It was well I took this private room," he said, "seeing that we've so much to say that is not for the public ear—though they made me pay for four. How devilish absurd that you can't dine or breakfast here with a friend in a private room unless you have four in the party ! I order for four and pay for four, and that stops their mouths, but it's an imposition !

"Well," he resumed, after having unburdened his mind on the subject of private dining-rooms, " you don't believe in my discoveries ? As I said just now, I don't blame you. I didn't believe in them myself till you told me my poor Camilla was dead. Now I am sure ; but at the same time I am going to convince myself by evidence such as will convince you. I have a very clear conception of the situation of the rooms in which the tragedy took place, and I intend to draw a plan of them and to write out an accompanying description. I shall make this in duplicate, and I shall give you one copy, retaining the other myself. Then I shall go to Annapolis in a day or two—and I'd like you to go along —and inspect the place. If it agrees with my description, you'll admit that there may be something in my vision, won't you ?"

"Yes," answered Jack, unhesitatingly. " If your written description agrees with the reality, I shall be very much disposed to believe in the rest."

CHAPTER XV.

"Now give me a sheet of paper and pen and ink," said Mr. Oldmixon, "and while you read the morning papers, I'll make my diagrams."

Jack rang the bell, and ordered the articles in question.

"Now," he said to the servant, "you can draw away that table, and don't let any one come up here again; and don't come yourself unless I ring."

"Very well, sir," answered the man, gathering the breakfast things together.

After he had gone Jack arranged the materials on the table, and betaking himself to his newspaper, left his uncle to draw the plans which he had in his mind as representing the topographical features of the rooms in the hotel at Annapolis.

"You must know, Jack," said the old gentleman, after he had been at work a few minutes, "that I have never been to Annapolis. I was born in Baltimore, as you know, but I was brought to New York when a baby by the removal of my parents to this city. Therefore my ideas of the place have no other source than the perceptions that occurred to me at Saratoga. How are Government 4s?"

"An advance of one eighth since yesterday."

"Good! If you have any money to invest, put it

10*

in Governments.   When they get to be bad the bottom
will be out of everything else."

After another five minutes or so he suddenly inquired:

" Jack, did you ever see a basilisk ?"

Jack laughed.   " No," he answered ; " I don't think
I ever did."

" Well, you never will, for there's no such thing.   I
am aware that there is a species of lizard, having a
membranous bag on the top of the head, to which the
name is applied.   It lives partly on the land and partly
on the water, but it has no right to the designation."

" What does he mean by that kind of talk ?" thought
Jack.   " Is he conscious that his mind is out of order,
and is he trying to divert my attention or to mystify me
in some way ?"

" The basilisk," continued Mr. Oldmixon, " was a
fabulous beast invented by the ancients.   You will find
a full account of it in Pliny's ' Natural History.'   Or if
you propose to read it in the original," laughing as he
spoke, " I have in my library a beautiful edition, printed
at Treviso in 1479, and ornamented with illuminated
capitals.   I was reading it this morning.   Liber VIII.
Capitulum XXI.

" I suppose there was no such animal," he went on,
after Jack had disclaimed all intention of trying to read
Pliny's description of the basilisk in the original Latin,
" but that the ancients meant the account of it to typify
a particular kind of a man, so low, so vile, so disgustingly
fearful, that there was no living animal to which he could
be compared.   So they invented the basilisk, and when
they found a creature having the external characteristics
of a man, but yet in his character so despicable, infamous,
abject, villainous, and incarnately devilish that it would

be a libel on the human species to consider him a man, they called him a basilisk. Well, that's what Hogarth is."

"So," thought Jack, "that's what he was after. I don't know what to make of him. He appears to me to be at once one of the most benevolent and one of the most diabolical of men; one of the wisest and one of the most foolish."

But Mr. Oldmixon had not yet finished with the basilisk, and Jack's thoughts were again interrupted by his uncle's remarks relative to this mythical animal.

"The basilisk," he said, still going on with his drawing and writing, "was a kind of serpent inhabiting the deserts of Africa. It had a sharp-pointed head with fiery eyes, and was nearly black in color. All other snakes got out of its way, and were frightened at the hissing sound it made. It killed everything it touched, and plants and animals died if only its breath reached them."

"What a horrid creature!" exclaimed Jack, laughing.

"Horrid creature!" returned Mr. Oldmixon. "You may well say that. But that's the sort of a beast Hogarth is. To call him a dog, a snake in the grass, a wolf in sheep's clothing, a vulture, would be to insult animals that are respectable when compared to him. Therefore I call him a basilisk.

"I'll soon be done now, and then we'll see who's right about this matter. I venture to say that when we go to Annapolis we'll find things exactly as I've put them down here."

"It will be a very remarkable circumstance if we do," said Jack, his interest at last thoroughly awakened.

"And then you'll have to admit that I have some

grounds for saying that Hogarth murdered his wife, and that I am justified in running him down to his death."

"I don't know about that, Uncle Victor. I should not like to see my brother die on the gallows, no matter how wicked he might be."

"Not if he had murdered the woman you loved!" exclaimed Mr. Oldmixon, rising in his excitement and pacing the floor hurriedly. "I don't know that you are in love—for special reasons very important in their nature I hope you are not—or that you have ever been. It may be difficult, therefore, for you to sympathize with me in this matter. It is only those that have suffered that can feel for another's woes."

"I think," answered Jack, "that it was a dreadful thing for Hogarth to lose his wife, and the sudden way in which she died makes it all the more terrible; but even if he killed her it appears to me that we are not the ones to secure his punishment."

"Speak for yourself, Jack—speak for yourself! By the by, did you ever see a weasel?"

"Well, Uncle Victor," said Jack, laughing again, in spite of himself, "you have the most astonishing way of unexpectedly changing the conversation, of any person I ever met. As to the weasel, I suppose I have seen it, but I can't distinctly recollect at this moment. I have no very clear conception as to what kind of an animal it is, except that I have an idea that it never sleeps. Isn't there a saying about 'catching a weasel asleep'?"

"Yes, that's the weasel. It's remarkable for its sharpness, agility, quickness of action, and perseverance, and it is so distinguished for these qualities that the common people have a notion that it does not sleep; hence the proverb 'catch a weasel asleep!' applied to

men that are always ready—on the *qui vive*—for whatever may turn up. I suppose weasels, however, do sleep,
though no one ever seems to have caught one in that
state. Jack, I'm a weasel."

As Mr. Oldmixon spoke these last words he dropped
his pen, and rose from his chair, with two half sheets of
paper in his hand. He had made the diagram and
explanations, and also a copy for Jack.

If Mr. Oldmixon had begun the renewal of his
acquaintance with his nephew by saying that he was a
weasel, Jack would certainly have been astonished; but
now the observation produced no more effect upon him
than to cause him to wait with some little interest for
the explanation that was certain to come. It had already
been given in part by the fact that the old gentleman had
called attention to certain qualities of the animal in question which would be valuable in a detective; and when
he stated that he was a weasel he meant Jack to understand that he intended to pursue Hogarth to the very
end, with all the astuteness and perseverance he could
bring to bear. But he perceived, from his uncle's manner, that there was something else that likened him to
a weasel, and that was yet to be mentioned. He did
not have long to wait.

"Yes, I am a weasel," repeated Mr. Oldmixon.
"The weasel is one of the most remarkable animals that
a wise and a beneficent Providence has seen fit to place
on the earth. Jack, it was the only animal that was able
to kill the basilisk. You will find it all in Pliny.
Hogarth is the basilisk, I am the weasel. I shall kill
him. No, no," he continued, seeing the look on Jack's
face, "don't misunderstand me; I'm not going to take his
life with these hands, but I am going to bring him to

his death for that murder in Annapolis. Now, take this paper and follow me while I describe the one I retain. They are exactly alike. If not, please call my attention to any differences that may exist."

Jack took the paper, and while his uncle spoke studied, with the most absorbing interest, the diagram drawn upon it. Here, at least, he thought was something that admitted of verification.

(Jack's copy came into my possession not long ago, and I am therefore enabled to produce it for the more complete elucidation of the subject.)

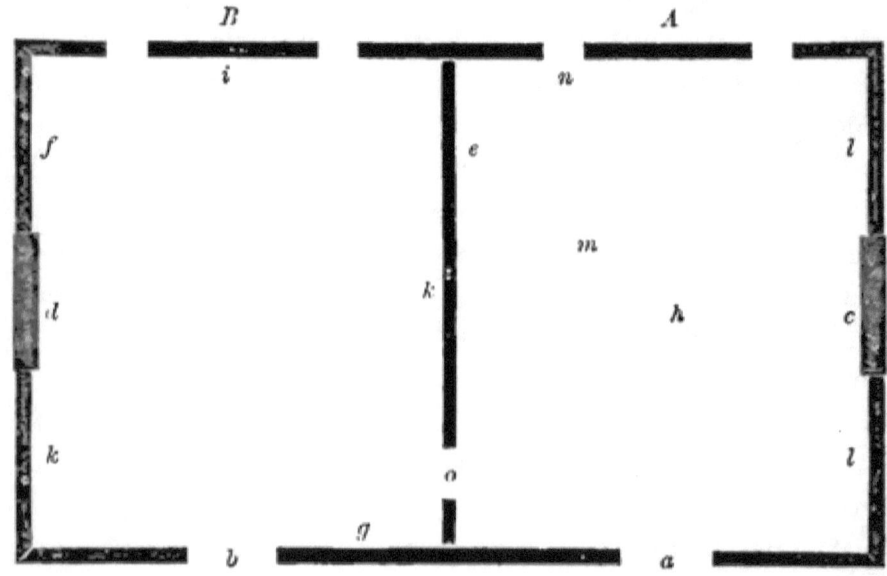

" There were two rooms," began Mr. Oldmixon, " of about equal size. Each fronted on the street, and each had two windows. The one marked *A* appeared to be a sitting-room ; the one marked *B* was a bedroom. The entrance to the room *A* was at *a*, and the entrance to the room *B* at *b*. The fireplace in the room *A* was at *c*, and that of room *B* at *d*. At *e* and *f* were wardrobes ;

that in room *A* was of modern workmanship, and was made of mahogany, but that in room *B* was smaller, and was an old piece of furniture, made of oak, black now and with a brass ball at each one of the upper corners. At *g* in room *B* was the bed, and at *h* in room *A* a round table with a yellow marble top. At *i* in room *B* was the dressing-bureau, at *k k* the washstands, and at *l l* in room *A* trunks. There were several chairs in each room, but I do not give their positions, as they have probably been changed. One, however, I *do* give. At *m* in room *A* Camilla sat in a rocking-chair, and the window at which Hogarth stood is marked *n*. The doorway between the two rooms is marked *o*. Now, does your diagram coincide with mine?"

"Yes, exactly," answered Jack, glancing over the two, as Mr. Oldmixon laid his on the table. "They are alike in all essential respects. It is all very wonderful that you should have such a distinct impression of a place that you have never seen."

"Yes, but it will be still more wonderful if, when we arrive in Annapolis and visit that hotel, we shall find that I have described those rooms without making a single mistake. I don't ask you to believe anything till I prove it. Perhaps you are right to be sceptical. The man's your brother, and my information comes in a queer way.

"Now, let me show you how the wretch did the horrid deed. Take your diagram, and follow me.

"Camilla sat in the chair at *m*," he read, "and the basilisk stood at the window at *n*. She was rocking herself. Suddenly he turned, bounded toward her, seized her, and carried her through the doorway *o* and threw her on the bed *g*. He stuffed the handkerchief

into her mouth just as he reached the bed. There were
two pillows on that bed. He took the one nearer the
door, and as her face lay toward him he pressed this
pillow against it, and held it there for probably three
or four minutes—until, in fact, she ceased to struggle.

" Is that the way it reads in your copy ?"

" Yes, word for word."

" Very well. Now, take care of it, and get ready to go
with me to Annapolis Monday next. I would leave to-
night, but I have some business that will keep me for
two or three days. I suppose Hogarth is in town."

" Yes, Brooks said he had seen him, and I saw him at
the funeral."

" Jack, my boy," said Mr. Oldmixon, after a few
minutes' pause, during which he had appeared to be
exercising his mind very deeply over something—" Jack,
my boy," he repeated, with a little tremor in his voice,
" you wouldn't betray your old uncle, I'm sure. What
has passed and what is to pass between you and me is
sacred."

" What you have said to me," interrupted Jack, " and
what you may hereafter say, and everything connected
with the subject we have discussed this morning will
never reach Hogarth through me."

" Thank you, Jack. That is just what I expected of
you. My dear boy," leaning over the table and looking
at his nephew with an expression of the most intense
cunning on his countenance, " I'm going to resume
relations with Hogarth."

" What, after all that you've said against him ?"

" Yes. That's the reason I want to have him about
me. Don't you see, my dear boy ?"

Jack was for a moment speechless. He could only

look at his uncle astonished, almost awed, by this new act in the drama.

"You are a little bewildered, I see, my dear boy," said the old gentleman, blandly. "But what else can I do? The weasel cannot catch the basilisk unless the weasel and the basilisk are brought together. Of course no one but myself saw Hogarth kill his wife, and the source of my information is such that it would not be received in a court of justice. I have but one way of proceeding, and that is to make the scoundrel confess; and that, by the blessing of God, I intend to force him to do. You know, dear boy, that alienists tell us that there is very little difference between insanity and genius. You shall decide, after I get through with this job, whether I am a lunatic or an exemplification of that rare form of mental development to which we apply the word genius."

"You must be your own judge, Uncle Victor," said Jack, "of your own conduct and of its propriety; but don't ask me to play the hypocrite with Hogarth. I cannot forget how he has treated me all these years, and I do not propose to forget it till he has atoned for it by expressing his regret; but I can't in cold blood act the traitor."

"Do as you please! do as you please! Only don't, by word or deed, interfere with me. Now, let's drop him and his misdeeds, for I have something to tell you that more intimately concerns you.

"I have made my will," he continued, "and I have left everything I possess in the world to you."

"I hope I appreciate your goodness to me, Uncle Victor," said Jack, much moved by this evidence of regard, "but—"

"Yes, yes; I know what you are going to say, but it would be no use for you to ask me to give anything to Hogarth. I'll never do it. But, Jack," and again the look of cunning and shrewdness came over his face, "if you should hear that I have made a new will and left my estate to Hogarth, don't be surprised, and don't believe it. You understand, don't you?"

"Yes," answered Jack, "I think I do. You intend to circulate such a report yourself, in order to deceive Hogarth."

"Sharp boy! sharp boy!" exclaimed Mr. Oldmixon, rubbing his hands together. "I shall say nothing. You can imagine what you please. But you're improving, Jack. I should not wonder if, in a short time, you get to be as sharp as your old uncle. Ha! ha! ha!" and Mr. Oldmixon laughed uproariously.

Jack muttered something about such a thing being impossible.

"Now," resumed Mr. Oldmixon, "I took an inventory of my estate yesterday, and I find that I am worth, at present valuation, seven hundred and sixty-five thousand dollars, besides an insurance on my life for twenty-five thousand, which brings the total close up to eight hundred thousand. It's not much of a pile, Jack, as piles go in these days, but it's not a bad plum by any means. It yields me an income of a little over forty thousand a year.

"Well, my boy, I was seventy-five last birthday, and, in the ordinary course of nature, I can't hold out much longer. I missed my chance for being hanged, I don't intend to blow my brains out, I mean to take care that Hogarth doesn't smother me, so that there is nothing left but a natural death, and that may come now at any moment."

"A man with your good health and good habits," said Jack, "may expect to live up to his expectancy, as the insurance companies put it. You have a good long lease of life before you yet."

"No, no, my boy!" observed Mr. Oldmixon, with a melancholy shake of the head. "I'm not in good health. I don't go round complaining like most of the old hacks you meet, but, in spite of my good looks, I'm standing on the brink of a volcano, and the least false step may cause me to fall into the crater. A man with a heart like mine is never safe.

"However," he went on, "I have something more important than my death to talk about. Do you ever think of getting married, Jack?"

Jack blushed scarlet at this direct question.

"I see you have," said his uncle, who had been watching him closely. "Your face speaks for you. Well, my boy, it's nothing to be ashamed of. Every young man ought to get married, and the sooner the better. I've done my duty in trying. Forty-three times, Jack, have I made the attempt to get a wife, and here I am nearly seventy-six years of age, and still an old bachelor."

"I can't think you have faced the matter with your usual energy," said Jack, with a smile.

"Well, well, perhaps not. I might have gone farther and fared worse. Ha! ha! But to go on: Thinking as I do about the advantages of matrimony to a young man, you will not be surprised when I tell you that I have made it a condition of your becoming my heir that you shall marry within one year of my decease."

"You may be putting me off for a long time, uncle," said Jack, laughing. "Suppose you should live ten or twelve years yet—as I hope and trust you may—am I to remain single during all that time ?''

'' No, no ; you misunderstand me ; you can marry as soon before my death as you please—a year after that event is the extreme limit. But the matter would not make much practical difference. I shall not live over a year at the outside. I am glad that you approve of the condition, for you take a load off my mind. There's only one thing more.''

'' What's that, uncle ?''

'' It's a delicate subject, Jack, I admit, but it's one in which my whole soul is interested. I have recently become acquainted with a lovely girl, gentle, intelligent, respectable. I want her for my daughter, and I want you to help me by making her your wife.''

'' I'm afraid I can't oblige you in that matter,'' said Jack, with decision and frankness, '' for I have recently become attached to a lady whom I intend soon to ask to become my wife.''

'' Give her up, Jack, or at least don't deny my request till you have made the acquaintance of the lady I refer to.''

'' It would be quite useless for me to become acquainted with the lady you have in your mind,'' said Jack, emphatically, '' for I shall never renounce the one I love till she tells me that there is no hope for me.''

'' O Jack, Jack ! is the chief object of my life to be defeated through your obstinacy ?''

'' If the chief object of your life is to marry me to a woman I do not know and have never even to my knowledge seen, I am quite sure that it will never be realized.''

'' I counted on you, Jack, so fondly,'' said Mr. Oldmixon, mournfully. "You have made me very unhappy, my boy. Still, I do not despair yet of bringing you to my views. You will not refuse to meet the lady, I suppose?"

"No, Uncle Victor; I will refuse to meet no one that you desire me to know. It would be a deception, however, if I were to let you think that meeting this lady will incline me to accept your proposition, that I shall marry her."

"Are you really very much in love, Jack?"

"Yes, uncle, I think I am."

"Is the lady beautiful?"

"She is to me the loveliest woman I have ever beheld. She has one of those speaking faces that send an impression into your heart that stays there forever."

"Have you known her long?"

"Not very long; long enough, however, to be very much in love with her, and to paint her portrait."

"Oh, you've painted her portrait! I don't think it's exactly the thing for a painter to fall in love with a woman who comes to him to have her portrait taken."

"But I didn't, and she didn't. I mean, I didn't fall in love with her because I painted her portrait, but I painted her portrait because I fell in love with her."

"Oh, that was the way of it!"

"Yes, that's the way it was."

"I should like to see this wonderful woman."

"I will show you her portrait first, and then you can judge whether or not it will be worth while for you to see her. May I ask," he inquired, "who the lady is that you have done me the honor of selecting to be my wife?"

"What is the good of your knowing anything about her? Didn't you just tell me it would be no use for you to make her acquaintance, for that you could not give up your present attachment ?"

" Yes, uncle ; on that account it would be useless ; but for your sake, as I just said, I am willing to make her acquaintance."

" I don't see what good could come of talking about her under the present circumstances. Her name is not one that you have probably ever heard. She is not in your station of life, as the saying is, though, so far as I can see, she's as good as any one. So, if I were to tell you her name before you see her, it would very likely prejudice you against her."

" I should not object on the score of what is called social position, if she were desirable as a wife in every other way. Shall I tell you who the lady is that I wish to marry ?"

" What's the use, Jack ? I should only feel more uncomfortable about the matter. But, my dear boy, do you distinctly understand that your becoming my heir is contingent on your marriage to the lady I have selected within one year from the date of my decease, if not before my death ?"

" Yes, uncle ; but I should think very meanly of myself if I could be influenced by such a consideration, and I should think equally meanly of you if you thought I could be so influenced."

Jack's blood was up at last. He had been indisposed to resent, more than by a positive refusal, his uncle's scheme to marry him to a woman that he did not know ; but now that the matter was put so clearly and significantly before him, he intended that there should be no doubt as to where he stood and what he meant to do ; so he added :

" And if my position as your heir depends upon my acceptance of a wife of your choosing, I desire you to omit my name from your will, for my mind is quite made up on the matter ; and even if it were not," he continued, warming with his subject, " I should make my own selection, regardless of all the heirships in the universe."

" By heavens ! my boy, I like you for that !" exclaimed Mr. Oldmixon. " Even if you do disappoint me, and you do not become my heir, let us be friends, Jack," holding out his hand, which his nephew cordially grasped. " I shall not change my will. If you comply with the conditions, you will get the estate ; if you do not, it will go to her. Perhaps, after all, you may change your mind."

Jack smiled incredulously, but said nothing.

The utterance of a single word—a word that each wished to speak—would have destroyed the misunderstanding existing between these two. It is not the only instance within my experience in which two persons have earnestly desired the same thing, and yet each thought the other desired a different thing, and in which one word, spoken by either, would have led to a perfect understanding and the avoidance of an infinitude of sorrow.

CHAPTER XVI.

"I COULD NEVER MARRY HIM, FATHER."

THE little farm that Mr. Henschel had purchased had a frontage of something like a quarter of a mile on Long Island Sound, and ran back about half a mile to the railway between New York and New Haven.

The house was placed on an elevation a few hundred yards from the water, a fine and what had once been a well-kept lawn, with a turf of over a hundred years, extending down to a sea-wall that bounded the entire water-front. It had at one time formed part of a large tract owned by the De Villon family, Huguenots, who were part of a large party who, in the troublous times at the period of the revocation of the Edict of Nantes, had fled from France to find a refuge on this side of the Atlantic Ocean.

The house occupied the exact spot upon which the original De Villon had built his residence. This latter, after standing in good condition for over a hundred years, was torn down by Colonel Guy de Villon some fifty years before Mr. Henschel appeared upon the premises, and a well-appointed stone structure, that looked as though it would stand till the end of time, had been erected on the foundations.

It was ascertained that these could not be improved, they being far more solid than such as are made in our day, so they were utilized as far as possible.

The walls of the new house, therefore, stood on the old stone work, except that at each end Colonel Guy de Villon had added a wing, thereby very considerably increasing the capacity of the new building over that of the original structure.

For several years the house had been uninhabited. The De Villons had left it many years ago to reside in New York, and then tenant after tenant had occupied it, each for only a short time, for there were ugly stories afloat relative to its unhealthfulness. It was said, among other things, that no family had ever lived in it a year without one or more of its members dying, and that sickness had begun almost immediately after occupancy.

As an explanation of this bad sanitary condition, it was alleged that the first De Villons had used the cellar as a mortuary vault, and that several dead bodies had been buried there. Another, and perhaps a still more powerful reason why the house had remained for nearly thirty years without an occupant was the belief, generally prevalent in the neighborhood, that it was haunted. Nothing so effectually conduces to the depreciation of the value of real estate as a well-authenticated story of this kind, and the story of the supernatural doings in the De Villon mansion rested upon testimony as strong as any that had ever before been offered in support of a like allegation. Not only had mysterious sounds been heard, but mysterious objects had been seen, felt, and smelt. Thus there had been moans, knocks, and, most wonderful of all, a bugle blast, or what sounded like it, coming apparently from the cellar precisely as the clock struck twelve.

Pale and dishevelled women had been seen by the passers-by flitting from window to window, clasping

11

their hands as though in an agony of grief, and tearing
their hair in the intensity of their sufferings. Similar
figures had been seen by the occupants walking in the
long halls and passages, or sitting sometimes in front of
the fire.

They had been felt, for young Tompkins, whose
father had, many years ago, declared that he was not
afraid, and that he and his family would live in the
house, had, on returning late at night from a convivial
party at New Rochelle, been seized by one of these
dishevelled women and led by the wrist down into the
cellar, where he was found the next morning more dead
than alive, and fully convinced that the house was
haunted. Nothing, he declared, would induce him to
pass another night under its roof, and shortly afterward,
other signs being produced, Mr. Tompkins and his family
had moved out. And they had been smelt ; or, at least,
odors more or less resembling those that are popularly
supposed to be indicative of the proximity of supernatural
beings, inasmuch as they were sulphurous and phosphor-
ous in character, had been wafted through the house in
a way that defied explanation. As there was no other
apparent source of these awful smells, the conclusion
was inevitable that they were due to the presence of beings
that had not yet entirely gotten rid of their corporeality.

All the senses—sight, hearing, touch, and smell—except that of taste appeared to unite in supplying evidence
of the existence of ghostly dwellers in the De Villon
manor house. The fact that this one sense furnished
no testimony ought not, of course, to have militated in
the slightest degree against the prevalent belief, for how
in the world can a ghost be tasted ? People don't run
round, even when they are scared, and it is midnight,

with their tongues lolling out of their mouths, searching
for ghosts ; and no being of the kind has ever been
known to jump down a person's throat, no matter how
wide open the jaws may have been.

There is evidence tending to show that demoniacal
personages of various degrees of eminence in the infernal hierarchy have entered the human body by the
mouth, and have, under the influence of the forms for
exorcism prescribed by the Church, departed through
the same channel ; but even if the possessed had been
in a frame of mind to exercise the sense of taste, I
respectfully submit that devils are not ghosts. Yes,
it will have to be admitted without further question
that no one has ever tasted a ghost—that is, the spirit of
a person once a dweller on earth.

The matter, however, was not discussed in any degree
of captiousness by the citizens of Westchester County,
in the State of New York, whose destiny had made
them neighbors of the De Villon property, for nearly
every one admitted that the stories told of the old house
were true. In fact, there was but one sceptic, and he
was a physician, who not only did not credit the tales
of the ghostly dwellers of the De Villon mansion, but
was generally thought not to believe in anything.

It was in vain, however, that old Dr. Maddox
denounced the faithful believers with all the vigor of
which he was capable and in language scarcely fitted for
ears polite.

It was in vain that he declared that there were no
dead bodies buried in the cellar ; that the deaths that
had occurred were due to bad drainage ; that the diabolical smells had the same origin, and that Dick Tompkins
was as drunk as a fool when he had come home that

night and imagined that a ghost had led him into the cellar.

It was in vain that he declared that the pale and dishevelled women seen at the windows were some old muslin curtains that had been left there, and that all the rest was imagination, controlled by fear.

Whenever have statements such as these made by unbelievers had any influence in convincing those whose minds are governed by faith, not fact? Never, so far as I know.

So the reputation of the De Villon manor house remained unchanged, very much to the disgust of the representative of the family and present owner, who could neither rent nor sell it.

But the bad name did not extend to the whole property, comprising at one time more than three thousand acres.

Little by little this had been disposed of, till now nothing remained but the house and about sixty acres around it. This it was that Mr. Henschel had bought.

Originally he had contemplated purchasing a smaller piece of ground, with a much more humble house, but Dr. Maddox had called his attention to the De Villon property, that could be had for a mere song, and that only required the expenditure of a few hundred dollars on the drainage to make it as healthy a residence as any on the Sound. As for the ghosts, he knew his old friend Henschel was not such an ass as to believe in them.

" You can get it," said the doctor, " for ten thousand dollars—you can sell it in five years for sixty thousand or more. I would have bought it long ago myself but for the facts that I am an old bachelor with no one to leave it to when I die, and that I have as much now, in the way of wealth, as I want."

The consequence was, that Mr. Henschel and Barbara had made a visit to the place, and after a thorough examination, in company with Dr. Maddox, had bought it of the agent for the sum of nine thousand dollars, Mr. Henschel offering eight, and the agent finally lowering his price to nine, or, as he said, "splitting the difference."

"That thousand dollars," remarked Mr. Henschel to Barbara, as they drove to the railway station on their way back to down, "will about pay for the new drainage the house wants. What do you think of it, Bab?"

"I think we shall be very happy there, father. It's a fine old house, but very large for us two."

"Yes, it's large; but there's never any harm in looking ahead. You'll marry some day or other, perhaps, and I shall only allow you to do so on condition that you don't leave me."

"O father, how can you think of such a thing!"

"How can I think of it, my dear? Didn't I have to make constant efforts not to think of it when that young professor was down here from Cornell, and was making excuses for coming every day to see you?"

"But I couldn't have married him, father, because, because—"

"Yes, I know, you sent him off. I suppose you didn't care for him, but he would have been a good match for you. Still, as things go—"

"Not if I didn't love him, father?"

"Oh, no, of course not; but I would have been well pleased if you could have loved him, my dear."

"It was impossible; I don't think I shall ever care enough for any man to marry him."

She spoke these last words as though they were a thought expressed aloud, and not intended for any one to hear.

If Mr. Henschel heard them, he took no notice of them.

"Then, there's Peter," resumed Mr. Henschel.

"Yes," she answered, with a little laugh, "there's Peter; but he is uneducated; you surely would not like me to marry Peter?"

"No, no, my dear, I did not say I would; I only mentioned his name as one of those you could have, by simply giving him a chance to ask you. But there's still another, Mr. Oldmixon."

"The old gentleman!" exclaimed Barbara, laughing again, but this time more than before, and coloring a little. "I haven't seen him since the day he told me of his troubles; I shall probably never see him again, and he's seventy-five years old."

"Ah! but, my dear, I didn't mean the old gentleman, as I suspect you know very well. I meant the young one, who's painting our portraits and workshop. How about him, Bab?"

"Nothing is so entirely out of the question as my marrying him," answered Barbara, very gravely. "Mr. Oldmixon is pleasant enough to talk to, but he is not the man I could marry, even if I were the woman he would care to marry."

"I am sure he cares for you, my dear; I haven't reached my age without learning the value of glances and smiles and words and actions. He's been coming now every day for the last week. When will he finish?"

"Probably to-morrow; but if he cares for me in the way you think, I shall let him understand that it is no use. I like him as a friend, but I couldn't marry him if he was the only man in the world."

"Why not, my dear? He's handsome, correct in his conduct—that I can see, too—making a name for himself very rapidly, able to take care of you, and if he should love you, what more could you ask?"

"I could never marry him, father; it is impossible. We cannot probably always tell ourselves why we arrive at certain conclusions relative to persons of our acquaintance; why we like some and dislike others, and so on. You know, father, I talk to you very frankly; I suppose if I had a mother I should speak to her as I speak to you. I see that you would be pleased to have me married to Mr. John Oldmixon. It can never be! Never! I like him very much; I take pleasure in his society—I would not wish to be cut off from it—but that is all; as to marrying him, it is out of the range of possibility. Besides, I am very sure he has never thought of me in that way."

"Well, well, perhaps I am mistaken. Shall I ask him to visit us at our new house?"

"If he shows that he would like to come I see no reason why you should not. You like him, I like him. One is not bound to marry any gentleman that one likes."

So, as the reader knows, the invitation had been given and accepted.

It took a couple of weeks to put the old house in such a sanitary condition as to make it safe for the Henschels to move into it. It was in good repair in every other respect, except that here and there a pane of glass was broken and the plaster needed mending, and then, of course, it was entirely without furniture.

They decided not to do more at present than to

furnish the main building, and indeed there was more of this than they had need for, there being four large rooms on each of the two floors. But, as Mr. Henschel said, he was not going to confine himself and his daughter to quarters as narrow as those they had occupied for so many years in New York. Peter had agreed with his capitalist, and Mr. Henschel had received his own price for the stand and the business, so that he was that much better off, in the way of ready money, than he had been before. There was no need for them to stint themselves. He was not what is called rich, but he had enough to make him and his daughter comfortable, without the necessity for either of them turning their hands to any labor for the purpose of getting money by it.

So the house was well furnished, and many little luxuries of a kind that they had never been accustomed to were added, in the expectation that it would be rendered still more attractive, as they were made happier, by experiencing the sense of possession and by the contemplation of objects that were in themselves beautiful.

" It's only an investment," Mr. Henschel said, when talking with Barbara about some Russian, French, and American bronzes he had purchased for the new home, and which had cost a considerable sum of money.

" They're not only beautiful to look at, but they'll serve you for study, my dear, now that you are going to become a sculptor. For a little while, that is," he added. " I had a conversation with Mr. Maurice yesterday, and he said all you wanted from him was a knowledge of how to use the tools and the material, and that you would learn that in a very short time. You'll teach them all after a while."

" Ah ! father," she answered, " that remains to be

seen. When do I take my first lesson from Mr. Maurice?"

"Well, I think we had better get fairly settled in the new house first. I suppose that will take a couple of weeks yet; then you can take the south-west room on the second story—the one just behind your bedroom—and fit it up as a studio. You can have that side of the second floor, and I'll take the other side. I think I'd like to practice a little taxidermy now and then, just to keep my hand in. By the by, Bab, you haven't given the place a name yet."

"Am I expected to name it, father?"

"Of course; I always intended that."

"Then I'll call it 'Lasata.'"

"And what in the world may be the meaning of Lasata?"

"It's a name I heard on the Plains. An Indian woman used it in speaking to me, and the interpreter explained to me that it meant 'the place where you rest after hard work.'"

"Admirable, my dear, from one point of view, but there will not be much rest for you, I'm afraid. People with your mental organization never rest till the grave closes over them. They change the form of their work, but that is all; however, Lasata it shall be."

So they left the house in New York and took possession of the one they had agreed to call Lasata. The sign remained over the old shop, but above it appeared another, with smaller letters, bearing the inscription, "Dibble & Swain, Taxidermists, Successors to."

Nothing had been seen of Jack since he had finished his picture. Every morning Barbara went in to Mr. Maurice's studio and took her lesson in modelling and

11*

in the use of the chisel. This gentleman had for many years been a friend of her father's. He was nearly, if not quite, as old as Mr. Henschel, but for all that he was capable of doing good work, and had recently executed a symbolical statue of " Argenta," in solid silver, for a wealthy citizen of one of the mining States, that had been highly praised in art circles. As a teacher he was unequalled. He not only took infinite pains with his pupils, but he seemed to have the power of imbuing all those possessed of any degree of receptivity with a portion of his own genius. In Barbara he evinced from the very beginning a great interest. She had all the art-instinct that he liked to see in his pupils. And indeed, as he had told her father, there was not much for him to do beyond teaching her the *technique* of the arts of modelling and sculpture.

By eight o'clock every morning, except Sunday, Barbara was at Mr. Maurice's studio, and here she remained till four o'clock, when she took the train for Mamaroneck, the more convenient station to Lasata, though New Rochelle was nearer. Here her father always met her in the little one-horse chaise that held two, and which he drove himself, while Barbara sat by his side. Usually before going home they took a little drive up the road that ran along the Sound, for a mile or two, and then turning off to the west brought them into a thickly wooded and semi-mountainous district, which was now rather barren of verdure, though it was well stocked with evergreens, but which in the spring, the summer, and the early autumn there was every indication was as beautiful a region as one would wish to see. It was generally quite dark when they got home, for the winter was now upon them ; but the cool,

bracing evening air was a luxury that they did not care
to forego ; and then Mr. Henschel could not easily have
dispensed with the pleasure he received at hearing Barbara's recital of her doings during her stay in the city.
What she was working at, what Mr. Maurice had talked
about, what she was likely to undertake next, and other
like matters were subjects about which he was never
weary of conversing. Then when they got home they
had dinner, and after that, while her father smoked his
pipe, in the room that they had fitted up as a library,
Barbara read sometimes aloud, or they talked, or she
played backgammon—of which he was very fond—with
him, till it was time to go to bed. There was very little
opportunity, therefore, for her to engage in any work of
her own in her studio. Occasionally, when she did not
feel tired, she would do a little at modelling in clay before
she went to bed, and in very bad weather, when she did
not go to town, she had a good long time to give to it.

They had been at Lasata somewhat over a week, and
yet nothing had been heard of young Mr. Oldmixon, as
they called him, till one morning, on arriving at the
studio, she found a note for her from Jack, which Mr.
Maurice told her had been left by the gentleman in
person, just after she had departed on the previous day.
It read :

"DEAR MISS HENSCHEL : I have been very much engaged in looking after my uncle, who has not been well
for several days, and besides that I have been out of town
with him, and was detained nearly a week by his illness. I only got back yesterday, to find that you had
gone away from the old place. Mr. Swain was kind
enough to tell me that I would find you at Mr. Mau-

rice's studio every day till four o'clock. I write this to leave, in case you have gone before I arrive, as I may possibly be a few minutes late.

"I have not forgotten that I am under promise to tell you how I caught the silver fox. If you have still any interest in hearing the wonderful story, let me know what evening I shall come out to your new home and tell it to you. Also at the same time inform me how I am to get there, and at what hour I can get back.

"With my regards to your father, believe me, dear Miss Henschel, Yours sincerely,

"JOHN OLDMIXON.

"P. S. I gave Archer, who stands in the very front rank of American painters, and who took a gold medal at the Paris *Salon* last year, a peep at the 'Taxidermists.' He looked at it for fifteen minutes, then he turned round, grasped my hand, and said, 'Oldmixon, I would rather have painted that picture than anything I have ever done.' As to what he said about the portraits, I shall have to keep that till I come to tell you how I caught the silver fox. J. O."

Barbara was glad to hear from Jack. She had wondered for several days what had become of him, and she had been disappointed that he had not called or sent a message of any kind. Had her acquaintance with him been of the ordinary description, she would not have troubled herself to think of him ; but she recognized the fact that it was something more than that. She had helped— although he probably knew nothing of the circumstance —to make him his uncle's heir, and their association, while he was painting his picture, had been of so intimate a character that she had learned a good deal about his disposition, his ways, his strong and weak points, his acquirements, that had tended to make her regard him as something more than a mere acquaintance. She liked him, but she had never once thought of him as a possible lover. She knew he was to be rich, and she had formed the idea that he did not know this fact, and that of itself would have operated as a bar to the development of any stronger feeling in her heart than that of friendship. It would have seemed to her as though she were taking an unfair advantage of him. No, she had never thought of him as a possible lover, but she had thought of him as an impossible one, and she had done so with regret and with the wish in her heart that matters had been so ordered that she could feel herself free to encourage Jack in making the demonstrations of affection that she knew would come at the slightest sign from her that they would be agreeable to her.

She had made up her mind that it would be very difficult, if not impossible, for her to maintain the course that she had resolved to pursue, unless she was cut off altogether from Jack's companionship. She had joined in the invitation that her father had given, but she had done so out of politeness and from that desire, inherent in her, never to say or do anything calculated to wound the feelings of her friends. She had really, however, at the time scarcely supposed that she would see much of Mr. Jack Oldmixon, and she doubted if he would even take the trouble to renew the acquaintance. Then she had felt that it was strange when, after several days, she heard nothing of him, that he had not called or made some effort to find her; and then she began to think that he had not acted altogether well, and that something, if only courtesy, was due to herself and her father.

This letter was at once an enlightenment and a solace to her. It explained his absence, and it relieved her mind of all her half-formed apprehensions that she and her father, having served his purpose for his picture, were no longer of sufficient importance to him to cause him to put himself to the trouble of making them a visit. Her mind was busy all through her work that day with reflections excited by this letter, and she read it over two or three times, in order to be quite sure that she had mastered all the meanings it was intended to convey. It was a very frank and clearly written letter, and she eventually arrived at the conclusion that there was no occult significance in its lines. Evidently the writer desired to renew the acquaintance, evidently he liked her, and evidently if he once began coming to Lasata he would continue to come, so long as he was permitted to do so and things were made pleasant to him. Well, she would not answer him till she had shown his letter to her father.

The old man was at the station, waiting for her as usual, and as usual they took their little drive before proceeding home. She said nothing to him then about what was on her mind, as she thought it would be better to wait till after dinner, and he could, with his pipe in his mouth, give his undivided attention to a matter that struck her as being one of great importance. Then, when that time arrived, she opened the subject in the direct way that was a characteristic of her method of dealing with all things, both great and small.

CHAPTER XVII.

"I've had a letter from Mr. John Oldmixon," said Barbara, while her father was lighting his pipe preparatory to sitting down to his evening newspaper.

"Have you, Bab? I've been wondering what had become of him."

"He's been out of town, and his uncle has been ill; but here's his letter. I wouldn't answer it before letting you read it, and deciding for me what kind of a reply to make."

Mr. Henschel's interest was at once excited. He thought the communication was a proposal of marriage, as almost any one else in his situation and with his knowledge of the circumstances would also have thought, and he instantly resolved that if this were the case he would advise his daughter to accept the hand tendered her. He was a practical man, not indisposed, however, to underestimate the advantages of a marriage in which there was love on both sides, but, at the same time, fully aware of the temporal benefits likely to occur to his daughter by a marriage with so eligible a *parti* as was Mr. John Oldmixon. He took the letter and read it; and though there was a little disappointment at the fact that his expectations were not realized, he was, nevertheless, well satisfied with it as an entering wedge to the conclusion he so greatly desired.

"It's a nice letter, Bab," he said, handing it back to her and relighting his pipe—his engagement with the letter having interfered with the combustion-process necessary to the usefulness of this important source of comfort—"and such a one as a gentleman should write. Not too effusive and not too formal. You haven't answered it, I think you said?"

"No, father; I didn't know exactly what to say. You know he can't very well come up here in the evening and go home that night. To do so would only give him about a half hour at the house."

"And you'd like to have him longer, eh, Bab?" said Mr. Henschel, with a knowing laugh.

"I didn't say that, father," answered Barbara, with a slight, very slight blush. "I was only thinking that it would scarcely be worth his while to come here and then have to hurry to avoid missing the train. Conversation under such circumstances can never be satisfactory."

"True, true," said the old man, musingly. "Then you had better invite him to stay all night."

"But we've no place to put him, father, and—and," she added, hesitatingly, "wouldn't it be going too far on our slight acquaintance with Mr. Oldmixon to ask him to pass a night in our house?"

"I don't know exactly how that would be, my dear. It won't do for us to be too forward with our invitations to men who, like Mr. John Oldmixon, may think they are better than we are, and—"

"O father!" interrupted Barbara, alarmed at the conclusion he had reached, and eager to defend Jack from what she felt was an unjust imputation, "I didn't mean that. I'm quite sure Mr. Oldmixon has never had any such notion."

" Probably not, my dear. I didn't say he had, but we can't be too much on our guard. We are proud people, Bab. Our family does not rank with the great ones either in Denmark or here, but we've always done our duty in the stations to which we have been called, and if we choose I doubt not could take our place among the aristocracy in this country. We're respectable, and we're rich—that is, rich enough," checking himself, " and that's the thing that tells.

" But to go back to Mr. John Oldmixon," he continued, after a little pause, during which he puffed strenuously at his pipe, in the expectation apparently that the more tobacco-smoke he got into his air-passages the quicker he would reach a satisfactory conclusion on the question under consideration—" to go back to him, I don't think we shall run any risk of being repulsed by meeting him half way. Therefore, write to him, my dear, and invite him to come up on any evening that suits him and to stay all night. Perhaps you had better give the invitation in my name."

" But we've no place to put him, father. You have the two north rooms, and I have the two south rooms."

" Why not fit up the room behind this as a bedroom? We want a spare room, for we must expect to have a guest with us occasionally. Yes, write, and I'll go to town to-morrow and get furniture for the room. This is Wednesday—well, Bab, what do you say to asking him to come on Saturday afternoon and to stay over through Sunday till Monday morning? Would that be having too much of him ?"

Barbara laughed. " If you'll promise to do the most of the entertaining, I have no objection," she answered.

"I think, however, that he will not be able to leave his uncle for so long a time."

"Well, he must be the judge of that. So write your letter, so that you can mail it in the city to-morrow. He'll get it sooner than if you send it from here."

Barbara seated herself at the table, and in a few minutes handed her father the letter she had written.

"DEAR MR. OLDMIXON : You are very kind to write and remind me of your promise to tell me how you caught the silver fox. We shall be glad to see you, and father bids me say that he will be very glad if you will come up in the 4 P.M. train on Saturday and stay over till Monday morning.

"We are both sorry to hear of your uncle's illness, and hope it is nothing serious.

"Hoping to see you Saturday evening, and informing you that you will have the opportunity of escorting me if you come in the 4 P.M. train, I am

"Yours sincerely,

"BARBARA HENSCHEL."

"That will do," said Mr. Henschel, as having finished reading the letter he handed it back to Barbara. "He'll be sure to come in the four-o'clock train," he added, laughing. "I'll send Ben down with the carriage, and you can drive him over while I stay at home to receive the guest. Will that suit you?"

"Any way of yours will suit me, father," said Barbara, who felt in unusually good spirits. "Now, shall I beat you at backgammon?"

They sat down to play, and they played many games, but she did not beat him. On the contrary, she got but

two or three games out of a dozen or more, and those she
won rather by persistent good luck than by good manage-
ment. In fact, her mind was not on the work before her.
She was thinking of the visit that was to be made to them
the following Saturday, and of what she should do toward
making the time pass pleasantly for the visitor. It was
rather too cold to go out on the water, even if the sun
should have the best sort of an opportunity for sending
down his rays to the earth, and the probability was that,
like most December days, Sunday would be bleak. She
might drive him around the country, or, better still, might
walk with him, for then her father could go along, and
she would not be under the necessity of being alone with
him. She dreaded this latter contingency. She was
afraid for herself—afraid that she would become more
deeply interested in him than would be conducive to her
happiness, for she had fully resolved that nothing should
persuade her to marry Mr. John Oldmixon; and to love
a man that she could not marry would be misery to her.

And then this must be his last visit, as it would be
his first. On that point her mind was clear; but she was
aware that it was one that she would have to argue with
her father, and that to gain it she would be obliged to
enter at length into her reasons.

Mr. Henschel never attempted to set himself in opposition to her fully matured and deliberately expressed
opinions; but as he was a reasonable human being, and
one that specially prided himself on the logical manner
in which he exercised his intellectual faculties, it would
not do for her to simply say, " I prefer not to have Mr.
John Oldmixon come here again." She must be able to
give reasons for such a dogmatic utterance, and as she
was a sensible woman, and one not prone to act from

whim or caprice, it was in the highest degree probable that her father, even if not convinced of the validity of her arguments, would allow her to have her own way in a matter that concerned no one so much as it did herself.

She had no very strong reasons for believing that Jack loved her, but she had a dim suspicion that he did. She too, like her father, had observed looks and tones and manner, all of which went to show that the young man's feelings were deeply involved. Then had come this letter, and that had tended to strengthen the misgiving into almost a belief, else why should he seek her out when there had been such an excellent opportunity for him to pass out of the current of her life altogether?

She finished her games of backgammon, and Mr. Henschel, who was delighted—as all old people are when they win games that they play merely for amusement—with his success, and who had not noticed the fact that Barbara's thoughts were not on her play, attributed the result to his own skill and knowledge.

"You don't play backgammon as well as you mount animals, Bab," he said, laughing, as they stood together in front of the fire before going up-stairs, "and probably not so well as you model. And as to modelling, didn't you tell me a few days ago that you were about to begin a new subject? What is it?"

"It's an animal, father. How the wind blows to-night! I hope it is not storming on the Sound. I saw the steamers go by awhile ago, one after the other, the big Fall River boat leading, and then the New London and the Stonington boats following, with several smaller ones at respectful distances."

"No, I don't think it is blowing very hard on the Sound. I'll go out and look around a moment, and

you'll feel easier if I come back and tell you there's no
danger of wrecks to-night."

She looked worried. She did not feel apprehensive
about a storm on the Sound; she had only been trying to
direct her father's attention from the subject she was
modelling; and she had succeeded so thoroughly that he
was going out into the cold night air in order to be able to
assure her that there was no rough weather, and thus to
enable her to sleep with a mind free from apprehension.
This was more than she had bargained for, and more than
she could honestly accept.

"No, father dear," she said, laying her hand on his
arm and looking pleadingly into his face, "don't go out;
it's cold—too cold for you to expose yourself. I'll tell
you what I am modelling. It's the silver fox, and I'm
doing it altogether from memory, for Mr. Oldmixon has
the specimen I mounted. It isn't storming on the Sound;
it was scarcely fair in me to intimate that it was; I only
said it," she continued, stroking his face with her hands
and smiling, "to divert your attention, for I did not want
to tell you what I was modelling. I was afraid you would
think I had chosen to model the silver fox because that
was the animal I mounted for Mr. Oldmixon, and—
and—"

"Never mind, you little witch," said Mr. Henschel,
laughing heartily; "it just shows how you can twist
your old father around your little finger. You could
make him believe that the moon's made out of green
cheese, if you were to try."

"She loves him," he continued to himself, after he
had bid her good-night and was crossing the upper hall
to his own room. "She may say what she pleases, but
she loves him. Probably she thinks she does not; but I

know something of the ways of women. Well, well, I hope so. I'll let her alone, and she'll do what's right; but I think she loves him, and there are very few women that can resist that feeling when it comes up in their hearts."

Preparations were at once made for Jack's visit. Mr. Henschel spent the whole of the next day after the reception of the letter selecting furniture, and Barbara "knocked off work," as she called it, two hours before her usual time for stopping, in order that she might assist in the selection of a rug for the floor, a brass bedstead, a dressing-stand, a table, a luxuriously upholstered chair, and several other articles that the emergency demanded. Then Barbara suggested a book-rack for the table, and her father was for going at once to get books to put into it ; but she reminded him that she knew what books Mr. Oldmixon liked best to look over in a desultory way, and that she had them at home.

It was a long time, however, before they could succeed in finding a pedestal of the kind that Barbara had set her heart on, and which she informed her father was for the silver fox. "I shall have it done by to-morrow evening," she said, "and I suppose it might as well stand in the spare room as anywhere else."

"Oh, yes, by all means!" replied her father. "That is the best place for it when we have visitors ; at other times we'll put it in the library."

And then Saturday came. The painter had touched up several spots that required his services, and had painted the floor a dark chocolate color where it was not covered by the Kensington rug ; the furniture was in place, some extra preparations had been made in the way of eatables, and last, but not least, the model in clay of the silver fox had arrived the night before, and had been set up on its pedestal in the centre of the large bay-window that occupied the greater part of the front of the house on that side of the doorway. Mr. Henschel thought she had been even more successful than with the mounted specimen, inasmuch as she had had more freedom for the exercise of her artistic instinct in working the clay than in moulding the skin of the dead animal. At any rate, she had produced a work that was full of her genius, and that Mr. Maurice, in a note to her father, said was sufficient of itself to stamp her as an artist of the highest merit. "I advise," he continued, "that it be cast in bronze. The more works like that that are spread over the country, the better it will be for the people." All of which was very pleasant both to Mr. Henschel and to Barbara.

She had been seated but a few minutes in the car that was to take her to Mamaroneck—the station at which she usually got out—when she was joined by Mr. Jack Oldmixon. There cannot be in a place, crowded as every car is on the late trains that go out on the New Haven Railroad every Saturday afternoon, any conversation but such as may be heard without restraint by every passenger within ten feet of the speakers. Barbara was in the first place surprised at Jack's appearance; he looked low-spirited, and as though he was suffering. In fact, he at once apologized for what he called his stupidity in having passed Barbara several times without seeing her, by saying that he had a bad headache. However, by the time they arrived at Mamaroneck he declared that, in spite of the noise and the increased effort he had been obliged to make in talking so as to allow what he said to be heard, he had gotten entirely rid of his headache, and never had felt better in his life.

Ben, a stout Westchester lad that Mr. Henschel had hired to look after the horse and do all other kinds of outside work, was at the station with the little carriage, and was to run home through the fields while Barbara drove Jack by the road, a distance of nearly three miles. Now that they were rattling along over the hard, smooth country road, Jack felt that he might say some things that he could not have said in the cars without having them heard by twenty or more people.

"I'm very glad to see you again, Miss Henschel," he began ; "I've missed those delightful morning sittings ever so much, though doubtless you were bored by them more than your good-nature allowed you to show."

"Did I look as though I were at all bored ?" inquired Barbara, with a smile. "If I did, my looks did me injustice."

"No, you did not !" exclaimed Jack, with emphasis, "but it is very pleasant for me to hear you say you were not wearied."

"But you talked so much that I could not get tired."

"You might have got tired of my talking."

"Perhaps I should have been if you had always talked about the same thing ; but your range of subjects was so very extensive that I was kept wide-awake, wondering what was to come next."

"I had to do that to get the facial expression I wanted. I tried many subjects before I succeeded."

"Oh, indeed ! Then I was showing off for your benefit !"

"I'm afraid that is an honest way of putting it," rejoined Jack, with a laugh. "But, then, in art, as in everything else, '*finis coronat opus*.' "

"I don't know what that means," said Barbara,

"but I'm sure it's something horrible. There now!" as the wheels went with a bump over a big stone that lay in the way, "that comes from your bothering a country girl's head with Latin. While I was trying to make out what you said, I missed seeing that stone. But pray, what subject did you finally decide upon as the one that made me show off to most advantage?"

"Ah! Miss Henschel, there is just where I think I have shown what little talent I possess. I tried at first to get a particular expression, and then I changed my mind, and endeavored to make your face a combination of all your expressions. You know an English scientist has been photographing groups of particular kinds of criminals and other sorts of people. He takes, for instance, the photographs of fifty burglars. Then he makes a compound picture of these fifty photographs, and obtains a representation of the typical burglar. You look at that, and though it is not exactly like any one of the individuals taken, it is the sum total of them all, and from it you would know any one of the rest at sight; and so on with murderers, pickpockets, and others. Now, that's what I tried to do with you, Miss Henschel. You are fifty persons—that is, you have fifty different expressions—and everybody that knows you and that sees the picture sees an expression he has seen on your face. If I had taken you in any one of them, don't you see it would only have represented the fiftieth part of you? That wouldn't have done at all, would it?"

"Not unless a part is better than the whole," replied Barbara, laughing merrily, "and perhaps in this case it is. You know, with some things the less you have of them the better."

"True; but you are not one of them. Look out!" as

12

the wheels barely missed going into the ditch at the side of the road. "A little more, and we should have been upset."

"Yes, and then you'd have had fifty pieces of a young woman to pick up in reality; but you see, Mr. Oldmixon, what comes of trying to do two things at once, when either is sufficient to require all the power of the female mind. But finish telling me about the picture."

"I merely endeavored to combine your fifty expressions into one which represented them all. I've got you now, Miss Henschel, not as you are at any one moment, but as you are at fifty moments. I wrote you part of what Archer said of it, but I didn't tell you what he said of your likeness."

"Something nice, I suppose, or you wouldn't mention it."

"Yes, it was nice. But Archer is one of the most emphatic men I ever knew. He's a wicked old fellow, too."

"Then, what he said was nice, emphatic, and wicked! What a remarkable combination! I am curious to hear it."

"Shall I tell you?"

Barbara looked at him for a moment. A pleasant smile was on his face. "I think I can trust you not to tell me anything I ought not to hear," she said.

"Thanks! He said, 'Oldmixon, that's the sort of a face a man is ready to die and to lose his soul for.'"

Barbara was silent. Things were going altogether too fast, and she thought she must put a brake on them, or there was no telling what would come next; and yet it was all very pleasant—so pleasant, that she could not remember that she had ever passed so delightful a half hour as that that was now coming to an end. Yes, it was

coming to an end, for she was within a hundred yards of
the house, and she could see her father's tall form as he
walked up and down the front porch, waiting their arrival. It was at least three minutes since Jack had told
her of Archer's remark, and during all that time she had
been deep in thought; still, it was not too late for her to
say something that would express her disapproval of such
speeches. She was on the point of saying, "I should be
very sorry if any one would be so foolish and wicked for
me," and then the idea occurred to her that it would be
very absurd for her to assume that Mr. Archer had her
in his mind when he spoke, and that to him the face had
no individuality, but simply represented a conception of
the artist's mind. Yes, it would certainly be better for
her to say nothing, and at the moment she came to this
determination she drove through the gateway and up to
the side of the porch, where her father stood waiting to
receive them.

"You're a little late, Bab," he said, as Ben took the
reins from her hand. "Welcome to Lasata, Mr. Oldmixon!" Jack was out in an instant, and was giving his
hand to Barbara in order to help her to alight from the
carriage before Mr. Henschel had ceased speaking. Then
he turned and shook hands warmly with his host, expressed his great delight at having been invited to Lasata
—the meaning of which name had been explained to him
by Miss Henschel—and passed high encomiums on that
young lady's skill in driving.

Barbara, who had not quite got through kissing her
father, laughed at this last part of Jack's speech.

"Yes," she said, "my skill certainly saved us from
being upset; for if I had had a little less we should assuredly have gone over. Therefore, father, thank your stars

..nat you have a daughter that knows enough about managing a horse not to kill either herself or the gentleman she is driving.''

"She'll kill me," thought Jack, "if she refuses me to-morrow, for to-morrow I shall have to ask her to be my wife. I didn't intend to go quite that far this time, but she's so lovely and sweet that, by Heaven! I can't resist any longer."

Then, when he entered his room to get ready for dinner and saw the model of the silver fox on its pedestal, he was so delighted that he rushed back to the hall where he had left Barbara talking with her father, to express his joy.

"I can only now thank you for the remembrance," he said; "I will tell you to-morrow, when I have examined it by daylight, what I think of it as a work of art. It was very kind, Miss Henschel, for now I know that those hours in which I was painting my picture were not wearisome to you."

He took her hand in his while he was speaking, and held it till he had finished. Then he raised it to his lips, and without another word went back to his room.

"He's a graceful man, Bab," said Mr. Henschel, looking well enough pleased with the act of courtesy, while Barbara, totally unused to such a proceeding, seemed doubtful as to how she should regard it. "No gentleman of the court of Denmark could have done it better. I saw the king kiss the queen's hand once, but he was awkward compared to Mr. John Oldmixon."

CHAPTER XVIII.

"WHY SHOULD SHE NOT?"

THERE was no chance that evening for Jack to make even an approach to the citadel he had determined to capture if he could. Besides, he wanted still a little time for reflection as to the best way in which to make his attack. A great deal, he knew, depended upon the tactics, just as it does with an army about to make an onslaught on another army. If it bungles it is very apt to be defeated, even though it be of superior force.

He had had a better opportunity while at dinner and during the three hours after that meal, which they all spent together in the library, for becoming acquainted with Barbara than he had ever before enjoyed. The conversation had been devoted to a variety of subjects in which he and Mr. Henschel and Barbara were interested, and there was scarcely one upon which she had not had something to say. Jack was not a very deep young man, but he was well educated in a certain direction, and his residence abroad had given him the opportunity—which he had not neglected—of picking up a good deal of information upon subjects a knowledge of which goes very far toward giving a man a reputation for being well-informed, and still further in the direction of making him agreeable in conversation. He was, therefore, sufficiently competent to form an opinion of Barbara's acquirements and good sense. He had made up his mind on these points some time ago, but this night had enabled him to confirm his opinion beyond all danger of reversal. To be sure, a young man in love does not approach without prejudice the consideration of the subject of the intellectual qualifications possessed by the object of his heart's desires. As a rule, he is utterly unable to see anything in her most insane moods and imbecile actions that is not indicative of the highest degree of mental development. But this was not the case with Jack. He had fallen in love with Barbara by no means altogether because she was pretty. If she had not possessed a charming mind, he knew very well that she would not be beautiful. It was her mentality speaking through her face that made her countenance such an enchanting picture to look upon. If Barbara had been a fool, she would have been a very commonplace-looking young woman, and then Jack certainly would not have fallen in love with her.

Barbara, as the reader already knows, had not gone deeply into learning; what she knew, however, she knew well, and her range of subjects, though probably not so extensive as that of which the young lady graduates of Macassar College are mistresses, was large enough, and she had the inestimable advantage of knowing something below the surface of the matters she had studied.

Jack was, of course, delighted. He had come to Lasata expecting to be delighted, and he had not been disappointed. To every word that Barbara spoke he listened with the most rapt attention. She had those predominating attractions in a woman—a clear and distinct enunciation and a soft, melodious voice. Consequently, though she never spoke in a loud tone, every word was as distinctly heard as though it had been gently spoken directly into the ear. It was happiness, therefore, for Jack, who had been for many days past in almost constant association with his uncle, and the unwilling recipient of that old gentleman's snarls and groans over the state of the world generally, and of his nephew Hogarth in particular, to sit in this peaceful atmosphere, where all was gentleness and refined repose, and listen to the mellowed voice and the musical laugh of the woman he thought the loveliest in all the world.

It was late—late, that is, for Lasata—when the party broke up. Barbara held out her hand to Jack as she bid him good-night and wished him pleasant dreams. So intoxicated was he with the impression she had made upon him, that if they had been alone he would at once have told the story of his love. As it was, there was nothing to do but to make some pleasant commonplace speech, and to wait for a better opportunity. He pressed her hand a little, but of course there was no response through that medium, and then he went into his own room.

Like a skilful and far-seeing general on the eve of an important battle, Jack sat down to think over the situation of affairs and to lay out his plan of operations for the next day. It has been said that the woman does not live and never has lived that could conceal her love from the man that possesses her heart. Probably this is true, but it is equally so of the other sex. When a man loves a woman, the woman, if she be not a fool, will certainly discover the fact. Either may pretend to a love they do not feel, and thus deceive not only the immature, but even those that are experienced in the wiles of men and women ; but when the passion is really present, it will reveal itself in spite of all efforts that may be made to keep it secret. Indeed, nothing so effectually makes it known as the attempts that may be made to conceal it. The

struggle is so wildly energetic and the results so entirely
one-sided, that he or she must be very blind or very cal-
lous if the true state of affairs is not soon made apparent.

Jack threw himself into the comfortable chair that had
been provided for his use, and gave himself up, with as
much disinterestedness as was possible under the circumstances, to a calm and impartial review of the position in
which he was placed and of the events and situations that
had brought him to the present crisis. As the result of
his cogitations, he arrived at the belief that Barbara loved
him ; but there was so much apprehension and fear
that he might be mistaken in this conviction, that, on the
whole, the effect was not so consolatory as he could have
wished. As is usual in such cases, he was afraid to trust
implicitly to the evidence of his own senses. He was
very much in the position of a physician that attempts to
prescribe for himself, and whose judgment is almost invariably warped by the personal interest he has in the
case. Still, after making all due allowances for the inevitable errors in this direction to which he was subject, he
could not fail to see that Barbara was kindly disposed toward him, and that this bias was so strongly pronounced,
that if it was not already love as he understood the subject, it practically amounted to the same thing in the
heart of a girl as true and as pure as was Barbara Henschel.

But there was a family matter—one that had within the
past few days given him much anxiety—which he felt he
was bound, as an honest man and a gentleman, to place
fully before Barbara when he asked her to be his wife.
It was this that had made him look badly, and as though
he were ill, when Barbara and he had met in the car on
their way to Lasata, and which he had explained by alleg-

ing a headache. His head did ache. There had been
quite enough since he had last seen her to make both his
head and his heart ache, and for all that he could perceive
to the contrary, there was ample warrant for the belief that they would ache still more before certain matters were settled. All this he intended that Barbara
should know. It should never be in the power of any
one to say that he had induced her to promise to become
his wife when there were circumstances existing that, had
they been brought to her knowledge, might have caused
her to turn from him with horror.

In the mean time the woman of whom he was thinking,
and with whom his happiness was so intimately bound,
was sitting by the window of a room that overlooked the
Sound. The night was bleak; there was no moon, and
the stars were obscured by thick black clouds that looked
as though they might be full of snow. Far off in the
distance, on the opposite shore of the Sound, was a light-
house upon which there was a revolving lantern, that she
had ascertained, by actual count, flashed its bright bar of
light over the water every two minutes. She sat watching this object, her thoughts being a strange medley, of
which the light, Jack, and herself were the central features, and wondering how the affair which she now felt
was hers—for good or evil, she did not know which—
would end. Would it be always bright, as was the light
when the open side of the lantern was turned toward her,
or would it be dark, as was the lantern when the opaque
side prevented the emergence of the rays from the lamp?
Or would it be for a while light and then dark, and so on
to the end?

She knew Jack loved her, and she felt sure that if he
were given the opportunity he would tell her so before
12*

the time came round on Monday morning for him to go
back to New York. She had resolved that nothing should
ever induce her to marry him, but now she felt the determination becoming less, as she found that she loved
him more than she had thought she should ever love him.
She felt that it was now possible that she would marry
him if he asked her, and she found herself with the questions in her heart, Why should she not? What did she
owe to his uncle that she should sacrifice her happiness
and that of the man she loved for any fancied loyalty to
him? True, she knew that Jack was to be his uncle's
heir, and she thought he was ignorant of this fact. She
had virtually promised not to speak of anything Mr.
Oldmixon had told her, and therefore it left room for the
suspicion in the minds of some persons, perhaps even in
that of Jack himself, and certainly in that of Mr. Oldmixon, that she had taken advantage of her knowledge to
inveigle this presumptively rich young man into a marriage when he did not know his pecuniary value. She
might tell him, she thought, and then he would be free,
with his eyes open, to do as he pleased; but reflection told
her that this would be dishonorable, and no woman ever
had a more chivalrous sense of honor than had Barbara
Henschel—a sense in which her sex is, as a rule, deficient.

But what were the opinions of old Mr. Oldmixon and all
the rest of the world when set up against Jack's? And
again the question came with irresistible force, Why
should she make him and herself miserable to please
other people? True, why should she? Had she been
disposed to do so, she would have been the only woman
within my knowledge willing to do such a thing. Women
will eagerly sacrifice themselves for the man they love,
but they will not sacrifice him. The women that go

into convents and kill themselves for love are either those
whose passion is not returned, or they are insane melan-
cholics that have brooded over delusions until their reason
has been overwhelmed. No woman of sane mind, knowing that the love she receives is as warm as that that she
gives, ever sacrificed herself and her lover to an idea or a
principle. She is not going to make him unhappy, whatever else she may do. She may allege a thousand reasons why she should not marry him, but the real reason is
either that she does not love him or that she knows he
does not love her, and this she generally keeps to herself.
If these be absent, there will be no holding back or
going into convents or a resort to Paris green, but she
will marry him by hook or by crook, openly or secretly,
though all the world should stand in the way. Barbara
felt very much in that way. She now perceived that when
she had spoken so decidedly to her father to the effect that
nothing could persuade her to be Mr. John Oldmixon's
wife, that she did not love him as she now did. She
knew now that she should be obliged to marry him if he
asked her, and if she was entirely satisfied that his love was
good and true. Doubtless there would be more or less
trouble; but her lover was a man who had shown his ability to hold his own in the face of adverse circumstances,
and even to make his way in spite of them; and she knew
that she had a force of her own that would enable her to
yield efficient assistance. She was not one to succumb to
the attacks of adversity. She had always shown pluck
and determination when these qualities had been required, and though she had never suffered any great
misfortune, she had the mental organization that is
ready to meet misfortune whenever it presents itself.

"I love him," she said to herself, just as the light

from over the Sound flashed in her eyes, " and that's the end of the contest. It's gone," as darkness once more prevailed on the water, " but it will shine again. Oh, Jack"—he had told her that his intimate friends called him by that name—" I tried my best not to love you, but it was no use. I thought you loved me almost from the first, and now I know you do, just as surely as though you had already told me. And if you do, I'll be yours, Jack, even if it should be wrong for me to marry you. It can't be *very* wrong ; I don't see how it can. If he loves me and I love him, whose business is it but ours ?" And with this satisfactory conclusion of the matter, Barbara went to bed, and with a much better prospect of getting a good night's rest than had Mr. Jack Oldmixon in the room just under hers.

As a matter of fact, Jack did not sleep well. He did not go to bed till he had exhausted all the capabilities of the subject that occupied his mind, and had discovered that there were no new lights in which he could view it. Indeed, it would have been a very wonderful topic if he had been able to extract anything original out of it, for he had thought of scarcely anything else, since his last meeting with Barbara, in the old shop in which he had painted his picture. There had been other matters forced upon his attention and they had worried him, but he had tried to dismiss them from his mind, and though not altogether with success, yet to such purpose that they rarely obtruded themselves upon him, and then only as passing shadows, that fled away as quickly as they had come.

The next morning, in spite of a rather restless night, he looked and felt better than at any time since his return from Annapolis. He was one of that class of persons who

become perfectly composed, when a crisis that concerns
them has come, although they may be greatly disturbed
while awaiting it. He had taken occasion before leaving
his room to make a thorough study of the silver fox ;
just as conscientious a one as though he was capable of
passing an impartial judgment on that work of art. I
am afraid that no matter how bad it might have been,
Jack would have found something in it to admire ; as it
was, however, it would have been impossible for him to
go wrong in any laudation of Barbara's first work that
he might give. It was, as Mr. Maurice had said, a production that would have made a reputation for any sculptor, and Jack was fully competent to discover as much
for himself. Of course, it was a pleasure for him to give
his opinion, as he did at the breakfast-table, and equally
a pleasure for Barbara and her father to hear him express
it with such evident heartiness and sense of its truth as
he exhibited.

The day was by no means an unpleasant one, considering the bad prospect for clear weather that the night
before had offered. It was not warm, but the sun was
shining brightly, and there was no cold, cutting wind to
make walking uncomfortable.

There was at the distance of about a mile from Lasata
a little church to which Mr. Henschel and his daughter
were in the habit of going every Sunday morning. Of
course, he had been brought up according to the tenets
of the Church of Denmark, which, though mainly Luther-
an in its doctrines, has nevertheless its bishops, with an
apostolic succession even more unquestioned than that
of the Church of England, and its Protestant Episcopal
daughter in the United States. On his arrival in their
country, they had looked about among the forty or more

religious sects that they found ready to receive them into their folds, and had come to the conclusion that the Episcopal came nearer to what they had been accustomed to at home than any of the others. They had accordingly given in their adhesion to that ecclesiastical organization, and had taken care that their children should be educated in its communion.

Barbara took her religion as she did everything else—healthily. She had been confirmed, and she devoutly believed all the articles of the Christian faith, but she believed them according to her own light, and not that of any one else. She found nothing in the doctrines or ritual of the Church that required her to dispense with her own reasoning powers and to commit her judgment and her conscience to others. She did not, therefore, do her duty to God and to her neighbor through any fear of eternal damnation if she neglected it, or hope of everlasting happiness as a reward for its performance. She did it because it was right. She was happy in her religion. If she had believed that the Creator of the world would punish eternally any of the beings that he had put into it, she would not have been happy. Into minute theological points she did not care to venture. She went to church and said her prayers, and felt happier for the exercise.

The fact of Jack's being in the house was no reason why she should not go to church that morning. There was nothing to do but to ask him to accompany her father and herself, and there was nothing for Jack to do but to accept. If the truth must be told of this young man, it must be said that he was not much of a church-goer. In fact, religion had never been one of the strong points of the Oldmixons ; and though, in answer to Barbara's question, he said that his mother had been a member of the Church of Scotland, he was forced to admit that her early death had prevented her giving him much religious instruction, and that he had never sought for it elsewhere. He added, however, that he was perfectly willing, nay anxious, to take his first lesson that morning, under the auspices of Miss Henschel.

It had been decided that as the morning was pleasant they would walk, so at ten o'clock they departed for the church. Jack thought, as he started off by Barbara's side, that never had she looked more beautiful than she did then, with her dark brown frock and seal-skin jacket, and a black broad-brimmed felt hat with a red-winged blackbird—of her own mounting, as she told him—set in front, with its wings in the attitude of flight. If Mr. Henschel were only out of the way, what better chance for laying his heart and hand at Barbara's feet than would be the walk home from church ? But how to get him out of the way was a matter that appeared to be at first sight altogether beyond his powers. Jack was not much of a diplomatist ; his nature was altogether too frank for the double-dealing or secretiveness necessary for the one that works by intrigue. But this very deficiency in the power of device was often the means of his obtaining success when others, in like circumstances, by using strategy would have ignominiously failed. Upon the present occasion he wanted Mr. Henschel out of the way, and it did not take him long to arrive at the conclusion that the best way to secure that gentleman's absence was to tell him all the essential facts of the situation, and request him to allow his daughter and him— Jack Oldmixon—to walk home from church without the presence of a third party. They were just passing out of the gate when this idea occurred to Jack, and to act upon it at once was a necessary concomitant.

"May I say a word to you, Mr. Henschel?" he said. "I beg your pardon, Miss Henschel," he continued, addressing Barbara, "but if you will kindly continue to switch at that cedar-tree with your parasol for two or three minutes I will promise to bring your father back in safety." He led the way round the house to the front porch, and then, without any preliminary words, opened his case.

"Mr. Henschel," he said, "I don't know whether you have observed the fact or not, but I love your daughter and I want to make her my wife. My time here is very short, and I propose, with your consent, to tell her this morning what is in my heart, and to ask her to marry me."

Mr. Henschel knew perfectly well that Jack was in love with Barbara, and, as the reader knows, he fully approved of that young gentleman as a husband for his daughter, but the present announcement took him by surprise, and it was a moment or two before he could sufficiently recover his presence of mind to give an answer. When, however, he did speak, there was no uncertain sound in his voice or meaning in his words. He believed, in spite of what Barbara had told him, that she would eventually be willing to marry Jack, and he thought that the last twenty-four hours had been sufficient to produce a weakening in the determination she had expressed to him. He had noticed that even when most emphatic in the declaration of her intention never to become Jack's wife, she had not denied loving him. There was probably, he thought, some chivalric idea connected with Jack's heirship of old Mr. Oldmixon's estate that caused her to take an exaggerated and mistaken view of her duty, and that would probably disappear under the cogency of her lover's arguments. He held out his hand to Jack, and, of course, it was grasped warmly, for it was evident before a word was spoken what the answer would be.

"Mr. Oldmixon," said Mr. Henschel, while the tears started to his eyes, "I am not so old as to have lost my perceptive faculties. I have known for some time that you loved Barbara, and if I had not approved of you as a husband for my girl, I wouldn't have asked you to come here. It would not be proper for me, in the absence of absolute knowledge, to say anything about your chances, but I am sure you can trust her to tell you the truth. You can speak to her whenever you choose, and I hope she'll take you for her husband. She's a good girl, and, what's as important in a girl as it is in a man, she's got a good stock of common-sense. I suppose you want me to get out of the way this morning, and give you a chance to speak to her?"

"Yes, that's what I want," said Jack, who had all the time kept hold of Mr. Henschel's hand, and who now gave it an extra grasp. "You know how grateful I am for your confidence in me. I have asked you for the greatest treasure you possess, and I don't believe you will ever have cause to regret having given her to me."

"With her consent, of course," interrupted Mr. Henschel. "You may tell her I approve, after she has accepted you; but no persuasions through me."

"I will say nothing of your consent till she has given me hers," said Jack, with an eagerness that showed his willingness to promise almost anything that might be asked of him.

"Now that that matter is settled," observed Mr.

Henschel, with a happy smile on his face, "what further is it that you want me to do?"

"I want you," said Jack, not in the least abashed, "to leave us at the church door when the service is over. You can probably," continued this outspoken young man, "find some one in the congregation to whom you would like to say a few words. There's the doctor, for instance; you might tell him how well the new drains work."

"The doctor! Doctor Maddox! He hasn't been inside of a church for twenty years, and he told me a day or two since that he never expected to go again. I might say a word to the clergyman. But," he added, with a slight laugh, "it might be too soon to do that yet; however, I'll find some excuse, never fear."

"Thanks. Now, let us join Barbara—Miss Henschel, I mean," correcting himself; "she will wonder what has become of us."

CHAPTER XIX.

"I LOVE YOU."

THE little church which the Henschels attended was constructed with a due regard to the principles of ecclesiological art. In the first place, there were no shams about it, and, in the next, no vain attempt had been made by the architect to copy, on a diminutive scale, any famous church edifice. I have seen in one of the largest cities of this country what is called an exact imitation of St. Paul's in London. It is a brick building, perhaps at the outside fifty by a hundred feet in extent, and surmounted by wooden cupolas covered with tin. Of course it is an abomination in the sight of every person with a soul above that of the snobbish architect that built it.

St. Ethelwold's made no pretension to being any better than it really was. It was built of a dark granite, and in the early English style, and was devoid of plaster, the bare stone, laid as it was in courses, producing a much more impressive effect than if it had been covered up and stencilled all over with gilt crosses, or lambs holding flags with their forelegs, or other symbols.

Jack sat next to Barbara ; she gave him a prayer-book, and all through the service found the places for him. No one could have been more devout, so far as externals went, than was he. He stood up and sat down, and bowed his head, and even made the responses, under the guidance of his fuglewoman, in a way that would have done credit

to a much more habitual worshipper. And, indeed, Jack
felt all the solemnity of the occasion with a depth and a
sincerity that he would not a month before have thought
it possible he could feel in any church in Christendom.
Although, as we have seen, not a church-goer, Jack was
not deficient in that natural religion in which all well-
constituted men, even though they be agnostics, abound.
The solemn, the beautiful, the reverential in sight and
in sound never failed to move him, and to excite in him
chivalrous or other noble thoughts in consonance with the
emotions that swayed him. Now, the dim light entering
through stained-glass windows, the measured voice of the
clergyman, the lofty words of the ritual, the spirit of
adoration that pervaded the congregation, the swelling
sound of the organ as it pealed forth its sacred melodies,
and, above all, the worshipping woman kneeling at his
side, whose low, sweet notes fell on his ears with a power
that brought the tears to his eyes, all excited in his
heart emotions that made him feel, for the time being, at
least, as though he were lifted up from a world of sin and
borne into a sphere where everything was pure and good.
" Lord, have mercy upon us, and incline our hearts to
keep this law." He glanced down at Barbara as these
words of supplication came from her lips in response to the
clergyman in the chancel pronouncing each commandment
of the Decalogue. Her head was bowed upon her closed
hands, which rested on the pew-railing before her. He
could not see her face, but the graceful curve of her white
neck, the well-rounded outlines of her figure—she had
taken off her seal-skin jacket—the knot of red hair—the
loveliest hair he thought that he had ever seen—that was
not covered by the shapely little hat with its dainty
bird that her own dear hands had mounted, the earnest-

ness with which each prayer was uttered, the distinctness
of her enunciation, impressed Jack with such a sense of
her beauty and goodness, that he wondered if it were
really possible that she could ever be his. He had never
felt his own unworthiness so keenly as he did then. It
seemed to him for a moment as though it would be almost
a sin to link with his own the life of the gentle girl
against whose name in the Book of Life the recording
angel had entered nothing but good, and yet who humbly
prayed to God for strength to keep his commandments.
How infinitely better than he was this kneeling, adoring
woman, who laid bare her heart to the Maker of all things,
as she might have done to her earthly father, and suppli-
cated him for a power she did not need ! "Lord, have
mercy upon us, and write all these thy laws in our hearts,
we beseech thee." Were they not already written in her
heart ? Doubtless she had never broken a single one of
them, while he, who had certainly violated two or three,
perhaps more, had never, so far as he could remember,
uttered a prayer for forgiveness or for strength to resist
temptation. Well, hereafter it should be different with
him. Her God should be his God, if she should grant
him her love. Yes, for he was willing to bargain with
Providence, or, in fact, with any other power that could
give him what he desired. Emotional religion is not,
after all, of the most elevated kind, or the most permanent in its duration.

Jack listened to the sermon, but with less attention
than he had bestowed on the service. The clergyman
was young—younger than himself—and it was not likely
that a man like Jack, who had seen a good deal of the
world in various parts of its surface, could look up to him
with sufficient confidence to accept him as a moral guide.

Jack was sure that he knew more about the human heart than did the speaker, and, moreover, that his knowledge came from personal experience, while that of the other came from books. It was very much as it is with the young men and young women who nowadays take to writing novels as soon as they have escaped from college or boarding-school, and who undertake to describe life and character from what they have read in other novels or have seen enacted on the stage by actors, who themselves have gotten their small knowledge from books. Clergymen, like novelists, should be over fifty years of age.

It must be confessed that while the young theologian was laying down the religious and moral law with a positiveness that ought to have been the result of personal experience, Jack was not so successful in following him as were many others of the congregation, who were accustomed to receive the words of warning and advice that fell from the lips of the ministrant as though they were veritable droppings from the sanctuary. He was thinking how he should begin the observations that he had to address to Barbara. At first he was disposed to adopt the same plan that had proved so successful with her father—that is, to come right out with the gist of the whole matter by telling her that he loved her. That, after all, was the one thing before which all the rest that he had to say went down like grass before a lawn-mower. But, upon reflection, he came to the conclusion that it would be better to inform her fully of certain family affairs that troubled him and that might influence her in the answer she might have to give him. Better to start squarely by letting her know just who he was and what disadvantages might attend upon marriage with him.

The advantages might safely be left to her to discover for herself.

The sermon was not a long one, and they rose at its conclusion to receive the blessing, and then to the music of the organ to make their way out of the church. But just as they had reached the door, the sexton came up to Mr. Henschel and informed him that Mr. Wilton, the rector, wished to speak with him in the vestry.

"He wants to see me about becoming one of the wardens in the place of Mr. Holtby, who died last week," said Mr. Henschel. "He spoke about it last Sunday, but I was not then prepared to give him an answer. Don't wait for me," he continued, with a significant glance at Jack. "Walk slowly, and perhaps I may overtake you. If I do not, I shall not be far behind you."

Nothing could have been more fortunate than this intervention. Jack and Barbara walked slowly, and in a few minutes found that all the rest of the congregation, most of whom came in vehicles of some kind or other, had passed them. At last they were alone.

They had talked of the sermon and of other indifferent subjects, till at last, Jack looking up and down the road, made the discovery that no one was in sight. His time had come, and then he found that all his preconceived plans of operation had vanished from his mind as completely as though they had never found a lodgment there, and that, after all, he must depend upon the inspiration of the moment. When did an earnest man ever fail at such a time? No one was ever more in earnest than was Jack. Without stopping to think or to arrange his ideas in any logical order, he began with what came first in his mind, and went on with a degree of volubility that, had

he been capable at the time of judging, would have
astonished him.

"At last we are alone," he said, "and at last I have
the opportunity of telling you what of all things in the
world is most in my heart. It will take but a moment
to say it. It is all contained in three little words—' I love
you.' "

Having gotten thus far—and it must be admitted that
anything else would only have been an amplification of
his "three little words"—Jack stopped, not only talking
but walking, and, at the same instant, Barbara stopped
also. From the time that he had spoken the first word,
she knew of course what was coming. There was nothing else that, after such a preamble, could have come but
the words "I love you," or others to that effect. For a
moment she felt weak and faint, but it was only for a
moment, and before he had half finished his short speech
she was taking in his words with a kind of calm delight
that appeared to pervade her whole being. When he
stopped walking she stopped as a matter of course; it
seemed to her that that was of itself a tacit admission
that in future he was to be her guide. She had not raised
her parasol, but she held it in her hand, and swung it
from side to side, while her eyes were apparently engaged
in diligently watching its oscillations.

"Did you hear what I said?" resumed Jack.

"Yes;" very low, but yet very distinctly.

"Have you nothing to say to me?"

She raised her eyes, and Jack saw that they were swim-
ming with tears; and thus, before she spoke a word, he
knew that the victory was essentially won.

"Yes," she said at last, "I heard what you said, and
I am very glad, for—for—I think I love you too. But

your uncle? Perhaps he may have other views for you."

Jack looked up and down the road, and seeing that there was no one in sight, took Barbara's head between his hands, and bending over—for though she was tall, he was a good deal taller—kissed her lips.

"I know I am not worthy of you, my darling," he said; "I was thinking all the time I was in church how thoroughly beneath you I am, but I'll try to make myself better. You've made me very happy; I've loved you, dear, ever since I first saw you. I never saw a woman as good and as lovely as you. And now you're mine! I can scarcely believe it"—and he kissed her again, as though to make sure that she really had said "yes" to him.

Barbara smiled. "Yes, I am sure I love you with all my heart," she said. "But there is something in the way that I have no right to mention to you. I don't know that it can come between us, but I wish it were not there, for if it were away my happiness would be complete."

"Something in the way!" exclaimed Jack, his thoughts at once reverting to his family affairs. "What is it, dear?" fearing, as he asked the question, that she would tell him of something she had heard about Hogarth or his uncle.

"Oh, I cannot tell you; I promised never to mention it."

"Well, dear," said Jack, a little crestfallen, "if you really made a promise not to speak of it, you are, of course, bound to keep your promise."

"I—I don't think I promised in words," faltered Barbara. "In fact, when the statement was about being

13

made to me, and the gentleman said, 'You must promise not to tell this to anybody but your father,' I didn't say anything at all, but I allowed him to go on and tell me, and that was the same thing as promising, wasn't it?''

She raised her eyes again to Jack's, as she asked this question, and looked at him inquiringly and doubtfully. He had never seen her more beautiful.

"Wait one moment," exclaimed the enraptured young man; "I can't answer any questions in the presence of such loveliness as yours. Oh, Barbara! my Barbara! have you the slightest idea that you are the sweetest woman that God ever made; the dearest, the most beautiful, the most incomparable, the—"

"Now," she said, laughing, "you don't expect me to answer that question, do you? But," she added more seriously, "if you love me, and admire me, I am very glad. Don't you think we had better walk on? We've been standing here almost long enough for father to overtake us."

"No," he continued, looking at her rapturously, "you don't know what a perfectly adorable creature you are. If you did, you would go away from this grovelling earth, to dwell with your fellow angels."

Again she laughed. She was very happy; she threw her arms around his neck, and drew his head to her breast. It was her first caress. "Oh, Jack!" she murmured, "my love, my love! Don't talk such nonsense. Don't you think I'd rather be with you than with all the angels that were ever born?"

"I didn't know," said the imbecile young man—all young men that are worth anything are imbecile at such times—"I knew I wasn't fit to associate with you, and I thought that perhaps you'd rather be with the superior beings that are like you. I suppose they are angels; they may be goddesses for all I know. That was the first time you called me 'Jack;' I was waiting to see when you meant to begin."

"I expect to call you 'Jack' many times."

"I hope you may do it for a thousand years, and then for another thousand, and so on for all eternity."

"Oh, you'd be tired enough of me before that."

Jack disdained any answer to this beyond a kiss.

"Now about that promise, or what you call a promise," he said, when he had the chance; "made to a gentleman, too! Upon my word, Miss Henschel! Have you any clear idea of what you've been doing?" He put on an air of mock severity as he asked this question.

"No, Jack," answered Barbara, demurely, "I don't think I have. I have only one idea now; there isn't room in my head for another—I know that you love me, and everything else in the way of knowledge has gone."

"That's all very well. That's the way I want to hear you talk; but don't you think you could muster sufficient intellect to tell me who the gentleman is that you gave that ghost of a promise to?"

"I think I might do that much. I made no promise, expressed or implied, on that point."

"Well, who was it?"

"It was your uncle, Jack."

"My Uncle Victor!"

"Yes, Jack."

"You know him then?"

"Yes, Jack."

"I am perfectly astounded! Have you known him long?"

"No, Jack."

" Have you met him often ?"

" No, Jack, only twice."

" How did you happen to make his acquaintance ?"

Barbara reflected for a moment before answering. They had resumed their walking, and they had yet about three-quarters of a mile to go before reaching home. She thought that what she had a right to tell her father she ought to be allowed to tell the man she was going to marry, especially as the matter concerned him. Yes, she would tell him. In reality, she had not actually promised. Scruples like hers disappear from a woman's mind in the presence of her lover.

" I think I'll have to tell you all about it, Jack," she said at last. " There's really no reason why you should not know, and if I don't tell you I shall be uncomfortable, and you will be unhappy, won't you, dear ?"

" Yes, very unhappy, my darling, very miserable. The very idea of your having a secret from me makes me wretched." (Jack did not look very wretched, but appearances are often deceptive.) " Besides," added the specious young man, " you didn't promise. If he had cared anything about it, don't you think he would have had you promise in words before he told you anything ? I think you ought to tell me, and then I've something in the way of a history to relate to you. How in the world did you make Uncle Victor's acquaintance ?"

" I mounted a canary-bird for him ;" and then Barbara told all she knew of Mr. Oldmixon, and all that he had related to her of his loves, his nephews, and his intentions.

Jack listened in astonishment. " So all this time," he exclaimed, " you have known of some of the most important events in my life, and it is to you that I owe the reconciliation with my uncle !"

"Yes, Jack, but you must bear in mind that at that time I had never even seen you. It was very venturesome in me to take your side when I knew nothing about you, don't you think so ?" looking archly at him as she spoke.

"I said you were an angel just now ; you are my guardian angel. I'm glad that I owe so much to you."

"But, Jack dear, that is the very thing that I thought might come between us. I was afraid that when you came to know all, as you would some day, you might think—I am not afraid now—but I was little fearful that you might think I loved you because you were rich, and—and—that's what I thought."

"You little goose ! As if I could ever think such a thing of an angel like you ! But if you have the slightest shadow of a fear on that account, you can get rid of it, for I am no longer my uncle's heir."

"Not your uncle's heir !"

"No, I have disinherited myself. It isn't often a fellow does that voluntarily," continued Jack, grandly, "but I've done it."

"On purpose ?"

"Yes, I've renounced all my prospects, or rather have declined them. You'll be happier, I hope, dear, without the money—that is, if I can do anything to make you so."

"Then you've given it all back to your brother ?"

"No ; some woman is to get it."

"Some woman !" exclaimed Barbara, surprised in turn.

"Yes, some woman—who, I have no idea, but I was expected to marry her."

" Expected to marry her, and without ever having seen her !"

" Yes, but of course I would not do it." Then Jack told how Mr. Oldmixon's will had made him only a contingent heir, how he had renounced the contingency, and how his uncle's estate would now go to the lady for whom he had been intended.

" And you don't know who she is ?"

" I have not the slightest idea."

" And you gave up all that large fortune for me ? Oh, Jack, how I do love you !"

" I'd renounce a hundred fortunes for you !" exclaimed Jack, magnificently.

" Oh, how I do love you for that !" repeated Barbara. " How very odd that your uncle should want to force you to marry a woman you had never seen !"

" Odd ! I think it was horrible ! He thought he could buy me with his money. I soon let him understand differently."

" Was he very angry ?"

" No, he was not angry ; he was grieved, sincerely grieved. I think he has a lingering hope that I will still marry her. You know I have up to a year after his death. If I don't marry her by that time she gets the estate."

" The horrid creature ! Do you think she's a party to the arrangement ?"

" I don't know. I shouldn't be surprised if she were. She's probably some woman he's been in love with, and who has rejected him."

" He said something to me about dividing his property between you and another. Then he changed his ideas and determined to give it all to you. I'm glad it's out of the way, Jack. We can do without it, can't we ?"

"Of course we can ; I can make all I want."

They were now near the gate that opened upon the lawn that surrounded the house, and looking in that direction they saw that Mr. Henschel was already at home, having probably taken a shorter path that led over the fields.

"Father will be glad to know that I am going to be your wife," said Barbara. "He likes you, Jack."

"Yes," said that young man, complacently, "I think he does."

"What do you mean, sir, by speaking in that self-sufficient manner and twisting your mustache in that idiotic way ?"

"I stole a march on you, Bab," he answered, laughing.

"Stole a march on me ! You don't mean to say that—"

"Yes, I do," he interrupted. "I spoke to him about you this morning before we went to church, and asked him to keep out of the way—"

"You arch hypocrite ! And what did he say ?"

"You know what he *did*. As to what he said, the general purport of it was that he would be glad to get rid of you."

"So you are a party to this nefarious scheme," she said to her father, as they entered the gate, and he came down the path to join them. "I should have thought that a man of your age— Oh, father !" she continued, as he clasped her in his arms and drew her to his heart, "I'm so happy ; I believe I loved him all the time."

" And now you *know* you do, Bab." He held out one hand to Jack while with the other he gave him Barbara's hand. " Take her, my friend," he continued ; " she's the greatest treasure I have in the world, but I think she's safe in your hands."

CHAPTER XX

It is safe to say that no three people in the State of New York that sat down to dinner that day were happier than our three friends.

Mr. Henschel was especially exuberant. He had had a bottle of champagne put into ice, and, in his old-fashioned way, he drank the health of Jack and Barbara and wished them many long years of happiness. It being Sunday, dinner, as was usual in the country, was early in the afternoon, and when it was over Mr. Henschel very considerately announced his intention of going to his own room and taking a nap. This gave Jack the opportunity he wanted to finish what he had to say to Barbara.

"I am bound in honor to tell her," he said to himself, "even if I knew she would break with me the next minute. I don't think she will," he continued, as he looked at her admiringly, while he followed her into the library. "She's such a sweet-tempered, charitable darling, that she'll probably feel sorry for me and love me, if possible, more than ever."

"What a good man your father is, Bab!" exclaimed Jack, as the old gentleman left the room. "I don't think I ever saw a finer specimen of nature's nobleman."

"For going away and leaving us alone?" inquired Barbara, laughing. "There isn't any hypocrisy about

13*

you, is there, dear ?　But he's everything that's good,
Jack—everything.　I should be a bad girl if I did not
recognize his goodness.　Of course you know that he's
only a Danish peasant, and I'm only a peasant's daughter."

"Oh," broke in Jack, "but such a peasant and such
a daughter !　Now sit down here, please, for I've a long
story to tell you—a sad story, a horrible story.　Nothing,
I trust, that will make you love me any the less, but
one that will grieve you, as the facts have grieved
me."

He made room for her on the sofa, as she took the
vacant place by his side.

"I am not afraid," she said, seriously, for she saw
that something of moment was coming, and her thoughts
turned on old Mr. Oldmixon, to whom she naturally
thought that what Jack had to say related.　"Perhaps I
can anticipate a part of what you are about to say—your
uncle is not well ?"

"No, he is not well ; but he is not, as you may think,
insane—at least, he is not a raving maniac.　I doubt very
much if he has been altogether sane since he was born,
but his insanity is not of the kind that overthrows the
reason, though it probably makes him do things that
otherwise he would not do.　It would be, I think, a very
difficult undertaking to attempt to prove in a court of
justice that Uncle Victor is insane.　There are hundreds
of his friends here who would come forward to swear
that they had never known a man with a more acute
mind, or one more capable of comprehension on a large
scale.　However, dear, what I have now to say is not in
regard to his mind."

He put his arm around her waist and drew her toward

him, so that her head rested on his shoulder, and then he began.

He told her of himself when a boy; of his uncle's treatment of him and preference for Hogarth; of his own early struggles and success; of his brother's marriage; his uncle's reconciliation; Mrs. Hogarth Oldmixon's death; his uncle's vision, or whatever else it was, at Saratoga; of his belief that his nephew was a murderer, and of his determination to bring him to justice. All this the reader already knows, and it is not necessary, therefore, to allude to it at greater length.

Barbara listened with the most rapt attention to every word, frequently interrupting him to ask pertinent questions, or to express her sympathy with Jack, as he disapproved of his uncle's course. When he had got through with the account of the conversation with his uncle at the Lucullus Club, during which Mr. Oldmixon had detailed the incidents of his vision, and declared his intention of going to Annapolis and of bringing Hogarth back into relations with him, Barbara's astonishment was at its height. She was not in the least degree superstitious. She did not believe in omens, or presages, or visions, or ghosts, or in lucky or unlucky days, but she was awed by Jack's account of his uncle's real or fancied experience on the lawn at Saratoga, and horrified beyond measure at the violence that the old man had exhibited toward his nephew.

"How prejudiced he is!" she said, raising her head from Jack's shoulder, for perhaps the twentieth time, to look into his face. "He is so different from you; you take after your mother, don't you, Jack?"

"Yes, I think I do."

"I'm glad of that; there's something very singular

about your uncle. I thought so when I first met him, and this impression was strengthened by our second interview, and now it is still stronger. How horrible that an uncle should be trying to fasten the crime of murder on his own nephew, and to say that he would like to see him hanged! And all because of his prejudice. I don't believe in his vision. I am sure he made it all up just to have some excuse for persecuting your brother, who, if wild, and not as good as he should be, is certainly not the wretch your uncle would make him out to be."

Jack was silent for a few minutes. He was a thoroughly generous and magnanimous young man. It was very painful to him to be obliged to say anything that reflected on his own brother, even though it were said to the woman who was now as near to him as was his own heart—the one that he had taken into his life as a part of himself, and with whom he hoped to live in happiness all the rest of his days. But he conceived that it was his duty to place her in possession of all facts that bore upon the character of the family into which he hoped, erelong, to introduce her. That family, he believed, was tainted with a tendency to insanity, and perhaps disgraced by an atrocious crime committed by one of its members. It might be that she, actuated by prudential motives, would prefer not to marry a man with such a family history as he had. He did not believe that she would take any such course with him, but it was possible she might, and, at any rate, the choice ought to be given her. She would love him all the more, perhaps, for his confidence in her reasoning faculties, even if she should repel with indignation the idea of separating from him.

" My darling," he said, as he drew her still closer to him, " you are so good yourself that it is impossible for you to suspect the existence of evil in others. It may be that a great crime has been committed. You shall hear what further I have to tell you, and then you will be able to judge for yourself.

" We went to Annapolis, as my uncle had arranged, and we stopped at the same hotel at which Hogarth and his wife had stopped. It was late when we arrived, so we did nothing that night toward the investigation of the matter of my uncle's vision ; but the next morning Uncle Victor went into the office, and I with him, and we had a long conversation with the clerk. Of course nothing was said relative to my uncle's suspicions. He told who he was—and the clerk had suspected that we were relatives as soon as he had read our names in the register—and of course it was natural that we should evince an interest in all the circumstances connected with the awful tragedy that a few days before had occurred at the hotel.

" We found at once that the sympathies of the clerk were strongly with Hogarth. Nothing, so far as we could learn, could have been more decorous than my brother's conduct on the occasion, and no one had ever shown more poignant grief."

" Oh, Jack, could he possibly have been guilty ?" exclaimed Barbara. " I cannot believe it ! It is too horrible a thought for me to conceive. It would have been such a monstrous and so utterly inhuman a crime that I cannot think it possible."

Jack said nothing in answer to this outburst of emotion, but as he went on his voice trembled and became more husky.

. " ' Did Mrs. Oldmixon,' asked my uncle, ' have no premonitory symptoms of disease ? Was she well all through that day up to the time of her death ? '

" ' They arrived here the night before,' answered the clerk, ' and ate a hearty supper. Mrs. Oldmixon expressed a desire to take a walk, and though it was after nine o'clock, her husband at once got ready to go with her. He was devoted to her. But then,' he added, with a smile, ' they had been just married. They were only gone a few minutes ; they had walked up to the church and then around the circle, and had come straight back to the hotel. It was all she saw of Annapolis, for the next day it rained in torrents.' "

As Jack uttered these words Barbara gave a start and turned pale. " Oh, Jack," she exclaimed, as she jumped up from the sofa in her excitement, " that is exactly as your uncle saw it in his vision."

" Yes, dear ; sit down and hear the rest."

" No, I cannot sit down ; I am too much excited. I must walk. Go on, please."

" As the clerk spoke these words, my uncle gave me a significant look, as much as to say, ' This is the first point.'

" ' May we see the rooms that my poor niece occupied ?' inquired my uncle ; ' we would like to spend a few minutes alone in them. It would be a melancholy pleasure for us to see the place where she met such an untimely death ! '

" The clerk called a servant. ' Show these gentlemen to No. 22,' he said."

" What !" said Barbara, " the same number that your uncle mentioned ! Oh," she continued, covering her face with her hands, " I know what is coming. It was true, everything was just as your uncle saw it! My poor Jack!" throwing her arms around his neck and bursting into tears as she lay on his breast. "I cannot tell you how much I feel for you, but you will know. And that poor woman! Oh, did he really kill her?"

Jack was too much overcome to answer. His voice was choked and the tears were streaming down his cheeks. The two "ninnies," some people may call them—but very human for all that; and is not the world mainly made up of "ninnies," in all their varieties?—stood for some time clasped in each other's arms. Jack did his best to soothe Barbara, and she was equally assiduous in calming him. The shock was over. She was in a great measure prepared for what was to come, and she had not faltered in her love, and, what was more, very evidently did not intend to falter. After a little while both became sufficiently composed to admit of the one telling the remainder of his story and of the other listening.

"We were shown up to the rooms, and, dismissing the servant, we entered. A glance was sufficient to show us, as we stood with the plans in our hands that Uncle Victor had drawn, that the rooms and the articles of furniture and the arrangements were exactly as we had them before us. There was the window at which Hogarth had stood, there the table in the centre of the room, there the chair in which his wife had been rocking herself, there every other article of furniture in the sitting-room, in the identical positions in which we had them on our diagrams.

"'It is the same,' said my uncle in a low but emphatic voice. 'Everything is, as you see, precisely as we have it here; and there,' he continued, as he pointed toward it, 'is the door through which he carried his poor wife to her death. Come, Jack,' he went on, 'follow me into the next room; there you will see the bed upon which he laid her, and the pillow with which he smothered the life out of her.'

"I went with him," resumed Jack, after there had been a little more comforting on both sides, "and there, sure enough, was everything exactly as we had it on our plans. Of course I was both astounded and horrified by the revelations of facts that were brought so vividly and truthfully before me. I did not know what to think. I had no precedent to which the experience through which I was then passing could be compared. I could only drop into a chair and cover my face with my hands so as to shut out the fearful images around me.

"But I could not dissipate the thoughts that were passing through my mind, or banish the picture of the awful deed as it had been described by Uncle Victor. Over and over again the scene was enacted before my mental eyes. I saw Hogarth standing at the window; then turn and seize his wife, his face distorted by the most frightful passion; then hurry with her to the next room, while she struggled to free herself from the grasp that she probably knew, from the look in his eyes, was meant to end in her death; then his throwing her on the bed and suffocating her with the pillow, without giving her the mercy of even a single breath. I trust I may never again have such images in my mind. They stuck to me for several days and nights, until I thought I should go wild. Indeed, my darling, it was the sight of your dear face yesterday in the car that finally sent them away, I hope, forever."

Barbara made the customary response to this state-ment, and, after a short delay, not improper under the circumstances, Jack again took up the thread of his discourse.

"My uncle acted with the utmost coolness and delib-eration; only once did he break down, and that was when he saw the bed upon which he firmly believed a murderous deed had been done. Then he fell on his knees before the bed and remained for several minutes with his head bowed upon it. Rising suddenly to his feet, he swore the most solemn oath, that there should be a life for a life, even if he himself had to be the avenger."

"I can scarcely realize it all," said Barbara. "It seems too horrible for belief, that your brother would commit so awful a crime. And I cannot and will not believe it. Is there no escape from the conclusion which at first sight appears to be the only one to be drawn?"

"Now, let us try and get the matter before us in a logi-cal way," said Jack, putting on an impressive manner. "My uncle describes to me rooms and furniture and arrangements, the ideas of which, he tells me, were given to him in a mysterious manner as he sat on the lawn at Saratoga. It would be too great a tax upon our faith in chance to say that the points of his vision and the actual facts as we found them at Annapolis agree merely through the accidental coincidence of a dream with reality. The items of agreement are too many for that alternative. So that, if we admit that my uncle told the truth as regards his vision or dream, or whatever else you choose to call it, we are bound to admit further that there is a strong probability of the truth of those parts that have not yet been confirmed."

" Yes, it would seem so."

" It is therefore, after all, a question of probabilities, and only of probabilities, even if we accept my uncle's assertions in their entirety. Nevertheless, the probabilities are so strong as to amount almost to a demonstration."

" I'm afraid that is so, Jack," replied Barbara, musingly.

" But now," continued Jack, becoming still more emphatic, " suppose that there is not a word of truth to my uncle's story, what then ?"

" Jack !"

" Yes, I say, suppose there is no truth whatever in the account he gave me, what then ? It was possible for him to have heard while he was at Saratoga of the death of Hogarth's wife ; to have gone to Annapolis, to have ascertained all about the matter—the rooms, the articles of furniture and their positions on the floors—to have taken the clerk into his confidence, and then to have come back to New York and to have concocted this story of a vision or of some other supernatural performance. I am sorry to say, from what I know of him, that I think he is entirely capable of doing all that for the purpose of avenging himself on Hogarth, who, he imagines, has terribly injured him."

" Is it possible, Jack, that he would commit so dishonorable an act ?"

" I think it quite possible ; though, at the same time, I am bound to say that I don't think he did. It is easier, however, for me to believe that such was his conduct than to believe in the story of the supernatural that he has related. It is only giving Hogarth the benefit of the doubt in a reasonable and just way ; and until I know that Uncle Victor did not leave Saratoga, and that he had no communication with Annapolis, I shall hold my belief in abeyance."

"That is right; we will not believe your brother to be a murderer till we have something more than your uncle's word for it—till, in fact, we have investigated him. Is that what you mean, Jack?"

"Something like that. I shall run up to Saratoga to-morrow and find out all I can in regard to his movements while he was there, and especially as to whether or not he left Saratoga at any time. If, as he says, he called out for help, the women that came to him will, of course, recollect the fact. Now, dear, I have only a little more to tell. We came back from Annapolis overwhelmed with the weight of the information we had obtained, but Uncle Victor was very quiet. He seemed to be lost in thought over what had occurred and in endeavoring to determine upon his future course. On our arrival in New York, he drove at once to his residence, making no allusions when we parted to what I knew was filling his mind, but merely requesting me to call and see him in the morning at as early an hour as possible. I went, and then he told me that he had written to Hogarth requesting him to let bygones be bygones, and to come and live in his house. 'You see, Jack,' he said, 'I know that he killed my poor Camilla, but my knowledge is not the knowledge for a jury. I'm going to wring the confession out of him, and to do that I am obliged to dissemble. Remember,' he went on, 'that, as I told you before, he's a basilisk, and the only animal that can destroy a basilisk is a weasel, and I'm the weasel in this case. The weasel, in the days when there were basilisks, made use of its cunning as its principal offensive weapon, just as it does now when it attacks chicken-coops. I have to do the same thing. If I did not, the scoundrel would escape me, and that he never shall.'

"It was in vain that I remonstrated; I left him more angry with me than he had been since our reconciliation, for I told him that I would not enter his house while Hogarth was there. I acted thus not only because my uncle was playing the part of a traitor, but for the reason also that I did not care to resume friendly relations with Hogarth after he had for so many years treated me with neglect and contumely."

"You were right, Jack dear," said Barbara, "both your reasons are good ones."

"Thanks! I am glad you think so. As matters now stand, Hogarth is apparently reinstated in his uncle's regards, and I am again discarded. I saw on the table the draft of what looked like a new will. He will execute this, show it to Hogarth, and thus, as he said, make him believe that he is the heir.

"That is all, my darling," continued Jack. "I thought it right that you should know that the family of the man that you have promised to marry is a tainted one, that the man's brother is suspected of having murdered his wife, and that he may end his days on a gallows. You may, therefore, if you marry me, live to see the day on which your brother-in-law will be hanged by the neck till he is dead. It is not a pleasant prospect," he went on bitterly, "and I should not blame you if, now that you know the truth, you should decline the honor of an alliance with a family with such a blurred escutcheon as ours."

Of course this was all talk on Jack's part. He knew very well that Barbara was not the kind of a woman to give up her lover for another's sins or crimes, but he wanted to receive the assurance of her devotion and constancy, and it is needless to say that he got them.

The next morning he escorted Barbara into town, and always afterward met her at the station and went with her to Mr. Maurice's studio, calling for her again in the afternoon and seeing her safely on the train. In this way he managed to meet her twice every day, to his and her unmitigated delight. On Saturdays he went to Lasata with her, passing Sundays in her company, and every day loving her, if possible, more devotedly than he had the previous day. It was determined that their marriage should take place early in the following March, and that the newly married couple should, as Mr. Henschel insisted, make the old manor-house their home. There was therefore going to be ample work for Barbara and her father in fitting up the additional rooms that would be required.

CHAPTER XXI.

"BY HEAVEN! THAT TOUCHED HIM."

Mr. Oldmixon sat in a revolving chair in front of a table loaded with books and papers. The room was his library, for Mr. Oldmixon was a man of literary and scientific tastes, which it was a pleasure to him to gratify, and which accordingly he did gratify to the extent of his power. He had always been a self-indulgent man, but as his tendencies had never been toward dissipation or immorality, the results of yielding to them had been favorable both to his mind and his body. At one time he had had serious thoughts of turning his attention to authorship, and many years before he is introduced to the reader had written several short stories and one novel. The former had, after some trouble in finding a medium for bringing them before the public, been accepted by a magazine which, a short time after publishing them, had gone the way of many of its predecessors, and been heard of no more. The channel for his lucubrations was therefore closed, and this fact had acted in so dispiriting a manner on Mr. Oldmixon, that he gave up authorship and turned his attention to reading and to the cultivation of gastronomic science. In order to indulge himself to the full in the new directions in which he had looked, he required two things—a library and a kitchen—and he had at once, with such knowledge of the necessities of the occasion as he possessed, and without advice from any one, set out to

supply himself. Relative to the library he knew tolerably
well what he wanted. The first thing, of course, was a
room ; and not having a suitable one in his house, he had
built an addition, which, when he had finished it and
stocked it with books to the number of over ten thousand,
he declared was the most complete private library for a
non-professional gentleman, such as was he, to be found
anywhere within the limits of the United States. "It's
not so big as some I've seen," he said one day to a distinguished gentleman to whom he was exhibiting his ac-
cumulations, "but it contains some of the rarest literary
treasures to be found on the earth. I never buy any edition of an old book but the first. I have seventy Elzevirs,
taller than any others to be found, and one hundred and
twenty-three vellum Aldine *editiones principes.* You
see, I've been all over the world ; I knew just where to
go to get my treasures. Do you see this Aldus?"

"What?" asked the distinguished gentleman, who had
been the governor of one of the States, and was then a
Cabinet Minister.

"This Aldus."

"I should call it a book," observed the distinguished
gentleman, taking it into his hands and turning it over
and over.

"Of course it's a book," said Mr. Oldmixon, in a tone
of disgust, "but it happens to be a copy of the first edition of Martial, printed by Aldus in the year 1501. As
you see, it's printed on vellum. It is one of five known
to exist, and it cost me just three hundred and fifty
dollars."

The distinguished gentleman threw up his hands in astonishment. "Three hundred and fifty dollars for that
little book ! What a waste of money !"

"Not at all, sir," replied Mr. Oldmixon, a little irritated by the disparaging speech of his friend; "books like this double in value every ten years. I expect to live twenty years yet, so that when I die and my library comes to be sold by my unappreciative heir, this little book will sell for exactly three thousand dollars. Not a bad investment, is it, even from your point of view? You wouldn't be likely to make as much out of a farm in Minnesota, would you? You've heard of Æsop, I suppose?" he continued, in a rather contemptuous tone.

"Oh, yes, the man that wrote the fables."

"The same. Well, here's a copy of the first printed Latin edition of his book. Look at it—look at it! Did you ever see anything more beautiful in all your life? What paper, what ink, what a register! Now, look at the colophon, and you will see that it was printed at Milan, in the year 1474—three hundred and two years before the Declaration of Independence, and more than four hundred years from this day."

"I can't read a word of it," said the distinguished gentleman, turning over the leaves, and laughing heartily.

"Of course you can't. There are two impediments to your doing so. In the first place, it's printed in Latin; and in the second place, it's printed in Gothic black letter."

"Very fine, I've no doubt, but I can buy a better copy for a quarter."

"If you wanted to read it, yes. But that copy cost eight hundred francs seven years ago. It's worth about fourteen hundred now—say two hundred and eighty dollars. But I see you don't appreciate these things. Here's a copy of Smith's 'Life of Andrew Jackson.' Observe the beautiful chromo-lithographs of the old hero," he went on, with an ironical expression in his voice that the distinguished gentleman, had he been observant, would have quickly detected. "See with what consummate skill the artist—printer I should have said—has colored the hair and cheeks and uniform of the gallant general! Is it not a beautiful production?"

"Splendid! I must have a copy of that. General Jackson has no more devoted admirer than myself."

"Take that copy, I beg of you. Smith presented it to me, but I shall feel highly honored by your acceptance of it, and," he added to himself, "I shall be devilish glad to get the vile book out of my library."

With his novel, however, Mr. Oldmixon had not been so successful as with his library. In fact, beyond the accomplishment of the work of writing it, he had not been successful at all. He had submitted it to a few literary friends, and they had unanimously decided against publication—one going so far as to say that he had never read a worse novel, unless it was "The Dwellers in Five Sisters' Court," that one Mudder had written. In such matters friends are very much like a council of war. The latter always advise against fighting, and the former always advise against publishing.

Then he had taken it first to one publishing house, and then to another, and each one had some reason for not desiring to bring it before the public, that the author was sure was eagerly waiting to snap it up, edition after edition. One thought it "too realistic" and another "not sufficiently realistic for this matter-of-fact world," while others simply sent it back with thanks, but regretting that their "readers" had advised against publication. One house had offered the use of their imprint, if he would pay all the expenses of publication, and give fifty

14

per cent of the retail price for their trouble in placing it in the market ; but this proposition Mr. Oldmixon had indignantly declined, saying that he was an author, not a publisher.

Then, declaring that the pirates—meaning thereby publishers—had entered into a combination to keep his novel from appearing before the world, he took his manuscript and locked it up, asserting that he would not look at it again for twenty years, and that then he should publish it without doubt, as all the houses that now refused it would be ready to tear each other's eyes out for the honor of having their firm-names associated with his.

But with his kitchen he was at first the recipient of more disappointment and misfortune than generally fall to the lot of a person that enters upon culinary operations. If he had known nothing about the theory of the subject, and had had the palate of a clodhopper, he would undoubtedly have gotten along very well ; but with the knowledge he had gained by reading, and by eating many good dinners in various parts of the world, and, above all, by the high state of development into which he had brought his gustatory nerves, his experience in the kitchen was at first anything but satisfactory. The man that does not know what good cooking is can always cook to suit himself. Mr. Oldmixon *did* know what it was, and hence his deficiency in technical knowledge was the cause to him of much vexation of spirit.

Nevertheless, he persevered, and at last hired a *chef* of the highest celebrity to give him lessons in the culinary art. The first step taken by this eminent possessor of the *cordon bleu* was to demand that a kitchen be built as an addition to the house, insisting that the basement hitherto used was altogether unfitted, by lack of air and light, for the occupancy of a true artist, such as he considered himself to be. Moreover, the library, a far less important affair than a kitchen, had had a building especially erected for it, and the department over which he was to preside should be equally favored. So, at an expense of several thousand dollars, an addition was built and was fitted up in accordance with the wishes of the gentleman who had condescended to act in the capacity of teacher to Mr. Oldmixon.

And a perfect affair of its kind it was, with its Parisian range, its bright copper saucepans, its marble mortar, and all the other utensils devised by ingenious inventors and needed for the various complicated processes necessary in the preparation of the delectable compounds that an advanced civilization has discovered. Here for three hours every day Mr. Oldmixon took lessons, until at the end of the year he had become as fully an accomplished culinary artist as the *chef*, his instructor. It was here, after he had acquired all that this eminent individual could teach him, that he had performed the experiments in gastronomic science that had given him such a high position with gourmands throughout the civilized world. It is scarcely necessary to add that it was here that he had developed the capabilities of the frog's liver, and had established the fact that at least a dozen wonderful dishes could be compounded with it for their basis.

As stated in the beginning of this chapter, Mr. Oldmixon was seated in his library in front of a table covered with books and papers. He was deeply engaged in perusing a voluminous manuscript that lay before him, and from time to time making corrections in its text. These latter appeared to be of a very extensive character, for not only did he erase and interline on almost every page, but not infrequently he cut out with a big pair of scissors large slips from the pages, and occasionally destroyed several pages in one lot, substituting new matter for that that he threw into the waste-paper basket. The twenty years had expired, and this was the novel that he had that long time ago laid aside, and which he was now revising, with the intention of again offering it to a publisher.

But he had very materially modified the determination which twenty years ago he had expressed. Then he had asserted that he would offer his book for publication on the termination of the period mentioned without the changing of a sentence, a word, or even a punctuation-mark, and that the fraternity that supplies the world with literary pabulum would eagerly strive for the honor of spreading his production over the land. He had, as I say, changed his intention, for now he was making alterations so extensive that it looked very much as though he were reconstructing the manuscript from the beginning to the end.

He had been engaged in this work since nine o'clock, and it was now nearly one. He looked at the table clock before him, and then, apparently surprised at the rapid flight of time, gathered his papers together, and putting them into a drawer, locked it and hid the key on one of the library shelves behind the books, or rather behind a particular book, the title of which he had in his pocket. He was obliged to resort to this mnemonic device, for his memory, as he advanced in years, was becoming treacherous. It now wanted five minutes of one. Mr. Oldmixon took up a volume from the table and began its perusal, seating himself in an arm-chair

big enough to hold two like him, and throwing his head
back till it was supported on the luxuriously cushioned
surface behind, at that angle that was most conducive
to the comfort of its possessor. Every now and then
he glanced at the clock, as though counting the minutes
that would elapse before some expected event. At last
the hands on the dial indicated one o'clock, and almost
at the very moment there was a knock on the door. Mr.
Oldmixon said "Come in," at the same time redoub-
ling his attention to the book he held in his hand, so that
the visitor had taken several steps into the room before
the old gentleman suddenly became aware of his presence,
and throwing the volume on the table, held out his hand.

"Punctual to the minute, my dear boy; that's what
I like to see. Your married life, short as it was, seems
to have improved you. Ah, my dear Hogarth, if she
had only lived, what a splendid fellow she'd have made
of you in time!"

"Yes, Uncle Victor," answered Hogarth, in tones the
lugubriousness of which would have moved an anchorite
to tears, and which really appeared to have that effect
on Mr. Oldmixon, as he hastily took out his handkerchief and applied it to his eyes—"yes, uncle, she is a
great loss to me. Although I think I appreciated her
while she lived, I never knew all that she was worth to
me till she was dead. I think if you had not again
taken me into your favor I should have terminated my
own existence."

"Ah! Well, well, death has to come in some form or
other to all of us, and those whom the gods love die
young. But don't talk of suicide! You make me
tremble, lest, in some one of your despairing moments,
you should be tempted to put an end to your existence."

Mr. Oldmixon was sitting in front of the mantel mirror, as was also Hogarth. By looking into the glass, the old gentleman could see the reflection of his nephew's face without appearing to be regarding it. In fact, he had arranged the chairs with direct reference to this matter ; and as he intended that every day at one o'clock his nephew should pay him a visit, he expected to be able to study at his leisure, and with the advantage of not being suspected, a face that he had resolved should be made to respond to the mental tortures he should inflict.

"I sometimes feel tired of life," said Hogarth, moodily ; "I had looked forward to many happy years of existence with the woman I loved, and then to have—"

"Yes, it is very hard," interrupted Mr. Oldmixon. "I wonder if she suffered much in dying?" he continued, looking into the mirror as he spoke ; "it is said that in some of these heart and lung diseases the agony is very acute. Now," he thought, "if the scoundrel has any feeling at all I shall perceive it."

But Hogarth remained quite unmoved under this attack. "I do not think she could have had any pain at all," he answered, coolly ; "she probably died in her sleep."

"I have just been reading here," continued Mr. Oldmixon, still looking in the glass at Hogarth, "that congestion of the lungs produces a sensation of suffocation, and from the little I know of that process it is painful. I was once nearly suffocated." "By Heaven!" he continued to himself, "that touched him." And it *had* touched him, for at the reference to suffocation Hogarth's face had become several shades paler, and he had moved uneasily on his chair.

" I did—did—not know that you had ever been nearly suf—suf—" he stammered.

" Suffocated !" exclaimed Mr. Oldmixon. " It is a rather difficult word to pronounce, but I never knew you to stammer before. You are weak and nervous, my boy. Say 'smothered' instead ; it is a good deal easier, and more appropriate. Yes, I was once nearly smothered."

Again Hogarth was moved. He glanced furtively at his uncle, and the corners of his mouth twitched a little, as though he were endeavoring to control himself.

He did not care to talk about the subject that Mr. Oldmixon had introduced, and yet he felt that if he did not ask for further information he would run the risk of exciting surprise in the mind of his uncle, and that this feeling might easily lead to the development of some other emotion—suspicion, perhaps. Still he remained silent so long that Mr. Oldmixon turned toward him, and repeated the assertion.

" Yes," he said, " I was once nearly smothered. Don't you care to hear about it ?"

" Certainly," answered Hogarth, with an attempt at a laugh, " although such things are not pleasant subjects of conversation. How was it ?"

" I was a young man at the time, not quite your present age, and was walking through a trench that had been dug for the purpose of receiving pipes for a water-supply. The sides were about eight feet high, and were not supported by boards, as they ought to have been. Suddenly one side caved in just opposite to where I was standing, and I was completely covered by the falling earth. I at once felt the most severe pain in my head, and at the same time a sensation of burning

in my chest, as though there was a fiery furnace there.
But these physical sufferings were nothing to what I
experienced mentally. I had the idea that some one
was sitting on my chest, and thereby preventing the
access of air! I thought I struggled with this murderer with all the strength I had, but I could not shake
him off. There he continued to sit, grinning with
diabolical malice at my feeble attempts to get rid of
him—attempts that I felt were every moment becoming more and more futile. Then I lost consciousness,
and when I came to myself I was lying on the bed in
my own house. Some men had seen the caving in of
the earth, and had come to my assistance. I was buried
nearly five minutes. The doctor said that a minute
longer would have been fatal, as there was no instance
on record of a suffocated person living five minutes."

Mr. Oldmixon spoke all this in an indifferent sort of
a tone, as though he were telling some commonplace
incident ; but he nevertheless did not fail to keep his
eyes on Hogarth through the medium of the mirror.
To his great disappointment, his nephew exhibited no
emotion whatever beyond a sort of languid interest,
perfectly explainable by the fact that the sufferer was
his uncle. He had recovered his composure. His mind
was now on the alert, and he did not mean to allow his
emotions to run away with him if he could help it. He
knew that this was his weak point, and that he had nothing to fear except from himself ; and he was aware of the
fact that if he wanted to prevent his exposure, he must
learn to restrain the manifestation of his feelings when
suffocation and smothering were the subjects of conversation. He was sensible that he had, when his uncle began to talk, allowed his face to express the fear he felt ;

but he did not believe that this had been noticed. The more he reflected upon the matter, the more he was convinced that his uncle could not possibly have any purpose in view not apparent in his words. Why should he have? What information could he possess relative to the crime that had been committed? All the knowledge of the act was locked up in his own heart, and there he intended to keep it. He was safe—absolutely safe, he thought, and he would show the world that he could talk of smothering with as composed an air as the judge on the bench or as the physician making a post-mortem examination.

"I am surprised," he said, with perfect coolness, "that you should have felt any pain. I have always been under the impression that that mode of death was rather pleasant than otherwise." Then, moved by a spirit of bravado that he could not resist, he added, with a little laugh, "If I were going to kill a man I think I should suffocate him."

"Or a woman?" inquired Mr. Oldmixon, with entire *nonchalance*. "Would you kill a woman in the same way?"

"Oh, yes, I suppose so," answered Hogarth, rising from his chair this time, for this blow was a little more than he had expected, and he felt that he must hide his face. "What would be pleasant for a man would be equally so for a woman. I hardly think that there is any difference in the power to feel in the two sexes."

"Probably not," said Mr. Oldmixon, dryly; "and I see, from a work on medical jurisprudence that I have here, that the post-mortem evidences of death from smothering—that was the word, I think, we agreed to use—are very uncertain, and that no positive opinion on the

14*

subject could be given by the most accomplished physician, unless he had some knowledge of the attendant circumstances. Therefore, my dear Hogarth, it would appear that you would choose well; for unless you had quarrelled with the lady or had done something else to excite suspicion against you, you would be absolutely safe."

Hogarth stood at the window, with his back to Mr. Oldmixon, while the latter was delivering these remarks, so that his face was invisible; but his uncle knew that this shot told, for he could see his whole frame tremble, his head fall toward his chest, and his fingers clutch spasmodically at the palms of his hands.

Hogarth was in reality completely stunned by this onslaught. He could not speak. He began to think that his uncle must have some knowledge of his crime, and already the idea suggested itself to him that if smothering were so safe an act for the criminal, why not try it on this man, who, purposely or ignorantly, was torturing his soul? It was a question to be deeply pondered. Certainly, however, this was not the time to make the attempt, when it was known to several persons that he was in his uncle's library. There was a time for all things, and doubtless there would be an opportunity for the deed he contemplated when it could be perpetrated without suspicion attaching to him.

As for Mr. Oldmixon, he sat and watched his nephew as he stood with his back to him. He saw the involuntary contraction of the fingers, produced by the emotion and the thought that at the moment swayed him. "The scoundrel is contemplating smothering me," he said to himself. "That is just the way his fingers twitched before he killed his wife."

CHAPTER XXII

MR. OLDMIXON's house was a large one, and there was, therefore, ample room in it for Hogarth. His uncle had given him the whole of the third floor, consisting of four large rooms, with their appurtenances.

No one could have been more surprised than was Hogarth when he received his uncle's letter, stating that he regretted that he had required his lawyer to write the communication that had been sent to Annapolis, that he should make a new will, similar in its provisions to the first, and that the change in his disposition had been effected by knowledge that had come to him that he had been mistaken in regard to certain circumstances that had influenced him to break with his nephew.

Hogarth had at once obeyed the command to call on him that Mr. Oldmixon gave, and also the further direction to live in the same house with him. The warmth of his reception convinced him of its reality, and he now saw his way clear to the acquisition of his uncle's estate, an event which, he was assured, could not be very long delayed. Certainly the old gentleman had begun to show within the last few weeks the inroads that his advanced age was making on his constitution.

" A month or two longer," thought Hogarth, as he looked at him, " and then all will be mine."

He had asked for no explanation of his uncle's course toward him. He was back in his old place, and apparently more fixed than ever, and that was enough for him. Inquiry might provoke discussion, and he was too wise a man to raise issues that were unnecessary and the outcome of which no one could predict. Things were well enough as they were, and he was one of those men that " let well enough alone." He had only been an inmate of his uncle's house two days when the interview, the particulars of which are given in the immediately foregoing chapter, took place. It was the first time that Mr. Oldmixon had opened his batteries, and, upon the whole, he was well satisfied with the result. He had made an impression on his enemy, and that, under the circumstances, was a good deal. However, he had done this with his small guns—guns that were not intended to do more than to harass and worry, without inflicting any serious damage. After he had bombarded with them for a few weeks, and had gotten his man into a state of semi-insanity, he would make use of his heavier ammunition, and he did not doubt that the result would be in accordance with his wishes. The climax would come. In what exact form, of course he did not know ; but it would be sufficiently decisive.

For a moment, occasionally, he felt some slight degree of pity for his victim. To be subject, day after day, to the influence of reminders of his crime, made in the most insinuating and apparently most innocent way, without the shadow of an object that could be perceived, was in itself a terrible punishment. Mr. Oldmixon was sufficiently well acquainted with the kind of nervous organization possessed by the Oldmixons—by all within his knowledge, except Jack—to know just what the effect of such continual reiteration would be. He had only to examine into his own nature a little in order to freshen his ideas on the subject and to convince himself that Hogarth had already begun to pay the penalty of his crime. Occasionally, as I have said, a little gleam of pity for his nephew would sweep through his mind; but one thought of what Camilla had suffered was sufficient to dissipate this feeling and to nerve him for fresh attempts in the direction of avenging her wrongs.

Several days elapsed after the incident recorded in 'the previous chapter before anything very notable occurred, though there was not one in which Mr. Oldmixon did not, though in the most ingenious and apparently unsophisticated way, make some allusion to suffocation as a means of causing death. Sometimes it was by one way, and sometimes by another.

"By the by, Hogarth," he said one morning, when they were at breakfast—he took his meals at home now, for Hogarth, not being a member of the Lucullus Club, could not enjoy the privileges of the institution—"did you read that account of the curious way in which a peasant in France killed his wife?"

"I suppose he suffocated her," answered Hogarth, crossly; "that mode of murder seems to be running in your mind pretty strongly now, Uncle Victor."

"It is, my dear boy, it is! But did we not agree that you should use the word 'smothered'? I remember that the first time I introduced the subject you could not readily pronounce the word 'suffocated.' Now you rattle it off as though you had been practising it. You didn't use to stammer before your marriage; but listen to my story. It certainly does present the most original method of smothering that I ever heard of. The man, a small farmer, quarrelled with his wife ; so what does he do but pick her up in his arms and carry her into the next room, where there was a corn-bin full of nice clean yellow corn, and plunge her head foremost into the mass of grain ! There he held her for five minutes, notwithstanding her struggles, and then, when he pulled her out, she was quite dead. Now, did you ever hear of such a mode of smothering a woman as that ?"

" No, no !" exclaimed Hogarth, roused to an emotion somewhat complex in character, for fear and anger and horror entered into its composition ; " I never did, and I never want to hear of such things again ; I am nervous and irritable, and not myself. I can't sleep ; my head is almost constantly aching ; my heart palpitates painfully under the least excitement—all, I suppose, caused by the death of my wife ; then these things that you are always talking about make me worse. I shall not sleep to-night, for seeing that man ramming his wife's head into the corn. I shall see her struggling limbs and her livid face when he takes her out of the bin. If I were well I should not care ; but till I get stronger, please, Uncle Victor, don't bring up such horrible subjects for con- versation."

" My poor boy," said Mr. Oldmixon, in a piteous tone of voice, " I beg your pardon ; I did not know that a subject so far removed from your life as is that of suffo- cation, or smothering, could cause you pain ; but I said nothing about the woman's face being livid ; what made you think it was livid ?"

" Oh, I don't know !" exclaimed Hogarth, wearily ; " it was only a guess ; her face may have been green, for all I know."

" Well, well, we'll not say anything more about it ;
let us talk of something more agreeable. I have my
will here in the drawer ; would you like me to read it to
you ?"

All this was more to Hogarth's liking than the subject
of murdering women by smothering them. He had an
intense degree of curiosity relative to the exact position
he occupied in his uncle's will.

He had not been able to obtain any information on
the subject, for his friend, Mr. Jeremiah Masters, upon
whom he had been accustomed to rely for information
as to what was passing in Mr. Ridley's office, had parted
from his employer, and had set up for himself ; and
there was no one else of whom he could make use. He
had been told over and over again by Mr. Oldmixon that
matters had been restored to the *statu quo ante bellum,*
but he did not know positively whether the will was
signed or not ; and until he possessed that knowledge
the matter of treating his uncle as he had treated his
wife could not come up in his mind for due deliberation
and final determination. Yes, he would like to hear
the will read ; but, at the same time, it would not be
prudent to display too much interest in its contents.

" Anything," he said, with a faint smile, " would
be preferable to the gloomy subjects that we have been
discussing ; but as to your will, uncle, you will do what
you think right, and I shall be satisfied."

" Yes, yes, of course ; but I think you might as well
know positively how great is my affection for you, and
how I have tried to show it in a practical way. Sit
down, then, my dear boy, and listen. This, to be sure,
is only the rough draft of my will ; and if you would
like to make any suggestions, I shall be glad to hear them.

I have such entire confidence in your good common-sense and ideas of justice.''

As Mr. Oldmixon spoke these words a tinge of sarcasm was apparent, or rather would have been apparent to almost any one but Hogarth. This young man was too greatly interested in the substance of his uncle's remarks to attend to the manner. The time had come in which he was to be made acquainted with his prospects for the future, and the character of those prospects was a subject of greater importance to him than any emotional expression that his uncle might choose to throw into his voice. If he had been a man of greater depth of character, he would have paid more attention to a feature that, more than the words themselves, shows a speaker's real thoughts.

'' I trust,'' he said, '' that you will never have cause to repent of your confidence. Doubtless you have heard stories to my disadvantage, and it is to them that I owe your disfavor of a few weeks ago. I am glad that, without any effort of mine, you saw that I had been wronged, and that of your own free and unsolicited will you rectified the injustice I was for a time made to suffer.''

'' Yes, my dear boy, that is all over. I am sure you are everything that is good and true. Now, there is Jack—''

'' Jack has no heart,'' interrupted Hogarth ; '' I have not forgotten the way in which he treated you many years ago. I suppose your recent experiment with him was not satisfactory.''

'' No, no ; it did not turn out well. We parted not such enemies as we were, but, nevertheless, we parted.''

'' He hates me as he does the devil.''

" Ha ! ha ! very good ; I wonder, now, if he *does* hate the devil."

" I mean," said Hogarth, laughing gayly, " as he ought to hate the devil."

" Oh, yes, of course, I understand," replied Mr. Old-mixon. " Now, here is the draft that I propose to send down to Mr. Ridley to-day," he continued, fumbling among some papers, and finally extracting one from the mass. " Give me your attention for a moment. It is short, and I think to the point."

" In the first paragraph I have given all my estate, of every kind whatsoever, to my beloved nephew Hogarth Oldmixon, and in the second I have appointed him sole executor. Now, what do you think of that ? Short and to the point, isn't it ?"

" You overwhelm me, Uncle Victor ; I can only hope that it may be many years before your will goes into effect."

" Thanks, my dear boy ; I know you are attached to me. Now," he continued, regarding Hogarth through the medium of the looking-glass, " I did think at one time of giving something to Jack—say a tenth part of the estate—enough to give him a support if he should become blind or otherwise unable to gain his living from his profession ; but—"

" You thought better of it," again interrupted Hogarth. " Jack is not capable of appreciating an act of generosity. He is not of an affectionate nature, and all he cares for in the world is himself. Self is Jack's god."

" Maybe, maybe!" exclaimed Mr. Oldmixon. " I'm not praising Jack ; I only thought that as he was my nephew and your brother, you might be inclined to urge

the putting of his name in the will.   But I leave it all
to you, my boy—all to you."

"Then I say no ; not because I am avaricious and
want all for myself, but solely because I know Jack is
not the kind of a man he ought to be.   He deserted you
while I stuck to you.   It would be a sort of a premium on
ingratitude.   Why, influenced by what I thought was
due to you and to myself, I stopped speaking to him
several years ago.   It would—"

"Say no more," broke in Mr. Oldmixon ; "it shall
be as you wish ; I was sure you would not be influenced
by any other feeling than a desire to do strict justice."

"Yes, that's it !" exclaimed Hogarth, taking eagerly
to the suggestion.   "If I looked at the matter from a
sentimental point of view, of course I should bear in
mind that Jack is my brother ; but this is one of those
subjects that sentiment has nothing to do with, and in
which impartial justice should be exercised.   From that
point of view I think it would be wrong to give Jack
one cent."

"I am sure you are right ; your instincts are those of
a born judge whose ideas are always on the side of right.
Now, will you be kind enough to take this down to Mr.
Ridley and request him to put it in proper legal form,
and to return it to me ?   Then, in a day or two I'll execute
it, and the matter will be off my mind.   I feel sometimes as though I should not live long.   You see, I am a
pretty old fellow, and my death may take place at any
moment.   In fact, I have a little difficulty of breathing
now," taking, as he spoke, his vial of the nitrite of amyl
from his pocket, and putting it to his nostrils—"a sort
of feeling of suffocation or smothering.   By the by, do
you know what burking is ?"

"No, indeed!" answered Hogarth, with a laugh. He was in great good-humor now, and felt inclined to be merry over everything. "How should I know? If I had your learning, I should be a much wiser man that I ever expect to be. What is it?"

"You see how my mind is running continually on one subject. I shouldn't be surprised if I became a monomaniac on it. There's insanity in the family, you know. Your father was certainly a lunatic, so was your grandfather, and so, also, was one of your aunts. I've been called 'queer' all my life. Now, there's Jack. He takes after his mother, and is level-headed, even if he is heartless and selfish, as you say. But to go back to burking. Burking is only another name for smothering. It is generally done by its perpetrators by simply putting the hand over the nose and mouth of the victim, so as to shut out the air."

"Smothering again!" gasped Hogarth, sinking into a chair, entirely overcome by the sudden revulsion of feeling that Mr. Oldmixon's words had produced. "Is that matter to be always on your mind, and are you always going to bring it up before me? My God! what do you mean?" he exclaimed, with sudden energy, springing up from his chair and approaching his uncle. "One would think that you are driving at me, and that you thought I had smothered some one. What do you mean? Tell me instantly, or—" He stretched out his hands as though to seize his uncle by the throat and force an answer out of him. The latter, who had also risen, stood by the side of the table, one hand resting carelessly on a little button raised about a half an inch above the surface of the green cloth, the other in his trousers pocket, apparently jingling a bunch of keys. Nothing could have exceeded the coolness and composure manifested by Mr. Oldmixon. He knew that Hogarth was entirely willing to strangle him then and there, but he was also aware that he himself held the trump card in the unexecuted will, and that all that was necessary was to bring Hogarth to a sense of that fact. Without, therefore, appearing to notice the excitement under which his nephew labored, he said, in the most unconcerned manner imaginable :

"Don't forget to see Ridley this morning, my dear Hogarth. I want to get through with that matter as soon as possible. You smother any one !" he continued ; " I'd as soon suspect the President of the United States of picking a pocket."

At the first words Hogarth's hands fell. It would not do to use violence yet. The will by which Jack got the estate was probably still in existence, and the new one was unexecuted. No, he must wait. Matters were not ripe yet for such extreme action.

"You irritate me very much, Uncle Victor," he said, in an injured tone of voice. "Your remarks are so pointed, that for the moment it seems as though you referred to me. Of course, when I come to reflect upon the subject, I know that my suspicions are unwarranted ; but reflection requires time. I am a very sensitive man, and my recent great affliction has made me still more so."

"I should not have told you what burking is unless you had asked me what the word meant. Did you never hear of Burke and his partner Hare, who, many years ago, made their living by suffocating people in the way I mentioned, and then selling the dead bodies to the medical colleges for dissection ? Read the 'History of

Burke and Hare.' I have it here, and will be happy to lend it to you."

" I do not want to read it ; it must be very horrible !"

" Yes, it is horrible," rejoined Mr. Oldmixon, shrugging his shoulders, " for all such descriptions excite the pity in a man's breast for the victims, as well as horror and detestation of the criminals. But if horrible to us when we simply read of the vile deeds, how much more fearful must have been the feelings of the wretches who murdered innocent people !"

" Yes," answered Hogarth, moodily, " they must have experienced that greatest of all mental torments—remorse."

" Of course—that is, if they had ordinary human emotions. Now, look at this portrait of Burke," taking up, as he spoke, the book from the table, and showing Hogarth the picture of a brutal-looking man. " Did you ever see a face so utterly devoid of the ' milk of human kindness' as that ? That man smothered about twenty people. He used a very simple process—only stopping the nose and mouth. Once, however, he put a pillow over the face, and that he thought was a better plan, as it prevented his seeing the last pleading look of the poor creatures. Yes," he continued, as though talking to himself, " if I were going to smother a person, especially a woman, I should prefer to cover the face with a pillow. I should not like to have that last look haunting my memory. Why, my dear boy !" as, looking at Hogarth, he saw his nephew standing erect, his eyes dilated, his hands outstretched, his lips moving, but no sound escaping, his face as pale at that of a ghost, and his mind apparently oblivious to what was going on about him. " Poor boy !" continued Mr. Oldmixon,

approaching the statue-like figure, " your troubles have
unnerved you ; come," laying a hand on his shoulder,
and shaking him gently, " rouse yourself. Your nerves
are indeed weak. Hogarth !" shaking him more violently, " what's the matter ? By Heaven ! I believe he
has a fit !" as his nephew remained rigid and unconscious, his eyes staring at vacancy. " Well, well," he
said to himself, " I must go a little more slowly. He's
not quite ready to confess yet, and I'm not quite ready
to have him die. I wonder how my nitrite of amyl
would do for him ?"

Mr. Oldmixon took the little vial from his waistcoat
pocket, and pouring a few drops on a handkerchief, held
it to Hogarth's face. Almost instantly the spasm re-
laxed, the extended arms fell, the stare ceased, and, with
a long inspiration, consciousness was restored.

" I had a dream, I think," said Hogarth, feebly, as
he lay down on a lounge, Mr. Oldmixon putting a pillow
under his head and giving him a glass of wine. " I don't
quite know what it was. My mind isn't clear yet, but I
thought I saw Camilla looking at me. Didn't you say
something about ' last looks ' ? I don't know—perhaps
I had better not talk till my mind gets clearer ; I might
say something that wasn't true, you know—something
that would do me harm. Of course dreams are not true.
Did I say anything ? If I did I take it back now. I—
I—" here his voice became inarticulate, and he fell into
a heavy stupor, from which he did not emerge for several
hours.

In the mean time Mr. Oldmixon called his valet to
look after Hogarth, while he, taking with him the manuscript with which he had been engaged just before his
nephew's arrival, went into a little room in which he

sometimes did his writing, and again busied himself in making alterations in the text of his novel.

Every now and then, however, he would stop, and, throwing himself back in his chair, indulge in serious reflections relative to the actual situation of the matter that so fully occupied his mind. Events were moving to suit him, and exactly as he had anticipated. He believed that Hogarth was on the verge of confessing, and that a little more torture would bring him to the speaking point.

"And he shall have it!" he exclaimed, rising from his chair and hurriedly pacing the floor; "I don't care about his speaking too soon. He hasn't suffered half enough yet. I'll bring him to the brink of acknowledging his guilt, and then I'll let up on him and give him a reviving inhalation, as the victims of bodily torture were brought back to consciousness by a restoring draught. I really thought I had lost him to-day.

"He came very near trying to kill me," he continued, after he had walked in silence. "One step farther, and I should have rung my electric bell and brought Thomas to the rescue. But pshaw! He will try nothing of that kind with me till the will is signed; and if I don't know enough to beat him at that game I'd better hang a millstone around my neck and throw myself into the river. If I, Victor Constantine Oldmixon, with the astuteness of the devil himself, can't get ahead of a clumsy knave like Hogarth, then there's no use in having brains.

"Poor Jack!" he went on, after another long pause; "I hope he knows that I haven't deserted him, and that nothing but a stern sense of duty would prompt me to have that beast—that basilisk—near me. Well, well, by

George ! I have almost forgotten my beauty, the most sensible woman I ever saw. Barbara ! What a pretty name ! I'll go and see her, and I'll let her into my confidence, as I did before."

He put his manuscript away, and going to his dressing-room, arrayed himself in the most unexceptionable attire for the street. Then he rang for his coupé, and after taking a look at Hogarth, who was still in a stupor and breathing laboriously, he ordered his coachman to drive to Mr. Henschel's.

CHAPTER XXIII.

HOGARTH HAS AN IDEA.

HOGARTH lay in a stupid condition till nearly four o'clock; then he began to regain consciousness. He sat up, looked wildly about him, put his hand to his head as though he might be endeavoring to recall the incidents that had brought him to his present condition, and then slowly arose to his feet. He staggered, however, and would have fallen if Thomas, who was on the alert, had not held him up.

"What a horrid headache!" he said, as the man assisted him to a chair; "can't you do something for me?"

"I don't know, sir," answered the man; "Mr. Oldmixon sometimes puts ice on his head when it aches. Shall I get some for you, sir?"

"Yes; break some ice and wrap it in a towel and put it on my head."

"I'm not clear at all," he said, after the man had left the room; "it seems to me that the last thing I recollect is that some one was trying to smother me, and that Camilla is somehow mixed up with it. I saw her face for one instant just before I covered it with the pillow, and I saw it again just now—just now!—my God, it is there before me at this moment! No," he added, more calmly, "it was only imagination. I can never see it again, and I never want to see it again—why, yes, there

15

it is !　It goes and comes like a hallucination, and that's
what it is, that's all—the last look given by a person that
is about to die, and given to the man by whom death is
coming !　I've seen it once, and, my God ! it seems as
though I could never again shut it out from my eyes.　I
was all right till I came to this cursed house to live, and
that fiend began with his devilish tricks.　I suppose it is
unintentional, or rather that he does it for his amusement, or perhaps simply from indifference to what I may
feel.　He cannot know anything ; that is impossible ;
and if he did, he wouldn't be such an infernal scoundrel
as to go to work deliberately to torture me in this way ;
no, he cannot know ; he cannot be unfriendly to me.　His
speech is kind enough, and then he shows his real thoughts
when he takes me back, invites me to his house, and
makes his will in my favor.

　" By Heaven ! the more I think of it the more I am
convinced that he is insane on the subject of smothering.
I believe he knows he is.　He hinted at something of
the kind just now.　I suppose if that is so that I shall
have to stand it for a while, till the will is signed, and
then—"　Again his fingers clutched at an imaginary
something, and were pressed convulsively against his
palms ; then they opened, and again closed, continuing
these movements for perhaps a minute, while he lay back
in the chair, with his eyes closed and his lips retracted,
so as to show his teeth.

　" Yes," he continued, after he had apparently exhausted the excitability of his hands, " I shall have to do it.
He has given me some valuable lessons, and, by God ! I'll
make use of them on him.　He's too uncertain a man to
be depended on.　He might change in a week over some
fancied insult or something else, and bring back that milk-

sop Jack. Well, I put a spoke in his wheel to-day, and
that's something. Ah! Thomas, here you are. Yes, that
will do; now put it on my head, and go and get me a
bottle of Vichy. You have Vichy in the house, I suppose?"

"Oh, yes, sir," answered the man, as he put the towel,
full of cracked ice, on Hogarth's head, making a kind of
skull-cap of it, and putting another towel around his neck
to absorb the water that ran down; "Mr. Oldmixon has
all the mineral waters; you can have any one you wish."

"I'll stick to the Vichy. I feel better already." As
the man left the room Hogarth got up and looked over
the papers on the library table till he found the rough
draft of the will that Mr. Oldmixon had left there. He
read it over very carefully several times. "Yes," he
said, as he folded it up and put it into his pocket, "it's
all right. I believe he's honest. It would be impossible
for him to do this if he knew anything, and was trying
to entrap me; he couldn't be such an infernal scoundrel!
I'll try and get used to his smothering mania, for that's
what it is, and the next time he mentions it I'll go him
one better. I'll tell a worse story than he can tell, and
I'll show him that I can play the game of bluff as well
as he. Thanks," as Thomas came in with the Vichy;
"set it down, and I'll help myself when I'm ready for
it. I feel pretty well now, so you needn't stay. Has
Mr. Oldmixon gone out?"

"Yes, sir; he went out an hour ago."

"Do you know where he went?"

"No, sir; but I suppose he went to the club."

"Oh, yes, I suppose he did. That will do. I'll go
to my room, I think, and get ready for a walk. If my
uncle comes in, tell him I shall be back in time for
dinner."

The man bowed and left the room, and Hogarth, after drinking nearly the whole of the bottle of Vichy, repaired to his bedroom, and began dressing for the street. He took off the brown velvet sack-coat that he generally wore when in the house, and was proceeding to put on a frock-coat of stylish cut, when a letter fell from one of the pockets to the floor. He stooped and picked it up, and immediately recognized it as the one that he had received from his friend Jeremiah Masters, informing him that Mr. Oldmixon had willed his property to Jack on condition that he should marry a lady unknown to the writer. Reading this letter again, his curiosity became excited as to who was the woman in whom his uncle took such great interest as to provide for her marriage to a man who was then his favorite nephew, and in case of his neglect or refusal to marry her, making her the residuary legatee of his entire estate. He had overlooked this circumstance, and the fact, now brought back to his recollection, gave him great uneasiness. He was by nature suspicious and prone to attribute concealed motives to persons with whom he had relations, so that it was not astonishing that the matter in question should have caused him additional discomfort. Had his uncle lost his interest in this woman at the same time that he had cast Jack off a second time? Would there be any such provision in the new will to be made in his favor? Why should there be this anxiety shown for her marriage, and this great consideration for her welfare by giving her nearly a million dollars?

He stood with his hand to his head, vainly endeavoring to answer these questions in a way satisfactory to himself. He was not yet quite restored to his normal condition. His head still ached with a dull, heavy pain, that rendered him, to a certain extent, stupid and incapable of grasping difficult questions like those that he had asked himself. Suddenly his face lit up with an expression that indicated that he had reached a solution of the matter. "By God!" he exclaimed, with all the emphasis of which he was capable, "I believe I've got it at last." The result did not, however, give him much pleasure, if a judgment could be formed from his countenance; but it certainly tended to quicken his movements, so that in a few minutes he had completed his toilet, and was on his way down-stairs to the library. "If my uncle were to die to-night," he said, as he went down the steps, "or if anything should prevent the execution of the new will, this woman, whoever she is, would get the estate. That is a matter for serious contemplation, and," he added, "for a little detective service. I must find out who this woman is; but how?" While still lost in the difficulties of this last interrogation, he entered the library, where he found Thomas engaged in removing the empty Vichy bottle and setting Mr. Oldmixon's table in order. "Perhaps," thought Hogarth, "this fellow may be able to give me some information.

"I suppose you never have lady visitors, Thomas," he said, "although, from the neatness that prevails over the whole house, I should think you had them very often."

"No, sir; I don't think any woman ever comes into this house except the laundress every week and the scrubbers every month."

"And my uncle, being such an inveterate old bachelor, visits no ladies, of course?" he said, interrogatively.

"Well, sir, I don't know about that," replied Thomas, with a grin; "Mr. Oldmixon's pretty well up in years now, but he likes a pretty face when he sees it."

"Oh, yes, of course! Every man does till the day of his death, if he lives to be a hundred. But he never took any decided fancy to any particular one, did he?"

"I ain't so sure of that neither," answered Thomas, still grinning with the consciousness of superior knowledge; "I guess there's one that he thinks a good deal of, but that's only a guess; and if he was to know that I'd said such a thing, he'd turn me off the next minute."

"Oh, that's all right! He'll never know from me; and besides," he added, laughing, "there's no great harm in a gentleman, even if he is seventy-five years old, admiring a pretty girl, is there, especially if the pretty girl admires him?"

"No, sir; no, sir; I guess there ain't no great wrong in it; but Mr. Oldmixon keeps this so mighty close that no one knows anything about it except Dan the coachman, and you couldn't get him to tell where he drove to if you was to prod him with red-hot irons, or give him a mint of money. Nothing ever has influence with Dan after Mr. Oldmixon tells him to hold his tongue."

"Well, Thomas, that isn't a bad trait in a servant; but in a little matter like this Dan might afford to be more communicative. Now, I want to play off a little joke on my uncle that I think will amuse him, and I'd like to know who the lady is that the old gentleman admires so highly."

"There ain't any use, sir, in going to Dan; nothing would make him open his mouth."

"Not even twenty dollars?"

"Twenty dollars!" exclaimed Thomas, with strong contempt in his tone. "No, sir, nor twenty times twenty, nor twenty times that. You see, Dan's lived with

Mr. Oldmixon over forty years. He gets the biggest wages of any coachman in the city, and Mr. Oldmixon's already given him two thousand dollars, which pays him more than a hundred a year from a mortgage that he put it in. But that ain't all. Last New Year's day he gave Dan a hundred dollars, and told him that if he was his coachman next New Year's day he'd give him a thousand more. Now, you see, all that keeps Dan's mouth shut. Then, besides, he's nearly Mr. Oldmixon's age, so that there's a fellow-feeling between them."

"So you think it's no use to try to find out anything from Dan?"

"I don't think anything about it, sir; I *know* it ain't no use. But," continued Thomas, who was under no such bonds to keep silent as was Dan, and who coveted the twenty dollars and doubtless more that Mr. Hogarth seemed disposed to give for information that would enable him to get off his little joke, "I know a point or two about that little affair as might lead, if you worked it well, to your knowing all about it."

"How's that, Thomas? I'll give you twenty dollars now for your 'point or two;' and if they lead to certainty, I'll make it a hundred more."

"Well, it's just this. Dan let out quite accidentally that Mr. Oldmixon was at a bird-stuffer's talking with a young lady once for half an hour, and once for an hour or more. But the minute I asked him what bird-stuffer, he was mum, and I couldn't get a word more out of him. Now, I know Mr. Oldmixon brought a stuffed canary bird home with him one day, and he's got it now in a silver box locked up in that old Dutch cabinet over there in the corner. Now, sir, while the silver box was being made for that bird, he kept it under a glass shade on that table there, and I've seen him kiss it two or three times when he didn't think any one was around."

"That's very strange," thought Hogarth; "I wonder if that can be the same bird that escaped from the window opposite, and that flew in here. Why should he have it stuffed? And why should he kiss it? Doubtless because that woman stuffed it. Now, who the devil can she be?

"You have no idea what bird-stuffer did the work?"

"No, sir; but it can't be very difficult to find out, for I think the same one—and she's a woman, that I know—did an animal for Mr. Jack."

"Oh, that's it, is it? But how do you know that the bird-stuffer is a woman?"

"How do I know it, sir!" exclaimed Thomas, as though there was in the question an imputation on his ability to acquire knowledge, "well, sir, I know it because she was here in this very room."

"In this room! Why, not ten minutes ago, you told me that no woman ever came here but the laundress and the scrubbers."

"So I did, sir," said Thomas, a little abashed, "but that was before—before—"

"Before I had promised you twenty dollars," interrupted Hogarth, with a laugh.

"Yes, sir."

"Well, now that you know what I'm going to do for you, I suppose you'll tell me all you know?"

"Yes, sir. The young woman came here with a sort of an animal she'd stuffed for Mr. Jack—one that he brought home with him from Canada."

"So she stuffed something for Mr. Jack, did she? Go on."

"Yes, sir, and she thought he lived here; she had lost the direction he gave her, and then she looked in the directory, and she came here, thinking this was his house."

"Well, and what did she say or do after she came here?"

"Not much; I didn't know that it was worth while to ask her any questions, or, of course, I could have got out of her all I wanted to know. I'd like to see the woman I couldn't get around when I tried," he added, complacently.

"You didn't find out her name?"

"No, sir, for I didn't think it was of any importance to know; but she's the one that Mr. Oldmixon spent so much time with, and she stuffed them two things, the bird for him and the badger—it looked like a badger—for Mr. Jack."

"How do you know that she stuffed the bird for my uncle?"

"Because it was on the table when she came here, and she saw it, and I asked her if she had stuffed that bird, and she said she had."

"That seems pretty straight," said Hogarth, as though speaking to himself. "Here, Thomas," he continued, addressing that individual—"here's your twenty dollars. Now, I've only got to find out where she lives, and that completes the affair so far as the identification goes. Can you give me no clew?"

"Oh, yes, sir! She told me she was in partnership with her father. Now, here's a business directory; look through it for the bird-stuffers, and note them that has partners. Then go to each one in turn till you find it. You can do it with a cab in an hour. Or I'll do it for you, sir, if you

15*

like," he added, having in mind an amplification of his
bonus.

" Yes, that will do exactly. Give me the book."

Taking the volume from Thomas, Hogarth turned to
the page containing the list of all the taxidermists doing
business in New York, and ran his eyes over the column.

" There are only three with more than one person in
the firm," he said ; " there's ' Tophan & Byles,' ' Jones
& Williams,' and ' Thomas Bangs & Company.' "

" That's it !" exclaimed Thomas ; " you see, it can't
be either of the others, for the names are different, and she
said she was in with her father. ' Thomas Bangs &
Company '—I'll bet that's the one."

" Seventy-three Lake Street," continued Hogarth,
reading from the directory. " Go down there this evening, Thomas, while we are at dinner ; and if she's the one,
leave a note on my dressing-table."

" There's something going on here that I don't understand," he said, as he walked down Fifth Avenue ; " if
anything happens before the new will is signed she gets
the money, unless Jack marries her, and then he gets it.
If she was to marry me now she couldn't marry Jack, and
that would cut him out altogether, and I'd get the estate
almost as completely as though he had willed it to me
direct. It's a complicated business, and I don't quite see
my way clear. I'm afraid the old man intends to do
something, and that this draft of a new will is all a sham.
One thing is certain : if he was to die to-night and I was
her husband, she'd have the money, and that would be the
same as if I had it. There's no getting over that. By
George !" as an idea suddenly occurred to him, " I'll go
and see Masters—five o'clock," taking out his watch and
holding it contemplatively in his hand. " It's rather

late to go down-town, and it's rather early to find him at
home. I'll risk it." He put his watch into his pocket,
and crossing the street at Madison Square, took a cab from
the stand there, and told the driver to go to 107 East
Henson Street.

"I ought to have gone to Masters long ago about the
matter," he said, as he took out his cigar-case and, lighting a cigar, lay back in the vehicle and smoked, more for
the sake of the company the act gave him than from any
other gratification. "He's a bright man in such things,
and he's a friend of mine too. Besides, he's not troubled
with scruples when his interest is at stake. Neither am
I under like circumstances."

It took but a few minutes to reach Mr. Masters's residence. It was a house that had once been occupied by
people of a good class, and was in a street that had once
been respectable, but which was now filled with all descriptions of disreputable and semi-disreputable persons,
who carried on various kinds of business that, if not positively unlawful, required the constant vigilance of the
police to keep them from becoming so. No. 107, in
which Mr. Masters lived, was on one side bounded by a
low concert and drinking hall and on the other by a
swindling policy shop and gambling establishment, fre-
quented habitually by the worst characters that a large
city like New York is able to produce.

The house had that dilapidated appearance that is so
characteristic of New York houses when they begin to
decline in respectability. Hogarth ascended the front
steps, which were already showing signs of a departure
from the degree of rectangularity that well-ordered con-
structions of the kind exhibit. He had some little difficulty in ringing the bell, and then, when he finally suc-

ceeded in producing a faint sound, was forced to wait several minutes and to pull the handle repeatedly before he heard the footsteps that announced the coming of some one to open the door.

"I'm sorry to have kept you waiting," said the slovenly and otherwise unprepossessing woman who let him in; "the girl is out on an errand, and I was up-stairs attending to my brother, who is not well to-day. Do you wish to see him on business, sir?"

"I did wish to see him on a matter of business," said Hogarth, "but since he is not well, I will call again. Please give him this card, and ask him to send me a line telling me when and where I can see him."

The woman took the card, and looking at it, exclaimed, "Oh, you are Mr. Hogarth Oldmixon! He'll see you, I am sure. Just step inside and wait in the parlor till I tell him you're here. Things don't look very nice," she continued, as she ushered Hogarth into a shabbily furnished room, "for Jeremiah's sickness has prevented me looking after matters. Take a seat, please, and I'll let him know at once."

Hogarth sat down on the hair-cloth-covered chair that she pushed toward him, and endeavored to amuse himself till Miss Masters returned by looking around the room. There was nothing, however, to attract his attention, not a picture, not a book, not an ornament of any kind. There was a white marble-top table, a hair-cloth sofa, four chairs of the same description, an ingrain carpet, and that was all. Fortunately for his peace of mind, he did not have to wait long, for in two or three minutes Miss Masters re-entered the room, and informed him that her brother would see him at once. Hogarth followed her up one flight of stairs and into the room in which

Mr. Jeremiah Masters sat, arrayed in a gaudy dressing-gown, and, like his sister, presenting a decidedly unkempt appearance, and looking, besides, as though he had just got out of the tumbled bed that occupied the greater part of the room.

"Leave us, Belinda, please," he said, addressing his sister; "Mr. Oldmixon probably wishes to consult me upon matters of private business. I didn't want to miss the chance of seeing you," he continued, after the lady had departed, "for I thought, from the fact of your coming here, that something important might have occurred. Am I right?" He looked sharply at Hogarth as he put this question, and then, without waiting for an answer, went on:

"I woke up with a horrid headache this morning, and didn't go down to the office; but I don't know any man whose affairs want looking after as much as yours do, and I am perfectly willing to devote my time, sick or well, to your service. Now, is there anything special?"

"Yes; I have the rough draft of my uncle's new will in my pocket, and I'm to take it to-morrow to Mr. Ridley to have it engrossed into proper form. Would you like to see it?"

He handed the paper to Mr. Masters, and the latter read it over two or three times.

"It seems to be sufficiently explicit," he said, as he handed it back to Hogarth. "I have known cases, however, in which the lawyer drawing up the will had received private instructions to leave out some requisite feature, so as to make the instrument invalid. The testator in such a case makes a great show of executing a will, for the purpose of deceiving interested parties, while all the time there is another will, properly drawn and executed, hidden away, to be brought out when the proper time comes."

" Do you think my uncle would do that with me ?"

" I think your uncle is so entirely unscrupulous that he would do whatever he wanted to do."

" But with what object ? Men don't become reconciled with nephews they have discarded and in whose favor they have made new wills for nothing. And as to motive for so much hypocrisy, I don't see it. Do you think he is a man to act the liar and the traitor simply from the love of evil ?"

Mr. Masters, before answering this question, stroked his chin with each hand alternately, as though, by thus stimulating the cutaneous surface of that part of his body, his thoughts would follow more rapidly. It was not a nice-looking chin. It was unshaven, and it was unclean, and it was misshapen ; but the gentle friction produced by its possessor's fingers appeared to excite the necessary cerebral action ; for after about two minutes devoted to this process, Mr. Masters spoke :

" Do you think you know your uncle ?"

" Do I think I know him ? Well, I ought to know him, seeing that I've lived in the same house or in intimate association with him almost ever since I was born."

" You might easily do that, and still not know Mr. Oldmixon. To my mind, he is the most secretive and the most unknowable man I ever saw. Where is the old will ?"

" I don't know. Perhaps it's destroyed."

" I know it isn't destroyed. At least, it was in existence at this time yesterday, for I saw it."

" You saw it ! Where ?"

"I was in Mr. Ridley's office; he had sent for me in regard to a case that he had when I was with him and that I understood. I saw a copy of this very draft that you have on his table, and I saw the other will there too. That will at this moment is worth all the rough drafts in the world."

"Are you perfectly familiar with the terms of that will?" asked Hogarth, anxiously.

"Perfectly."

"But you don't know the name of the woman to whom the estate goes in case Jack does not marry her?"

"No; the name was left blank."

"Then I am wiser than you, for I know."

"You do! How did you find out?"

"By a process of reasoning from certain premises. She's a bird-stuffer, and her name is Bangs."

"It may be," said Mr. Masters, reflectively; "Mr. Oldmixon, I know, had at about the time the will was drawn up some dealings with a taxidermist."

"Yes; she stuffed a canary bird for him."

"True; I recollect now. I heard him speaking of it to Mr. Ridley and extolling the workmanship. But are you sure of the name?"

"Not entirely, but I shall be by to-night. Everything, however, points to Miss Bangs as the legatee."

"You'd better go and marry her; for, as sure as I believe in the existence of the world, I don't believe that Mr. Oldmixon intends to make a new will."

"What makes you think so?"

"My general knowledge of his character, which tells me that when he makes an ostentatious show of doing anything he generally means to do the very reverse. The suddenness with which you were called back after I had heard him denounce you as the greatest scoundrel the world had ever produced, and when nothing had occurred to cause him to change his opinion ; the fact that your brother Jack and he are on the most affectionate terms with each other, while he pretends to you that he has quarrelled with him.''

" You don't say that he and Jack are friendly !'' exclaimed Hogarth, rising from his chair, and pacing the floor hurriedly.

" Yes, I do ; they met at Mr. Ridley's yesterday, and were discussing this very matter of the will.''

" Then the old villain means to play me false ! He has some devilish scheme on hand that I have not fathomed. Is there no way to be even with him ?''

" I can counsel you to nothing unlawful. But there is no reason, so far as I can see, why you should not marry the girl. She knows nothing about being Mr. Oldmixon's heiress, and your brother has refused to marry her.''

" Jack has refused to marry her ! By Heaven ! why have you kept this from me, when you must have known how anxious I was on the subject ?''

" Because, my friend, I am engaged in making my living by practising the profession of the law. There are matters that I am going to give you the right to use for a consideration, and that consideration is the sum of one hundred thousand dollars, to be paid to me within thirty days after you marry the heiress.''

" But you have told me, and I can use them for nothing.''

" Oh, no ; for unless you sign this little document to the effect that, for value received, you promise to pay, thirty days after sight, to Jeremiah Masters or order, one hundred thousand dollars, value received. I shall immediately inform your uncle of this interview, and notify Miss Bangs of your designs. Sign it, and we are friends, and you shall have my best services ; refuse, and your game is at an end."

Hogarth was no fool. He saw that he was in the power of this man ; so, after some further conversation, he signed the note, and prepared to take his departure to begin the operations upon which he trusted for success.

" There's one thing more I'd like to know," he said, " and that is, why Jack refused to marry the girl ?"

" Because he's in love with another woman. I heard Mr. Ridley and Mr. Oldmixon talking it over ; and though your uncle regretted the fact, he declared that it should not cause him to change his will. In fact, it's the girl he wants to have the money, and neither you nor your brother."

" I wonder why he takes such an interest in this woman ! Do you know ?"

" No, I don't."

" I believe she's his mistress."

" I think you are mistaken."

" I'll probe the matter to the bottom. But I'm ready to marry her. I'm not squeamish."

" I'm sure you're mistaken."

" There's nothing else that could account for his interest. He simply wants to provide for her handsomely, and get her a husband at the same time. Jack has found out his little game, and has refused. *He* is squeamish, but *I*'m not. So long as she's to have nearly a million dollars I'll take her, even if I have to father a lot of bastards into the bargain."

CHAPTER XXIV.

Mr. Oldmixon was in great good-humor, and as he drove down the street on his way to the house where he had last seen Barbara Henschel, he fairly chuckled with delight at the success that he had thus far obtained from his procedures against Hogarth. It may as well be said here that Mr. Jeremiah Masters was entirely right in his suspicions relative to Mr. Oldmixon's contemplated action. That gentleman had not the most distant idea of making another will. The one that Mr. Ridley had in his fire-proof and burglar-proof safe was exactly in accordance with his wishes, as much so as when he had signed it. To be sure, Jack's refusal to marry the woman he had selected for him had discomposed him somewhat; but he had reflected that, after all, his chief object was to give the estate to Barbara, and that if Jack did not choose to share it with her, or rather to get it for himself, the loss would be his.

Then he reflected that the end as regarded his scoundrelly nephew Hogarth was approaching very rapidly. The constant iteration and reiteration of the same subject was beginning to affect the fellow. At first he had disregarded it; then he had attempted to brave it out with a bullying air; but at last he had succumbed, and henceforth the contest would be all on one side.

As he thought of the matter he endeavored to form

some idea of the manner in which the climax would appear, and he came to the conclusion that it would be in the form of insanity. Already he saw indications of the approach of that disorder, and these occurring in a person so strongly predisposed by hereditary tendency as was Hogarth appeared to him to point, with irresistible force, to the speedy advent of a condition the existence of which in his nephew would be an ample atonement for the crime he had committed.

"It's about the worst thing that could happen," he said to himself, as his coupé rolled down Fifth Avenue, "but not a bit worse than he deserves to receive at my hands, and I don't mean to let up a bit. He shall have the full measure to which his crime entitles him, and if he dies in a lunatic asylum well and good.

"What a mean, contemptible dog he is! See how he tried to cut off poor Jack without even a dollar! And he's getting dangerous too. He would have killed me if it hadn't been for the hold of the will that I have over him. He's not going to kill the goose that lays the golden egg. Not a bit of it!

"Jack's a stupid fellow, if he is a great painter," he continued, the idea being probably excited by the fact that, looking out of the window of the coupé, he saw the "Vandyke," where Jack had his lodgings and studio near by in a cross street. "Here's the prettiest and the best girl in New York offered him for a wife, and he refuses her as though she were an Irish bog-trotter or a German sausage-maker. She's too good for him. I wonder who the devil he's after! If he isn't entirely caught, I wouldn't despair yet of bringing him to Barbara Henschel's feet. I'll have to let them see each other. If he once gets a good look at her and hears her talk and sees her smile she'll fetch him, as sure as my name's Old-mixon. By George! I must bring it about some way or other."

The coupé here turned out of the avenue, and after going a few blocks stopped in front of the late residence of Mr. Henschel and his daughter. Externally it looked just as it did when Mr. Oldmixon last saw it, for he did not raise his eyes sufficiently to observe that the sign was changed. He entered the front door and encountered Peter, who was engaged at the desk behind the counter making up his accounts for the week, and looking not very cheerful over the array of figures.

" I would like a few minutes' conversation with Miss Henschel, please," said Mr. Oldmixon, putting on his most seductive expression and assuming his most dulcet tones.

" Well," rejoined Peter somewhat sulkily—for the information given by the figures was still working on him—" you'll have to want at present, I guess."

" What do you mean?" inquired Mr. Oldmixon, less suavely.

" I mean that, as Miss Henschel isn't here, it stands in reason that you can't talk with her now."

" Not here !"

" No ; she's left here, she and her father, and devilish sorry I am too."

" Well, my friend, I'm sorry also ; and as ' misery loves company,' suppose we sympathize with each other, and that you put me on equal terms with yourself by telling me all you know about her disappearance. Why she went, where she went, when she went."

This speech put Peter into a better humor, and he proceeded, with much verbiage and circumlocution, to

put Mr. Oldmixon in possession of all the facts connected
with the transfer of the business and the change of residence of the Henschels that were within his knowledge,
ending with the statement that since they had retired
from the establishment the orders for work had fallen off
to such an extent as to make him seriously apprehensive
for the future.

Mr. Oldmixon was surprised to hear of the departure
of his friends, but the place to which they had gone was
not so far distant as to render it difficult to reach them.

"Miss Henschel's in town every day," resumed Peter;
"she's taking lessons in sculpture from Mr. Maurice.
It's easy enough to find her, however. You can get out
either at New Rochelle or at Mamaroneck. The first's
a little nearer to their house, but the other's more convenient for some reason or other. I'd like to go up myself some day, to see if I can't get them interested in the
business again."

"I don't think you'll succeed. She's got too much
talent for taxidermy, and ere long will astonish the world
with her work as a sculptor."

"Yes, that's so, I believe," said Peter, with emphasis.
"But," he added, bending over toward Mr. Oldmixon
and speaking with all the earnestness of which he was
capable, "do you know what's going on?"

"I haven't the slightest idea."

"Well, there's a firm here in the same business, by the
name of 'Thomas Bangs & Company,' composed of father
and daughter; and the girl has been going round claiming
that she did some of the best work that Miss Henschel
did. Of course she lies about it; but exposing liars is
hard work unless you turn your whole attention to it."

"What's that? You don't mean to say that this

Bangs girl asserts that she mounted certain specimens that were in reality mounted by Miss Henschel ?"

" Yes, I do. That's exactly what I mean to say. You recollect that canary bird that Miss Henschel mounted for you ?"

" Certainly I do. I am not likely to forget it, I think."

" Well, she has circulated a story that she mounted it, and she's got a good deal of work through the falsehood too."

" You don't tell me so ! Where does she live ? I'll go straight there and denounce her. The horrid huzzy ! How dare she attempt to filch the reputation of the most accomplished taxidermist that ever lived !"

" She lives not far from here, in Lake Street ; but it isn't worth your while to go after her, for she's a perfect termagant, and would just as soon attack you with a broomstick or throw a pail of dirty water on you as not. No, sir ; let her alone. Of course she can't play that game long without being found out."

Mr. Oldmixon looked at his faultless coat, trousers, and waistcoat, and arrived at the conclusion that it would not be expedient to expose them to the danger of being ruined by the viragoish Miss Bangs. He declared, however, that he would have a lot of notices printed informing the public that his bird was mounted by Miss Henschel, and would hire a boy to stand on the pavement in front of the Bangs establishment and distribute them to the passers-by. This idea struck him as a particularly brilliant one ; and after chuckling over it with great delight, quoting several proverbs and other wise sayings that reflected upon the wickedness of stealing a person's reputation, he made a note of the railway stations nearest to the Henschels' residence, and then took his departure.

On the pavement, before getting into his carriage, he looked at his watch. It was twenty minutes of five o'clock. Doubtless Barbara had left Mr. Maurice's studio and had gone home. How would it do for him to go to New Rochelle that evening? He stood for a moment, apparently undecided what to do. Then, telling his coachman to drive rapidly to the Grand Central Railway station, he entered the carriage, and pulling down the blinds, gave himself up to the thoughts that the occasion suggested.

In the first place, he was determined that if possible he would see Barbara that night and tell her of the plans for her enrichment and marriage that he had formed. He would also inform her of his suspicions against his nephew Hogarth, and of the scheme for rendering him insane that was then being carried out in apparently the most successful manner. And, above all, he desired to ask her advice in regard to another matter that he had in contemplation. He had the utmost confidence in Barbara's good sense and independence of character. She had aided him materially in his other difficulties, and he resolved, as he lay back in his carriage, his mind undisturbed by the crowds on the streets or by the scenes constantly to be witnessed in the thoroughfares of a large city, that he would implicitly follow her advice in all the affairs that he intended to submit to her judgment.

Arriving at the Grand Central station he ascertained that a train would leave at five o'clock, but that he could not get back that night unless he was content to stay no longer than half an hour at Mr. Henschel's country residence. He knew that it was about three miles from

either New Rochelle or Mamaroneck, and he was not
sure that he would find a carriage at either place to take
him to his destination. Still he resolved to risk it ; so,
sending word by the coachman that he would not be at
home to dinner, and finding that he had but three minutes to spare, he bought a ticket for New Rochelle and
entered the train.

It was half-past five when he arrived at New Rochelle,
and quite dark. He saw, however, to his great satisfaction,
that there were a number of carriages at the station ; but
upon inquiry he found that the hackman he was about to
engage knew nothing of the Henschels. As the reader
is aware, Mr. Henschel and his daughter always made use
of the Mamaroneck station in going to or from Lasata,
and this was three miles farther on. However, he at
last found a man who professed to know where Mr.
Henschel lived, and who did, after a good deal of bun-
gling, finally succeed in finding the place. Looking at
his watch, Mr. Oldmixon found that he would have but
about half an hour to stay, and then, if he wished to
catch the last train for the night, he would have to take
his departure. He was quite sure that this would be
altogether insufficient for him to say all that he had to
say to Barbara, but he hoped to be able to continue the
conversation the following day at Mr. Maurice's studio.

Telling the man to wait for him, Mr. Oldmixon entered
the grounds surrounding the house. There were lights
in several of the rooms, but the curtains were drawn,
and he could not see in, though he tried his utmost to
get a glimpse of the interior of the front room on the
left of the entrance, in which there was a bright light,
but over the windows of which curtains of some thick
material hung. Finally he rang the bell.

In a short time it was answered by a neatly dressed housemaid.

Now, Mr. Oldmixon did not wish to see Mr. Henschel, but he judged, very properly of course, that it would be more in accordance with the rules of propriety for him to ask for that gentleman than to request to see his daughter. He did not suppose that Mr. Henschel would make any objection to Barbara seeing him in private on receiving an intimation that such an interview was desired. His age, he thought, was sufficient warrant for requesting such a privilege. Still, when he was informed that Mr. Henschel had gone to New Haven, and would not be back before half-past seven o'clock, he was not at all distressed.

"Is Miss Henschel at home?" he next inquired.

"Yes, sir; walk into the parlor. Who shall I say called?"

"Here is my card," he said, opening his pocketbook and looking in its compartments for a piece of pasteboard with his name on it. "No, I have no card," he continued, as he did not find what he sought. "Tell her, please, that Mr. Oldmixon would like to see her."

At the name the woman started; but as Mr. Oldmixon had turned to go into the parlor he did not observe her surprise. The only "Mr. Oldmixon" she knew was Jack—a very different looking personage.

Barbara, who had not long since arrived home, was in her own room dressing for dinner when the maid entered with the exclamation, "O Miss Barbara! there's a gentleman down-stairs who says he's Mr. Oldmixon."

"Mr. Oldmixon!"

"Yes; but he's not our Mr. Oldmixon. He's old enough to be his grandfather, I think."

16

"Oh," said Barbara, with a smile, though at the same time her heart sank within her, "I know who it is; say I'll be down in a few minutes."

Yes, her heart sank within her, for the idea at once occurred to her that Mr. Oldmixon had called to remonstrate with her for becoming engaged to his nephew; perhaps even to denounce her for having inveigled the young man into her matrimonial net, to the great detriment of his worldly prospects. How he had discovered the matter she could not imagine, for Jack, who had escorted her to the Grand Central station, had told her—almost the last thing he had said—that he had not yet informed his uncle of what had taken place between himself and Barbara, but that he intended to do so on the following day. In some way or other, however, the secret must have reached him, and he had come here, possibly to entreat her not to interfere with the plans that he had formed for securing Jack's happiness, and failing by persuasion to move her, to fulminate his wrath not only against her, but against his nephew also.

Believing all this, Barbara saw that the situation was going to be a trying one; and knowing as she did Mr. Oldmixon's impetuosity and unreasonableness, she recognized the fact that she would require all her strength of mind and powers of resistance to withstand his assaults. She had plenty of courage, and she was fully resolved that nothing he could say should cause her to yield one iota unless it was supported by a message from Jack. If *he* desired to be free he should be, so far as she could give him freedom. That alternative was, however, one that did not cause her a moment's uneasiness. Not much over an hour ago he had given his views on the subject of constancy in a manner so emphatic that their expression carried conviction to her mind so strongly that nothing that the uncle could say would shake her confidence in her lover.

She looked very lovely as she went down the broad old oak staircase to the room below. She wore her hair as usual, very simply arranged, and her dark brown cashmere frock, trimmed with knots of dark blue ribbon, became her wondrously well—fitting her as it did to perfection, and setting off her tall, lithe, and well-developed figure as scarcely any other color or material could have set it off.

She nerved herself for a long and a severe contest as she turned the knob of the door, and then she stood before Mr. Oldmixon.

The old gentleman had evidently been on the watch for her, for he was standing in the middle of the room, facing the door. As she entered he advanced as rapidly as his not very active legs permitted, and holding out his hand, said :

" My dear Miss Henschel, how delighted I am to see you ! First of all, however, tell me that you pardon my intrusion on your leisure and privacy. Till I obtain your forgiveness I shall not feel that I have any right to be here. But you are so kind and gracious that I do not despair. You are one of those of whom Madame de Staël spoke,

'Whoe'er feels deeply, feels for all who love.' "

Barbara perceived before Mr. Oldmixon had spoken half a dozen words that she had altogether mistaken the object of his visit, and that whatever that object might be it had no reference to the matter that was nearest her heart. Indeed, she discerned, with the penetration that bright women generally possess, that he had come for some purpose of his own, and that she was again to be called upon to act as adviser.

" I am very glad to see you again, Mr. Oldmixon," she said ; " I have often wondered what had become of you, and I should have been still more anxious if—if—"

She was going on to say " if Jack had not kept me advised about you," when she reflected that the time had not yet come for any reference to Jack, so she ended her remarks by asking him to sit down.

" I have been quite ill, Miss Henschel," continued Mr. Oldmixon, after he had made himself comfortable in the large arm-chair that Barbara selected for him, and she had taken one immediately in front of him, " and I have had a good deal to trouble me. My poor Camilla died only five days after her marriage. Died, did I say ?" turning toward Barbara and speaking in a whisper, though a loud one—" she was murdered !"

" Oh, Mr. Oldmixon, are you sure of that ?" said Barbara, who, as the reader knows, had been told by Jack of all Mr. Oldmixon's suspicions and of their verification. It was about the only thing she could say without betraying her knowledge.

" Absolutely certain," replied Mr. Oldmixon, with all the impressiveness he could muster. " It was

> 'Murder most foul, as in the best it is,
> But this most foul, strange, and unnatural.'

Fortunately, I know who is the criminal, and it is of him and his punishment that I come to speak to you—among other things—to-night.

> ' Murder, though it have no tongue, will speak
> With most miraculous organ ! ' "

"Oh, not to me, Mr. Oldmixon!" exclaimed Barbara, with something of horror in her voice; "surely you can advise with others on such a subject to more advantage than with me. I am a woman, and should not have such matters brought before me. I cannot—"

"For Heaven's sake, Miss Henschel, hear me!" said Mr. Oldmixon, excitedly. "You are the only one, man or woman, to whom I can go with confidence that I shall get what I ask for—sincerity. I am very unhappy. I wish—I wish—that I had never been born."

Here Mr. Oldmixon "went to pieces," as the saying is, and wept and sobbed with a violence that alarmed Barbara. What was she to do? She knew the whole story as well as he knew it, and to have him go through all the harrowing details was more, she thought, than she could bear. But here she was in the presence of this sobbing, sorrowing old man, who had come for the purpose of pouring all his woes into her ear, and he was the uncle of the man she loved, and who loved her! Barbara was a woman of decision when circumstances required promptness of mental action. She never lost her presence of mind in the face of danger nor the ability to reason with clearness in situations characterized by great emotional disturbance. It was at such times, too, that the frankness and truth of her disposition came out with most distinctness. She was not one to evade an issue or to cover it up with a mass of verbiage meaning nothing; but she met it without reserve, candidly, and with such artlessness that all interested perceived that she was abandoning herself to the dictates of her own unsophisticated nature.

Her mind was a comprehensive one, and took in at one view all the points of the matter before her. This

old man, now convulsed with excess of emotion, was
Jack's uncle. He was seventy-five years of age. He
was entitled to be treated kindly and without hypocrisy
or deceit, even of that passive kind that is manifested by
silence. Surely she could be ingenuous and outspoken
with him, obeying the dictates of her heart whithersoever
they might lead her !

CHAPTER XXV

"STOP, IF YOU LOVE ME!"

"I know all about it," she said, gently, and with that sweet inflection in her voice which, more than mere words, expresses sympathy and sincerity. "What do you wish me to do?"

"You know all about it!" exclaimed Mr. Oldmixon, dropping his hands from before his face and looking at her with the utmost astonishment depicted on his countenance.

"Yes," softly and with downcast eyes.

"What do you know? Who told you anything?"

"I know of your vision or dream, or whatever else it was that you had at Saratoga; I know how completely it has been verified, and—and—" still more softly and sweetly, "Jack—I mean Mr. John Oldmixon told me."

"Jack! my nephew, Jack Oldmixon! You don't mean to say that you know him?"

"Yes, I know him."

"You know him!" exclaimed Mr. Oldmixon, rising to his feet and approaching her. "Are you going to tell me that, O Barbara!" laying his hand on her head. "Is it possible that you—that you are the woman that Jack loves, and that I've been such a damned old fool as not to see it!"

She raised her eyes to his ere he had finished speaking,

and the smile that had before made Mr. Oldmixon her
slave was again on her face.

"Yes," she said, "I—I think I'm the one."

"Excuse me for swearing before a lady. I don't
think I ever did such a thing before, and you are the
one that I respect and—and love more than any other
that I ever saw; but I was so overwhelmed with joy at
hearing of the consummation of my dearest hopes, that
the oath slipped out before I knew it. My dear, dear
child, I am, next to Jack, the happiest man in the
world. How did it happen? Tell me all about it."
He started off to pace the floor at his fastest gait, and
had crossed it several times before Barbara began to
answer him.

"I don't think Jack could help it," she said—and
now the reaction set in, after the way with nice women,
and tears filled her eyes—"and I know I couldn't;
for I tried my best not—not to love him."

"You're a dear, sweet girl! I never did such an act
of self-denial in my life as when I selected you for Jack.
It went hard with me, but I did it, and, my dear, before
God, I believe he's a good man, and that he will make
you happy. If I had been forty years or even twenty
younger, I would have seen him in the lowest section
of purgatory, or even of a still more uncomfortable
place, before I would have given you up."

"It was very funny," said Barbara, who had during
this speech recovered the sunniness of her disposition,
"that you and Jack should have so misunderstood each
other, when one word from either would have made everything clear. To think," she added, with a happy smile
that lit up her face with a radiance that would have
captivated a much less impressionable man than was

Mr. Oldmixon—"to think that you should both have meant me, and that each one should have thought the other meant some one else!"

"Yes, it was very remarkable; and yet, when I come to think of it, not so very odd, after all. Men are such stupendous asses! They so rarely confide in each other; and then young men are still more asinine. The chances are a thousand to one that if I had told Jack that I had discovered an angel that I wanted him to marry, and that her name was Barbara Henschel, he would have turned up his nose and have said, 'No, thank you, I prefer Miss Bangs.'"

Barbara laughed merrily at this. "Where did you ever hear of Miss Bangs?" she said. "She was my rival in taxidermy."

"Yes, I know; that is why I happened to hear of her; she is claiming to have done some of your best work, and is, as the present proprietor of your late business told me, injuring his establishment by her lies."

"Oh, well," answered Barbara, "such conduct can be only temporarily successful; but what a despicable creature!"

"Yes, yes," said Mr. Oldmixon, absently, as though his thoughts were on something else. "It is very strange, very strange," he continued, as if speaking to himself; then he drew a long breath and looked around the room with a puzzled and somewhat wild expression on his countenance.

For a moment Barbara was alarmed. The light from the lamp on the table fell upon his face, and she saw the change that had come over it. Then when Mr. Oldmixon the next instant took the little vial of nitrite of

16*

amyl from his waistcoat pocket and held it to his nostrils, she felt reassured, for she had seen him before in similar attacks, and the inhalation of the medicine had always appeared to give him relief.

"You are not ill, I hope, Mr. Oldmixon," she said, as she rose and stood by his side. "Can I do anything for you? Will you have a glass of wine?"

"No, no; it is nothing, I assure you, but I have just had another most remarkable experience. There's been no one else in this room since we came in?"

"No, no one."

"Not Miss Bangs?"

"No, certainly not Miss Bangs."

"Well, while you were speaking just now of Miss Bangs's conduct, I thought I saw her talking to my man Thomas. They did not appear to me to be in this room, although I asked the question in regard to her, for I thought that if she *had* been here the fact would constitute a basis for what I imagined I saw. She and the man seemed to me to be talking together in a shop, not unlike the one you had. There was a counter at one side of it and cases around the walls containing mounted specimens of animals."

"That is a description of their shop."

"Yes, so I suppose. The girl was stoutly built, had black eyes and hair, and was greatly over-dressed. Around her neck she wore a heavy gold or yellow metal chain, and she had large earrings of similar metal in her ears."

"As well as I recollect, that describes Miss Bangs. But I have only seen her once, and that was over a year ago. You probably have had a short dream."

"No, it was not a dream; it was just like my experience at Saratoga, though shorter and less vivid. I saw the two distinctly, but, as on the other occasion, I could not hear a word. Do you believe in the possibility of my sitting here and seeing what is going on in Lake Street, in New York?"

"No; I do not believe in what are called supernatural occurrences; and for you in this house to see what is going on in New York would be supernatural."

"Yes, judging from the standpoint of the little that we know of nature's laws. But there may be natural events which occur so seldom and only to certain persons that we regard them as supernatural simply out of our ignorance. If I did not really see Miss Bangs and my man Thomas talking together, how could I have described the place and the lady so accurately? For to my knowledge I have never seen her or her shop."

"I do not know, but it is possible that you have been in the shop, and that you have seen Miss Bangs, and that talking of her to-day with Peter and then again with me, and perhaps having some ideas of her running through your head, you had the hallucination of seeing her. This house was supposed by the whole neighborhood to be haunted, and the most wonderful and apparently direct stories were told of the ghostly inhabitants; but we have never seen or heard anything of them. Dr. Maddox helped us to get rid of them by showing us how to improve the drainage."

"Then you don't believe in what the Scotch call 'second-sight'?"

"I am not sure that I know what it is," answered Barbara, laughing; "but if it means sitting in this room and seeing a man and a woman talking together in Lake

Street, in New York, nearly twenty miles from here, I certainly do not believe in it."

"Well, well, I was hoping that you believed in it, for it appears to my mind the only explanation of my vision at Saratoga, all the particulars of which were confirmed by my visit to Annapolis. Except one," he added, after a moment's pause, "and that will be verified, I think, within twenty-four hours."

"Dr. Maddox would probably be able to explain it to you. He has given great attention to such subjects. It takes very little in some people to cause hallucinations."

"Yes, but this was not a hallucination, for it was verified. Hallucinations are false. This was real."

"I do not know enough of the subject to be able to talk about it, but I can conceive of a train of thought originating in your mind and giving a corresponding character to the hallucination. Were you never in Annapolis?"

"I thought until a day or two past that I never had been there, but I have discovered that I was in the place about thirty years ago. I found a note addressed to me there by a lady whom I knew; and then the fact of my having stopped at the very hotel at which my Camilla was murdered came to my mind. I'm quite sure, too, that I occupied the very room that she did."

"And you knew when you were sitting on the lawn at Saratoga that your nephew and his wife had gone to Annapolis?"

"Yes, I knew that they were probably there at that moment, but all my knowledge cannot account for my seeing him kill her."

"No; but that has not yet been verified. You do not

know that he did. I wish," she added, " that you could get the idea out of your mind. Think what an awful thing it will be for you to discover ! Is it not better to remain in ignorance or doubt, rather than to confirm your suspicions against a man who is your nephew and —and Jack's brother ?"

Now, Mr. Oldmixon had come to see Barbara with the intention of discussing this very point with her, and more than half inclined to yield to the suggestions or entreaties that he felt sure she would address to him. But, like Pharaoh, his heart had been hardened, and the process of induration had been brought about by the real or imaginary sight of Thomas and Miss Bangs conversing together, in the reality of which he fully believed. He was just as sure that, on his return home, he would extract the truth from his man as he was of his existence. Furthermore, although he had had no supernatural evidence of the circumstance, he was confident that Hogarth and his man were in collusion, and that the former had, under the idea that Miss Bangs was the woman to whom his uncle had devised his estate, conceived a purpose of marrying her. This latter notion had entered his mind while he was in the shop conversing with Peter. At first he had rejected it, but it had forced itself, or been forced so strongly upon him, that he had at last accepted it as true, and all the way out to New Rochelle he had been thinking it over as an event that would not be at all displeasing to him. He chuckled to himself at the thought that both his nephew and Miss Bangs would be punished by such an act, and he determined that, so far from doing anything to prevent it, he would facilitate its consummation by every means in his power. There was only one thing that was likely to stand in the way, and that was the fact that in all probability matters with Hogarth would be brought to a crisis long before a marriage between him and Miss Bangs could take place.

No, he would not relax in the severity of his method with his murderous nephew; not even Barbara's efforts to induce him to be merciful should be successful. He would go on till the wretch confessed, and then the further consequences might be what they might be; he would not regret them.

It did not take a tenth part of the time to determine what answer to give Barbara as it has taken me to write the account of the mental process by which his conclusion was reached. He rose from the chair as he spoke, and looked at his watch.

"Good Heavens!" he exclaimed, "I have been here nearly half an hour, and have barely time to catch the train. Barbara, my dear—I may surely call you Barbara, now that you are going to marry my dear boy—I shall see Jack to-morrow, and tell him how nicely we have been brought to an understanding. As to the other matter, if Hogarth is innocent his innocence will appear; if he is guilty, he will deserve all he can receive in this world or in the next. Good-by; God bless you, my dear." He held her hand in his, and drawing her toward him, kissed her forehead. Then he turned away, and was going to leave the room when a thought occurred to him that caused him to retrace his steps. He came closer to her and spoke almost in a whisper, though with great energy and distinctness.

"That's a bad woman," he said, "that Bangs girl. Hogarth has got an inkling of the contents of my will, but he has made a mistake in the woman. He thinks I have made her the heiress of my estate, and he intends to marry her if he can."

"But how do you know all this?"

"I don't know. It all seems to come to me as a kind of inspiration that I cannot explain, and, after all, it may be only a guess. I shall find out the truth as soon as I get home; for Thomas is a great coward, and I shall make him tell me everything he knows."

"Oh, yes!" exclaimed Barbara. "Find it out, and then save her from such a marriage if there is any danger of it."

Mr. Oldmixon looked at her very sharply for a moment before he spoke.

"That's a very creditable notion of yours, my dear," he said at last. "All women should be merciful, especially to their own sex. But this girl is a mean, contemptible, dishonest, unscrupulous, and degraded person, who is altogether unworthy of your consideration. She has been stealing your reputation and lying like a Turk to advance herself at your expense. She's entitled to no mercy, and, by Heaven! she shall not have any. She shall marry Hogarth. I'm going to do all in my power to help the match along. No, no!" as Barbara attempted to speak, "she shall have her reward. Good-by! Another minute and I'll miss that train. I'll be up again in a few days;" and he was gone without giving her the opportunity of saying a word.

Barbara stood for a moment undecided what to do. Then she ran down to the door and called after Mr. Oldmixon, but the carriage was driving rapidly away from the house, and he probably did not hear her voice. Doubtless he would not have returned even if he had heard her. More than ever before did she recognize the

fact that his mind, if not positively deranged, was
certainly a very different one from any other with which
she was acquainted. His likes and his hates were equally
powerful ; he was as unscrupulous in his way as he
thought Miss Bangs to be, or even his nephew Hogarth.
In the accomplishment of his ideas of revenge or punishment he stopped at nothing. He was, she thought, a bad
man. She did not want his money, and she resolved
that if, by any chance, it came to her direct—and she
could not get it unless Jack were unfaithful to her, and
that was an impossibility—she would give it away to
some charitable institution where it would serve in
some measure as an atonement for the sins of its former
possessor. As it was, she resolved that she would beg
Jack to refuse to be his uncle's heir unless he at once
renounced all his schemes against Hogarth and Miss
Bangs. And furthermore she determined that she
would see that young woman in the morning and put
her on her guard against Hogarth. She had never made
Miss Bangs's acquaintance, and from what she had heard
of her, did not wish to do so. But she reasoned, if Miss
Bangs was the quintessence of vulgarity, and if she had
been mean enough to claim as her own, work that she
had not done, it was no reason that she should be inveigled into a marriage with a man whom everybody
united in regarding as thoroughly wicked and disreputable. Miss Bangs's offence had been committed against
her, and it was for her to resent it, and not Mr. Oldmixon, who, she perceived, was more anxious to spring
a trap on his nephew than to further the ends of justice.

She thought she saw, too, that Mr. Oldmixon in all
things was morbidly anxious that his plans should
succeed, and that this was the chief, if not the only

motive that prompted him to favor her marriage with
Jack. He had seen her, had taken a fancy to her, and
had then, without consulting her, set about to arrange
for her marriage with a man she had never seen. The
more she thought of this matter, the more indignant she
felt at the liberty he had taken. True, events had
moved in accordance with his wishes, but, she thanked
God, entirely independently of any agency of his.
When she had discovered that she was the woman that
he wished Jack to marry she felt glad, especially for her
lover's sake, that a possibly disturbing factor had been
taken out of their path. She had perceived rather the
ludicrous side of the situation to the exclusion of other
and more important points. Now, however, reflection
was coming to her aid ; and as she walked up and down
the long parlor, and bent her mind to the consideration
of the issues before her, she felt annoyed with herself
that she had not seen more deeply into the subject at
first, and given Mr. Oldmixon some knowledge of the displeasure she felt at the liberty he had taken in attempt-
ing to dispose of her in marriage without her consent.

But Barbara was not one of those persons that see
only one side of a question. She believed that Mr.
Oldmixon really liked her. Whatever might be his
reasons, the fact was undoubted. She felt kindly toward
him for this. It was her nature to try to like those that
liked her. Besides, he was Jack's uncle, and as such
entitled to her prepossessions and to all the respect that
she could conscientiously give.

And one point had more influence with her than any
other. The more she saw of Mr. Oldmixon, the more
she was convinced that he was not entirely responsible
for his actions. She believed that he could control

them within certain limits, but that after a time the impulse to persevere became overpowering; his ideas were then to him imperative conceptions that he could not resist, and which carried him along in spite of the efforts he might make to break from them. From this point of view he was more to be pitied than blamed, but she did not lose sight of the fact that there was a time when he might have controlled them, and when he wilfully allowed his evil impulses to govern him.

As to his pretended visions or second-sights, or whatever else he choose to call them, she did not believe in them at all. She perceived that there was a certain basis of reality about them that was clearly the result of vivid recollections that had faded from his mind. She saw, too, that he was full of suspicions against those persons he disliked, and especially against his nephew Hogarth, whom he evidently thought was capable of any atrocity that could be conceived by the mind of man. Endowed with high imaginative powers, he had engrafted on his recollection of localities, such as that of the hotel at Annapolis and Miss Bangs's shop, some one of the many fancies that were continually forming in his brain, and had adopted it as truth. "Perhaps," she thought, "it may be that his intuitions—as I have heard they sometimes are in insane persons—are wonderfully acute. I do not know that they could be so penetrating and exact as to indicate to him not only the fact that his nephew Hogarth murdered his wife, but also the way in which he did the deed and all the steps of the procedure; but it may be possible. I cannot tell. If it should turn out that he is right, it will be very wonderful; but till I know that his nephew is a murderer I shall try to keep my judgment in reserve. Thus far nothing has been established by either of his visions that might not have been based upon actual knowledge. Yes, there is one thing : it was a clear day at Saratoga, and he saw it raining at Annapolis at the time of Mrs. Oldmixon's death, and it *was* raining. But this," she added, after thinking for a moment, " may have been a coincidence. It would be very horrible if he should drive Hogarth to confess ; and oh !" she went on, clasping her hands together in her excitement, " how infinitely more horrible it would be if he should, by his persistence, make an innocent man insane, and drive him to the confession of a crime he never committed !"

Once this idea had found a lodgment in her mind she experienced an impossibility of getting rid of it. She was sure that she had arrived at the correct view of the result of the mental tortures that Mr. Oldmixon was inflicting upon his nephew, but she did not see her way clear to helping the sufferer. She had every reason for believing that he was a bad man. Enough was known of him from evidence that was indisputable to satisfy her on this point ; but notwithstanding this fact she felt that her sympathies were strongly exercised in his favor, and that it was her bounden duty to do what she could to save him from the fate that was impending over him. Of course she thought of interesting Jack in some scheme that they might both agree upon and that would be calculated to circumvent his uncle's machinations. And, above all, she must warn Miss Bangs of the plot against her.

Mr. Henschel came home in time for a late dinner, and then Barbara, who had no secrets from her father, told him of Mr. Oldmixon's visit, of the nature of her conversation with him, and of the fears that she entertained. Mr. Henschel was, in his way, as straightforward as his daughter was in hers, and his advice was that she should write a letter to Mr. Oldmixon, in which she should unburden her mind of what was on it, and appeal to him to allow Hogarth to rest in peace. She wrote the letter that night. It was long, and covered every part of the matter with that thoroughness that only those who know what they want to say and know how to say it are able to exhibit. Among other points that she brought forward was one that related to the policy of Mr. Oldmixon's course. "What advantage," she wrote, "can it be to a family to let the world know that it has a murderer among its members, and to incur the odium that attaches to a public trial and a shameful death on the gallows? You may talk to me of the virtue of a Brutus who could condemn his own son to death; but, then, Brutus was a judge charged under his oath with the administration of the law. Even in his case I think he would better have shown his humanity by resigning his office and leaving to some other less interested magistrate the awful duty that he took upon himself. But you have no excuse for your conduct. You do not know that your nephew is guilty, but you have started out for the purpose of proving him so by his own confession, or at least of making him confess, no matter whether he be guilty or not guilty. It will not be difficult for you to succeed in this, for I have read that, many years ago, the reiterated accusation of being a witch or a sorcerer was sufficient to wring confession from innocent women and men, even though they knew that the stake and the fagot were waiting for them. If physical torture will force an innocent person to confess, how much more will mental torture bring a like result?

" I thought once that I should like you. You are the uncle of the man I love better than I love any other person in all the world, and as such you are entitled to my affectionate regard. You are possessed of many engaging qualities ; you have exhibited toward me a degree of kindness for which I am grateful, and I am anxious to stand well with you. You have several times spoken of my influence with you and of the pleasure it gave you to do anything that would aid in securing my happiness. This is the first time I have appealed to you, and I do it now, not only because of the object I have in view, but because you have, by your goodness to me, allowed me to think that I should not have to ask in vain. Therefore I beg of you, by whatever consideration you may have for the honor of your family, by whatever regard for the principles of justice, by whatever affection for me, to stop all further efforts to fix the crime of murder on your nephew. If he is guilty, God will in His own due time search him with a thoroughness compared to which your attempts to reach the truth are vain and blind and shallow. Besides, has He not said, ' Vengeance is mine, I will repay ' ?

" In my own humble way I have written. I cannot plead eloquently with you, for I am not skilled in niceties of speech, and perhaps in much that I have said I have shown a lack of that tact that goes for so much with those that are suppliants. But I have at least written honestly, and with a desire to have you do what I conceive to be right. May He who is all goodness and mercy incline your heart to that charity ' that thinketh no evil.'

" Your sincere friend,

" BARBARA HENSCHEL."

She left her letter so that it would be taken to the post-office the first thing in the morning, and then went to bed content with what she had done thus far, but resolved to bring all the batteries to bear on Mr. Oldmixon that she could place in position in · order to make him renounce his scheme for extorting confession from his nephew Hogarth.

CHAPTER XXVI.

MR. OLDMIXON, immediately on his return to his residence, went to the library and rang the bell for his man Thomas. He had stopped at the Lucullus Club and taken his dinner, so that it was nearly ten o'clock when, in answer to his summons, Thomas entered the room. Mr. Oldmixon was seated at his table engaged in turning over the leaves of the manuscript of his novel, to which he was apparently giving the deepest attention. The man had been standing for several minutes waiting for his presence to be recognized, but Mr. Oldmixon seemed to have no thought for anything but the matter before him, for he went on making interlineations and erasures, as though entirely oblivious of the fact that he had rung for the man. At last, having—possibly by some intuition—become aware of the fact that the man was in the room—for he had not looked toward him—or else satisfied with the part of indifference he had been acting, without raising his eyes from the papers before him or ceasing his work he said :

" Thomas !"

" Yes, sir."

" How long have you been in my service ?"

" Eleven years, sir, next Christmas. You know, sir, I came on Christmas, because you wanted two men for that day, and you were so much pleased with me that you sent the other man away and gave me the place."

" Oh, yes, so I did ! Well, Thomas, I am very much afraid that on that occasion I made a big fool of myself, and that instead of your being a good, honest, and faithful fellow, you're the damnedest scoundrel that lives outside of the penitentiary."

" Sir !"

" Yes, Thomas," continued Mr. Oldmixon, with the most indifferent manner imaginable, and still going on with his work, never having yet even so much as looked at the man, " I am forced to the conclusion that, as you are such a devilish traitor and villain, it will be conducive to the cause of morality, as I know it will be to my interests, that you should within the next half hour take your horrid person off my premises. You will find a month's wages there on the corner of the mantelpiece. Go, and never let me lay eyes on you again."

" But," stammered the astounded Thomas, " what have I done, sir ?" And then bursting into tears, " It's too bad that, after I've done my duty for eleven years, I should be abused in this way and dismissed without being told what for !"

" Oh," exclaimed Mr. Oldmixon, rising from his chair and approaching the man till he stood at the distance of a couple of feet from him, while he fixed his eyes on him as though he would, if he could, pierce him through and through—" oh, you're in an inquiring frame of mind to-night, are you ? Well, you shall be gratified. You went to see a woman named Bangs this evening—a bird-stuffer in Lake Street !"

" Yes, sir ; I—"

" That will do. Who sent you ?"

"I went, sir—"

"Who sent you?" thundered Mr. Oldmixon.

"Mr. Hogarth, sir," answered the man, thoroughly terrified at the violence exhibited by his master.

"What for?"

"Oh, sir, I only went to see if she was the young woman that brought an animal here that she had stuffed for Mr. Jack! She thought this was where he lived."

"Then she has been in this house?"

"Yes, sir, and she saw the bird that you had mounted, and she said she had done it."

"She said she had stuffed that bird!" shrieked Mr. Oldmixon. "Oh, the liar—the horrid liar!" And he raised his hands as though completely dumbfounded at the enormity of the offence.

(As we know that Mr. Oldmixon was already aware of this claim of Miss Bangs, it is safe to assume that the emotion exhibited was not so sincere as it appeared to be.)

"Yes, sir," continued the wily Thomas, relieved to find Mr. Oldmixon's anger diverted from himself, "she said she had done it, and she told me the same thing to-night."

"And you came home and told it to Mr. Hogarth, I suppose, and that was what you went to find out, eh?"

"Yes, sir; I didn't think there was any harm in it. Mr. Hogarth wanted to know if she was the one that came here."

"Now, sir, what did Mr. Hogarth tell you was his object?" resumed Mr. Oldmixon, satisfied now that, having sufficiently terrified the man, he should get the truth.

"He said, sir, that he had a little joke to play off on

17

you, sir. That was all, and I didn't suppose there was anything wrong."

"How much did he give you for being a traitor to your employer?"

"Sir, I—"

"How much did he give you?" repeated Mr. Oldmixon, in a louder and more severe voice.

"Twenty dollars, sir."

"And how much more are you to get?"

"A hundred dollars, sir."

"Ah!" said Mr. Oldmixon, resuming his seat and going on with his work, satisfied that he had gotten all the information to be obtained from the man; "you may remain in my service on one condition, and that is, that you say nothing of all this to Mr. Hogarth, that you tell me of everything he says and does in regard to this Bangs girl, and that you take this piece of paper to him and tell him you found it lying on my desk among some other memoranda. If you do these things faithfully I will not only keep you in my service, but I will give you two hundred dollars, and perhaps—only *perhaps*, remember—I may mention you in my will."

"Thank you, sir," replied Thomas, with the cheerfulness natural to a man who had happily escaped from a dangerous position. "I'll do anything you wish me to do, sir. Shall I give him the paper now, sir?"

"No; wait till to-morrow morning. Then go to him very quietly, and when no one is near, and slip this piece of paper into his hand, saying that you found it on my desk, and that you think it may be of some importance." Mr. Oldmixon looked over the paper carefully, and this is what he read:

"*Memorandum for Mr. Ridley.*—Entire estate, real,

personal, and mixed, to go to my nephew John Oldmixon, provided that before my death or within one year after that event he marries —— Bangs.

"In case he shall, from any cause whatever, fail to marry said —— Bangs, then the said —— Bangs to receive the entire estate as aforesaid."

"Did you find out Miss Bangs's first name?" he said to Thomas, while he still continued to look at the paper.

"Yes, sir; it's Lena."

Mr. Oldmixon took a pen and filled in the blanks. "Lena Bangs," he said; "that's all right now. Now, sir," turning to Thomas, "you may have heard that I'm a crank, or not quite sound in my mind, or something of the kind. Well, perhaps I'm not quite right in the upper story, but I'm just the sort of a man that will poison you, or bring you to some other violent and sudden death, if you play me false in this affair in the slightest particular.

"You are to give this paper to Mr. Hogarth, as I have told you; you are to listen to what he says and observe his actions, and then you are to come and report everything to me. Now go."

He handed the paper to Thomas, and the man, with a low bow, went off, glad to have escaped so easily, and wondering how Mr. Oldmixon had obtained the knowledge of his doings that afternoon.

The next morning, as Hogarth was leaving his room, he saw Thomas standing near the head of the stairs, as though waiting for him.

"I got your note," he said, as he joined the man. "You are quite sure she's the woman?"

"Oh, yes, sir; there's no doubt of that. But I've something else, sir. Last night, after Mr. Oldmixon had gone to bed, I discovered that he had done something that I never knew him to do before—he had forgotten to lock his desk. I looked through it, and I found this piece of paper, and as I thought it might be of importance to you, I took it."

As he spoke he handed the slip to Hogarth.

The latter ran his eye over the writing, and at once his countenance showed the pleasure that the perusal gave him.

"This," he exclaimed, "is worth all the rest. Now, I know just what I've got to do. Thomas, I'll reward you handsomely for this. Now, take it and put it back exactly where you found it. My uncle might miss it, and then there would be trouble. I know it by heart, and it's of no further use to me."

Before becoming acquainted with the writing on the little slip of paper Hogarth had felt a degree of mental discomfort such as he had never before experienced. He had passed a wretched night. All through the hours that ought to have been passed in sleep he had been in that state of semi-unconsciousness during which the imagination, little, if at all, controlled by the judgment, runs riot with the thoughts. Fancies of the most horrible description had taken possession of him, and several times he had, in his fright, jumped from the bed and rushed terror-stricken to a distant part of the room in his effort to escape from the phantoms that he imagined he saw hovering over him, but which, as they disappeared as soon as he was fully awake, he knew must be only the fictions of dreams. The moment he lay down again they reappeared, and though he tried to fight them off by appeals to his reason, they were so vivid and the impression they produced was so strong that a long contest was impossible, and, time after time, they forced him to accept them as realities.

But there was one that, amid them all, kept its place. Lying or standing, asleep or awake, he saw the face of his wife as she had given him that last look ere he had hidden it with the pillow and shut out its gaze from earth forever. There was no body, there was not even a head; there was nothing but the face, with its terrified, despairing, pleading expression—a face that showed that its possessor knew that her last moment had come, that had perceived the look that was on *his* face, and was reflecting the knowledge that there was no mercy for her.

"My God!" he exclaimed, after he had passed several hours of agony, "is there no escape for me?" He shut his eyes, but the face was still there, immovable, unchanged, without the slightest variation in its expression, and looking, for all the world, as though it were carved in stone. He covered his own face with his hands, with the bedclothes, but *hers* was still before him.

"I cannot stand this very long," he said, as he arose from the bed for perhaps the twentieth time that night. "I shall lose my mind if I am always to be haunted in this way. And I had got over it all till that torturer began his schemes and brought back ideas that I had banished, as I thought, forever. I am afraid of him. Yes, that is it. His allusions are so significant that he must, in some way or other, have discovered something. But how?

"My God! he may have heard me talk in my sleep. There is no other way. Some night, or perhaps on several nights, he has been in this room, has stood by the side of my bed, and heard me tell the whole story in my dreams. And that is what he invited me here for. He had suspicions, and he was determined, if possible, to verify them.

"Well, he has gained his point," he continued, as he lit the gas and walked up and down the floor, "but the battle is not yet over. I may still escape, and there are two ways open to me. One involves his life; the other, my own. Either would give me peace. Which shall it be? My God! which shall it be?"

Unconscious of the hideous sin he had committed in asking God to decide for him whether he should perpetrate a murder or a suicide, he sat down in front of his dressing-table, and in the full blaze of the gaslight studied his face.

"It looks like the face of a guilty man," he said, with a despairing expression of voice. "I would pick it out from a thousand as that of a man with a crime on his soul and in terror for his life."

He sat for a long while before the glass, apparently thinking deeply of the alternatives that had been presented to his mind. Then he unbuttoned the collar of his night-gown, and turning his head to one side, looked at his neck, and then felt it carefully with the ends of his fingers.

"It is here," he said, in a whisper; "I feel its throb." His dressing-case was before him, and opening it, he took out a razor, while the fingers of the other hand remained on his neck over the carotid artery.

"It would be the easiest thing in the world to do," he said. "A single motion of the hand, and all would be over. No pain, no consciousness after the gash is made, and a sudden and absolute cessation of all misery."

He laid the edge of the razor on his neck and held it there, while he watched it rise and fall with the pulsations of the artery beneath it.

"Why don't I do it?" he said, hoarsely. "I'm not afraid of the future. Hell can't be worse than this night, and, after all, there may be no hell. It would be leaving a certainty of torment for an uncertainty, and that would be a good exchange. A little stronger pressure of the hand, and then oblivion.

"No," he exclaimed, throwing the razor into a corner of the room and springing to his feet, "it were better his life than mine. I'll drown my sorrows in another crime, just as the drunkard straightens himself up with another drink. His face would not trouble me, and perhaps it would drive hers away. Yes, his doom is sealed. I'll marry the Bangs girl, secretly, before she knows that she is his heiress, and then I'll quickly extinguish his life, as I did that of—of—the other. It's the best way, and, as he has so assiduously endeavored to teach me, leaves no signs. Besides, he is known to have heart-disease. I'll go to his room at night, as he has come to mine. I'll pay him off in his own coin, and with compound interest."

Strange as it may seem, Hogarth felt a degree of mental repose after he had arrived at the determination to smother his uncle, such as he had not experienced before for several days. The phantoms disappeared, and even the face became less distinct, until, passing through all stages of haziness, it finally disappeared altogether. It was now broad daylight, and he had not had ten minutes' complete sleep during the whole night. He did not care to go back to bed, for his mind was so full of the thoughts engendered by the determination to which he had come, that he was sure sleep would be unattainable; so he went into the dressing-room adjoining, and turning on the cold water in the bath-tub, got into it and stayed there long enough to have seriously injured the health of weaker or less excited persons, but which, on him, had no other effect than to cool his heated skin and lessen the force and frequency of a pulse that was feverish in its quality.

When he emerged from the bath, the temperature of which was not many degrees above the freezing-point, and after he had brought about the proper degree of reaction by rubbing himself with coarse towels, he felt like a new man, and fully equal to the performance of the task that he had assigned to himself. He dressed himself, and going out into the hall on his way to the breakfast-room, encountered Thomas, as we have seen, and had received intelligence that had still further added to his sense of *bien aise* and strengthened him in his resolution to bring matters to a crisis. This piece of information was the only thing needed to make him absolutely sure that he was on the right track. Evidently it had been a memorandum for Mr. Ridley for his guidance in preparing the draft of the will, and it settled the point definitely in favor of Miss Bangs. He therefore entered the breakfast-room feeling that he was now more than a match for his uncle, and resolved to let nothing that might be said to him disturb the equanimity that he knew was essential to the success of the schemes he had in view.

Mr. Oldmixon was sitting in an arm-chair near the window, reading a morning newspaper. On his nephew's entrance he threw it aside and greeted him with all the fervor of which he was capable.

"Come in, my dear boy. I'm glad to see you looking so well. 'Pon my honor, I never saw you look better. What do you say to going to the theatre this evening?"

"I should be delighted," answered Hogarth. "Shall I get a box as I go down-town this morning?"

"Yes, suppose you do. By the by, you've got to go down to Ridley's office, haven't you, about the will? Don't forget that, whatever you do. You know I may go now at any moment, and there's nothing like having things in readiness. You can take my coupé, as I think I'll stay at home this morning. Stop at Booth's Theatre on your way down, and get a box for to-night. Salvini plays Othello"—he glanced furtively at Hogarth as he spoke these words — "and he does the smothering scene with wonderful naturalness. You'll know as much about it, my dear boy, after you see him press the pillow over Desdemona's face, as though you had done the very same thing yourself."

This was the most direct speech on the subject that Mr. Oldmixon had yet made to his nephew, and the effect was even more decided than he had anticipated. He saw from Hogarth's manner that he had come into the room prepared to resist all assaults of the kind and resolved to brave it out to the last, and he, in his turn, had determined to give him, at the very outset, a blow that would probably have some effect in lessening his self-confidence.

At the mention of the play of Othello, Hogarth's face had blanched with fear, for he well knew what was coming. He had, more than a year before, seen the terribly realistic acting of Salvini, and the remembrance of it had more than once since his own murderous act

17*

been brought to his mind. Before his uncle had finished
speaking he was trembling like an aspen leaf—all of
which was duly observed by Mr. Oldmixon—and had
determined that nothing should make him see the great
actor again in that part. As the last words fell upon his
ears the pallor of his countenance approached that of
death ; he rose to his feet, and then, with a low, inarticulate cry, he dropped upon the floor, as though he had
been shot, and lay there, his face changed to a livid hue
and frightfully distorted, his limbs jerking spasmodically,
as though moved by a powerful galvanic battery, and his
mind a blank to everything that was going on about
him.

Mr. Oldmixon sat and looked at the struggling form
before him, apparently unmoved by the frightful sight.
He seemed to be engaged in studying the various contortions that the arms and legs were undergoing, and
imagining to himself what would be the next expression
that the face of the unconscious man would assume.
Then suddenly an idea occurred to him.

" This will never do !" he exclaimed—" dying without confessing. Oh, no ; I can never allow that !"   He
got up from his chair with as much celerity as was
attainable, and rang the bell.   Then he took the little
vial of the nitrite of amyl from his waistcoat pocket, and
pouring a few drops on his hand, held it over Hogarth's
mouth.   By this time Thomas had answered the bell.

" Mr. Hogarth has a fit, or something of the kind,"
said Mr. Oldmixon to the man.   " Loosen his cravat
and bring that pillow from the lounge and put it under
his head.

" He's coming round," he continued, as he noticed
that the purple hue of the face was disappearing, and that

the convulsive movements were less violent. "He'll be all right in a moment or two. Go and tell Dan to come and help you to carry him up to his own room and lay him on the bed."

But before Thomas could go on this errand the sick man opened his eyes, and looking wildly about him, began to talk incoherently, a word or two only being occasionally distinguishable, while the rest was a mass of thick guttural gibberish. Then he raised himself on his elbow, and with Thomas's assistance managed to assume the erect posture and to stand supported by the man's arm, though his legs trembled as though they would every moment give way under him.

"Do you feel better, my dear boy?" said Mr. Oldmixon, in a sympathizing voice. "I was just about to have you carried up-stairs to your room, where you will be more comfortable. But perhaps you would prefer to stay here? Yes? Put the pillow back on the lounge, Thomas, and help Mr. Hogarth to make himself comfortable. I had no idea you were subject to such turns. You will have to see a doctor. Don't send for Jimnay, whatever you do. He's an ass, and liked to have killed me a week or so ago. Besides, he's got the dyspepsia, and a doctor with a bad stomach always has a bad heart. Get Milledge; he's the only doctor in New York that knows anything. He'll charge you twenty-five dollars for the first visit, but when he's gone you'll feel that you've had the worth of your money. Shall I send for him, my dear boy? So sorry you should be so afflicted!"

By this time Hogarth had been led to the lounge and was about lying down on it. He turned toward his uncle as the question reached his ears, and looked at him stupidly for a moment; then he let his head fall on the pillow, and in an instant was in a heavy sleep, or rather stupor, if a judgment could be formed from the character of his breathing and the dull, stolid, vacant expression on his turgid and still livid face.

Mr. Oldmixon went on with his breakfast, and having finished it, he gave a look at his nephew, who was still insensible and breathing heavily. " It's only the stupor after the fit," he said to himself, as he went to the library. " I had an aunt that used to have one every Sunday morning, just as regularly as the day came round, and the stupor lasted till late in the afternoon. It's epilepsy, and it's in the Oldmixon family, along with the other nice heritages they possess. I'll not bother him with a doctor. But, by George! how that Shaksperian shot told! If it hadn't been for the fit he would have confessed then and there. It was on his mind to do so —I know by that look that he gave me just before he went to sleep. He couldn't collect his thoughts. He knew there was something, but he couldn't tell what it was. I heard him say ' Camilla ' and ' pillow ' while he was still on the floor and trying to talk. O you scoundrel!" he continued, as he seated himself at his desk and began working on his manuscript, " you black-hearted murderer, I'll bring you to it, if you have to suffer the torments of the damned, and then you will not have half atoned for your cruel crime. I should like to be present with him at Salvini's performance of the part of Othello. By Heaven! I believe it would kill him."

He had not been engaged more than a few minutes when Thomas entered with the morning's letters. There were half a dozen, all for Mr. Oldmixon. He scarcely looked at them, but went on with his alterations in his manuscript, so that a half hour had elapsed before he turned his attention to the communications, still unopened, that lay before him.

Then he slit up their envelopes with a paper-knife, and read a line or two of each, so as to see that it was of no importance, till he came to one post-marked New Rochelle, and directed in a handwriting which, though he had never seen it before, he knew was Barbara's.

"Ah!" he exclaimed, pressing it to his lips, "the angel writes to me. What is there that I would not do for her? Nothing—absolutely nothing! If she were to ask me to put a millstone around my neck and jump into the East River, I'd do it at once. Let me see what the sweet girl wants."

He opened the letter as he had the others, but, unlike his actions with them, he read it through carefully to the end. Then he laid it down on the desk, and shutting his eyes, lay back in the chair to think. For nearly an hour he remained abstracted from the consideration of every other subject but the contents of Barbara's letter. Then, taking the letter he read it again, still more slowly than before, and holding it in his hand, paced the floor, stopping now and then to read parts of it again. At last he appeared to have made up his mind what to do, for he went to his desk and wrote two letters—one to Barbara and one to Jack.

That to Barbara was as follows:

"MY DEAR BARBARA: I have read your dear letter, and have been greatly impressed by what you say. I should be very glad if I could see you again. Will not you and your father dine with me at six o'clock on Friday evening next? I make the hour early, because you will then be able to return home by the eleven P.M. train.

After dinner I shall be delighted to read you a chapter
of my novel. My carriage will meet you at the station,
and will take you back. I have invited Jack, and of
course he will come. You will also have an opportunity
of making the acquaintance of my nephew Hogarth, in
whom you are so much interested.

" Yours affectionately,

" VICTOR CONSTANTINE OLDMIXON."

To Jack he wrote :

" MY DEAR JACK : Dine with me to-morrow at six.
I have invited Barbara and her father. I wish your
opinion on certain parts of my novel, which I am now
preparing for the press. I propose to read them to you
after dinner.

" You will also meet your brother Hogarth. I am
sure it is only necessary for me to tell you this in order
to increase your anxiety to be present. The virtue of
forgiveness is one that need not be urged upon so good
a man as you. Come, therefore, with the resolution to
take him again into your heart. Bury the hatchet, Jack.
I am burying all mine, and getting ready therefore to face
my Maker ; but I find the process requires a larger grave-
yard than I at first expected. However, the work goes
bravely on.

" Your affectionate uncle,

" VICTOR."

Then, having sealed these letters and sent them to be
mailed, he dressed himself with his usual care and strolled
down to the Lucullus Club-house.

CHAPTER XXVII.

Mr. Oldmixon's dinner was for Friday, and it was on Tuesday of the same week that he sent out his invitations. On the following morning—Wednesday—Barbara went to town as usual, having received Mr. Oldmixon's letter the previous evening, but concluding that she would not answer it till she had seen Jack. On the day following Mr. Oldmixon's visit to her he had, as was his habit now, met her at the station, and had walked with her to Mr. Maurice's studio. These morning walks in the fresh, bracing December air were the chief pleasures that the two young people had, except those offered by Jack's Saturday-evening visits to Lasata and his stay through Sunday till Monday morning. During this walk she had informed him of all that had taken place between her and Mr. Oldmixon, and of the discovery she had made that she was the woman for whom his uncle designed him and who was to receive his estate, should Jack neglect or refuse to marry her. Of course this information pleased the young man exceedingly, and he was not inclined to regard the matter in the light of a liberty, almost amounting to an insult, as had Barbara. It took from his mind all the regret that he had experienced at not being able to oblige his uncle, and he was, besides, enough of a man of the world to know the advantages that Mr. Oldmixon's estate would be to himself and his wife. Then, after settling that point eventually to their satisfaction, Barbara had asked his advice in regard to her going to see Miss Bangs and putting her on her guard against the devices of Hogarth. She had thought of the subject a good deal since Mr. Oldmixon's departure, and the more she had considered the matter the more she was disposed to enlighten her taxidermist rival and the robber of her reputation relative to the scheme of which it seemed as though she was about to be the subject.

Jack, however, after as long and mature thought as was possible while walking down Fifth Avenue, with Barbara by his side, had expressed his decided opinion that interference now would be premature.

" It isn't likely," he said, " that Hogarth, under any circumstances, will marry Miss Bangs at once. In fact, I do not see how he could, even if he wanted to. He has probably never seen her in his life, and though it is likely that as soon as she makes his acquaintance and finds out who he is she will agree to marry him, several days must elapse before the arrangements can be effected. Now, you see, my dear Bab," he continued, assuming his most argumentative manner, " the only reason why Hogarth wishes to marry Miss Bangs, if he really has such a desire—and of that you must admit that we have no positive evidence—is that he supposes her to be the heiress of my uncle's property. Of course, from his standpoint such a marriage would have to be kept secret till my uncle's death, for certainly if Miss Bangs were the heiress, as we will say Hogarth supposes her to be, the will would certainly be changed by my uncle as soon as he became aware of the marriage. Hogarth is too shrewd a fellow not to look out for all possible contingencies.

Now, it strikes me that the one absolutely sure way to prevent the marriage would be to inform Hogarth that Miss Bangs is not the heiress, that my uncle has no intention of making her such, or of in any way altering the will already made. He would believe this if the information came from me, and I will tell him at once. Then, don't you see, Miss Bangs would not be brought into the matter at all, unless Hogarth should want to marry her out of love, which it is very unlikely he will care to do."

"I think you are right," said Barbara, after she had thought for a little while of what Jack had said; "but lose no time; events seem to me to be coming to a focus, and there is really every reason why you should act speedily."

When he met her the next morning they had both received their invitations to dine with Mr. Oldmixon on the following Friday. Jack had already accepted his, but Barbara had, as we know, determined to advise with her lover on the subject before deciding to partake of Mr. Oldmixon's hospitality. Jack was of the opinion that she ought to go. It would please his uncle, and it would please him. What more could she want?

"I'll meet you and your father at the station and take you over to Uncle Victor's house, and then when the dinner is over I'll take you back. Besides, we shall of course sit together at the table."

"It will all be very nice, but I do not like the idea of meeting your brother; in fact, I am afraid of him."

"I don't like the idea either," rejoined Jack, "but Uncle Victor is evidently in a forgiving mood, brought about, doubtless, by your letter, and I don't think it would be advisable for me to say or do anything that might prompt him to change his present disposition. He has appealed to me to make friends with Hogarth, and I have decided to do so. My brother has heretofore been my worst enemy, but I suppose that that is no reason why I should not be ready to meet him half-way in a reconciliation."

"That is right," exclaimed Barbara, with emphasis. "I am glad that my letter has apparently not been without influence. Then we will all go, and may the dinner be the means of restoring peace among us!

"And, Jack," resumed Barbara, with an arch smile, after they had walked a little farther, "don't you think that, as your uncle is going to tell us his story, you might inform us how you caught the silver fox? You know we are still in ignorance of the process of capture."

"By George! I forgot all about the silver fox. Of course, I'll tell you. You see, Bab, we've always had so many things to talk about and so little time at our disposal, that it has always escaped my memory. It's a wonderful story, and will make each individual hair of your head stand on end."

"Then I shall look like a comet, or a blazing star, or some other fiery contrivance."

By this time they had reached the door of the apartment house in which Mr. Maurice had his studio. It was not often that Jack went any farther, for he thought it only right that Barbara should be allowed all the time and opportunity to advance in her new profession, without let or hindrance from him. But to-day she was so anxious to show him her work on a head of her father that she was modelling, and he was so anxious to see it, that it did not take much persuasion to induce him to go up with her.

Mr. Maurice had several young lady pupils whose instruction was generally left to Mrs. Maurice, until, at least, they had acquired the rudiments of the art, and had shown some degree of talent for the work before them.   It very often happened that a pupil never got farther than the instruction that the lady was able to give her; for if she showed an incapacity for advancing, Mr. Maurice very frankly, but very kindly told her of the fact, and advised her to take to some profession for which she might be better adapted than she was for sculpture.   Barbara, however, had almost immediately passed from Mrs. Maurice's ministrations to those of her husband.   She had from the very first shown a genius for her chosen art, that had at once surprised and delighted him, and he had, in consequence, taken that loving interest in her advancement that was in itself an incentive to her, only second in power to her own inherent love for the work to which she had resolved to devote herself.

For several days past her father had either accompanied her to the city, or had come to the studio in order to give her the sittings she required in modelling a bust of him.   She had taken the utmost interest in this production, and it promised to be in every way worthy of her genius.   Mr. Henschel's head was one that an artist could not fail to notice and to admire.   It was not unlike, in general characteristics, that of some mediæval saint, with its long white beard, and its face expressive both of that sternness and gentleness that the holy worthies of the middle ages are represented by the painters of the time to have possessed, and which those of the present day deem it essential to give them.

Jack did not stay long at the studio.   He admired the head, which was already well advanced toward completion, talked a little with Mr. and Mrs. Maurice and heard with pleasure their encomiums of Barbara, and then went to the Lucullus Club to meet his uncle, with whom he had an appointment.

As he walked down the street, Jack wondered what was the particular matter about which his uncle wished to see him. In his letter of acceptance he had very magnanimously expressed his approval of the plan of reconciliation, but he was, of course, anxious to know something more definite in regard to what was expected of him, and he hoped to be able to get some information on the subject that morning. But he felt now that it was not to talk about that that his uncle had requested this interview, but doubtless for some purpose of his own that interested him greatly, and in which he desired his nephew's co-operation. On that point he did not feel much doubt.

In talking the matter over with Barbara, they had both alluded to the fact that, while Mr. Oldmixon had pointed out to Jack the duty that was upon him, of forgiving his brother, he had markedly refrained from saying anything about what he himself contemplated doing. In his letter to Barbara he had avoided the subject altogether. This struck them both as being suspicious of the fact that he was not so forgiving as he apparently desired others to be. Jack had seen enough of his uncle to be aware of the fact that he could be intensely secretive when he chose to be so, and that he was at all times utterly unscrupulous as to the means he took to accomplish his objects. He seemed to have no conscience whatever in the matter of deceiving those whom he assumed to love and respect, and for whom he probably *did* have a high regard ; nor to be actuated by any other principle than an intensely morbid impulse to accomplish his ends without reference to the morality of the means employed.

As to whether Mr. Oldmixon was correct in his belief that Hogarth had murdered his wife by smothering her with a pillow, Jack was more in doubt than he had been. The fact that his uncle had, many years ago, been at Annapolis, as he had admitted to Barbara, and had probably occupied the very rooms he had so minutely described, had somewhat weakened the conviction of his brother's guilt that he had, after the visit to that city, been forced to form. Still, he was by no means satisfied of Hogarth's innocence. There was a degree of positiveness about his uncle's assertions that impressed him very strongly, and he could scarcely go so far as to ascribe the correctness of his topography of the rooms in the hotel at Annapolis to recollections revived after having been dormant for over thirty years, and when the fact of the visit had altogether faded from the memory.

But, whether his brother were guilty or not, Jack was perfectly clear as to the impropriety of his uncle's taking the part of a detective or that of a questioner in a torture process. In this he had not changed since Mr. Oldmixon had first revealed his intentions, and he was delighted to find that Barbara was equally emphatic as he was himself in her denunciations of his uncle's procedure. There was a bare hope that the old gentleman had renounced his intentions, and that the dinner would witness the restoration of peace all around, to the extent that peace was possible in a family in which there were so many disturbing factors as there were in his. So far as he was concerned he was prepared to get on good terms with Hogarth, but as to being friendly with him, as one brother should be with another, Jack felt that

that would be impossible. He had no respect for Hogarth ; he knew that he was, in every relation of life, a bad man—one that had, in fact, scarcely a redeeming quality, if, indeed, he was not wholly and incorrigibly depraved. To be on relations of intimacy and confidence with such a man was out of the question. But Jack intended to again insist upon Hogarth being made co-heir with himself to his uncle's estate, or failing in attaining his wish, to make over by deed of gift one exact half of the property so soon as it should come into his possession. It would seem as though a man or a woman cannot be so utterly wicked and degraded but that there are some good people constantly on the watch to protect their interests.

When he arrived at the Lucullus Club House he found that his uncle was already there and was expecting him in the reception-room.

"I've only just come, my boy, so that you haven't kept me waiting a moment," said Mr. Oldmixon, as he shook his nephew heartily by the hand. "It's an infernal outrage that I can't ask you any farther into the Club House than this reception-room, unless I invite you to dinner, and it's too early for that. Here we're liable to be interrupted any moment. By George ! I'll start a club in which members shall have the privilege of asking their friends into a private room when they want to have conversation that they don't want all the town to hear."

"That wouldn't be a bad idea, Uncle Victor," said Jack, laughing. "Still, it's so early in the morning that we're not likely to be disturbed."

"Well, my dear boy, sit down. If any fellow comes in we'll jump into my carriage. I told Dan to be here by eleven o'clock." He dropped into a large arm-chair, in which he was nearly wholly concealed, and Jack took one equally comfortable near him.

" Everything's going on well," resumed Mr. Oldmixon, as he handed Jack his cigar-case and took a "weed" for himself. " I've almost brought that scoundrel Hogarth to a confession. Every time I mention smothering to him he goes off into some kind of a fit—epileptic, I suppose—and doesn't get over it for several hours. I wish you could have seen the effect yesterday when I invited him to go with me to see Salvini play Othello and smother Desdemona. I was afraid at first that he was going to die without making a confession in so many words, but fortunately he came to himself again. Jack, my boy, I'd give ten thousand dollars if I could get him to go and see Salvini in Othello ! He'll never do it. It would be the last of him, and I believe he would end with a full confession."

" Oh, uncle ! can't you make up your mind to cease your warfare on Hogarth ? What is to be gained by it beyond the horrid satisfaction you may obtain of having your suspicions confirmed ? Surely, for that poor reward, you are not going to make Barbara and me, and eventually yourself, unhappy !"

" Barbara ! Oh, Jack, my dear boy, to think that you and I should have been two such fools as almost to quarrel about a matter upon which we were both agreed ! I was just going to tell you how much pleasure the discovery I made gave me, when you introduced this Hogarth affair. Jack," continued Mr. Oldmixon, in a subdued voice, " get married as soon as you can. Perhaps if Hogarth should be hanged for his crime she might feel inclined to back out. Take her at once, my boy, before he makes confession. Don't you think you could get

her to go with you this morning to a parson and have the
knot tied? I asked you to meet me here for the purpose
of putting this matter before you. My dear boy, hurry
matters up at once, or I am afraid she'll slip through your
fingers after all."

Jack was astounded. He looked at his uncle, unable
for a while to speak a word. Then he said, very slowly
and very sedately :

"I think you do not know Barbara. If Hogarth and
you were both to be hanged, she would not give me up.
I would not dare to insult her by proposing such a scheme
as the one you suggest. She is as gentle, as refined, as
truthful as—as—I can't find anything to compare her
with," he added, as his ideas of lovely beings failed
him.

Mr. Oldmixon rose and shut the door.

"Jack, my boy," he said, as he laid a hand on Jack's
shoulder, while his emotion almost choked his utterance,
"don't, for God's sake, look at the matter in that way !
I adore her as much as you do, and would be the last man
to say a word or advise an act that could properly be
construed into one of disrespect. But, my God, Jack,
I am afraid ! Think of the disgrace of having a brother-
in-law hanged ! Would you marry her if her father was
a convict or was about to be tried for his life ?"

"Yes," exclaimed Jack, interrupting him. "I'd
marry her if every relation she ever had in the world had
been hanged."

"But she's so good herself, Jack, so pure, that I'm
afraid that when she hears the whole truth about Hogarth, and he has been hanged in the jail-yard at Annapolis, she'll fell wronged and disgraced, and will pine
away and die of her grief."

"I tell you you don't know her," cried Jack, excitedly. "I've talked the whole matter over with her, and
she's as true as steel. I'll never insult her by proposing
a marriage that would disgrace an immigrant just landed
from the steerage. Please God, she shall marry me in
her father's house, in decency and in order, or not at all!"

"My poor boy, you don't know women as I know
them. No matter how good they may be, they have
their peculiarities, and the better they are the more dis-
tinctively peculiar they are. Barbara comes of an honorable stock, humble though it may be, and she and her
father are as proud as Lucifer, and whatever she may
say now you may depend upon it that when your brother
stands, as he will, under the shadow of the gallows, she'll
give you up, if it kills her to do so. No, no!" seeing that
Jack was about to expostulate, "hear me out to the end
before you say another word. See here!" taking as he
spoke a bundle of papers from the breast-pocket of his
coat. "I shall not live more than a month or two longer, at most; I feel certain symptoms about my heart
that warn me of my approaching end. By my will all
my estate goes to you or Barbara—it makes no difference now which of you gets it—but, lest you should be
apprehensive that I might play you a trick, I have here
deeds and bonds and certificates of stock amounting to
six hundred thousand dollars that I am going to make
over to you now, by deed of gift. The papers are all in
order, I executed the deed this morning before a notary,
and all you have to do is to marry Barbara to-day, or to-
morrow at farthest, and the whole of it is yours. I have
kept back about two hundred thousand dollars, enough
to yield me all the income I shall want while I live, and
which will also go to you when I die."

18

Jack rose from his chair long before Mr. Oldmixon finished speaking, and was pacing the floor in a state of extreme agitation. His uncle's pertinacity and evident sincerity troubled him greatly, though the magnificent offer made to him did not at all shake him in the determination he had already expressed. It was only another evidence to his mind of the unchanged resolution of his uncle to bring Hogarth to confession and disgrace, if it were in his power to do so, and he shuddered as he thought of the indignity that the whole matter was likely to fix upon the Oldmixon family and all connected with him. He felt assured that his uncle was entirely certain of Hogarth's guilt, and that he meant to expose him at the earliest possible moment, probably at the dinner to which he and Barbara had been invited, and which he now determined that neither he nor Barbara would attend unless assurances were given that no such act was in contemplation.

"I cannot accept your offer, Uncle Victor," he said, at last. "I am sensible of the existence of a sincere desire on your part to secure Barbara for me as a wife. You need be under no apprehension in regard to the matter, for she will as certainly marry me as that the sun shines in the heavens. I have no fear, but if you feel that there is the slightest uncertainty on the subject, you have it in your power to banish it by simply resolving to let Hogarth rest in piece, to be punished by his own conscience and as God may otherwise direct."

"My dear boy!" exclaimed Mr. Oldmixon, in a hoarse voice, "I can't do that. It is impossible. I have tried to bring my mind to such a conclusion, but it is out of the question. I can't do it." He looked helplessly about him as he spoke these last words, his gaze resting at last on Jack as though he was appealing to him to give him the strength he required.

"Then, Uncle Victor," said Jack, who notwithstanding that he pitied his uncle, was convinced, from former experience, that the exhibition of compassion was not at all calculated to make him yield, "there is but one thing for Barbara and Mr. Henschel and me to do, and that is to stay away from your dinner. It would be very distressing to all of us to be present at such a scene as you possibly have it in your power to get up. It would be peculiarly unbecoming in you to develop your opinions in Barbara's presence. She is about to become a member of the family, and, though I think it right that she should know—and she does know—that there are skeletons in our closets, I think it exceedingly scandalous to drag them out and exhibit them to her in all their disgraceful proportions, and at a dinner, too, where very different means of entertainment should be provided by the host for his guests than that of exposing a supposed murderer, and he his own nephew."

"Well, Mr. Jack Oldmixon," exclaimed the old gentleman, who, while Jack was speaking, had recovered his equanimity, "if you think you have quite concluded your discourse, perhaps you will allow me the opportunity of saying a word. Who said anything about exposing the villain, the basilisk, at my dinner-table? Do you take me for such a vulgar wretch as to interfere with the appetites of my guests by harassing their minds with ideas of that scoundrel's crimes? Do you suppose that I could run the risk of having my *boudins de perdreaux à la Richelieu* or my *pain de gibier au suprême*, upon which so much care will be exercised, unappreciated, perhaps even to be handed round without being tasted?

No, you do not know me if you suppose for a moment
that I would commit an outrage of the kind, and I feel
hurt, yes, angry, that you should think me such a savage
as your suspicions imply." And Mr. Oldmixon's eyes
filled with tears so rapidly that repeated applications of
his handkerchief were necessary for their absorption.

"I beg your pardon, Uncle Victor," said Jack, humbly, "I did not intend—"

"No, no! of course you 'did not intend,'" rejoined
Mr. Oldmixon, in a tone of voice that was intended to
convey the idea that the feelings of the speaker were injured to a degree that would not readily be lessened.
"It is always the unintentional word that cuts the
deepest. You shall all eat your dinners in peace, and
with that amount of enjoyment that the goodness of the
feast and the excellence of the company will warrant.
After dinner I had proposed to read a few pages from
my novel, hoping that they would interest those that I
had brought together ; but if this plan is disagreeable to
you it can easily be changed, and we can have a recita-
tion from you, or a chapter from the Bible, if it suits you
better, read by that eminent biblical expositor and exem-
plar, Mr. Hogarth Oldmixon."

"Again, I humbly beg your pardon," reiterated Jack,
"and express my regret at my error. Of course we will
have the novel ; I am anxious to hear a specimen of it
read and by such a good reader as you are ; and Barbara,
likewise, is greatly interested."

"Then you want to hear a chapter or so from my
novel, and you are quite sure Barbara would also be
pleased with the reading ?" said Mr. Oldmixon, much
mollified by Jack's soothing speech. "My dear boy, you
shall both be gratified ! I shall select the most interest-

ing chapter of the book, one that I am sure will keep your attention riveted ; for its dramatic intensity is so pronounced that the minds of those persons hearing it read will be so engrossed that thoughts other than those excited by my ideas will be impossible."

Jack made a satisfactory rejoinder to this burst of self-adulatory enthusiasm, and soon afterward took his departure. Mr. Oldmixon returned his deeds and valuable papers to his pocket, apparently feeling little or no regret at his failure to induce Jack to receive them as a bribe for hastening his marriage with Barbara. Then he took two or three strides across the floor, as though to get rid of some surplus energy before going out into the public rooms of the club house, and finally, with a look of self-satisfaction, not altogether free from that species of facial expression that is designated Mephistophelian, or diabolical, or Satanic, or by some other adjective expressive of the personality of the Prince of Darkness, he put on his hat, buttoned up his coat, and, passing through the hall to the street, ordered his coachman to drive him to the National Academy, where there was an exhibition of pictures—among which was the one Jack had painted for Mr. Van der Linden, and which he had not yet seen.

CHAPTER XXVIII.

HOGARTH IS SATISFIED.

THE episode of Othello had a greater effect upon Hogarth Oldmixon than any other that had been introduced by his uncle, and it was not until late the following day that he had entirely recovered from the mental and physical disturbance consequent upon the paroxysm with which he had been visited. He had now no doubt that his secret was known to at least one person, and that there was a systematic attempt being made to cause him trouble. What the ultimate object of his persecutor was he could not divine; he did not believe that it extended to the point of delivering him up to justice to be tried for his crime. He was not able to conceive of the possibility of his own uncle, who, up to quite a recent period, had been his friend and protector, acting the part of a detective policeman and doing all in his power to bring him to the gallows. He was quite sure that no one saw him kill his wife, and that the persecution to which he was subjected was altogether based upon conjecture and suspicion. He was also very certain that his own conduct, in the face of his uncle's tortures, had had the effect of strengthening the belief of his guilt that was entertained by his tormentor, and had consequently served to encourage him to still more positive efforts to make him say or do something that would place his criminality beyond a peradventure. Hitherto, however wanting in the confidence of innocence his conduct might have been under the taunts and innuendoes heaped upon him, he had never positively committed himself by words, or even let drop an expression that could, by the most eager detective, have been construed into an acknowledgment of guilt. He had been several times on the point of confessing, and of throwing himself on his uncle's mercy, but had up to the present time maintained sufficient command of himself to keep silent. The impulses he had experienced to reveal all were born of the occasions, and were instinctively self-defensive, unprompted as they were by deliberate thought ; but as he lay in bed on the morning of the day of his uncle's dinner and looked up at the ceiling in a meditative sort of a way, he was not quite sure that it would not be well to seek out his persecutor as soon as possible and make a clean breast of it. This was the only alternative that then presented itself to that of murdering his uncle and marrying Miss Bangs, whom he was certain was the woman to whom the estate had been devised, in the event of Jack failing to marry her.

The question was certainly a momentous one : confession of one murder or the perpetration of another ; and Hogarth thought it over as thoroughly as the state of his brain permitted. His head still ached, he had passed a restless night, and his mind was by no means clear that morning, so that he was not able to bring to bear the full force of an intellect that, in a state of health, generally served him well. But he did his best in the effort to arrive at a decision that should be final. He felt confident that matters were approaching a crisis, and he had some apprehension that with the evidences of criminality that his uncle had already obtained he might at any moment denounce him. He did not, it is true, think that there was much danger of such a course being pursued ; but Mr. Oldmixon was a singular being who could never be depended upon for doing what others thought he ought to do, and, besides, Hogarth did not know the extent of his information. He must have something positive, he thought, or why should he have begun such a systematic and well-formed an attack ? He could not have been more explicit in his assaults if he had seen the murder committed, for at one time or another he had insinuated every feature of the deed as it had actually occurred. The thought of all this was very terrible to Hogarth. He perceived that his uncle was merciless, and that his words and acts that had the appearance of kindness were intensely hypocritical and a part of his general plan of deception. He now saw why he had been invited to the house, and he thoroughly comprehended the fraud of the new will, the rough draft of which was still in his coat pocket undelivered to Mr. Ridley, but which he would take down to him to-day.

Perhaps it would be better to defer deciding the matter till he had seen Mr. Ridley, and observed that gentleman in the presence of the draft of the new will that he had been authorized to deliver to him. That would only be postponing the further consideration for a few hours, and then he would probably be in a better position for arriving at a conclusion than he was now. Mr. Ridley was a very different person from his uncle, and would not lie or knowingly be a party to a fraud. One thing was certain, he could not much longer endure the daily tortures that his uncle was inflicting on him. He felt that his mind was giving way ; for, though he had not since his decision of a few days ago seen the face that had haunted him, he had had other mental troubles of fully as serious a character. He had been disposed to attribute the disappearance of the face to the fact that his mind had lost its uncertainty when he had resolved that his uncle should be smothered, but he had since then been fully as perplexed as ever before in regard to the course to be pursued, and yet the face had not returned. As he lay in bed he speculated in regard to the appearance and disappearance of the hallucination that had so disturbed him, and though he could give no satisfactory explanation of the phenomenon, he fully recognized the fact of its unreality. " I suppose," he said to himself, " that I had been thinking so much about the matter and had got into such a worried condition of mind that my brain wouldn't work right. Well, I don't believe it would trouble me much now if it were to come back ; there is such a thing," he added, with a little laugh, " as getting used to being haunted."

Mr. Oldmixon, of course, had told him of the dinner that was to take place that evening, and had also informed him who were to be the guests.

" You know, my dear boy," he had said, " that I am a very old man and shall not probably stay much longer with you all. I have become reconciled to Jack, and I wish you to do so likewise. Surely you can afford to be magnanimous to your brother, seeing that you will succeed to the whole of my estate."

Hogarth had with as good a grace as was possible expressed his willingness to resume relations with Jack, but had added that he was feeling so badly after his recent attack that he begged to be excused from being present. He would meet Jack, he said, the following

18*

day, and then they could exchange regrets and become friends again.

" No, no," replied Mr. Oldmixon, "that will not do at all ; I never saw you looking better than you do now. I not only want you to see Jack, but I am especially desirous to have you meet the lady he is going to marry."

" Jack is going to be married !"

" Yes, he chose to select his wife without reference to my wishes, but that is no reason why the family should not treat her kindly, especially as I believe she is quite a good sort of a girl in her way. She's a sculptor, I believe, a pupil of Maurice's.   Jack seems to be infatuated with her, and though—well, well," he added, as though interrupting himself in what he was about to say, " it isn't necessary now to go into all that, since such a great change has recently taken place in our family affairs."

" What change do you mean ?"

" Why, your coming back to me, of course. You have always, except for a few days, been my favorite nephew."

" Oh, yes ! I'm much obliged."

" Don't forget that draft of the will ; Ridley is waiting for it."

So the conversation had ended, and Hogarth, as he lay in bed, recalled all the details of it.   He did not wish to go to the dinner, or to resume relations with Jack, or to make the acquaintance of Miss Henschel, but he saw no way of avoidance, unless upon the plea of illness, and he did not believe that that excuse would be accepted, unless he was obviously too ill to be present. No, there was no escape for him.

He did not expect any trouble from his uncle during

the dinner. He was sure that, no matter how determined the old gentleman might be in the matter of making him feel uncomfortable, he had not yet reached the point of being willing to expose him to strangers. Evidently, whatever suspicions or facts he had he had thus far kept in his own bosom. The time for making the world acquainted with his hypothesis or knowledge might come, but it had not yet arrived.

He turned over and looked at his watch that lay on the table by the side of the bed. It was ten o'clock, so he got up, took his cold bath, as was his habit, and, dressing himself at once for the street, went down to the breakfast-room. As he expected, Mr. Oldmixon had not yet left his bedroom. He ordered a cup of coffee and a roll, and, having soon disposed of the light repast, left the house and started to go down-town to Mr. Ridley's office. The coffee made him feel better than he had felt before getting up, and the cold air of the December morning tended still further to dissipate the sense of constriction and pain that he had experienced in his head. He hesitated as to whether he should take the elevated railway from Forty-second Street or walk all the way down. Finally, considering that he was not yet quite himself, and that a walk of three or four miles would stir his blood and probably carry off his bad feelings, he decided to use his legs instead of the agency provided by the Metropolitan Elevated Railway Company. By the time he arrived at his destination he felt something like his normal self, and fully equal to a contest of subtlety and sharp practice with even so redoubtable an adversary as he knew Mr. Ridley to be. It was nearly twelve o'clock when he knocked at the door of the lawyer's anteroom, and, in compliance with an invitation to that effect given by the small

boy that attended to the door, entered, and took a seat till
Mr. Ridley should be disengaged.

He sat at a desk in one corner of the room, while the
small boy was diligently occupied, in a diagonally opposite
corner, in reading some one of the story-telling weekly
newspapers published in the city of New York in which
pursuers of literature of his class take special delight.
Hogarth had nothing to read and no other way of occu-
pying the time till Mr. Ridley had gotten rid of his
present visitor than by looking around him. He had
diligently pursued this occupation for several minutes,
and it was beginning to be monotonous, when, having
completed the survey of the more distant objects in the
room, he turned his attention to those nearer to him, and
first of all to the desk at which he was sitting. Apparently it was one at which Mr. Ridley sometimes sat, for
there were several letters addressed to him lying on it,
and a partly-written one which he had probably been engaged in indicting when interrupted by the visitor now
engaging his attention.

As the reader is already well aware, Hogarth Oldmixon
was altogether devoid of those conscientious scruples that
prevent a man, even though sorely tempted, doing an
unmanly action. The sentiment of honor, if it had ever
had a lodgment in his breast, had vacated the tenement
early in his career, and there had been no other feeling
of a like character to take its place. He was governed
altogether by the most complete and overpowering sel-
fishness, and by no other emotion whatever. He looked
closely at the papers lying on the desk, and at one end
observed a little pile of letters that had probably been
received by that morning's mail, as he noticed that several
of them were still unopened. He glanced furtively at

the boy and perceived that his head and face were entirely
concealed by the literary production he was reading.
Then he moved his hand very quietly on the cloth-covered
surface of the desk till it rested on the pile of letters.
He had no distinct object in view in meddling with the
letters, but he *did* have a faint, shadowy sort of an idea
that by so doing he might effect something to his advantage, but what he could not for the life of him have told.
To separate the letters so as to see the direction on each
was an easy piece of work, and he did it without attracting
the notice of the guardian of the room. They were all
directed to "Theobald Ridley, Esq., Counsellor at Law,"
and in handwritings that he did not recognize, till he
came to the very bottom one of all. Then he started,
for he saw that that bore a superscription that he knew
was written by his uncle.

There was, of course, a good deal of risk to be incurred
if he should determine to purloin that letter in order to
make himself acquainted with its contents, and yet he had
determined, on the very instant, that when he left that
desk the letter should be in his pocket. There was no
difficulty in stealing it. The boy was still intently engaged with his story paper, and all that Hogarth had to
do was to keep his eyes fixed on the absorbed youth
while his hand conveyed the coveted letter from the desk
to the breast-pocket of his coat. Then he got up, walked
several times across the floor, and finally asked the boy
whether he thought Mr. Ridley would soon be disengaged,
receiving an answer to the effect that he—the boy—did
not know. How should he?

"Perhaps," said Hogarth, taking a visiting-card from
his pocketbook, "if you were to take this to him, he
might hurry a little."

"He told me I wasn't to bring no cards to him," answered the boy.

"Oh, he did! Then I suppose the visitor will be with him a long time."

"I don't know about that," rejoined the youth, evidently not pleased at being disturbed from his engrossing occupation of reading of the adventures of a prairie scout of blood-thirsty proclivities. "Sometimes they stay long, and then again they don't." As the words were uttered, the bell from the inner office rang, and the boy quickly disappeared into the precincts of the apartment that Hogarth was longing to enter.

He was back again in a moment, and, going to the desk at which Hogarth had been sitting, picked up the package of letters lying there, and again went into the room in which were Mr. Ridley and his visitor.

But his absence was of short duration, for he reappeared in a couple of minutes, and, with a look of anxiety on his face, looked carefully through all the papers lying on the desk.

"Mr. Ridley says he hasn't got all the letters that came this morning," he remarked, as though speaking to no one in particular. "I took him in eleven, and he says there were twelve. I don't see any other, and he says I've got to find it, or clear out and never show my face here again. I guess a boy can't find a letter when there ain't no letter to find."

Hogarth began to feel that it was just possible that he had committed an act that was calculated to precipitate the impending catastrophe. He might, by a little skilful manœuvring, have restored the letter to its place, or have let it drop on the floor, and then have pretended to find it, but he was of the opinion that it was essential for him to know what his uncle was, at that time, writing about to Mr. Ridley, and he knew, or at least thought he did, that although he might be suspected of having taken the letter, it would be impossible, unless he were searched, to connect him with its disappearance.

But while the young man was overturning the papers on the desk and working himself into a fever of apprehension, Mr. Ridley, impatient doubtless at the delay, came hastily out of his sanctum.

"What's the reason—"

But before he could get any further in his angry interrogatory, his eyes lighted on Hogarth, and a marked change immediately ensued in his countenance and manner. For a moment he stood irresolute, and then, while his face was flushed and he stammered a little in his speech, he addressed himself to his visitor.

"I did not know that you were here, Mr. Oldmixon," he said, "I am very busy with a client, but I'll see you directly. A letter has been lost, but, fortunately, it's of no great consequence *now*" (with a decided accent on the "now"). "I don't like to miss things out of my office, for it gives rise to suspicions that may be unjust. No," he continued, as he turned over every scrap of paper on the desk, "it certainly is not here. Has anybody else been in this room?" he went on, addressing the boy, whose looks expressed his fears more strongly than any words could have done.

"No, sir, nobody's been here but that gentleman," indicating Hogarth by a nod of his head. "He was sitting at the desk just after he came in—"

"Yes," said Hogarth, speaking for the first time since Mr. Ridley's appearance, "I was sitting at the desk, but I took no notice of anything on it. I saw your boy there come in and take something from it, but I don't even know whether it was a bundle of letters or an inkstand."

"Of course not! of course not! How should you? Well, it isn't, as I said before, a matter of much consequence so far as the letter is concerned. I'll see you in a few minutes, Mr. Oldmixon;" so saying, Mr. Ridley returned to his inner room, and Hogarth felt that a load was taken from his mind.

But if he had known who the client was that Mr. Ridley was giving so much of his time to, and the nature of their conversation when the lawyer rejoined him, he would not only not have felt relief, but he would have experienced a decided aggravation of his uncomfortable sensations, for the person was no other than his uncle, and the ideas interchanged between the two gentlemen were not such as would have been reassuring to the nephew.

"It's all explained," said Mr. Ridley, in a low voice, after carefully shutting the door behind him. "Who do you think is outside?"

"Hogarth, of course," replied Mr. Oldmixon, promptly, "and he has the letter in his pocket."

"Yes, I suppose he has. He was sitting at the desk, it appears, and doubtless saw it, and, surmising that it concerned him, he has purloined it with a view to reading it at his leisure."

"What is to be done?"

"I don't see that we can do anything. His getting hold of the letter, while giving him no clear idea of your plans, will make him understand that there is or was a plan of some kind. You are quite sure as to the contents?"

"Yes, I am certain that all I said was that I did not want any policemen, and that I did want the band."

"Well, I should think he would be somewhat thrown off his guard by that, and would conclude that you had given the matter up, if, as you say, you have reason to believe that he has his suspicions of you."

"It may have that effect. It is well that I got here before him. He must have walked all the way down. He's come about the will, but in regard to that you need no further instructions. Now, I want to get away without being seen by him."

"You can do so by going through that end door. It opens on the hall near the elevator. As you close the door behind you I will ring for him."

This was accomplished without any interference with the arrangement, and Hogarth entered the room at the ringing of the bell and took the seat that Mr. Ridley pointed out to him, and that had, not a minute before, been occupied by his uncle.

"I am sorry to have kept you waiting, Mr. Old-mixon," said the lawyer, "but the matter was one of importance. I suppose you have brought me the draft of the new will that your uncle informs me he intends making."

"Yes, he requested me to bring it to you several days ago, but I have not been very well, and was, therefore, unable to attend to it till to-day."

As Hogarth spoke he handed the memorandum to Mr. Ridley, and the latter ran his eye over it rapidly.

"This is very short," he said, laying it on the table before him and placing a paper weight on it, "and will require but an hour or two for its engrossing. Did your uncle say when he wanted to execute it?"

"He told me that he would like to have it as soon as possible."

"I can send it to him this afternoon, or, if you would

like to be the medium for conveying to him the paper that makes you his heir, I will have it ready for you by two o'clock if you will call here at that hour."

"That will suit me very well. It is not yet quite one. I will amuse myself on the Battery till two, and then stop here on my way up-town. My uncle has a family dinner-party this evening, and perhaps he would like to execute the will at that time." Then bidding Mr. Ridley good-morning, Hogarth went out by the same door through which his uncle had departed.

But instead of going to the Battery, as he had said was his intention, he stood on the sidewalk, apparently undecided what to do with himself. He had his uncle's letter in his pocket, and he was desirous of seeing Miss Bangs, and, if possible, of making the acquaintance of the lady that might, he thought, in the course of events, be his wife. It was important for him to know how much she knew of Mr. Oldmixon's intentions, and, if she knew anything of them, what she purposed doing in regard thereto. It was not very far to Lake Street, so he concluded that he would go there in a cab, and read his uncle's letter on the way. He did not recollect the number of the house in which the girl lived, but he told the driver to take him to "a bird-stuffer's, named Bangs, in Lake Street," not doubting that, as the street was a short one, the man would find the place. No sooner was he inside the vehicle than he drew down the blinds, and, taking the stolen letter from his pocket, tore open the envelope without hesitation and read as follows :

"DEAR RIDLEY : I write in haste to countermand the order for policemen, but I shall want the band.

"Yours truly,

"VICTOR CONSTANTINE OLDMIXON."

And this was all.

But what did it mean? He read it and reread it without being able to form a satisfactory idea of the purport of this note of less than three lines. Did it refer to him at all? And if it did, in what manner? Evidently, policemen had been ordered for some purpose, and they were not now required. Had his uncle contemplated causing his arrest, and had he subsequently abandoned the idea? If it related to him at all, this was probably what it meant, and so far it was satisfactory. Perhaps his uncle had failed to get the evidence that he had thought he should be able to obtain, and had abandoned his warfare against him. This also struck him as being plausible, and was, therefore, a still more satisfactory conclusion than the other. These two deductions seemed to him to dispose of the first clause of the letter. Before going on with the rest of it he suddenly opened the cab-door and called to the driver :

"Never mind going to Lake Street," he said. "Go to the Fifth Avenue Hotel.

"I shall not have to think of Miss Bangs if he signs the new will," he said, as he threw himself back in the vehicle. "It will be time enough to take her up after to-night. I think I'm pretty safe for to-night. If he makes fresh war on me, I'll accept the other alternative before to-morrow morning. Now, let us see what the rest of this means :

"'But I shall want the band,'" he read. "What kind of a 'band' will he want? By George! if he were twenty-five instead of seventy-five I should think he was going to serenade a lady. Perhaps he is, after all, bent on some such expedition, or he may intend to have music for his dinner this evening. A 'band' for 'policemen,' however, is a good exchange. I don't see that this concerns me at all, so I think I can safely let it go without bothering myself about it."

When he drove up to the Fifth Avenue Hotel, he went into the bar-room and drank a "brandy and soda." Then he returned to Mr. Ridley's office. The clock on Trinity Church was just striking two as he entered the elevator. He did not see Mr. Ridley, that gentleman having gone out, so the boy said, to get his lunch. But a large envelope unclosed was handed to him, and this, as he ascertained, contained the will drawn up in due form, and with the attesting clause expressed in the terms required by the laws of the State of New York.

The morning had been a satisfactory one to him, all things considered. He had obtained some valuable information, he had had no unpleasant experience with Mr. Ridley, and the new will, ready to be executed, was in his pocket. He took it out of the envelope as he drove up-town, the blinds of the cab still down, and read it over very carefully from beginning to end. It was in exact accordance with the memorandum given him by his uncle, and which he had delivered to Mr. Ridley— and, as he observed with pleasure, the date was filled in and it was that very day. Clearly, the will was intended to be executed before twelve o'clock that night. If his surmises should be fulfilled and he be made his uncle's heir, the old man should be a corpse before sunrise to-morrow.

CHAPTER XXIX.

At five minutes before six Mr. Oldmixon was pacing the floor of his drawing-room, dressed for dinner, and waiting to receive his guests. He appeared to be in a particularly pleasant frame of mind, for he smiled often, and rubbed his hands together, as was his habit when feeling pleasantly inclined, and looked at himself admiringly as he passed and repassed before the large mirror that was placed over the mantel-piece. At three minutes before six he went into the dining-room and surveyed with a critical eye the preparations that had been made for the dinner, and, if one could judge from the smile on his face, the arrangement of the table was satisfactory to him. He had, as was his custom, given great attention to the setting of the table, and to all those æsthetic accessories that add so much to the enjoyment of a dinner. He was to occupy the head of the table, Hogarth the foot, immediately opposite to him, Barbara was to be on his right, her father on his left, and Jack on Barbara's right. There was a wide space between Mr. Henschel and himself, and Mr. Henschel and Hogarth, but this he could not avoid without inviting another guest, and, as this was a family dinner, he did not care to introduce a stranger. He had thought of asking Mr. Brooks, but, after a full consideration of the subject, he had determined to confine the party to himself and the four persons that he had originally invited.

Mr. Oldmixon's domestic service was not extensive, so he had for this occasion hired two men to officiate in conjunction with Thomas in the dining-room. They appeared to understand their business well, but they had probably been more or less tutored by Thomas, who was an experienced butler, understanding just how wines were to be served, and all the other details connected with an elaborate dinner. As regarded table furniture, there were few in New York that could equal Mr. Oldmixon in the elegance and elaborateness of such equipments, his glass, china, silver, cutlery, linen, being costly and beautiful—two qualities which, in such things, do not always go together.

There was to be only one lady at the table, and at her plate was laid a beautiful corsage bouquet of Jacqueminot roses, and a little morocco case containing a gold locket set with large diamonds on one side, and on the other marked with the letters B. and J., interlaced with the consummate skill of the engraver into a monogram that would have defied the abilities of all professional untiers, even of those who, like Alexander the Great and the Gordian knot, would have taken to the sword for its unravelling. For the more this knot should have been cut, the more difficult would have been its segregation. Inside, on one face, was engraved the sentence, "To Barbara from her Uncle (in anticipation) Victor," and on the other a canary-bird, an exact portraiture of the specimen Barbara had mounted for him, and underneath which were the words, "By their fruits ye shall know them."

It must be confessed that the distinguished jeweller that took the order for this locket looked a little surprised at the directions given him, but from politeness and policy refrained from saying a word or even offering a suggestion.

Mr. Oldmixon had been at some pains to ascertain Barbara's floral favorites, and, being told by Jack that they were Jacqueminot roses and violets, had, in addition to the bouquet of roses, provided a large five-rayed star of violets, which occupied the centre of the table with a point reaching across to each guest's plate.

It was six o'clock.   Mr. Oldmixon, at the first stroke of the old Dutch clock that stood in the hall, repaired to the drawing-room to be in readiness to receive his guests. Hogarth was the first to arrive. He knew his uncle's strictness in regard to punctuality in arriving to a dinner, and this was a day on which he did not intend to annoy him in any way. He had often known his uncle, after waiting ten minutes for a dilatory person to put in an appearance, order dinner, with the remark that he wouldn't wait "longer than ten minutes for the angel Gabriel, if he was starving and had to blow his horn at daybreak ;" and then, to enjoy the confusion and awkward excuses of the procrastinator, " I made him feel uncomfortable at any rate," he would say, " so that we're square on that score."   Hogarth had not seen his uncle since his return from his visit to Mr. Ridley, and had not yet, therefore, delivered the draft of the will.   He now came forward, faultlessly attired, with the document in his hand.

" I went down to Ridley's this morning," he said, " with the rough draft that you gave me, and he was kind enough to have it engrossed so that I could present it to you this evening. But of course you will not care to bother over it now. Shall I lay it on your desk in the library ?"

"No, no, my dear boy, give it to me now," exclaimed Mr. Oldmixon, holding out his hand for the paper, and then running his eye over it, while Hogarth stood by, watching him closely. "It is all right," he continued, "and to-night, after dinner, we'll all go into the library and I'll execute it. Then, my dear boy, I shall be more than ever attached to you."

"You are very kind, Uncle Victor, and I thank you sincerely; but," looking at the clock on the mantel-piece, "is it not time for Jack and the other guests to put in an appearance?"

"Yes, and there they are," as the front-door bell was heard to ring. "Jenny (Jenny was one of the maids) will look after Miss Henschel. Now, Hogarth, my boy, I'm sure I need not ask you again to meet Jack half-way."

"You will have no reason to be dissatisfied with me, I think."

A few minutes afterward the new arrivals entered the room, Barbara escorted by her father, and Jack bringing up the rear.

Mr. Oldmixon had probably never in the whole course of his life been in a condition of greater pleasurable excitement than he was now. He went forward to meet his guests, and welcomed both Barbara and her father with as much grace and dignity as he would have done had they been a king and his daughter. After the first formal greetings and introductions, he spoke in more familiar strains, and then, on the appearance of Thomas with the announcement that dinner was ready, he offered his arm to Barbara to conduct her to the dining-room.

Jack, on seeing Hogarth standing near his uncle, had gone toward him, and holding out his hand, said:

" How are you, Hogarth, old fellow ?"

The other took the proffered hand, and muttered a few words about being " glad to see you," or something of the kind, and then the two had entered into conversation upon indifferent subjects.   All of which was very well. At such times the less that is said about bygones the better ; but a disinterested observer would have noticed that there was an absence of frankness in Hogarth's manner which all his efforts could not prevent his showing.   As to Mr. Oldmixon, he had watched with the most intense interest the behavior of the two brothers in the presence of each other.

" Jack is a whole-souled, generous fellow," he said, "but the other is a mean, contemptible cad, who hasn't the magnanimity of a scullion."

Hogarth had been watching his uncle as sharply as his uncle had been watching him, and he had not failed to notice the great impression that the new arrivals made on him.   He saw him bow low before Mr. Henschel and his daughter, and observed with surprise the look of admiration on his face as he spoke a few courteous words to Barbara—for to his eyes she was not a beautiful woman. "She has red hair," he said, "and that is enough ; she must have the temper of the devil !   Her figure is good, eyes fair, mouth and teeth not bad, skin clear and delicate, holds herself well, is self-possessed, looks as though she had been accustomed to this sort of thing all her life, but probably dines on bacon and cabbage every day ; is dressed in excellent taste, neither too much nor too little ; but, for all that, her hair is red, and so are her eyebrows.   From all red-haired women the Lord deliver me ! I wonder where Jack picked her up," he continued, as he brought up the rear of the procession to the dining-

19

room. "He's welcome to her, for all I care ; she'll tear his eyes out if he ventures to differ with her."

By this time they had seated themselves at the table, and the gentlemen were putting their *boutonnières* in their places. Barbara, who was wearing a bouquet of violets that Jack had given her, put that of Jacquemi-not roses at the side of it, and was unrolling her napkin when she perceived the little morocco box that it had partially concealed. At first she did not appear to understand why the casket should be there. She looked inquiringly at Mr. Oldmixon, and then at Jack, but their faces wore the blankest of expressions, and she saw that no information was to be obtained from them. Apparently making up her mind that it was there unintentionally, or at least that it was not meant for her, she ceased to regard it, and turning to Mr. Oldmixon, complimented him on the beauty of the table decorations.

"I never saw anything more beautiful in the way of flowers," she said, "than that bed of violets ; and these roses," looking at the bouquet that she had fastened to her dress, "are simply lovely."

"I am glad you like them, for I got them to please you. Now," he continued, "won't you kindly open that box by your plate, and tell me if I have succeeded half so well with its contents as I have with the flowers ?"

Barbara looked a little surprised, but, at a glance from Jack, who had a pretty exact idea of his uncle's intention, she opened the case, and, while a blush of pleasure overspread her face, took the locket, to which a gold chain of elegant design was attached, out of its resting-place and held it in her hand admiringly.

"It is a token of affection," said Mr. Oldmixon, "from your uncle that is to be."

"It is very beautiful," she said, "and I shall always prize it as a gift from one who has ever been kind to me."

Mr. Oldmixon was in ecstasies. "Pass it around, my dear," he exclaimed. "Let Jack and Hogarth and your father see it."

Jack admired it, and thanked his uncle warmly for his affectionate remembrance of the woman who in a few weeks would be his wife. Hogarth received it next as it went on its rounds. Neither of the others had had time to open it, but Hogarth saw that it was very valuable, and the idea galled him, for he thought that the money spent for it had, as a matter of fact, been so much taken from his inheritance.

"It must have cost at least a couple of thousand dollars," he said to himself, "and the old fool gives that splendid jewel to a girl that probably would have been just as well pleased with one of plain gold. The idea of giving diamonds to a woman of her class in life is ridiculous."

He opened it as he thought all this, and read the inscription, then he examined the other inside face, and saw the bird engraved there, and the words around it. He recognized it as an exact representation, so far as the engraver could make it such, of the canary-bird of which his uncle was so careful. A deadly sickness came over him, and a paleness that could be felt overspread his countenance. He did not dare to raise his eyes to those of his uncle, which he instinctively knew were fixed upon him with a malicious expression, that all their possessor's power could not conceal. He could not even venture to speak lest the tone, or the hoarseness, or the tremor of his voice should betray him. He could only stretch out his hand with the locket toward Mr. Henschel, and hear indistinctly, as though they came from a long distance off, the remarks made about the locket.

It had gotten back to Barbara, and she was examining the interior.

"It was very kind of you," she was saying, "to put the canary-bird where I could always have the opportunity of seeing it, and of being reminded of the occasion that first made us acquainted."

Yes, his worst fears were realized. She was the "bird-stuffer" to whom the money was to go, unless Jack married her, and he was going to marry her and become the heir himself. There was no doubt now that he had been made a fool of, and that the will that he had had drafted and that his uncle now had in his pocket was intended to assist in a fraud then being perpetrated upon him. "Yes," he thought, "in all probability the hypocritical old scoundrel has originated the whole story about the Bangs girl with the idea of getting me entrapped into a marriage with her. He has doubtless put the notion of deceiving me into her head, and if I had gone to see her to-day I should have found her fully supplied with a set of well-concocted lies prepared for the direct purpose of victimizing me. I had a narrow escape of it! But my hour is at hand, and then I shall show him as little mercy as he has shown me.

"As to his signing the will he has in his pocket, of course he will do nothing of the kind; or, if he does, there will be a trick of some sort about it that will render it invalid. I see no hope whatever of my being the heir. It is impossible. He has brought Jack and that girl here for the sole purpose of declaring him or her the inheritor of his estate, and at the same time to mor-

tify me.   His death will do me no good except to rid me
of a tormentor.   It would only put them sooner in possession of the property."

Hogarth was not the man to perpetrate a useless crime ;
he recognized the fact that there was an element of danger even in smothering his uncle in the dead of night.
He saw how shrewd and apparently prepared for him on
every point the old man was ; how he had divined his
thoughts, and met him at every turn of his career, since
they two had lived under one roof.   It was more than
likely, therefore, that he had become aware of the murderous intentions of his nephew, and that he was so closely
guarded that an attempt against his life would not only
result in failure, but would be apt to be followed by the
immediate arrest of the perpetrator.

He sat through the dinner in a half-dazed state, talking to no one, and replying in monosyllables and vaguely
to the remarks that were occasionally addressed to him.
He was aware that all present but himself were laughing
and talking as though they were in the height of enjoyment.   He heard his uncle, who seemed to be in an almost abnormal condition of good-humor and merriment,
explaining several of the dishes to Barbara and descant-
ing on their delicacy and rarity.   To him everything
was tasteless, but he swallowed great draughts of wine,
and after a time the effect was felt in a diminution of his
fears and an increase of his perceptive and intellectual
powers.

He was very confident that his uncle had some scheme
in view in having him meet Jack and Barbara, and he
was well aware of the fact that he should need all his
powers of resistance and of attack in order to maintain
himself in the contest that was impending.   He thought

seriously of getting up from the table without ceremony or excuse, and walking deliberately out of the room, never again to make his appearance in the house, or, indeed, anywhere where he would be liable to meet any one now at the table ; for he felt quite convinced that he had nothing to his advantage to expect from his uncle. But even this attempt he all at once became aware would not probably be successful, for, happening to raise his eyes, he saw one of the waiters exchanging glances with Mr. Oldmixon, and he at once formed the idea that both of them were detectives, and that they would stop him before he could leave the house.

This idea, once it had found a place in his mind, disturbed him greatly, and caused him to watch the two men, who were apparently skilled in the business of serving an elaborate dinner. The face of one of them seemed to be familiar to him. " Where had he seen it before?" he asked himself. He scanned it closely, but he did not readily associate it with that of any particular person or event. But suddenly the idea flashed upon him that it was that of the cabman who had driven him that morning when he had started from Mr. Ridley's office to go to see Miss Bangs, and had, after reading the stolen letter, changed his destination to the Fifth Avenue Hotel—the same man who had subsequently driven him home. He had done a good deal to change his countenance. He had shaven off his beard, or had, perhaps, only removed his false whiskers. He had made his face look much paler than it had appeared in the morning, and he had altered the cut of his hair, but, for all these differences, he was sure these two men were the same.

Had the fellow seen him reading the purloined letter? " My God," he exclaimed, under his breath, " where is the letter ? Did I leave it in the cab ? Yes, I laid it on the seat while I lit a cigar, and I never touched it afterward. That man took it, and my uncle probably has it in his pocket at this instant !''

He knew that he had committed an offence against the laws of the United States that subjected him to a long term of imprisonment, and he did not doubt that the two men were there disguised as waiters for the express purpose, on a single word from his uncle, of arresting him and taking him to Ludlow Street Jail, there to await his trial on the charge of stealing and opening a letter not addressed to him. Still, what could he do ? There was nothing for him to do but await developments. He was in the toils of his implacable enemy, and he knew that when the explosion came there would be no mercy.

He gave some attention to what was being said in the hope that there might be something let drop by his uncle that would give him an inkling of what was to come, but the old gentleman was apparently thinking of very different affairs than those that occupied Hogarth's mind. He was telling Barbara of the origin of the Oldmixon family.

" Yes, we are certainly distinguished," he said, with a hearty laugh. " I think I once told you something about our origin. The founder of the family was a reprobate called Nick. He began life by robbing a church when he was only sixteen years old. For this he was tried, found guilty, and sentenced to be burned at the stake. But while he was being conveyed to the place of execution, he broke loose from the guard, and, after running nearly a mile with soldiers, monks, and all the rag-tag and bobtail of the town after him, he plunged into the sea and swam out to a vessel lying at anchor half a mile from the shore. They were all afraid to follow him, and thus he escaped. The vessel was a noted pirate, and, after a short time, Nick became the captain of the vessel."

"How long ago was that?" inquired Barbara, amused as much at Mr. Oldmixon's delight as at the story itself.

"Well, let me see—that must have been in the year 989, during the reign of Ethelred, the last of the English kings, before the final Danish invasion. Wasn't it, Jack?"

"Don't ask me," answered Jack, with a laugh, "I don't pretend to your antiquarian knowledge of the Oldmixons."

"But, to go on," resumed Mr. Oldmixon, "Nick became a great pirate, or viking, as perhaps he was called in that day, and after he had advanced in years he was of course called 'Old Nick.' When he got to be too old to steal anything more as a pirate, he settled down on an estate that he bought with his plunder and set up as a reformer. I may, by way of parenthesis, remark that the like process goes on in our day very often.

"But, although he built an abbey and endowed it with a vast property, he always went by the name of 'Old Nick,' and a son that he had was designated 'Old Nick's son.' This son killed his father, and was altogether one of the most diabolical of the family. Being rich, however, he was able to buy immunity from punishment both in this world and in the world to come. He was at the same time very pious, and somehow or other became a mitred abbot. It wouldn't of course do for a mitred abbot to go by the name of 'Old Nick's son.' It was too infernally suggestive of his devilish traits, so he changed the name to Oldmixon, and by that cognomen we have been known ever since."

Everybody but Hogarth laughed at this apocryphal narration. He tried to smile, but the effect was a sickly one, and he gave up the attempt before the angles of his mouth had begun to expand.

It was impossible at such a small dinner-party as that for there to be any private conversation. Barbara could not, therefore, tell Jack what she thought of his brother, and perhaps she would not have told him had she been afforded every opportunity for so doing, for she did not like him. She liked neither his appearance nor his manners. With a woman's quick intuitions she saw that there was something preying on his mind—something that engrossed his attention to the exclusion of everything else, and that filled him with a fear that he could not conceal.

The dinner had nearly come to an end, and Mr. Oldmixon, to Barbara's great satisfaction, had made no attack on Hogarth. Indeed, he had scarcely spoken to him during the repast, beyond occasionally asking him his opinion of a dish or a wine, and then always addressing him as " My dear boy," or " My dear Hogarth."

But while the coffee was being handed, Mr. Oldmixon seemed to awaken to the consciousness of Hogarth's presence, and to the fact that he had scarcely done his part toward making the evening pass pleasantly. He sat right opposite to his uncle, and the latter, as he sipped his coffee, looked at him with the most pleasant expression imaginable on his face.

" What has made you so silent, my dear boy ?" he said. " One would think, from your lugubrious expression and melancholic manner, that you were about to be led out to execution. Let me see," he continued, in a meditative way, " the last Oldmixon executed was Sir Guy, who, unfortunately, took it into his head to poison his wife. He

19*

used arsenic for the purpose, and of course the chemists
and doctors discovered it, and Sir Guy was hanged in
chains.   We know better nowadays.   When we want to
kill our wives we don't poison—we—we," hesitating and
looking smilingly at Hogarth, " we employ some method
not so likely to lead to detection.   Now, if I had a wife
that I wanted to get rid of, I'd smo—" He checked himself suddenly and said, " have her struck by lightning."

   " Struck by lightning !" said Hogarth, who had noticed the break in the word " smother," but who, thinking that his uncle had stopped out of consideration for
him, was desirous of keeping him in that vein.   " How
could you accomplish that ? Suppose you tell us," he added, with a degree of recklessness that he was sorry for ere
many seconds had passed, " for Jack's benefit.   He's the
only one here likely to require the knowledge."

   Mr. Oldmixon at these latter words seemed to be upon
the point of losing whatever of self-restraint he had been
exercising during the dinner, and of bursting out into
some passionate speech against Hogarth. His red face
became still redder, his eyes glared, his mouth twitched,
and he seemed to be trying to speak, and yet to be unable
to utter a word. At last, however, he appeared to have
obtained sufficient control of himself to go on with the
conversation, though it had evidently been a hard struggle,
and his voice trembled at first with the effort that he
made to appear. calm.

   " Jack, my dear Hogarth," he said, " will never need
any method of getting rid of a wife, for you see he is not
an Oldmixon so far as his character and disposition are
concerned.   Indeed, in his mental organization he takes
after his mother, who was a very excellent and sensible

woman, altogether too good for the man whose wife she
was."

"Thank you, Uncle Victor," said Jack, with feeling.
Barbara gave him a look of thankfulness.   Hogarth, beginning now to perceive that he had precipitated matters,
looked as black as a thunder-cloud.

"But you, my dear boy," continued Mr. Oldmixon,
"though you have no *further* use for any wife-ridding
process, may, perhaps, in your future career marry again—
though I am free to say that I think that contingency
very remote—and it is therefore just possible that if, only
upon the principle that variety is as well the spice of
death as it is of life, you may find the procedure I have
in mind not only simple but effectual."

Hogarth laughed long and loudly at this speech, but it
was easy to see that his laughter was forced.   He had determined to brave the matter through to the end, and to
force his uncle once and for all to show his cards and
play his game.   He began to suspect that, after all, there
was more guessing than knowledge.

"One would think," he said, still laughing, "that you
were accusing me of having gotten rid of my wife by
some easy process.   It is well for me that all those that
hear you are friends, otherwise I could scarcely hope to
escape suspicion.   However, you scarcely intended what
your words seemed to imply.   So, by all means tell us
your quick and easy process for getting rid of a wife."

"Ah, my dear boy, I thought I should at last interest
you ; but come," he added, looking around the table, "we
have finished dinner.   Let us go into the library, where I
have a little business to transact, and some selections from
my novel to read, and where, if my dear Barbara does not
object, the gentlemen can smoke their cigars.   Come !"

"I hope you will excuse me, Uncle Victor," said Hogarth, thinking that here might be an opportunity for escape, "I am not feeling very well."

"No, I cannot excuse you, for the business mainly concerns you, my dear boy. This paper requires to be executed," taking, as he spoke, the draft of the will from his pocket. "You will have to come." He said these last words very emphatically, and with his eyes fixed on Hogarth.

Hogarth looked around him. The two detectives officiating as waiters were not present ; doubtless they were stationed so as to arrest him, should he attempt to leave the company. "Very well !" he said, with some desperation in his voice, "I have no objection. Perhaps I can stand not only your process, but even your novel."

It was a challenge, and so Mr. Oldmixon regarded it. "Thanks, my dear boy. You are very kind. Come !" and then, giving his arm to Barbara, he escorted her to the library, the rest following, and the two strange waiters —as Hogarth, who looked behind him, ascertained— watching them from the dining-room, into which they had entered as the others left it.

"The dinner is over now," said Mr. Oldmixon to Barbara. "I think you will admit that I have kept my promise as well as was possible under the circumstances. But for God's sake don't interfere with me further !"

She did not know what to think. She was sure a catastrophe of some kind was impending, and yet she was powerless to interfere without probably making matters worse. She looked imploringly at him, but he turned away his face, unwilling or unable to meet her appeal.

CHAPTER XXX.

"Now," said Mr. Oldmixon, gayly, after they were all seated, and the gentlemen had, with Barbara's permission, lighted their cigars, "first let me tell you how to get rid of a wife that you are tired of. You may laugh," he continued, smiling at the looks of merriment he saw about him—for even Hogarth was laughing—"but it's a serious matter. It's a process that never fails. You must have her struck by lightning."

"So you told us just now, Uncle," said Hogarth, "but the process must be rather difficult to carry out. You might, to be sure, invite her to climb one of those tall poles in the street, and touch the wire, but not many wives are endowed with sufficient strength and agility to do that. Your plan would require a previous education in gymnastics that few women are likely to have. Now, there, for instance, is Miss Henschel—"

"Now, my dear Hogarth, for Heaven's sake," said Mr. Oldmixon, with both hands raised in a deprecating manner, "don't bring Miss Henschel into this discussion. I admit once and for all that your experience with wives is sufficient to give you some idea of their strength and agility, but my plan requires no such acrobatic feat as climbing an electric lamp-pole. It is much simpler.

"I was once in the city of Merida, in Yucatan," he went on, having succeeded in silencing Hogarth, "when the Alcalde, standing in the doorway of his palace talking to me, saw his wife—an American woman, by the by, and not disposed to submit to marital restraint—curveting around the plaza on a wild mustang that she was endeavoring to break. He called to her to stop, but she paid no attention to him, save by smiling defiantly at him, as, in making the circuit of the plaza, she came repeatedly near to where we were standing.

"'I wish he would throw you,' said her husband. But he did not, and the lady continued to smile.

"'I wish the ground would open and swallow you up!' exclaimed the angry husband, the next time she came round. Still the lady smiled, and the ground did not open.

"Then he wished that the devil and all his demons would fly away with her. But it is needless to say that they didn't. Probably they were otherwise engaged, or maybe he was not sufficiently influential with his Satanic majesty. Had he been an Oldmixon, now, he could have raised the devil without much trouble.

"It was a clear day. The sun was shining in all the fervid heat and glare of the tropics, and there was not a cloud as large as a man's hand to be seen anywhere. My friend, the Alcalde, had not succeeded in arresting the circus-like performance of his wife, who, with even if possible greater speed than before, was rushing around the plaza. On she came like an Amazon, her horse's mane and tail streaming in the wind, and her whole soul bent to the excitement of the occasion. As she came opposite to us, and scarcely twenty feet distant, she turned and smiled defiantly at her husband.

"'I wish the lightning would strike you dead!' he exclaimed, furiously. The words were scarcely out of his mouth when there was a blinding flash, a terrific peal, and the wife lay on the ground, while the mustang swept like a whirlwind around the plaza, apparently uninjured. She was dead, and her husband had killed her."

"It is horrible!" said Barbara, covering her face with her hands, "but of course it was a mere coincidence."

"I think not," remarked Mr. Oldmixon, calmly. "It has succeeded every time, to my knowledge, that it has been tried."

"But how often has it been tried?" inquired Jack, laughingly.

"Once, only once," answered his uncle, "but then see what chances there were against its success, and how can you doubt that the imprecation and the death bore to each other the relation of cause and effect? I have been several times on the point of trying it against people that disgusted me, but there's always been something to prevent me. I would have tried it on that fellow that put currant jelly on canvas-back duck, only I didn't want to make a scene at the club. Besides, it might be dangerous to others, unless employed out in the open air, and in a house would probably ruin the furniture. Then, again, it must be a horrid thing to have a person's death on your mind. And perhaps, after all, it is only efficacious against wives."

"Yes," said Jack, "all the conditions must be observed; in which case the wife would have to be riding around a plaza on a wild mustang."

Hogarth had made no remark at the end of the story, except an exclamation that sounded something like "bosh," and that was probably intended to intimate his belief that the whole recital was a fabrication of his uncle's. Whether the story were true or not, Mr. Old-

mixon did not deign to say. It had served his purpose of introducing the subject of the killing of wives,
and of showing that Hogarth's nerves were strong
enough, except when his own particular method was
referred to.

"Now," he continued, after going to his desk and
laying the draft of the new will on the table, "I propose to carry out the plan, my dear Hogarth, that we
were talking about this afternoon. Will you kindly
ring the bell?"

Hogarth did as he was requested, and almost instantly the two waiters made their appearance.

"I want you to witness a document," said Mr. Oldmixon. "This," he continued, "is my last will and tes-
tament; as you see, I sign it," writing his name as he
spoke. "Now, will you kindly sign here?" indicating with his finger the place where he wished them
to put their signatures. "Thanks!" as they affixed
their names; "I think that makes the paper complete."
Then, speaking a few words in a low tone to one of the
men, he signified to them that their presence was no
longer required, and they left the room.

"My dear Hogarth," he resumed, "I trust you may
live long to enjoy the fortune that is here bequeathed to
you. I do not expect to cumber the earth much longer,
so that it isn't likely that you will be kept out of the
estate for any considerable period. I suppose you might
as well keep this, as it concerns you more than it does me or
any one else." With which words he handed the paper to
Hogarth. "Now, if you please," he continued, "I will
read you a few extracts from my novel;" and turning to
his desk, he took out of a compartment a manuscript, of
which he at once proceeded to turn over the leaves, ap-

parently with the view of selecting the parts that he especially desired to bring to the notice of his guests.

Hogarth had taken the will, but, without looking at it, and without one word of thanks or of anything else to his uncle, had laid it on the mantel-piece near where he was sitting. Indeed, as though divining that something of a serious nature was impending over him, he had become as livid as a ghost, and apparently so overcome with terror that he shivered as if suffering from an ague attack. As to Jack and Barbara, nothing could have been more unpleasant than their situation, for they also were quite sure that Mr. Oldmixon had some plan that he was carrying out as a finality in the matter of his contest with Hogarth, and that the *denouement*, when it came, would be of such a character as to render their position still more embarrassing. Mr. Henschel was apparently unaware that there was any "reading between the lines" going on. He thought it singular that Mr. Oldmixon had changed his mind in regard to his will, for he had supposed that Jack was going to receive the bulk of the estate, but from the placid manner that his son-in-law in expectancy took the matter, he supposed that some compensation had been, in some way or other, provided, and that the principles of justice had not been violated.

After some little delay, and after repeatedly looking at the clock that stood on the desk, Mr. Oldmixon found the part that he was looking for, and, amid the most complete silence, began to speak:

"I must premise," he said, "by stating that I am going to read only a single scene from my book. It is one, however, that will give you some idea of my style and powers of description, and I think may be taken as a sample of the whole book." Again looking at the clock, he read :

" ' Hugo was a man in whose person were united most of the vices that in general are only met with in many men. He was, as it were, a microcosm of diabolism, and to offset his plenitude of wickedness there was not one single redeeming virtue. In early life he had shown the inherent depravity of his character by torturing all the animals that came in his way and that it was safe for him to attack, for with all his cruelty he was cowardly to such a degree that it often happened that boys and men weaker than himself thrashed him for some insult or outrage that he had perpetrated while he, like " the poor craven bridegroom, said never a word."

" ' It argues little for the existence of that keenness of perception with which women are said to be endowed, that a man like Hugo should have been able to win the affections of a woman the opposite of himself in all mental qualities. But so it was. Certainly he could only have done so by assuming virtues that he did not possess. As we shall see hereafter, it was no unusual thing for him to take upon himself the livery of heaven while diligently engaged in serving his master the devil.'

" That," he continued, laying down his manuscript, " will serve as an introduction of the two principal characters of the work ; of course there is a good deal more in regard to them, but I refrain from reading it now, being desirous of bringing up at once one of the principal incidents, if not the chief one of the story.

" Hugo and Cecilia were married and left soon after the ceremony on their wedding-tour, and, in the course of it, they arrived, late one evening, at the little city of Acropolis. They did not do much sight-seeing that night, and the next day the rain poured down in torrents, so that they were confined to their rooms in the hotel. Now we resume the narrative :

" ' It was not a large room in which Hugo and Cecilia were spending the afternoon, but it was comfortable, and fitted up in a manner a little better than that usually followed in the hotels of country towns. Adjoining it was the bedroom ; a door communicating between the two was open.

" ' He was already beginning to weary of her, and perhaps she had discovered that he was not the paragon of perfection that she had taken him to be. She was sitting in a low rocking-chair, while he stood with his back to her, looking out of the window at the rain, as it filled the gutters and rushed down the steep incline of the street with almost the force of a mountain torrent. He had said many bitter things to her that afternoon, and, moreover, she had detected him in several of the lies that he had told while wooing her, so that the feeling between them was very far from being of that kind that generally exists, at least through the honeymoon. Something that she said appeared to rouse all the evil passions that were slumbering in his breast, for suddenly he turned upon her, and with an expression upon his face that the arch-fiend of hell might have envied, he seized her—' "

" Stop !" cried Hogarth, rising from the chair on which he was sitting, and coming into the middle of the room. " By some means or other, aided, perhaps, by that demon that you say I am like, you know that I killed my wife —"

" Ah, you confess it then, murderer !" exclaimed Mr. Oldmixon, jumping up also, and meeting his nephew half way, till they stood not three feet apart, confronting each other. "I thought I should torture you into revealing your crime, and at last my hope is realized."

"Yes; I carried her into the next room, threw her on the bed, and smothered her to death with a pillow."

"My God!" exclaimed Barbara and Jack in a breath, while Mr. Henschel, looking horror-stricken, could only mutter a few inarticulate expressions.

"I knew it!" cried Mr. Oldmixon, excitedly. "The wretch confesses! He smothered her! Oh, double-dyed villain that you are, why the great God does not strike you dead as you stand there is a mystery to me! Liar, swindler, murderer, thief!" As he uttered this last word he threw the purloined letter on the floor before his cowering nephew. "For some inscrutable reason of His own, God sees fit to let you live till such time as He shall put it into your heart to take yourself out of this world; and may He do it speedily! Go!" he continued, while all the rest of the company were standing horrified at the awful scene before them. "Go, wretch, basilisk, whose very look chills the marrow in the bones of honest men. If by the rising of to-morrow's sun your apology for a soul inhabits your vile body, the hangman shall separate them."

Hogarth heard all this with head bowed, and eyes closed, and trembling in body and limb. Barbara, unable longer to endure the agony of the situation, had fallen upon the sofa, and was being ministered to by Jack and her father. She was sobbing hysterically, and the two men were on their knees before her, oblivious now of what was passing between Hogarth and Mr. Oldmixon, who still stood, the one with bowed head, the other with form erect, eyes flashing, lips compressed, breathing hurriedly, and with one arm extended toward the door.

"You meant to smother me to-night as you smothered

your wife," cried Mr. Oldmixon, still pointing toward the door. "Will you go?"

Without a word further, Hogarth moved slowly toward the door; as he reached it, he raised his head. "My God!" he exclaimed, "that face again!" As his hand rested on the knob, and the door opened to allow him to pass, Mr. Oldmixon stepped back and touched a little white button that, fastened to a wire covered with silk, lay on the desk. Instantly a band of musicians, stationed somewhere outside, began to play.

It was the " Rogue's March " to which Hogarth slunk
out of his uncle's house uninterfered with, according to
their instructions, by those that watched his departure.
He stood on the porch for an instant, and then, hastily
descending the steps, walked rapidly toward the North
River.

The music ceased, and Mr. Oldmixon, overcome by the
excitement and exertion, dropped panting into a chair.
Barbara was better, and Jack, seeing that his uncle was
overpowered by the force of the event that had taken
place, hurried to see if assistance was required. Mr.
Oldmixon held out his hand.

" My dear boy," he gasped, " I'm afraid this has been
a little too much for me. My nitrite of amyl!" Jack
felt in his uncle's waistcoat pocket, but did not find it.

" I left it in my other waistcoat when I changed my
clothes for dinner," said Mr. Oldmixon, feebly. Jack
was off in an instant to get it. " Barbara, my dear, come
here, kneel here by my side," as she approached him with
streaming eyes and clasped hands. " I'm sorry, dear,
that I had to give you pain, but I could not help it.

We're a bad lot, my dear, all but Jack. He'll be kind to
you, for he's a good, manly fellow, and—and you'll be—"
speaking with greater difficulty—"very happy. My time
has come. I know it, for things are beginning to look
strange and—and—don't put out the lights!" he exclaimed, with more strength. "No, no, never mind; it
is getting dark to me, that's all. A nice dinner party!
A very nice dinner party! No one but a lunatic would
have acted as I did. Ah, Jack," as his nephew returned
with the nitrite of amyl and held the vial to his nostrils,
"it's very little use to me now. Hand me that paper
that the basilisk left on the mantel-piece. By George! I
can see once more! The amyl did some good, after all.
Open it, Jack. It's only a piece of blank paper. I had
to pretend it was a will, or the fellow would have left
before I got through with him. My poor child," turning
to Barbara, "how I did shock and grieve you! But I
couldn't help it, dear. It had to be done, and I had to
do it—I had to do it. That band and the 'Rogue's March'!
Quite original! Not another man in the world would
have thought of such a thing. The basilisk! What did
I tell you, Jack? I said the weasel would finish him,
didn't I?"

The last words were spoken in so low a tone that Jack
and Barbara, who were kneeling at the side of the chair,
could scarcely hear them. The nitrite of amyl appeared
to have lost its power, or rather the old man had lost *his*
power to breathe it into his lungs, and he lay back in the
chair, gasping in quick and short inspirations for the air
that was all around him, but which he was unable to get.
Then suddenly his face flushed as a candle, just before it
dies out, brightens into a little flash of life.

"Give me your hand, dear," he said, in a clear and

distinct voice. "A good girl! a good girl! There are not many things in this world better than a good woman. It's all right about the will. You and Jack—Ridley has it—Look at me! I want to see your face the last thing on earth. I'm sorry I did it, but I had to do it—band and all—I had to do it. Ah!" he continued, as, with his eyes fixed upon the door, he raised himself a little in the chair, "I see him. The death look is in his face. He is going toward the river, and she—she beckons him on. Camilla! In a few minutes you will be avenged. His life for yours! His life for yours! But I shall not live to see it. No—no," as he sank back, speaking scarcely above a whisper, and in a despairing tone. "I shall not live—quite—long—enough—" Once more he turned to Barbara: "My dear, God bless—!" His eyes closed, his jaw fell, a little twitching of the corners of the mouth caused an expression that was almost a smile, and his head fell forward on his breast.

"Oh, Jack!" cried Barbara, throwing herself into his arms, and sobbing as though her heart would break, "he is dead!"

"Yes, dear, he is dead. God give him peace!"

THE END.

L A L.

A Novel.

By DR. WILLIAM A. HAMMOND.

SIXTH EDITION NOW READY.

SOME OPINIONS OF THE PRESS.

ONE OPINION.

"'Lal,' the heroine of Dr. W. A. Hammond's story (Appleton), is short for Laila Rookh. The shortened name carries to the ears an impression which the book confirms. A more disagreeable book to one who loves art it would be hard to find. The veneer of philosophy which covers the cheap material out of which the book is constructed only makes the novel more objectionable. Every canon of good taste is violated, and one has not even a piece of rough humanity to fall back upon. The book is a piece of artistic falsehood."—*Atlantic Monthly.*

OTHER AND DIFFERENT OPINIONS.

"The unfolding of the character and conscience, the taste and intelligence, of this frontier wild flower, the brutal ordeals to which she is subjected, and from which she extricates herself unharmed by her own pluck and energy, the blossoming of her love for the hero of the tale, and the discovery that she was not the child of the ruffian Bosier, but had been stolen by him in infancy from parents of great refinement and intelligence, are woven into a romance of genuine but unequal power, and in which, besides this growth of a soul and birth of love, are also depicted some dramatic scenes of far Western life, illustrative of its lawlessness and sense of honor, its fierceness and gentleness, its strange commingling of vices and virtues, its hospitality, generosity, and quick recognition of physical or intellectual excellence."—*Harper's New Monthly Magazine.*

[OVER]

" The wildness of the mountains, the startling depravities of the mining-camp, the savage cruelty of man, the terror of private vengeance—it is with themes like these that Dr. Hammond mingles the tenderness of women's hearts, the heroism of personal courage and chivalrous devotion to duty, and the eccentricities of genius devoted to high intellectual and social ends."—*Literary World* (Boston).

" The comprehension of the trials and temptations of Western roughs, of their singular intellectual ability when it comes to circumventing each other, of their remarkable codes of honor, and the way in which they deceive their own consciences, as well as their friends and enemies, betrays a remarkable knowledge of human nature. We have here all the good points we have been taught to associate with this roughest sort of life."—*Critic* (New York).

" It possesses the great merit of being interesting from beginning to end. The characters are striking, and several of them have an element of originality; the incidents are abundant and effective; the situations are well devised, and, if there is not much intricacy in the plot, there is a certain bustle and rapidity of movement which answers instead of more complicated machinery. Here, it will be seen, are some of the most important qualities of a good story; and we risk nothing in predicting for ' Lal ' a notable success."—*New York Tribune.*

" Dr. William A. Hammond's ' Lal ' is at once an enjoyment and a surprise —though why an eminent physician, and one of broad culture and literary attainments, should not write a vigorous and successful novel if he sets his hand and mind to it is more than we can say, except that many have been called but few shown themselves chosen. The wild surroundings of mountain and mining life in the West are boldly gathered about Dr. Hammond's heroine, and the Polish patriot, representing the refining influences of European civilization, is brought into fine relief in his isolation amid such savage scenery and semi-savage existence."—*Independent.*

" The scenes in ' Lal ' suggest the scenes in Bret Harte's stories. Dr. Hammond has journeyed through the country where Harte found his rough-diamond heroes. He has done more than journey through it; he has lived in it, suffered its hardships, studied its characters, and acquainted himself with all its picturesque oddities. He writes, therefore, from his own point of view, and it is quite true that his point of view is his own. His method is in no sense imitative. Dr. Hammond is too aggressive and too brilliantly able to be an imitator, even when he is treading on the ground of another. ' Lal ' is a vigorous, well-written, stimulating work."—GEORGE EDGAR MONTGOMERY, in *New York World.*

12mo, cloth. Price, $1.80.

New York: D. APPLETON & CO., 1, 3, & 5 Bond Street.

DR. GRATTAN.

A Novel.

By DR. WILLIAM A. HAMMOND.

FOURTH EDITION NOW READY.

SOME OPINIONS OF THE PRESS.

ONE OPINION.

" ' Dr. Grattan,' by William A. Hammond, a novel in which a noisy style, cheap learning, and physiological jugglery combine to swamp the story and leave the reader in doubt whether he has brought enough away to warrant the trouble he was forced to take to get the treasure."—*Atlantic Monthly.*

SOME OTHER AND DIFFERENT OPINIONS.

" And it is not pleasant, in such a generally fair and helpful review as that of ' Books of the Month ' (' Atlantic Monthly '), to stumble on such an unfair and misleading judgment as is given of Dr. Hammond's last novel."—*Literary World* (Boston).

" Dr. Hammond is earning a conspicuous place among our American novelists, as well by the rapidity with which he writes as by the ability with which he portrays anomalous mental states and conditions. His new novel, ' Doctor Grattan,' ministers to the curiosity and entertainment of the reader, while putting him in possession of some highly interesting information derived from the author's professional experience. Its scene is laid at the foot of the Adirondacks, fine descriptions of which, and of the forest and village life in and around them, are given in the course of the narrative. As the story unfolds, close and very charming glimpses are given of the household life and the frank and loving comradeship of Doctor Grattan and his energetic and beautiful daughter, who soon become prominent actors in the drama, but toward whom we are drawn with a feeling of cordial interest even before we are invited to witness the incidents and companionships that later on introduced new influences into their secluded lives, and invested them with a glamour of mystery and romance. The story embodies two cleverly developed love stories, which are told with great straightforwardness and refreshing freedom from tantalizing eventualities."—*Harper's Monthly.*

"Dr. Hammond constructs the plot of this story with the skill and apparent ease of the veteran novelist. He deals mainly in improbabilities, but he manages to give to these the semblance of reality by the minutely circumstantial manner in which the story is related. His coolness and accuracy of statement overcome all doubt as to the fact he is giving. We have the exact hour and minute of an occurrence, as if the good doctor were standing by with his watch in his hand. Particulars are given us even where a general statement would have been all that we could reasonably have asked for. This impresses the mind of the reader with a sense of the author's accurate knowledge and unswerving allegiance to the truth. . . . The book is written in a style clear, vigorous, and direct. The language is free from technicalities which, from the nature of the case, might have been looked for. Evidently the author aims to secure readers, and he does not hesitate to employ legitimate means to that end. He shows such care as respect for his readers requires, and only that. He is cramped by no pettiness or squeamishness. He succeeds as well in the telling of his story as in the contrivance of its plot."—*Boston Evening Transcript.*

"'Doctor Grattan' is really a capital book. It is a novel with the scene laid in America, yet not an 'American novel' as we know that product, for which Mr. Hammond (like the hero of 'The Witch's Head') expresses his open contempt. The interest of the story lies in the question as to whether Mr. Lamar, the father of the heroine, has been a slave-dealer for many years of his life, or whether he has merely brooded on the subject till he has imagined that he has dealt in human merchandise. The problem is most cleverly worked out, and it would be unfair to Mr. Hammond to disclose the solution. Doctor Grattan himself is a pleasant, practical man, who makes an excellent and original hero. But Mr. Hammond must be congratulated on his women."—*Saturday Review* (London).

12mo, cloth.   Price, $1.50.

New York: D. APPLETON & CO., 1, 3, & 5 Bond Street.

D. APPLETON & Co. WILL PUBLISH EARLY IN THE AUTUMN

A STRONG-MINDED WOMAN; or, TWO YEARS AFTER.

A Sequel to "Lal."

By WILLIAM A. HAMMOND, M. D.,

AUTHOR OF "LAL," "DOCTOR GRATTAN," "MR. OLDMIXON," ETC.